PRAISE FOR THE CALENDAR GIRL

"Carlan has captivated me with…
Mia and her feistiness."
~ **Karen's Book Haven**

"Five amazing stars! This might be the best one
yet! So many secrets and plot twists…"
~ **Ramblings From Beneath the Sheets Blog**

"This series freakin' rocks! I have loved going on this
"journey" with Mia and watching her grow…"
~ **Crazy Daisy Book Whore Blog**

CALENDAR GIRL

VOLUME THREE

DEDICATIONS

Rosa McAnulty

*July is dedicated to you, my Puerto Rican princess.
Thank you for making sure that the language
and mannerisms of the Puerto Rican culture were
authentic and true to the character. Thank you for
being an amazing member of my team, support
system, but most of all, for being a friend.
BESOS, Angel.*

August

Ketty McLean Beale

*August is dedicated to you.
In a sea of strangers, you sought me out,
offered friendship, a smile, and a wicked sense of humor.
I'll never forget how you made my first
experience connecting with my peers a memorable one.
'Never will I ever'…forget you.*

Karen Roma

*September is dedicated to you, my Australian friend.
Your reviews are always honest,
whether you connect to the story or not.
Still, you never give up on me.
In the end, I think the constructive feedback
makes me work harder, and strive for more.
You make me better.
Thank you, Angel.*

TABLE OF CONTENTS

July

CALENDAR GIRL

AUDREY CARLAN

WATERHOUSE
PRESS

CHAPTER ONE

Blond. Blue-eyed. Tall. Goddess. Jesus H. Christ. The universe was laughing at me as I stood stock-still and looked the modelesque woman up and down. She looked like she could be Rachel's ungodly perfect sister, and I thought Rachel was stunning. Nope. Totally wrong.

The woman stood next to a shiny black Porsche Boxster, jittering around as if incredibly anxious. Her fingers tapped a solid beat against the sign she held up with my name on it. A not-so-subtle shift from one sky-high stiletto to the other only added to the fierceness rolling off her in waves. Then again, that could've been the Miami heat. Good Lord, it was sweltering, yet this woman was perfectly put together, as if she'd walked right out of a rock video. Skinny jeans so tight I could see the nice curve of her booty. Her tank top had me drooling, complete with a monogram across a set of large tits that said *Hug Me and Die*. There were at least ten necklaces of varying beads, lengths, and sizes wrapped around the smooth column of her neck. She had kick-ass rock-star hair pulled back into a complex system of twists and loose pieces that looked rocker-chic.

After I inspected her for what felt like minutes, she fixed her steel-blue gaze on me. A puff of air left her lungs as she tossed the cardboard in the car window and sauntered over. She scanned me from my flowing black locks, over my sundress, and to the simple flats I wore on two big feet.

"This will never do." She shook her head with exasperation. "Come on, time is money," came the flippant retort over her shoulder. The trunk popped open, and I tossed my suitcase in.

"I'm Mia, by the way." I held out my hand as she slid on a pair of ultra-cool aviators, turned her head, and looked at me over the top of them.

"I know who you are. I'm the one that chose you." Her tone held a twinge of distaste as she started the car and hit the gas, not even waiting for me to get the seatbelt fastened. My body jolted forward, and I braced on the smooth leather dash.

"Did I do something to piss you off?" I readjusted the belt and watched her profile.

Her breath came out in a long, slow exhale before she shook her head. "No," she groaned. "I'm sorry. Anton pissed me off. I was in the middle of something big when he told me to come get you because *he* needed our driver so *he* could fuck a couple groupies in the back of the Escalade."

I cringed. Great, sounded like my new boss for the month was a slimy douche. *Not another one.* "That sucks."

She took a quick right turn onto the freeway. "Can we start over?" Her voice now held sincerity and apology. "I'm Heather Renee, by the way, personal assistant to Anton Santiago. Hottest hip-hop artist in the nation."

"Is that right?" Wow. I hadn't realized he was that big-time. I didn't usually listen to much hip-hop. More of an alternative and rock chick.

Heather nodded. "Yep, every album he's done has gone platinum. He's the "It" boy in Hip Hop, and good grief does he know it." She grinned. "Anton wants to meet you right away, but you can't wear that." Her gaze moved down to the plain green sundress I wore. It highlighted my eyes and made my hair look phenomenal. Plus, it was comfortable to travel in.

"Why not?" I tugged at the hem of the dress, suddenly feeling self-conscious.

"Anton is expecting a bombshell model with curves that don't quit." Once more her eyes ran over my outfit. "You've got the curves going for you, but that dress is too Sandra Bullock girl next door. You'll need to wear one of the outfits I bought for you. At the house, you've got a closet full of clothes waiting. Wear them. He'll expect you to look like eye candy at all times."

Scowling, I focused my attention outside as the Porsche cruised Ocean Drive. The art deco buildings overlooking the Atlantic slid by over an enormous stretch of land.

"So there's water on both sides?" I noticed when we had passed over one of the main bridges.

Heather made a hand gesture. "Biscayne Bay Lagoon and the Atlantic sit on both sides of the strip. As you can see"—she pointed up and over to sets of tall buildings—"most of these are hotels, like the Colony Hotel and other iconic landmarks. Then you have the folks"—her eyebrows waggled—"that can afford to live here, like Anton."

Scanning each building as the Porsche jetted down the road, the wind blowing through the windows ruffling my hair, I noted myriad rich colors in palettes I didn't often see. In Vegas, everything seemed brown or terracotta-colored. In LA, you had everything from brilliant white to a variety of muted tones that fit with the California vibe. Here though, colors seemed to burst out in pale sunny oranges, blues, and pinks mixed with white.

"See all these places?" She pointed out the businesses such as the Colony Hotel and Boulevard Hotel with a whisk of her hand into the flowing wind. I nodded and stretched over her form to see better. "They all light up in neon colors at night. Kind of like in Vegas."

Vegas. I was sure my eyes widened as a steady thud picked up in my chest. A pang of need suddenly coiled around my heart. I needed to call Maddy and Ginelle. Man, Gin would be so pissed when I told her what happened in Washington, DC. Maybe I could get away with never bringing it up? That idea certainly had some serious merit. "That's so cool. I'm originally from Vegas, so it will be nice to see the buildings lit up." I sat back in my seat and enjoyed the breeze, allowing the tension I'd picked up from DC and Boston, when I had to leave Rachel and Mason behind, to dissipate.

Fumbling, I pulled out my phone and turned it on. Several pings rang out. I scanned them, a message from Rachel telling me to text when I'd arrived. A message from Tai asking if the new client was a gentleman or if he needed to get on a plane again. And a text from Ginelle. *Oh, snap.* This was not good.

My stomach felt like a pit the size of the Grand Canyon, a never-ending cavern of dread filling the wide open space.

To: Mia Saunders
From: Skank-a-lot-a-Puss
You were attacked? In the hospital? Why the fuck did I have to hear about it in a text from Tai's brother! If you aren't already dead I'm so going to kill you!

Sucking in a breath between my teeth I typed out a reply.

To: Skank-a-lot-a-Puss
From: Mia Saunders
Just a little mishap. No big deal. Totally fine. Don't worry about me. I'll call you later when I get settled with the Latin Lov-ah.

To: Mia Saunders
From: Skank-a-lot-a-Puss
Latin Lov-ah? No shit? He's like the biggest thing in hip hop and habanero hot!

To: Skank-a-lot-a-Puss
From: Mia Saunders
I heard he's douchey.

To: Mia Saunders
From: Skank-a-lot-a-Puss
That man can douche me any time…preferably with his tongue!

To: Skank-a-lot-a-Puss
From: Mia Saunders
You're twisted!

To: Mia Saunders
From: Skank-a-lot-a-Puss
I'd like to be the rice and beans on the side of his entre. The churro to end his meal. The flaming flan he blows on and licks clean.

To: Skank-a-lot-a-Puss
From: Mia Saunders
Stop! Crazy whore. Jeez. You make me look like a fucking

saint.

To: Mia Saunders
From: Skank-a-lot-a-Puss
At least I know if I'm going to hell you'll be right there giving me a lift!

I laughed out loud as Heather said, "Work?" while gesturing toward my phone. I hit a button and put it on silent before sliding it into my purse.

"Sorry. Best friend. Checking in." I sighed and flicked my hair over one shoulder. The heat was getting to me. Leaning over, I adjusted the air vent to blast me with icy cold goodness. Ah, better. Obviously Heather wasn't worried about wasting the cool air by also having the windows down.

"You close?" Her lips pursed together as she turned into an underground parking garage.

My brows furrowed. What part of "best friend" had she not heard? "Yep. Close as you can get. Known one another forever."

She huffed and slammed the car into park. "You're lucky. I don't have any friends." Her words jolted through me like an electric shock.

"What do you mean? Everyone has friends."

Heather shook her head. "Not me. Too much work to do to cultivate relationships. Anton has to be the best. Even if I'm just his PA, I need to rock the house. Besides, my education is in business management. One day maybe I'll be making the decisions for an artist. If I want my dreams to come true, I have to work hard."

"Guess so." I shrugged and followed her as she walked briskly toward an elevator, passing a line of seriously impressive luxury cars.

"Damn," I whispered under my breath, taking in the Mercedes, Range Rover, Escalade, BMW, Bentley, Ferrari, and several other European cars I didn't get to check out. What I did see—the items that stopped me in my tracks, had me glued to the concrete—were the six hottest sex on wheels I'd ever seen.

BMW HP2 Sport—white with blue rims and an 1170 engine. I might have wet myself at that point. Then there was an MV Agusta F4 1000, the only bike in the world to have a radial valved engine. I twisted around, let go of the handle on my suitcase, and traced the third bike's sexy as fuck seat. The Icon Sheene all black with shiny chrome. I caressed it the way a lover would, with one finger tip, tracing its rounded curves and bold edge design. This bike cost over a hundred and fifty thousand dollars! *Fuck me. No, really, I need to fuck on this bike.*

Air, I needed air! I gasped and crouched down, still not capable of taking my eyes off the pretty. *Sweet baby, come to Mama.* I could happily live in this garage, just staring at the bikes of my dreams.

"Um, hello? Earth to Mia? What the hell are you doing?"

Her voice came through, but I didn't answer. It was like a pesky mosquito that no matter how many times you swatted it away it kept coming back.

I slowly stood, sucked in a replenishing breath, and scanned down the line once more. An orange-and-black sick tricked out KTM Super Duke was hanging out at the back of the line. Probably the most affordable of the lot, definitely on my list of amazing bikes I might one day be able to afford. "Whose bikes are these?" I asked, my voice having dropped an octave, in awe of the pure hot sex on two wheels.

"Anton's. This is his building. His music studio is here, dance club, gym, and of course, the penthouse is his home. The rest of his team each have an apartment in the building as well. You've even got your own loft apartment we use for visiting celebrities or folks who are working on one of his albums.

"Does he ride the bikes?"

She grinned. "Bike enthusiast, huh?"

"You could say that." I had to force the words out, even though I hadn't yet ripped my gaze from the line of man-made beauty.

"Maybe he'll take you for a ride."

That got my attention. "A ride."

She nodded, her smile so pretty it could be on advertisements selling products across the globe.

"Fuck that. I don't ride bitch, honey. I drive."

★ ★ ★

Heather gave me all of fifteen minutes to freshen up before she was going to take me down to meet Anton. I jumped in the shower, washed off the day's travel grime, and spotted the outfit she'd laid out. Outfit was too strong a description. What was sitting on the bed for me was a scrap of fabric, a pair of booty shorts, and stilettos that crisscrossed up the entire length of my calf to the knee. I slid on the shorts and checked the hemline in the mirror. A swath of ass cheek was clearly visible to any discerning eye. Fuck me. I turned to the front. The shorts were cut so high the lining of the pocket stuck out the bottom. The tank was cute. It was blousy, tied together by two thin ribbons at each shoulder. Closing my eyes, I counted to ten and gave myself a pep talk.

You can do this, Mia.
Just over a month ago you were traipsing around in a bikini with Tai and the modeling team. This is actually more clothing than that. Plus, you're not here for your stellar morals in decency, you're here to look hot and be a love interest in a rock video. Er, a hip-hop video.

A groan slipped out of my mouth as I pulled my hair up into a ponytail. It felt like a million degrees, or maybe my own internal temperature had hit a hundred.

Breathing slowly through my nose and out my mouth, I stood and walked out to the living space. Heather was there, taking a call. Her eyes took in my outfit from the tip of my toes to my hair. When she got to my head, an ugly frown marred her face. Never taking her ear off the phone she moved to me, tugged on the hair tie, and let the thick strands tumble around my shoulders. "Better," she whispered while fluffing it this way and that. Then she snapped her fingers and walked to the door.

"Did you just fucking snap at me?" The easy camaraderie that we'd had in the car ride from the airport was blown to bits.

Heather had the good grace to look chagrined. "Sorry," she mouthed. "Yes, Anton, I've got her now." The words held irritation as if it were a physical thing you could toss up in the air and catch on a whim. "We'll meet you in the dance room. Yes, five minutes."

"Mia, I'm sorry. He gets me all twisted in a knot. Unfortunately, he's on a bit of a tear. Didn't mean to be rude. Apparently the backup dancers sucked, couldn't move if they had bees in their underpants."

I tried to chuckle with her but couldn't really pull it off. Dread ricocheted down each rib to land heavily in my gut. He would most certainly not be happy when he found out this white girl could not dance. At least I was safe in the knowledge that there were no take-backs. He paid the fee regardless of whether I could dance. That was not part of my portfolio, and I'd never claimed it to be.

The elevator opened to a hallway where glass walls spanned the entire length from wall to wall. The regular lights were off in the room, black lights were flickering, and spotlights shone down on several figures, bodies writhing to the obscenely loud beat. A man in jogging shorts and a T-shirt clapped out beats and called numbers to the dancers in what I thought were placements for their feet or hands, but I couldn't be sure.

Heather brought me in to stand to the side. That's when I got my first good look at Anton Santiago. I took in his sleek, muscled form, and my mouth went dry. The room around me seemed to throb like a heartbeat as he slowly walked forward. Each beat of the music accentuated the movement of his shoulders, one in front of the other, and twisted his hips along to each hit. His body was covered in slick sweat from the protruding collar bone, over square pecs, and down the highway that was one helluva toned abdomen. Not only was he cut, his body just screamed, "Hold me, touch me, put your naked form all over me."

He spun around, the back-up dancers mimicking the move, and then he hit the floor…with his body. He did a series of pushups to the beat, and then one-handed, the muscles in his forearms bulging delectably. He did another, but with an added roll of his hips as if he were humping the ground. Sweet mother…I wanted to shimmy over there and lay down so he could practice that move on a living, breathing, hot-blooded woman. And I was hot. So fucking hot. I fanned myself as I watched his body twist, turn, and catapult into the air onto his feet where he repeated the hip rolling pelvic thrust to the sexiest lyrics.

"Ride it baby, ride…" *body roll*

"With me, I'll go all night…" *thrust*

"Let me do you right…" *body roll*

"And ride it baby, ride…" *thrust*

He cupped his package with his large hand, tugging up while his body arched into the air. He looked like a golden-brown god who'd just finished pounding his dream girl and was checking the status of his weapon before going back into a sex-driven battle.

The music came to an abrupt halt. "Okay, guys, that's enough for the day. Anton, we good," the guy in shorts called out.

Anton didn't say a word, just offered one cool as a cucumber chin lift. A gaggle of girls clambered up to him with water and a towel. "Oh, Anton, you were amazing. So sexy."

He stopped a few feet in front of me, eyes never leaving mine. Green to green. His blazing, mine turned way the fuck on. "Leave me."

"But I thought after rehearsal we were going to have

fun?" The two girls clamored for his attention.

His brows furrowed. "Anton don't do repeats. *Vete al carajo*," he said, and with a sweep of his hand shooed them away. By the grimace and sadness on their faces, whatever he said could not have been good. Later I found out it meant "fuck off."

"*Lucita*." He licked his lips in the way a man does that literally makes your spine tingle and your core *clench*. Yes, he made my pussy clench with a single lip lick. "Now that you're here, whatever shall we do with you?" His Puerto Rican accent did crazy things to my senses as his eyes scanned me from head to toe again. He might as well have reached out a hand and trailed it all along my skin for how much I felt that look.

Those green orbs glazed over with what could only be seen as pure carnal lust. We stood there, eyes locked on one another, as we had a visual silent war with one another. Nostrils flared, eyes squinted, and finally, I spoke.

"You could feed me. I'm starved," I said. Heather, standing a lot closer than I thought, snorted with laughter, breaking the tension between me and the Latin Lov-ah. Now that I saw him in front me, it made all kinds of sense where he got that name.

His head cut to hers. "Sorry, Anton," she said and looked away, failing to hide the smile on her face.

Anton held his hand out to me. "Mia, let's fill you up." The way he said those words literally made me think of a hundred other completely inappropriate things besides food. I licked my lips and smacked my chops.

"Yes, let's."

CHAPTER TWO

Anton led the three of us to the elevator and up to the penthouse, his private residence. The moment the doors opened, Anton walked through them, leaving the two of us behind. "You know what to do, H," he hollered over his shoulder, not even sparing a glance in his wake.

Heather led me in the opposite direction. "Come on, girl. I think we'll be needing a drink. A big one."

We entered an open floor plan kitchen. White cabinets spanned an entire wall, each with a unique black scrollwork handle, as if each one was individually made. An obscenely long counter stretched in front of the cabinetry and top notch appliances. Ten stools with rounded tops sat in a perfect line under the black granite slab counter. I pulled one out and sat, tugging down the itty bitty shorts as much as possible to make sure portions of my ass weren't hanging over the bull-nosed edge of the stool. Not a good look for anybody.

"Do you like pomegranate?" Heather pulled out two crystal martini glasses.

I nodded. "Very much."

She proceeded to pull out a giant bottle of Grey Goose Vodka, a metal shaker, and the juice.

"So what does Anton have planned for me?" I asked while she dropped the cubes into the shaker and then, with a heavy hand, poured the vodka, adding just a splash of the pomegranate concentrate.

Heather smirked and smiled. "You mean aside from fucking you?" The statement was more an accusation than a question. I balked, unable to believe the audacity of what she'd just said.

"Don't act all coy. I saw the way the two of you were eye-fucking each other in the studio earlier. I give it until evening before he has you laid out underneath him."

She pushed the martini glass filled to the brim with burgundy liquid over to me. "Bottoms up," she said and took a healthy swig.

I did the same, needing the liquid courage to set her straight. "You really don't think that highly of me, do you?" The words came out as venomous as a rattlesnake's bite.

Her eyebrows scrunched together. "Don't you fuck all your clients? You are an *escort*." That one word carried an enormous amount of scorn.

On that note, I smacked the glass down, red liquid sloshing all over the counter. "I fuck who I want, when I want to. It's not part of my contract. I'm an escort not a *whore*." I blew out a harsh breath and continued, "I offer companionship or fill a need, but that need doesn't necessarily include fucking my clients." My tone was rife with indignation although, technically, I had fucked some of my clients, but not all of them.

I say who, and I say when. Period.

Thoughts of the man who'd wanted to push the physical *who* and the *when* onto m, crept their sinister way into my subconscious. If I could, I'd bat the disgusting reminders back with a sledgehammer, lock them in a very dark closet, and throw away the key. *You will not control me.*

Revenge scaled along my chest and up through my throat, fueled by my lingering fear of what had recently occurred with Aaron. "Now I know why you don't have any friends. You're judgmental, pissy, and downright rude!"

Heather backed up a few steps until she hit the opposite counter where the stainless steel double-wide Sub Zero fridge shook. If I hadn't been paying close attention I wouldn't have recognized the shimmery blue of her eyes. She cleared her throat, raised a delicate long-fingered hand to her chest, and spoke. "I'm sorry, Mia. That was rude of me."

"Damn right it was rude!" My mouth hurt from clenching my teeth. I sucked back the rest of my drink, allowing the fiery burn to disguise the acid burn building in the pit of my stomach.

She licked her lips, and her eyes moved from side to side. "Again, please, I'm sorry. I didn't hire you to be his bedmate. He has plenty of those. You're going to be the main woman in the new video. A woman he wants, a seductress that he can't have."

A seductress. Now there was something I hadn't been. It sounded so ridiculous, especially in light of the heated conversation we'd just had, that I tipped my head back and laughed. A full-bellied, snorting, hiccupping guffaw that rose in volume and hysterics.

Heather's eyebrows drew up toward her hairline. "Um, okay…well, no more 'tinis for *you!*" She winked, effectively lightening the situation.

I placed my elbow on the counter and my chin into my hand. "Today has been odd. Hell, the past month was nuts. This just tops the crazy cake I call my life." I shook my head and ran my fingers through my hair. It was getting really long. Maybe I could swindle some time away from the Latin Lov-ah to score a haircut.

Regardless of what she'd said, Heather made us both another drink. "Can we call a truce? I really don't want you hating me, and I did misunderstand the meaning of what you do." Her blue eyes seemed round and big on her pretty face, innocent even.

I held out my hand. She glanced at it, a weariness making her movements slow when she clasped mine with her own. We shook. "Truce." I smiled. She grinned back and repeated the word.

"Two ladies shaking hands over a couple of alcoholic beverages can be cause to make a man nervous. What are you two conspiring?" Anton entered, wearing a flowing pair of white linen pants that had a drawstring hanging precariously close to his manhood. He'd paired the pants with a crisp mint green dress shirt that he left open, exposing his finely sculpted abdomen. Perfectly manicured toes peeked out past the loose-fitting pants. Damn, even his feet were lickable. That right there said more than it should about the insanely beautiful specimen standing before me. I watched him move with the grace of a cougar even with the bulk of his muscles to weigh him down. Anton wasn't short, but he wasn't extremely tall. I'd guess around five-foot-eleven, which was fine for me since I was only five-foot-eight, but I typically preferred my men taller like Wes and Alec.

Wes and Alec. Two men, two completely different feelings rushing through my system at the mere thought of them. One had lasting implications of a future together, and the other lasting desire.

Anton moved to Heather and placed an arm around her shoulders. "So, H, *Lucita* here is going to be the love interest that I cannot have in the video?" He squeezed Heather's bicep, pulling her into his side in a friendly hold, but his eyes never left mine. She nodded mutely and rolled her eyes. He brought his opposite hand up toward his face where he proceeded to pet the flesh of his bottom lip with the pad of his thumb as he assessed me. It was as if his fingertips were tracking all over my form the way his eyes moved over each new surface of skin.

Not gonna lie. I swooned. Hard. Damn, he had it going on in the looks department as well as the way he moved and spoke. The hint of his Puerto Rican accent, the way his words seemed to roll off his tongue like sex incarnate... did something to me. Something I *did not* want to feel after what I'd just gone through in June with Aaron. Nevertheless, low and behold, this guy, the Latin Lov-ah, must have had supercharged pheromones because I felt each and every one of them like a physical blow to my sex.

"You are *damn* fine, girl." He tipped his chin up at me. "You got moves?"

"Er, as in what type of moves?" I asked.

He spun away from Heather on the tips of his toes and moved in a series of fast circles until he made his way around the long counter and slid toward me on a clap, a shimmy of his hips, and a pop of his chest. Anton stopped a hair's breadth from my face, smelling of soap and coconut, reminding me of lying out on a sunny beach in Hawaii. I wanted to be lying on a beach in Hawaii right now, preferably underneath this sex god.

"Moves, *muñeca,*" he whispered. I could feel the heat of

his breath against my face, small puffs of air tantalizing my nerves and awakening lust receptors from their month-long sleep.

I held his gaze with my own and leaned close, resting my cheek against his so I could whisper into his ear. "What does *muñeca* mean?" The words were soft, almost a caress against his skin.

"Doll." His voice was gritty, as if he'd swallowed a spoonful of sand.

"And *Lucita*?" I let my lips hover close enough to his cheek that I could feel the stubble on his jaw.

He groaned and laid a hand on my hip, a featherlight hold that my mind dismissed casually. "Little light."

Little light? I moved my head back, breaking the intensity of the moment and the halo of lust surrounding our close proximity. "Little light?" I couldn't hold back the giggle that escaped. "Why?"

With the lightest touch of the tips of two fingers, he traced the ball of my shoulder and slid those digits down along the sensitive skin of my arm. Gooseflesh rose against the surface, a gnarled pair of claws worked their way up from where he held my wrist up my arm, over my chest to coil around my heart and squeeze. Blackness entered my vision, and the sound of a heartbeat thudded loudly. My skin felt tight, constricted, every nerve prickling with the desire to run, cower…escape.

"You ready to get pounded?" he growls, his breath hitting my face with little flecks of spittle.

My body presses against the concrete wall of the library. The sickening sound of his pants being unbuckled and the noise of the

zipper going down is like my own personal death knell. I scream
as loud as I can, but he swoops down so fast and bites the sound
from my lips and then slams my head into the concrete. Pain flashes
across my vision like stars in an open dessert sky.
　　"No!"

"No!" I screamed and pushed the hard body standing
too close and then jumped back until I hit the edge of a
couch. A couch? Huh? Moving my head back and forth I
shook off the web of memories clouding my judgment.

　　Holy fucking shit! What. The. Hell. Was. That?

　　Two pairs of horrified eyes watched as I came to.
"Mia…" Heather gasped, her hand over her mouth.

　　"*Lucita*, I…*perdóname*. I'm sorry. Did I hurt you
somehow?" Anton's voice was tinged with distaste and
something that I could only name as fear.

　　Shit. This was not going well. Why did I have that
flashback? What the hell had triggered it?

　　I shook my head. "No, no, sorry guys. I think I'm just
tired from traveling, and I haven't eaten, and I drank the
martini so quickly…yeah, I'm sure that's what it was." Had
to be.

　　Anton's lips tightened into a thin line. "Let's get you
fed. I will not tolerate my team not having their needs met.
Come. H, let's go to our favorite." He held out his hand
to me, and I placed mine within it. The familiar stirrings
of excitement were still there, but now with the edge of
nervousness. From the simple act of holding his hand. What.
The. Fuck. *This is not you, Mia.* I needed to figure this out
and quick. But how?

　　Not knowing what else to do, I followed Anton and

Heather out the door, my mind in a tizzy and the circle of fear still nipping at my heels.

★ ★ ★

Dinner was awesome. Delicious *Gnocchi al Gorgonzola* they called it at Il Gabbiano, the upscale Italian restaurant Anton took us to. I was completely underdressed, but so were he and Heather. As we walked into the place, several of Anton's security team were hot on our tails. We entered as though we were royalty. The restaurant manager spied us and made his way over as if he were barefoot walking on steaming black coals. He sat us with no waiting at a corner table with a beautiful view of the Atlantic ocean. Anton ordered several appetizers with a flourish and a pristine white smile. His pale green and brown gaze dazzled every woman within a twenty foot radius and garnered the attention of the other patrons. Both Heather and I ordered antipasti, I wanting something devilishly decadent and filled with a bazillion calories, so I ordered my all-time favorite puffy pillows of goodness, gnocchi covered in cream sauce. It was absolute heaven on the taste buds.

Anton ordered a shrimp and pasta dish and ate his food with speed and efficiency, as though it would jump off his plate back into the ocean. When I questioned his feverish eating, he frowned, wiped his mouth, and looked out over the Atlantic. Heather studiously changed the subject before he could answer. Apparently she knew something about this particular hot button item that I didn't. I glanced at her, and she shook her head minutely. The conversation turned to the music video and what the plan was.

That's when I had to drop the giant atomic bomb that I had absolutely no skills in the art of dance whatsoever.

"None?" Anton's eyebrows pinched together. I shook my head and bit my lip. He lifted a hand, scraped it across his five o'clock shadow, and inhaled. "We'll have to do something about this. You"—he gestured from the top of my head to the end of the table—"are *perfecto* eh…perfect as the seductress. H, you couldn't have picked someone better. We must solve this little issue." He rubbed his hands together. Anton's pupils darkened. "You thinking what I'm thinking?" He was speaking to Heather, not me.

Her lips tipped up, and she tapped her index finger against her lips and shrugged. "If she's available. The dance company in San Francisco just finished, and that wicked man who was stalking her group of friends is gone." She shimmied in her seat. "The news has cleared. Perhaps having her come on as the choreographer would fix the problems you're having with the backup dancers. I'll give her a call, see if she's interested in saving your ass. You know it's going to cost you."

Anton laughed. "Doesn't everything, H? I want her. I'm tired of dealing with this stupid fucker, and her contemporary work is best. Add the Latin fusion. She'll know how to spin the angles right. I want all eyes to be on Mia. Want her mouthwateringly desirable on the video. Every man will want her, and no man will have her." He grinned salaciously, popped an entire shrimp into his mouth, and dropped the tail onto the side plate. Anton was beaming, obviously excited about his new idea.

"So, uh, who's this choreographer?"

Heather sipped her white wine and wiped her mouth.

"A really gifted contemporary dancer who's been on stage with the San Francisco Dance Company the last couple years, so we haven't been able to steal her away." She pointed one finger at Anton while holding her wine glass. "Anton fell in love with her body and the way she moves when we saw her show last year."

That information surprised me. "You're into theatre productions?" I butted in.

"Yes, *Lucita*. It calms me and seduces my muse. I love to see others dancing, singing to the classics and new innovative pieces."

"Anyway," Heather interrupted, "we found out she teaches dance for the San Francisco Theatre exclusively. You know she won't leave San Francisco for Miami." She addressed that last part to him. Anton frowned. "Something about needing to be where her sisters are. But if we offer her enough and get on the horn quickly, she might be willing to head out for the time Mia's here while we're filming. Could really add the element we need to take the video to the next level." Abruptly, Heather stood up. "I'll call now." She looked down at her watch. "They're three hours behind so we're good." Without further comment, she left the table and headed for the open balcony.

I sipped my wine and looked out over the ocean. The breeze wafted around us, but the heat lamps near our table provided enough warmth. "That assistant of yours is pretty efficient."

Anton smiled. "She is. That's why I keep her."

"May I be frank?" I asked, pressing my lips together, waiting.

He leaned back, crossed an ankle to his knee, and spread

his arms out. "Of course."

"Why do you have that harsh tone with her? Don't you ever worry she'll leave you?" I truly wondered why anyone would stay with a man who acted like his shit didn't stink half of the time and the other half was laid back and easy going. It was as though there were two completely different sides to him.

"What would make you think that?" His eyes narrowed.

I shrugged. "I don't know. Maybe the way you bark at her over the phone, walk in front of her like she's your peon, and throw orders at her while walking away."

Anton scowled. "I value Heather's opinion over all others. Hers is the only one I give credence to…ever. I trust her implicitly."

"Could have fooled me."

Anton grabbed his drink and inhaled the rest of his Shiraz. "Has she said anything to you about leaving?" His tone proved that the idea of Heather leaving him was not a welcome one.

"No! Not at all. I do get the hint that she wants more."

"More?" The question hung heavy. "As in a relationship?"

I shook my head. Was he really that narcissistic? Scanning his body and the face angels would weep for, I guess he had a right to be. Sort of. "Not that I know of. I was referring to her work. Something she mentioned about her dream being to manage an artist. You seem to be lacking a manager at this time."

Anton's hand came up to his mouth where he stroked that supremely kissable bottom lip with the pad of his thumb. "I don't have one. Usually I just bounce all the decisions off of H, and she sets everything up."

Interesting. "So, she's kind of already managing you without the benefits or clout the title of Manager carries. Bummer for her." Nonchalantly I fiddled with my hair and adjusted my seat so I was facing the water to give him space. The ocean was absolutely stunning. A pang hit my heart as I realized how much I missed home.

Home.

Crap. It looked like I'd inadvertently answered a question I'd been mulling over for the better part of a few months.

Home was California.

CHAPTER THREE

The sun streaked through the curtains, blinding me in its glory. Day three and I finally felt as though I'd gotten enough sleep. Yesterday had been a whirlwind of meetings with the beautician, stylist, and crew. Tonight we would meet the choreographer. She would be flying in this morning and wanted a meet-and-greet with the entire team in the dance studio right away. Hopefully, that didn't mean she was going to be a hard ass drill sergeant type. Anxiety and excitement warred in equal parts, skittering along my senses as I wondered if she'd be able to get me shimmying in a way that wouldn't look like Elaine from that dreaded Seinfeld episode Dad loved.

This white girl can't dance. It's always been a bone of contention with me and my agent. I can carry a tune, act, and apparently model well enough, but I've never been gifted with the art of dance. Ginelle, however, can dance her way out of a hurricane. Her work with Dainty Dolls Burlesque put her on the map, and the stage loves her. Even pint-sized, she packs a lot in her tiny form and can move across the stage better than anyone I know.

Sadness swirled around me like a cloak. Gin would've loved being here to meet with a fancy choreographer from San Francisco. Once I found out who it is, I'd give her a heads up, see what she knew, if anything, about the mysterious woman that Anton was head over heels for. Well, as far as her dancing was concerned.

My phone pinged as I turned it on. I scanned the messages, bleary eyed from a full night's sleep. One message was from Maddy, updating me about school, thanking me for the most recent check I sent for books and food. It still irked me that I didn't have to pay for her living expenses anymore. I took deep breaths and let go a little more every day. I would never fully let go of my responsibility when it came to my baby sister. It was far too ingrained into the very fiber of my being. However, I had to constantly remind myself that she was an adult, one who was living with her now fiancé with her career and future goals all laid out in front of her. She was happy, healthy, and in a good place, with a guy who seemed to dote on her every whim. He'd better stay that way or I'd tie the fucker down and pluck out every hair on his chest one at time with my handy dandy tweezers.

The next message chilled my blood. Oh, that bestie of mine was going to get it. There was only one way that he'd know about my birthday and that was if someone had told him.

To: Mia Saunders
From: Wes Channing
Little birdie told me your birthday was next week and that you're in Miami. Carve out a day away. You can't possibly want to spend your birthday with a stranger. I'm coming to see you. Be ready. We've got months to make up for.

With a flourish, I rang the little snake that gave away the goods.

"H-ullo," a sleepy voice answered. "Mia, you okay?" she responded again, this time a bit more alert.

"How could you?" I grated into the phone, holding my cell as if it were a hammer ready to strike.

Ginelle sighed and mumbled. "Had to be done." She yawned.

"Really? Had to be done. Is that your response? I'm so mad at you," I whisper-yelled into the phone. Why I was whispering I couldn't say since there was no one in the apartment with me.

She groaned and yawned once more. "Mia, I did an eeny meenie miny moe of hot guys from the phone numbers I stole from your phone." I rolled my eyes and clenched my teeth. Just like her to steal their numbers instead of asking for them. "Wes was the one I landed on. You shouldn't spend your birthday alone." Her voice turned into a cross between a high-pitched yawn and her normal witty self. "I'd come out, but you know after May's vacation I can't take the time. What time is it anyways?"

I glanced at the clock on the side table. Eight o'clock in the morning on the East coast. Snickering, I responded, "Five your time. Serves you right. Now I have to deal with Wes."

"Deal with him? Hmm, I'd be doing a lot more than dealing with him. Why are you so mad, anyway?"

Good point. Gin meddled in my business all the time and never before had I been angry with her. Perhaps it was because I wasn't ready to see Wes so soon after the Aaron debacle and the fact that I was still working through my own issues over what happened. All of this on top of the big whopper that I was falling in love with the guy. Fuck!

That was the problem. My mind could push back, fight my heart all it wanted to, but the end-all be-all was that I was in love with the dirty blond sex god who looks just as good in a pair of low-slung swim trunks or a tux as he does buck naked. Definitely prefer the bare ass naked version. I licked my lips, remembering our last encounter in Chi-Town. It was intense, carnal, and seared into my memory for eternity.

"Hello, Mia? Dick got your tongue? I sure as hell hope so. You're grumpy since that political prick got his grubby hands on you."

"Gin! I was attacked. Have a little mercy."

Her voice went instantly soft. "I know, babe. I'm sorry. I just don't want you to let that fucker get the best of you. No man gets to have that power over you. Remember. That's what you told me after all the shit you went through with Blaine."

I groaned. "I don't know, girl. Anton here is mouthwateringly hot—"

In true Ginelle fashion, she cut me off. "Girl, what I would give to be in your position right now. No, not your position. You like playing all hard to get. See me and my awesome tits, come look at 'em, oh, no, you can't have 'em. Me, I'd be down on my knees in front of that hot piece of mocha-covered goodness sucking down his manhood like a frappuccino-flavored icy treat."

I busted out laughing. "You would, you skanky ho-bag."

"Who me?" She pretended to be surprised.

I groaned and flopped back onto the bed. "But Gin, here's the thing. The second he got close, I freaked. Had a full on flashback of that night with Aaron." Scowling, I picked at my cuticle, working a piece until it bled. The pain was nothing compared to the worry that I was more screwed up than I thought after what had happened.

"Hmm, I think you need to give yourself some time. Is he pressuring you?" Her voice turned hard, that high pitch hitting a crescendo. It was a warning that she was about to blow up.

"No, no, no. Not at all. Just in the beginning, there was some serious flirting going on between us, but now, it's like a wet blanket has fallen over my libido."

"Hmm, maybe Wes coming to town is the exact thing you need. You know, get your groove back."

"Are you seriously quoting movie titles?"

"Babe, I got nuthin' when it comes to you not wanting to bang an exceptionally ripped, powerfully gorgeous rich hunk of yumminess. Goes against everything that I am."

"True…big whore," I added for levity.

"Gotta stick to what I know."

I rolled my eyes and sighed. "Fine. You owe me, though." It took effort to sound hard and unyielding, especially to my best friend, but I felt I managed pretty well.

"So I'm forgiven for meddling?" she squeaked out in a tiny, almost nervous voice.

Staring up at the ceiling, I let the swirls in the plaster settle my mood. "Yeah, for now. But don't contact any of them again. I mean it, Gin!"

"Scout's honor!" she rushed to add.

"You've never been a scout!" I scolded her and laughed.

"Sounded good in the moment." She giggled.

"Whatever. Go back to bed 'hood-rat!" I grinned, and even though she couldn't see me, I'm certain she knew all was forgiven just by my tone.

"Aye, aye, captain coochie! Love you, bitch."

"Love you more, bitch-face."

We hung up, and I read Wes's message again. He'd be here in two weeks. My birthday was July fourteenth. Bastille Day.

Figured I'd better get this over with.

To: Wes Channing
From: Mia Saunders

Ginelle should have kept her mouth shut. You really don't have to come. I'll be fine. I love that you're thinking of me.

Love? There's that damn word again. Love. Did I love Wes? Truly? I didn't know. Maybe. Probably. Possibly. It was definitely not something I had any business thinking about when I was with yet another client. One that, true to Gin's words, was a mocha-colored hunk of yumminess. And also a *player.* Then again, wasn't I? I'd been with Wes, Alec, and Tai, and here I sat in another rich man's apartment considering how fuckable he was.

Lightning fast, I pulled up my Internet app and typed in the word *Player.* The Internet helpfully supplied the following.

Player

1. *A person taking part in a sport or game. Football player.*

2. *A person playing a musical instrument. A trumpet player.*

Not the type of player definition I was going for. Just under that definition was a link to a different website named "Metropolitan Dictionary." I clicked the link.

Player

A male who is talented at manipulating or "playing" others, and skilled at seducing the opposite sex by pretending to care for them when their only interest is in sex.

Hmm, was the term player only used to describe males? My get-out-of-jail-free-card holding side wanted to cash in that coupon as fast as you could say go, collect my two hundred dollars, and buy Park Place. Unfortunately, my self-loathing guilty conscience wouldn't allow me to think so highly of myself. That niggling simpering twit within had me visiting Intellectipedia. It had never let me down before.

The first definition said it all in black and white, noting exactly what I feared.

Player may refer to:

Player in the dating sense: a man or woman who has romantic affairs or sexual relations with the opposite sex with no intent to marry or carry on a monogamous relationship.

That was all I needed to see. Confirmed. *Mia Saunders, honey, you are a player.*

★ ★ ★

After spending an ungodly amount of time scalding my skin to a tantalizing and oversensitive pink hue, I made my way up to the elevator. The text I'd received from Heather directed me to dress casually and meet Anton on the roof. Why the roof, I had no idea, but I was on their dime, so followed the request without response. It had been an hour since my text to Wes, and he hadn't yet responded. I didn't know what I wanted him to say. Would he push back and force his way into my heart? A part of me wanted that so badly I could hardly breathe. Another part of me wanted to continue with the way our relationship was, at least for now. No expectations, no rights to one another, just friends. With benefits.

Friends with benefits.

Was that the relationship I really wanted with Wes? My Wes? Shit. And when did he become *my Wes*? I suspected somewhere between admitting I was falling in love with him and thinking of home being California. No, not just California. His place in Malibu. That's where I felt most like myself. Free to just be Mia.

With a snarl, I smashed the elevator button so hard my thumb smarted. I shook it out and watched the numbers climb. Why now? After dealing with a shitty experience, licking my wounds in Boston with Rach and Mace, to come here, find a hot guy who was overt in showing his appreciation for me, or at least my body, and everything built up to this? Had it always been coming to this point? Where I felt as though my emotions and fears were simmering like lava under the Earth's surface, a volcano that could erupt at any moment?

The elevator dinged, and I was catapulted into a very strange world. Plants, trees, and the humid air blasted against my skin, making it hard to breathe. The humidity was so thick you could cut it like a pat of butter.

"Jesus…" I swallowed reflexively, trying to bite back the fish–out–of–water feeling.

"*Lucita!* Over here," I heard Anton call, but only saw a

man's form, a blur of white as he moved from plant to plant. On closer inspection, his shirt, linen pants, even his boat shoes were white and smattered with dirt marking up the toes. A huge Asian-style sunhat peeked up over a large shrub as I made my way closer.

I stopped and stared at Anton as he pulled weeds, twisting the bottom and yanking them out, scraggly webbed roots and all. "What are you doing?"

"Gardening. There are gloves over there. Do you have a green thumb?" he asked, with what sounded like hope in his tone.

I shook my head. " 'Fraid not. I kill most things."

He stood tall, the linen shirt forming around all his muscles. A stirring of excitement started low in my belly but fizzled out when he stepped closer, within touching distance. Look but no touch. Interesting.

"Guess we'll have to change that, won't we?"

Shrugging, I pulled on the gloves. "Never gardened before. Back in Vegas, we have what's called zero-scaping. Rocks instead of lawn, cacti instead of bushes, and succulents instead of flowers. You don't have to do much to keep those suckers alive."

"Ah, but the joy comes from the tending and caring for something other than yourself."

Lovely way to think of it.

"Here, you see this plant?" I followed his fingers and assessed the wild green sprout that didn't look like the others. "This weed will end up infiltrating this entire box of Pawpaw." I crinkled my nose, not sure what the heck a Pawpaw was. He grinned. "It's a shrub, but it flowers. See this?" He held up a stem that had a flower unlike any I'd ever seen. It was a deep, dark eggplant color at the center, with three long petals that were light greenish yellow in color. Unique for sure. "The weed will infest the entire lot and destroy the beauty growing within. Kind of like negative thoughts."

Negative thoughts. "How so?"

He smiled softly, his eyes a bright green. "Sit with me, *Lucita*." I did as he bid, planting my bum on the small edge of the flower box. "Negative thoughts are planted like a seed in the brain, and then once they grow, they take over the whole mind, infecting your ability to see truth and beauty clearly. To see the honesty behind a person or situation. In the end, those thoughts take over, and you lose sight of the joy of having that person in your life. Like the weed. It will grow and infest the entire planter box until all the beauty is destroyed and all that remains is the one thing you didn't want in the first place. The weed, or in this case, the negative thought."

"You surprise me." I laid my hand on his bicep and squeezed. When he placed his hand over my knee I froze. Fear and ugliness crept from the center of his touch up my leg, over my body, where a tightness stuck in my chest. Without realizing it at first, I held my breath. His green eyes searched mine, and he closed his eyes, blinking slowly before letting my knee go. It was as if I could breathe again. I turned my head, braced my hands on my knees, and breathed in through my nose and out through my mouth, trying to be stealthy about it. Didn't work. He noticed but had the decency not to comment.

When I got myself back in order, he finally answered my question. He waggled his eyebrows and licked those plump, kissable lips. "I surprise most people." And there was the sarcastic side.

"So gardening is your hobby?"

He nodded. "*Si*. I love to see beautiful things grow. And I love to eat what I've grown." There was pride in his tone. This hobby seemed beloved to the Latin Lov-ah, and somehow it made him more real, a bit more earthy.

The word *eat* jangled around in my mind. Reminded me of the way he'd eaten dinner the other night and how he reacted when I told him I hadn't eaten. "Are you a food lover?" I asked, toying with a leaf of a bush I couldn't name. Everything was so exotic and new to my untrained eye.

Anton got up and moseyed over to another bush. "Food is a necessity. No one should be without it."

"Sounds like man who's lived without it and knows what it's like."

His jaw tightened and his lips thinned. Bingo!

"Are you going to tell me why you freeze when I touch you, even in a friendly manner? Though I'd like to touch you in other ways. If you were willing." His eyes blazed with intensity, proving that he did, in fact, fancy me the same way I fancied him, only it wasn't meant to be.

Walking through the lines of flowers and bushes, I ignored his question and his comment about being attracted to me. "What's this?" I pointed to a bush that had bright yellow fuzzy balls with fern-like deep green leaves connected to it.

"Sweet Acacia. It flowers all year long but don't touch…" he said just as I grasped the yellow bud and was pricked by its thorns.

"Ouch!" I pulled my finger back and flailed it into the

air. He grabbed it and popped the digit into his mouth. Three things happened all at once.

One, a fire lit in my belly, bringing with it all kinds of lustful desire and need so strong moisture set up shop right between my thighs.

Two, that scary, gnawing, anxious feeling wrapped its way around my entire body, effectively putting me into an immobile lockdown.

Three, my vision went black. When I opened my eyes I was back there. Against that fucking wall.

CHAPTER FOUR

"You think you're special, don't you?" Aaron's words are a piercing bite loaded with poisonous venom.

I shake my head and try to sound calm. "Not at all, actually." It's the truth, but based on his response, he doesn't agree.

He scowls, turns on a heel, and prowls forward until I lift my hands in front of me in defense. Aaron doesn't stop. Continuing forward, I find myself pressed up against the concrete wall of a darkened area. In a few more steps, his chest is against mine, all before I realize what is happening. Inhaling shallowly, I consider the best way to handle this, only the champagne is fogging my reflexes, making my limbs feel heavy and lethargic. "Aaron, you don't want to do this."

His face is closer now, and he slides his nose along my temple. Shivers of dread slither down my spine, prickling the hairs at the back of my neck. "Of course I do." His voice sounds dead, devoid of any real emotion. I push against his chest to see if there is any give. No dice. Fear, ripe and hot, tickles my senses, the fight-or-flight response building within. "Trying to escape, little whore," he says in a drunken slur.

"I'm not a whore, Aaron. You know that." I push and jolt my body forward, wanting, needing to get away. That's when things get worse.

Aaron lunges down and bites the space where my shoulder and neck meet. Hard. So hard I cry out, pain throbbing from the wound. He doesn't seem to care and uses his superior strength against me.

"I know my father hired you to be his whore in front of his fucked-up rich friends. I know that you work for an escort service and get paid by the month. Time to get Daddy's money's worth."

"*Dios mio,* Mia. Please! I'm here. It's Anton. Anton! I'm not going to hurt you!" Anton was holding me tight, arms locked around my body, preventing any movement.

That clawing feeling was so strong I used every ounce of strength, turned in his arms, and screamed. He released me as if I were a grenade that just landed in his hands. I ran to the trash can near the edge of the space and threw up. Violent heaving spasms racked my frame. There wasn't much there since I hadn't eaten breakfast yet. Thank God. Mostly just coffee and bile. Anton stood close but not so close that the fear hit me again. His arms were crossed over his chest, his hat off and hanging on a string behind his back. His eyes were dark and filled with sorrow, maybe even pity.

"Don't look at me like that!" I growled and wiped my mouth on the back of my arm. I needed another shower. Sweat beaded on my brow, and my stomach clenched once more. Woozily I made my way to another bench nearby and sat. Anton followed but didn't sit down.

He leaned down on one knee and waited until I lifted my chin, and our gazes held. "You can talk to me." His tone was compassionate, filled with worry.

Frustration and anger hit me with a wallop. "You gonna talk to me?" I smacked my own chest. "What's up with you and food, Anton?" I shot back.

Inhaling, he pinched his lips with his thumb and forefinger. Something dark turned his green eyes a hazy green. The lines in his face softened as he sighed. "I grew up poor. Very poor. So poor there were many days we survived on water and the scraps my siblings and I could scavenge in the dumpsters of the high-priced restaurants near our shack of a home. Puerto Rico isn't all sunshine, beautiful bikini-clad women, and endless beaches. There are many parts that are still very much like a third world country. The east side of the island is very dangerous, and that's where I grew up."

"How many siblings do you have?"

"Two. One brother, one sister. But *mi papa* died when we were very young. *Mi mama* did the best she could, but there were too many nights I went to bed hungry. Years' worth of a rumbling belly." He stood and spread his arms out wide, the picture of the king of his castle. "No more. *Mi mama* now gets plenty of money from me and lives a quiet, happy life, not wishing for anything. Same with my *hermanos*. My siblings," he clarified in English.

I closed my eyes and counted to ten, my only coping mechanism. When my heart rate settled, I opened my eyes and spoke. "My last client had a son, a politician, very high up in the ranks as far as American politics go. He attacked me physically, tried sexually. Got very close to raping me. Too close." Even the words tasted like putrid filth on my tongue.

"When?" The soft way he spoke made me believe I could trust him, share in a way I wouldn't normally have considered with someone I'd only known a couple days.

"Close to three weeks ago."

"*Coño*, that recent? Christ, Mia. Is the fucker in jail?"

And therein lay the problem. I shook my head, and his eyes narrowed. "I didn't press charges." Admitting it out loud hurt like a serrated knife to the gut. Even though I knew it was for the greater good, I still warred against the reality that he'd essentially gotten away with it. Yes, there were repercussions and demands being met that I set, but none that would ease that pit within, that hole in me that would only be filled with the knowledge that justice was served. "No. There were extenuating circumstances. I did what I had to do. There was no good option. If I'd taken him through the system, more than the two of us would have been hurt, and a lot of people would see harm beyond what putting away one sick fuck would do."

Anton nodded. "Sometimes the decisions we have to make are harder on us than anyone can ever comprehend." He said the words with absolutely no judgment. I'd just told him that a vile man attacked and almost raped me, and I willingly didn't put him behind bars. He knew nothing of the circumstances, but instead, chose to accept the decision I'd made as necessary. Why couldn't I?

Making his intent clear, he sat next to me and opened his hand. Offering support and comfort. Scared, but determined to get past this, I placed my hand in his. Did it feel the way it felt when I held hands with Tai or Mace? No, it didn't. Those two men knew what I went through, and for some reason, I wasn't affected by their touch in the days after the attack.

That now familiar fear tingled along my hand, and I squeezed his once and pulled away. "Thank you," I whispered.

His eyebrows rose into his hairline. "For what?"

"For not judging me." My voice cracked, emotion momentarily taking the reins.

Anton took a slow breath. "I do not live your life. I cannot possibly understand how a decision one way or the other could be better or worse, for it is not mine to make. Only you have to live with your choices. I can see that this one is weighing very heavily on you."

Nodding, I inhaled and pressed my palms together until my knuckles turned white with tension.

"So can we be friends without the other possibilities?" I asked, suddenly worried he might be upset with that particular decision.

"Are you attracted to me, *Lucita*?" Little light. Silly man.

"Yes," I said without reservation.

"Yet you will deny yourself the pleasures of mating with me?"

I smiled wide. The pleasures of mating? Where did he come up with this stuff? "Unfortunately, I don't think a new mate is in my cards at this time. Plus, there's sort of someone else." Okay, I admitted it. What the hell was I going to do about it?

Anton smacked his thighs and stood. "Pity. I was looking forward to bedding you."

"I don't think you'll be lacking any company for the foreseeable future."

"This is true." He waggled his eyebrows again. "Friends it is, then?" He held out his hand this time as if to shake on a deal.

"Friends."

He pulled up his hat and placed it on his head once more. "Now, as my friend, you'll help me pull all these weeds."

"I think I'd like that, Anton." A little work in the sun, sweating out the nasty toxins of the emotions too close to the surface would be cathartic. "On one condition…" I added a hand to the hip and cocked my head to the side.

He grinned, a devilish, boyish gleam to his eyes that made me regret the "no mating" decision. "State your terms, woman." His accent made his response sound absurdly suggestive.

"I want to drive one of your motorcycles."

Anton's head popped back and he chuckled. "You ride?" The shock evident in his body language and tone irked me.

"I don't ride, *doll*," I emphasized, using one of his endearments on him. "Baby, I drive."

His happy expression gave me hope. He pursed his lips together. "I look forward to paying up on our deal." He pointed over to a big basket. "Gloves over there, an extra hat, and a bucket."

"Score!"

★ ★ ★

Maria De La Torre.

That was the choreographer's name. Upon seeing her in person, I almost swallowed my own tongue. Her raven hair rivaled my own in the bad ass hair department, and for a dancer, she had curves that wouldn't quit. She was and more muscular than I was, and her body could have been etched in marble and worshipped for eons. She spoke English but switched into Spanish on a whim. Her ethnicity was unique. If I had to guess, I'd say Greek or Italian and maybe European Spanish. Definitely Mediterranean. All in all, she was downright exotic. When she moved, all eyes were on her. There was a fluidity and grace about her, unlike any of the other dancers here.

"Seductress!" Maria called out, looking at a piece of paper. "A Mia Saunders?" She scanned the crowd until all heads turned to me.

I walked to the front of the dance studio where everyone was sitting. I had been holding up the wall in the back, not wanting to get in the way. She questioned each dancer, had them do a series of choreography, and then straight up nixed half of them. Right on the spot, she sent their asses packing. Brutal but effective.

Maria's eyes were an ice blue as she took in my body. "You are not a dancer," she said directly without even asking me to repeat the steps the others had gone through. I almost felt relieved I didn't have to embarrass myself in front of the others.

"No, hired escort." I shrugged and placed my hands on my hips.

Her eyes narrowed, and a small V formed at the top of her brow. "Are you dating someone here?" she asked clearly. Thank goodness someone knew the actual definition of an escort and didn't automatically assume I was a whore.

I smiled. "Anton and Heather hired me for this role. You can discuss the whys and rationale behind that decision with them."

Maria tilted her head one way then the next. "Turn around." I did as she requested. "Again." I circled once more until I was facing her. "Can you dance?"

"Professionally?"

She laughed. "No, I know you can't dance professionally. Your body doesn't lie. Though I can absolutely see, based on your curves and your beauty, why you were chosen in the role of seductress. But I'm wondering, do you dance for fun, move your hips, hula, salsa, tango, anything?"

I shook my head, afraid of how she'd react, though she'd been perfectly professional the entire time, even when axing half the dancers. "Okay, I'll have to think on your role and how we're going to present you to the cameras. You wouldn't be here for a hip hop video if Anton didn't want you in that role. We'll work around any deficiencies."

That didn't sound too bad. At least she didn't cut me out of the production altogether. That would have been a lot easier, and I'd still have gotten paid, the whole no-take-backs clause perfectly in place. Somehow, the concept of failing or disappointing Anton, Heather, or my Aunt Millie, for that matter, by being sent home, didn't sit well with me. I was surprised to note that I was happy she'd kept me. The no-dancing bit and all.

Maria worked over the rest of the dancers. The room now held only a handful of backup dancers and me when Anton entered.

"*Mamacita*," he greeted Maria in an enthusiastic, friendly hug. "*Mama*, you are looking damn fine." He scanned the remaining individuals wandering around, stretching against the ballet barre, running through a series of steps. "Cleaned up shop, I see."

Maria grinned. "Anton, you knew I was going to fire most of the dancers. You don't need that many for what I have in mind. I listened to the song many times on the plane. Based on the concept I've come up with, you're mostly going to need her"—she hooked a thumb towards me—"and maybe a couple more than what are left here." Heather's eyebrows had risen, but she stayed silent, standing a step behind where Maria and Anton were holding their conversation. I held up the rear, not wanting to miss out, but still trying to be the proverbial fly on the wall.

"Let's go chat somewhere private. Unless you wanted to work tonight?" The question hung out there, waiting for her reply.

She tapped her lips with one finger. *"No, vamos a dejar descansar esta. Van estar muertos de los pies con lo que he planeado para el resto de la semana."* She spoke in rapid fire Spanish, and a twisted curl adorned her lips.

Anton shook his head, grinning as he led the three of them out of the office. *"Usted es una mujer malvada. Me encanta."* He led Maria toward the exit of the dance studio. When he reached the door he turned around, his eyes on me. *"Lucita,* you go where I go unless one of us"—he pointed to himself, Maria, and Heather in a crescent-shaped gesture—"says differently. *Entiendes?"*

I nodded, placed both hands in the back pockets of my jeans, and followed them. He held the door open. His eyes left my face, made a short path down, clocking my tits, and around to give my ass a once over.

Maria chuckled. "Oh, yeah, she's a *seductora* all right."

As we walked, I knocked shoulders with Heather. "Wish I knew what they said in Spanish back there."

Heather tweaked her hair while we walked, fluffing certain parts. "Oh, Maria basically said that the dancers didn't have to work tonight because they needed to rest. She plans on working their asses off the rest of the week." I opened my mouth but no words came out. "Then Anton responded that she was a wicked woman..." The timbre of her voice changed when she finished with, "...and he loves that about her."

"Damn girl, you know Spanish?"

Heather smiled. "Got Rosetta Stone the first week I started with Anton as his PA after graduating college four years ago. One week was all it took for me to realize if I was going to be any good in his world, I'd need to know exactly what he was saying—all the time. However, Puerto Rican Spanish is a bit different than Mexican or even European Spanish. For the most part, I get what they're saying even when the wording or style changes. Kind of like how there are different dialects and slang depending on where you live in the States, be it Easterners, Midwesterners, Southerners and such."

"Huh, that's really cool though. I can tell how much you mean to Anton."

Heather blushed and looked down before shrugging. "Perhaps you're seeing something that isn't there."

I scrunched my eyebrows together and stopped her with a hand to her elbow. Anton and Maria moved ahead taking the elevator. "You guys coming?" Anton held the door open.

"Um, give us a minute?" I asked.

"O-kay," he agreed and continued to chat in his native tongue to Maria.

"What gives? You're acting strange now that Maria is here."

Heather bit her bottom lip and leaned against the opposite wall. "With Maria here, all the ideas and concepts I came up with for the video are going to be completely forgotten. I'd convinced the old choreographer to add in some of the new things I came up with but now..."

Her words just stopped, disappointment dripping off each sentence like a rusty leaking faucet.

"Have you approached Anton about your concerns?" I asked.

She shook her head vehemently. "No, he wouldn't listen anyway. Now that she's here, all eyes and ears will be on everything she does and says."

I cringed. "But I thought you wanted her here. You were yippy skippy to call her up and bring her out."

"Because she's the best. Anton deserves the best."

Bringing my hands together in front of me into a steeple, I thought on this for a moment. Was there more to this than she was admitting?

"Are you in love with Anton?" The question left my lips before I could sugarcoat it or lead into it with more subtlety.

Heather's eyes widened and she leaned over, hands braced on her knees as her entire body shook. Then the roar of laughter ripped from her lungs as she stood back up. Her eyes were teary, cheeks pinked, and full piggy snorts left her nose as she howled in unfettered glee.

Apparently I got that *way* wrong. "I'm guessing that's a no then?" I asked.

"Sorry, no." She wiped the tears tracking down her face and took an enormous lung-filling breath. Honey, I would never fall for him. I want a man who makes me a priority, not an option." She chortled. "We both know Anton is lover to all, committed to none."

Lover to all, committed to none. No truer words had been spoken in my recent memory. Anton didn't seem anywhere near the type to settle down or commit to one woman for any length of time. "Then why can't you talk to him?"

"I don't know. Every time I broach the subject of creative direction of a particular project he stonewalls me before I can express my ideas. I'm at the point in my career, Mia, where I need to move forward or move on."

I nodded. "So what are you going to do?"

"Well, between you and me"—she looked down the hall way ahead of us and then behind, making sure the coast was clear—"I've been scouted by an agent for another musical group. Someone who's prepared to give me the Creative Manager role directly under the group's talent agent. It's for a hip-hop group out of New Jersey. A real up and comer. With the connections I've made and the concepts I already sketched out, the guy wants me bad. Willing to pay almost double my salary to get me to leave Anton."

My eyes widened. "Wow, Heather, that's incredible. What are you waiting for?"

Again, she bit down on her plump bottom lip. Her pretty blue eyes glanced sideways, and she kicked the toe of her shoe against the floor, dragging it along the carpet. "Um, it's hard. I've been with Anton for four years. It's always been about him. I mean, I have no real family. Only child. Parents died when I was very young. I was raised by my grandparents who have also passed."

"Okay so what does that have to do with you making the decision to work somewhere else? Somewhere you're going to be doing what you want, using the education you worked so hard to obtain, and the career you've already sacrificed your life to."

She pressed a hand through her unruly blond locks.

"Mia, it's so hard. Anton's the closest thing to family I have. Even if I'm not his number one priority, he's still mine." Her shoulders slumped. "He's my best friend, my only friend."

"Oh, honey," I rubbed her arm.

"How sad is that? I'm loyal to a man who doesn't give a hoot about me, yet he's all I've got."

Grabbing Heather by the biceps, I tugged her into my arms and hugged her. She held on tight. Interestingly enough, her touch didn't send me into a mini panic attack. Tears poured down her cheeks as she clung to me and sniffed against my neck. I patted her hair and told her over and over that it was going to be okay. Eventually, the sobs turned into giggles. Pulling back, I wiped the tears running down her cheeks with my thumbs and looked her in the eye.

"You are smart, beautiful, and Anton cares more about what you think than you know. Just talk to him."

She sighed deeply and nodded curtly. "I will. Thanks, Mia."

"It will work out as it's supposed to, but only if you're honest with yourself and Anton. He can't know how you feel if you don't tell him. And he's definitely not going to change anything unless he's aware of your needs and the fact that you've got other opportunities to consider."

"Do you think he'll be mad?" she asked as we walked to the elevator. I pressed the button, and it whirred to life somewhere above us.

"You know him better than I do. I think he'll be very concerned that you've not gotten through to him and you're considering leaving without giving him the opportunity to make things right. From what I gather, you're the only one he listens to."

Heather shook her head. "Nope. He does what he wants when he wants."

"I think that's a bit harsh and a smidge untrue."

She rolled her eyes and crossed her arms over her chest. "Maybe."

I smiled and walked through Anton's penthouse as the doors opened. "Come on, girl, let's see what the devil is up to with Ms. Dancing with the Stars."

Heather snorted. "Girl, don't let her hear you say that. She's liable to kick your ass! I heard she's got a mighty hot temper."

"Heather, honey, so do I. So. Do. I."

CHAPTER FIVE

When we entered the penthouse, Anton and Maria were not sitting idly at the table. No, they were in the center of the living room, having a dance off.

"Then your character does this"—Maria did a series of complicated steps, rolled her body, circled her hips, touched the floor, and bounced back up into another body roll followed by slamming her high-heeled foot down making a loud snap sound—"right at the *ride it, baby, ride.*"

Anton mimicked exactly what she did, only when he did the moves, all three of us were mesmerized. Standing in a pair of loose linen pants and absolutely nothing else but a diamond encrusted heart dangling around his sweaty torso, he was a thing of beauty. Masculine living, breathing art at its finest.

Heather cleared her throat. Two sets of eyes zeroed in on the two of us.

"Need us for anything?" The timid sound of her voice annoyed me. That was nowhere near getting her any credibility with the two hot-head type A personalities before us.

I butted in bravely. "What Heather means is, she has some ideas she was working on with the last choreographer that she'd like to share with the rest of the class." I glanced at Anton, and he watched me and tilted his head. I made a hello-come-on gesture with my eyes and slight shifts of my shoulders.

It took a minute, but he finally got the message. He picked up a hand towel that was dangling over the couch and wiped the sweat off his face. "Oh, yeah, H? How come you didn't say before?" His eyebrows narrowed in an unspoken accusation.

Heather's mouth tightened, and her jaw locked. "Anton, I tried many times to tell you my ideas. You told me to work out anything with the choreographer, and you'd see the end result."

That's when Maria and I both took in the staring contest the two of them had going on. "*Mi amiga*, since you have hired me as the new choreographer, how about you tell me your ideas and we can bounce them off one another over dinner. *Suena bien?*"

"I can call in some takeout?" I offered.

"That's my job." Heather sighed.

I shook my head. "Not tonight it's not. How does sushi sound?" I practically danced in my pants, which really was more a jumble of limbs complete with a shoulder shimmy. Maria watched the display and then groaned, whispering in Spanish so low I could barely hear it, "*Tengo mi trabajo por de lante.*"

"What did she say?" I pointed an accusing finger at Maria while speaking to Heather. Maria's eyes lit up with mischief and a saucy grin.

Heather clapped me on the shoulder and handed me her credit card. "Relax. She just said something about having her work cut out for her. Nothing offensive."

Shooting daggers her way, I snarled. "I've got my eyes on you."

Both Anton and Maria laughed and walked toward the kitchen. "Drink, Mia?" Anton called out.

"Yeah, whatever you're having is fine."

I turned and headed to the sitting room. I pulled out my phone, bringing up the Grub Hub app. Right off the bat, Yummy Chinese and Sushi Bar popped up with over a hundred Yelp ratings as well as an average of five stars. And the kisser...free delivery! Winner, winner, sushi dinner!

★ ★ ★

"No, no, no, you're not getting it!" Heather's words were biting and fueled by the top shelf vodka we'd been imbibing. She stood and walked to the center of the room. A third round of fruity martinis was laid out on the table in front of us, courtesy of a Mia's-badass-bartending-skills special. I patted myself on the back and waited for Heather to make her point. "My vision was a very Michael Jackson's *Billie Jean* meets Billy Joel's *Uptown Girl.*"

Maria scanned the notes in front of her, bobbing her head from side to side, the new song Anton had written playing on repeat to keep the muse enchanted. "*Si, si*, I feel you. Mia can be strutting her stuff like so." She mimicked a sexy, sultry walk. "Then Anton will follow behind her, keeping a bit with the Michael Jackson hip sway and fast feet but with his own hip-hop Latin fusion style," she said excitedly.

Anton pounced after Maria when she repeated the moves. While she swayed her hips, I paid close attention because this would eventually be my role when the cameras were on. "See, Mia, come here." I stood, rather tipsy, wiped my sticky martini fingers on my jeans, and followed her lead. She turned around and grabbed my hips as though she were a man dancing with me. "Now, pretend I'm not here and move your hips when I tap your side."

We walked a few steps, and she tapped. I swayed back and forth, picking up her rhythm. "Now stop and bend down, and touch your toes slowly, as if you're going to tie your shoe. Then caress your legs all the way up, past your waist and over your breasts."

I did what she said. "*Tan caliente,*" Anton murmured. He pressed his hands against my hips and rubbed his groin along my ass. He wasn't hard, but that icky vibe hit out of nowhere and I broke out in a sweat.

"An-ton," I warned. My lip trembled, betraying the fear that must have been evident in my eyes, saying something I wasn't able to vocalize, because his hands left me as if they'd been burned.

"Sorry, *muñeca*"

I turned around and placed a hand on his chest. "No, I'm sorry. We're just practicing. It will get easier. I promise." Closing my eyes, I sent a quiet prayer up above that I'd get past this touching thing and quick. My job depended on it.

From across the room, I could hear my phone beep announcing a new text message. Anton lifted his chin as if approving I take a minute. Hustling over to my purse on the counter, I yanked the phone out and read the message.

To: Mia Saunders
From: Wes Channing
No way, no how am I missing your birthday. Deal with it. I'll be in Miami in a week. We'll do it the easy way or the hard

way. Whichever you prefer, sweetheart, but you're not getting out of seeing me.

Little did I know I had an audience. Heather made no bones about reading the text over my shoulder.

"Who's Wes? Your boyfriend?"

Who was Wes? That was an excellent question indeed. My friend, lover, boyfriend, man of my dreams? In a way, he was all those things and more. "Um, definitely friend, sort of a boyfriend, I guess. We haven't really established any titles at this time. Just taking it slow. You know how it goes."

She snorted. "Me? Um, no. I'm queen of the one-night stand. With my job, there hasn't been room for a special someone, though I hope one day there will be."

Anton looped an arm over Heather's shoulder. "Oh come now, H. There was that one guy that was all over you a couple weeks ago. Remember? Straight lost his shit when I entered your apartment unannounced."

She groaned. "I remember, Anton. You don't have to remind me."

He laughed and smacked his thigh. "You were riding that fucking pony six ways from Sunday! Whatever happened to him?"

"You! You happened to him, Anton. Just like Reece, and David, and Jonathan. Every time I get close to a guy, you seem to screw it up with your demands, your entering my loft without knocking. Frightening them away before I ever even have a chance at more." She harrumphed and pouted.

Anton's eyes screwed into white-hot points. "You're shitting me? You're blaming me for being unlucky in love?"

She crossed her arms over her chest. "No. I am not shitting you! When the nation's biggest hip-hop artist trails into your home unannounced, looking the way you do and calling me *baby*, it doesn't leave the best impression on future suitors." Her hand came up to her forehead. and she pressed her finger and thumb into her temples. "Why do I put up with this?" she grumbled under her breath.

Anton's shoulders slumped, and he lifted her chin. "H, baby, talk to me."

"Talk to you! I'll talk to you. I've been offered another job. One I think I'm going to take. How about that for idle chat!" Her voice was loud in the cavernous room.

"What! You are *not* fucking leaving me!" he roared.

Oh, no. Both Maria and I backed up a couple steps until we hit the edge of the counter. Heather lifted a pointed finger. "I'm tired of you not listening to me. Not promoting me!" Her voice rose, and I lifted my martini to my lips. Maria did the same as we watched the fight unfold.

"Listen to *you*? You're the only one I listen to!" he countered. "And you've never asked for a promotion! What do you want? More money? Done!"

Heather's face contorted into a grimace, an expression so wrought with pain even I could feel the heat of her ire. "It's not always about fucking money! Uggh, you're so infuriating." She yanked on her hair and spun around to face the wall of windows overlooking the Atlantic Ocean. "Maybe it's best that I move on."

Anton took two steps and put his hands on her shoulders. "No. I won't let you go." The words were laced with regret.

"You may not have a choice. This is my life," she

63

whispered, tears filling her eyes.

"You're it for me. I can't work with anyone else."

"And I can't be your assistant any longer."

He grimaced. "You're not my fucking assistant. True, you handle me, but you handle everything! What do you want from me? Just ask H, and it's yours. I can't go where I want to go without you there by my side."

Maria nudged me. "Are they fucking?" If I didn't know better I would have assumed the same thing. I shook my head. "Maybe they should be," she remarked.

"Nah, its sibling rivalry. Kind of like a fight with your BFF. Do you have any friends?"

A huge grin lit her face and made her impossibly more pretty. Bitch. I wanted to hate her, but she was way too cool and had proved herself a force to be reckoned with. She was also utterly professional on top of being good at what she did. "Three soul sisters. Those bitches own me. Drive me absolutely *loco*. It's like that, only these two have never told one another of their importance. We're seeing the aftermath of that error."

Her lips formed a silent "O" as we continued to watch the smackdown. Unfortunately, it ended all too quickly with Heather storming off and slamming the condo door. Damn, I must have missed the good part.

"Shit!" Anton yelled. "*Terca puta mujer!*" he added.

I looked at Maria. "I think that's our cue."

She nodded. "When a man is hollering about a crazy stubborn woman, it's best that we don't get in the way of him letting off that steam."

We tiptoed silently out of the kitchen and left the condo. We were both staying in one of the furnished apartments for guests, so we got out at the same floor.

Maria went one way and I went the other. "Hey," I called out to her.

"Yeah?"

"Do you think I'll be able to do the job well enough?"

"Of course you will. You've got me to teach you." She winked, opened her door, and waved.

★ ★ ★

The engine rumbled underneath my bum as I pulled out of the garage and onto the streets of Miami. Anton rode the Icon Sheene. The bike was black with chrome accents. He wore black jeans, a white T-shirt, and a black leather jacket. I rocked my own pair of Lucky Brand jeans that were well worn and soft in all the right places. Namely the ass. The junk in my trunk looked damn good in these jeans, and I knew it. My hair was braided and tucked into the leather jacket I wore over the top of a red, white, and black White Stripes concert tank I'd gotten when Ginelle and I caught their show in Vegas back in the day. "Seven Nation Army" was still one of my favorites.

I sat on the KTM Super Duke tricked out in orange and black. It hummed between my thighs, caressing my sweet spot better than a lover could. There was just something absolutely beautiful and freeing about riding a bike.

Anton made hand gestures, leading me through the city of Miami and South Beach. At red lights, he'd tell me brief tidbits about different sections.

"This is where the locals and tourists shake their *culos*." He pointed to a never-ending stream of clubs down

Washington Avenue. We then traversed our way down Collins Avenue where he pointed out the many restaurants and hotels.

Of course, we rode down Ocean drive. One side was all boxy art deco styled buildings that Heather had pointed out when I arrived almost two weeks ago. The other side was a vast span of grass dotted with palm trees all the way up until the grass met the sand and then nothing but ocean.

We stopped at a tourist and local haunt called Gelato-Go. I'd never had the stuff, but Anton swore by it.

We entered the small café, looking a bit out of place. I think that worked best for Anton because he was usually so recognizable. He wore his sunglasses inside and didn't take them off. I pushed mine on top of my head to survey the options.

"So gelato is like ice-cream?"

He nodded. "It is. Italian-style ice cream, only it's not made with traditional cream. It's made with milk. It's also churned far less, leaving it with little air in it, making it seem more dense. I prefer it because the flavors are more robust, and it's healthier."

I scanned each option. The chocolate seemed far too dark, making me think it would end up tasting like the bitter ass cannolis you get in Italian joints. Blech. I hated cannolis.

A wiry, thin fella approached me. His hair was high and slicked back in a very stylish way. He wore a shirt that said, "Gelato-Go, Fresh every day, healthy, light, low-fat, delicious, and creamy." The name tag he wore boasted "Fresh Francesco", and although he could very well be Italian, it was hard to tell one way or the other.

"*Bella signora,* how may Francesco help you today?" His

66

accent was definitely Italian. That solved that mystery.

"I don't know. My friend here"—I pointed to Anton who looked more like the terminator than his alter ego Latin Lov-ah—"said your gelato was to die for. Since I've never had gelato before, what do you recommend?"

Fresh Franny grinned manically. "Oh, *signora*, you are going to love everything. We make fresh every day, homemade, and with less sugar and no fattening cream. You be keeping that body for years to come eating our treat!" he promised, and I laughed.

I pointed down to the green one that had flecks of things in it. "What's that?"

"Oh, good choice. Our very famous pistachio. We ship the nuts in from Sicily to make ours extra special."

Anton leaned over my shoulder and whispered in my ear. "It's pretty amazing and very flavorful. I'd probably recommend something a bit more simple. Do you like caramel?"

"Does a gambler love money?" I gave him my patented are-you-shitting-me look. He chuckled. Oh, how I loved that chuckle. It reminded me of good times and another smokin' hot dude who would be here tomorrow. "I'm pretty sure that ninety-nine percent of the population loves caramel. If they say they don't, they are lying. Usually driven by their need to avoid something that often makes them gain weight by just glancing at it."

Francesco watched patiently as we discussed the merits of every flavor. How strawberry was a far too boring flavor to get if I was going to try something I considered new and unusual. I wanted to go all out. Go big or go home, as they say. "Fresh Franny, I'm going to go with the caramel *dulce de leche*, please."

"Excellent choice!" He filled the biggest serving bowl full of the creamy dessert.

I was pretty sure my eyes were the size of pizzas when he handed it to me. "I should have told you the little one," I declared, sizing up the giant dessert.

He shook his head. His hair jiggled with the effort but stayed perfect. "Everyone comes back for more. You go big."

"If you say so."

"I do."

Anton, of course, ordered the pistachio, which pissed me off. He warned me off it, and then he ordered it! "Punk!" I swore at him.

"What?" He pushed his shades up into his hair and took a giant spoonful between his lips. Mmm, I could watch him eat ice cream all damned day. He looked that flippin' good. Suddenly, I was too warm. I took off my jacket and placed it over the back of the chair. He did the same.

For a while, we sat in silence and enjoyed the best freaking gelato ever. Of course it was my first, but I couldn't imagine anything better right then. The texture and silkiness was a cross between ice cream and frozen yogurt. Either way, I was a big fan.

"What are you going to do about Heather? She still mad?"

"Furious, and she's barely talking to me." He frowned and then took another bite. "I don't know what to do. I can't let her go."

"What if she needs to go?"

He narrowed his brows and cringed. "I'm already famous. Working with me gives her more of a name than a new wannabe star."

"And are you prepared to give her the clout she needs?"

"Clout?"

"You know, the respect. The role."

His eyes and nose scrunched up. "Is that what this is about? Her not wanting to be my assistant?"

I wanted to say, "uh, duh," but refrained as he was obviously clueless. "It seems to me that Heather is pretty smart." He nodded. "Beautiful." Again he agreed. "But she's so much more than just your assistant. That night, you yourself said she managed everything right. Or at the very least had a hand in everything."

"Yeah, so? What're you getting at? Lay it out for me, *Lucita*."

Taking a bite of gelato and letting it melt on my tongue, I swallowed and put down my spoon. "I think she wants to be your business manager slash agent. I don't know enough about the industry to say exactly, but if she's setting up your shows, running your team, taking care of you"—I picked up the spoon and pointed it at him—"then it sounds to me like she's already doing the job without the pay, respect, or title under her belt, and floundering to try and get it all done alone. Maybe she needs a PA!" I snorted.

Both of his hands came up to his face, and he slid them over his forehead and down past his nose and lips, betraying his frustration. "You're right, Mia. *Cristo en una cruz, tienes razón.*" I could pretty much figure it out without asking for a translation.

"The girl has no life beyond you. You know, she told me that she didn't have any friends except you. That you were her only family. Her best friend."

"She said that?" His eyes darkened, and he cupped his chin in the palm of his hand. I nodded. "Hell, H has always been my best friend."

"You ever tell her that?"

"I assumed she just knew." His tone revealed how destroyed he was by the knowledge of Heather's unhappiness.

I laughed. "You know what they say about people who assume right?"

His eyes hardened and one side of his lip curled as he shook his head.

"Assuming makes an ass out of you and me. Get it! Ass-ume!"

Anton shook his head and plowed into his green ice cream once more. "You're a nut. Anyone ever tell you that?"

"All the time, but usually, my best friend Ginelle comes up with more colorful language."

When I said the words "best friend," Anton's form slumped again. He picked up his unfinished treat and tossed it into the trash. A hard line formed between his brows, and a slight scowl marred his handsome face.

"Let's go. You have rehearsal, and I need to talk to my girl."

Internally, I did a mighty fist pump followed by a touchdown dance.

Then I looked at the Super Duke I was riding and did it all over again.

CHAPTER SIX

"Again!" Maria roared. "No. Stop the music." She waved her hand up high in the air, and the music cut out.

I stood in the corner, waiting for my turn to be battered. I'd been working on the same scene all day. Mostly, I did an ultra-sexy walk, followed by a hip swivel one way and then the other, bend down, back up, shimmy the tits, and arch back. Eventually, Anton would be following behind me, doing his moves with the backup dancers. Some of the moves I learned would be consistent with whatever he was learning and going to do with his body. In all honesty, it was nothing compared to the paces that Maria was putting these other dancers through, and I was already beat. It had been a long fricking day. I needed a shower, food, and bed. Besides, tomorrow was my birthday, and Anton had given me the full day off. That also meant that Wes would arrive.

Equal parts excitement and trepidation warred with one another as I thought about my laid-back movie-making surfer. I wanted to see Wes so badly I could feel the ache in my teeth. However, I also didn't want my heart to be broken when I told him I was ready to be exclusive. A one-woman gal. His gal. Hopefully.

In order to do that though, he'd have to cut Gina DeLuca loose. No more casual sex with the nation's hottest movie actress. Even the mere thought of her made the green-eyed monster rear her disgustingly ugly head. If we were going to do this, we had to commit. *Fuck. Commit.* That was one word I hadn't said in a long time or place anywhere near the opposite sex. Mostly because every time I did, I got screwed over one way or another.

"Mia, *hermosa*, come here." Maria pointed to a spot on the floor where a black X had been placed. This was where I needed to stop and do my own body roll against Anton in the video. She made sure I knew exactly how many steps it took, where each one of my limbs needed to be, and how all the other dancers would be placed. Between her and Heather, they had all the dancers lusting after me, dancing around my form while I walked, sat, and leaned against a wall. There were several different pieces I had to learn, but most of them I had down. She was a kind choreographer with a bottomless well of patience. Every time I messed up the other dancers would scowl, knowing they would have to do it again. Maria, however, had no problem running them through their paces over and over again. She insisted it perfected their parts.

Maria positioned me and then pretended to be Anton's character. "Go through your moves." Her eyes cut to the dancers. "I'm not doing this because Mia needs help. You all are slacking. I don't care if you're tired. I don't care if your muscles are sore and your feet hurt. You want to be in the biggest hip-hop video to date?" Her blue eyes turned ice-cold as she clocked each one of them with a glare. "This is what it costs. *Trabaja por el.* Work for it!" She repeated the admonishment in English as she often did. "Now, Mia, start from the beginning."

I went back to the corner of the room and took a deep breath, closed my eyes, and set my sights on what I wanted to accomplish. This was my first music video. My face would be on televisions, Internet feeds, and cell phones all over the globe. *You so got this girl. Nail it for Maria, for the dancers, for Anton…to hell with all that, I'm nailing this shit for myself!*

The music came on, the lights dimmed, and I swayed my hips and shoulders from side to side. Very Jessica Rabbit. When the right note hit, I strutted across the floor. Before I could move more than five steps, a pair of masculine hands was on my hips.

The base of the music hit harder, I closed my eyes and went for it, arching my back, allowing Anton to grind into my behind as I laid my hand on the back of his neck. The aroma of coconut drifted around me in a cocoon of fun in the sun. Hips hit, hands gripped, and Anton spun me around and then did a body roll from my thighs up past my pelvis to my belly where he arched back. I mimicked it, pushing my body hard. He fell back to the ground, the same as the dancers did, as if I'd knocked him out with my body. Then he was up on his knees pumping his hips up toward me in a graphic display of his manhood.

"Ride it baby, ride… *thrust*

"With me, I'll go all night…"

"Let me do you right…" *thrust*

"And ride it baby, ride…"

The music matched our movements perfectly. Toward the end of the song, Anton did some crazy urban ninja-style run-and-leap off the mirrors of the studio, landing on his feet where he tugged my waist, got to his knee, and draped me over it. My back arched almost painfully over his knee, and he laid a hard, smacking kiss on my mouth.

And that's when it happened…again.

I get a nice fist to his mouth, cutting open his lip before he restrains my hands with one of his, then gropes my body with the other. Wild drops of crimson trail down his chin, his teeth turning a sickening, vile red. Aaron crushes me against the concrete wall. A piercing pain grates along the tender skin of my back as the coarse surface abrades my skin raw. His lower half presses harder, over and over, while he dry-humps me, his erection like a steel pipe digging into my sex.

I start to scream, but he puts his mouth over mine so fast that nothing but a garbled sound escapes. I'm screaming bloody murder when I hear the sickening jingle of his belt being unbuckled and the noise of the zipper opening, each tooth unlocking as if in slow motion. Aaron retaliates by biting down on my lips and slamming my head against the concrete. I see stars and rainbows across my vision, and things are now hazy. He yanks on the hem of my dress, pulling it tight as he slides it up to my waist. The cool air slithers across my bare flesh. More swirls of distorted light still splinter across my vision. I blink several times, trying to stay conscious. Aaron slides his fingers down my stomach, reaching his target, and he cups my sex roughly, pressing into the soft tissue. I hear myself whimper as bile rises up into my throat, the intense burn gagging me so bad I want to vomit.

"I'm going to fuck you so hard, take you like the whore you are. Fucking white trash," he roars, spittle splattering against my face. This is the man who touched me while I slept, and when confronted, showed no remorse. Aaron Shipley, Senator for California, is about to rape me. Right here, out in public with a giant party going on not more than two hundred feet away.

I feel the head of his cock where he presses it against my legs as he grinds it along my thigh. I whisper, "No," and shake my head, only to receive a gut-twisting grin in reply. He puts a hand over my mouth, muffling the sound of my scream. I bite down on the flesh of his hand. Salt and the coppery taste of blood fill my mouth. He curses and smashes my head into the wall again. I can't hold myself up and slump against the surface. my body feeling almost weightless, and as the darkness takes me, I am sure he is going to rape me.

"Get your fucking hands off me!" I screamed loud enough to tear the house down.

"Mia, no, no! *Lo siento. Lo siento.* I'm sorry. *Lucita,* come back. Shit!" Anton cradled my head as I came around. My stomach rolled and churned. Staggering to my feet, I ran over to the nearest trash can and hurled my lunch. Maria stood over me, holding my hair back, whispering calming, soothing things into my ear.

When I'd finished, a towel and a bottle of water were thrust into my hand. I gulped the refreshing liquid, but it went down as if I were swallowing razor blades, until all the bile washed back down.

Maria's eyes were hard, now dark, and cold. She took my hand and brought me to a small room off the side of dance studio.

"Who's hurting you? I know people. Very, very rich people who will not stand for a good woman being hurt by a scumbag."

I shook my head. "Maria, no, it's not what it looks like."

Her hands flew to her hips, and she cocked her head to the side, black tendrils escaping her ponytail. "Really? Because it seems to me that someone hurt you bad enough that you are having flashbacks. Not to mention the fact that you freeze every time one of the male dancers or Anton touches you. So tell me, is that not true? Am I imagining this shit? I know exactly what a battered woman looks like, *hermosa,* because I was one. For many years. Not okay with allowing that shit to happen to good women and neither are my friends. Hell, Anton wouldn't stand for it."

Pushing my hair back, I took a deep breath and looked at her. "Anton knows. There's nothing any of you can do about it. It's been handled," I lied. Technically it had been handled so that wasn't a lie. The way I was dealing with the end result, on the other hand, had not been handled.

"I need more, Mia, because right now, I'm flaming mad. As in *muy caliente* and not in a good way. I want blood. So speak. Even if it hurts, even if you cry, want to hit something. You have to get it out. You cannot let this stay bottled in. Believe me, I've been through it, and I came out on the other side stronger and smarter." Her statement was almost a speech—no, a benediction. Something she believed one hundred percent. Something that was private, part of her very soul, and she was strong enough to share it with me.

"My last client had a son who attacked me, sexually and physically. I was in the hospital for a few days." Her eyes widened and blazed like a thousand fires set in a forest of dead trees. "I'm getting past it, but I'm having a little trouble with being touched. It's weird. I don't get it."

Maria came over to me and sat down on the desk in the center of the room where I leaned. "It's not weird. Once your trust has been broken by the opposite sex, it can be hard to get it back. Does Anton know?" I nodded. "Then he shouldn't have kissed you or held you that way."

I let out a frustrated breath. "Anton and I have been working on it. The dancing has been okay, even when he holds onto me, but the second he bent me over him in that way and kissed me, I-I went back there. To that night."

She nodded and put her arm around me. "For one, Anton shouldn't have done what he did." I tried to interrupt her, but she held up her hand. "No, he knew your issue, and then threw you over his body in a way that put you in a vulnerable sexual position. That wasn't smart. I'll talk to him about his improvisation. That little scene was not part of the choreography. As a matter of fact, that *cabron* isn't supposed to have gotten the seductress. The whole point is she's off limits!" Her indignation was high. Her perfectly sculpted black eyebrows narrowed, and her pretty mouth moved into a pout.

"He probably just got lost in the moment," I offered with a small smile.

She squinted. "Yeah, yeah. I'll deal with handsy." Once more, she squeezed my shoulder. "You will be okay. It's going to take time. You should probably find a professional to talk to about it. I will say telling me, Anton, and others who care for you will help."

That made me think of Ginelle. I needed to talk to her about it. Really talk to her about it, not sweep it under the rug and pretend it was nothing. I needed to lay it out so that I had her to bounce things off of. She'd be angry. More than angry. Downright homicidal, but she'd listen, let me vent, help me get past it. That's what I'd do. Later this evening I'd give her a call and hash it out.

"Now, we have this scene down. You're off tomorrow. Why don't you go to your apartment. Do you want to do dinner tonight?"

I shook my head. "Sorry, Maria. I'm beat. I'd like to take

a bath, make a PB & J, and veg out in front of the TV before passing out. Do you have any idea how hard you worked us? And physically, I didn't have a crazy involved part like the other guys!"

Her eyes gleamed, the previous ire cooling, bringing back her normal silver-blue eyes that I swear you could stare at for days and never tire of.

"Hard work is good for you. Makes you appreciate the end product more."

We stood and she led me back to the room.

Anton had been pacing the floor, almost wearing a hole in it. "*Lucita!*" His shoulders slumped. "I got caught up. *Lo siento.* Please, forgive me." He looked immensely sad, heartbroken, as if he'd done something horribly wrong. He hadn't. Sure, he might have lost sight for a moment, but his response to the mood of the room and the way the routine was going perfectly was natural. If I weren't so screwed up, it would have been fun, well received even.

"Anton, seriously, it's fine." I walked over to him and opened my arms. He walked into them and stood there, letting me hug him. When his hands weren't clasping me, it was easy to be near him. Comfortable. "You can hug me."

He lifted his arms and pulled me into his chest harder. The niggling fear and anxiety started up, but I pushed it down. Anton was a good man with a huge heart. He made a mistake that wouldn't have even been a mistake if I hadn't been the victim of an assault. "I'm sorry, Mia. It won't happen again," he whispered in my ear and released me.

Maria clapped her hands to get everyone's attention. "That's all for today folks. Go on home. Tomorrow you get a day off, and then it's back to a couple of days for rehearsal where we'll perfect the routines. Then we tape!" The ten dancers hooted and hollered, smacking high fives to one another, doing the man-hug thing.

"Are you sure you're going to be okay?" Anton asked as Heather entered the room. She noticed our position and frowned. I tried to smile at her as she approached.

She stopped about four feet from us, crossed her arms over her chest, and pursed her lips. "Word is you want to talk to me?"

Anton bristled. "Chilly reception," he murmured, and I laughed, hugged him once more, and pulled away.

"You getting food?" Heather asked.

I shook my head. "Nope, eating in tonight. Need to rest and take a hot bath to *soak these muscles!*" I spoke loud enough for Maria to hear. She did a tit lift and a head tilt while laughing, obviously proud of herself. Damn, the bitch was cool. Everything from her sumptuous body to her dancing ability, her beauty—she was all that and a bag of chips. I wondered if she had a guy. Alec would rock her world. Hell, Alec had rocked my world and often.

No more Alec.

I sighed and moved to Heather, hugged her close, and whispered, "Go easy on him. He may be clueless, but he loves you like a sister. Give him the benefit of the doubt, okay?" I pushed back and held her at arm's length. Her blue eyes filled with unshed tears and she nodded. "Okay, go get 'em tiger," I said and smacked her ass hard as I passed.

"Ouch! Bitch!" she yelled, though the enthusiasm in her tone proved she wasn't mad.

I flicked a hand behind my back, giving her the finger. "Sit on it and spin!"

Behind me, I could hear her say to Anton, "Can you believe her?"

Anton laughed, and then a muffled *oompf* filled my ears. I turned around to see Anton squeezing the life out of Heather. "Don't leave me, H. I need you."

"You don't need me."

"Bullshit! You take care of me."

I waited to see how she'd respond. "Yeah, you know what? I do. Time for you to realize that and make something of it, or I'm walking."

"You walk and I'll run after you. No other band is getting my manager," he roared.

"Manager?" The word came out broken and gritty, almost as if it hurt to say it.

"That's right. People want me to play their venues? They go through my manager. They want me to pimp their product? They go through my manager. They want me doing awards shows? They go through my manager. And that, *chica,* is you. From here on out, Heather Renee is the Latin Lov-ah's Manager."

She paced in front of him. "So, that means I get a raise?"

He nodded. "Big fucking raise, H. How's about fifteen percent on every gig."

A sharp whistle left Maria's lips.

"Seriously?"

"You bring me the jobs, you get paid. I looked into it, H. That's more than fair, plus we pay your expenses out of our business account when we travel. Your name will appear on the albums, the whole enchilada. So"—he held his hand out—"do we have a deal or what?"

Heather's eyes were wide. Her mouth opened and

closed like she couldn't catch her breath. "But…but…but, that's so much."

It was a rhetorical statement, but Anton answered anyway. "No, it's what's going to happen for me to keep my talent. Now, you gonna keep me hanging, or are we going to do this?"

Heather held out her hand. It trembled as she clasped Anton's. Without hesitation, he pulled her into his arms in what I knew was a bone-crushing hug. I'd been on the other side of those arms when he was worried or frightened. "Never doubt my love for you. H, you are the most talented woman I know. You keep me going. Having my sister, my *hermana*, my *mejor amiga* making sure I'm taken care of, getting us the best contracts, that's my dream come true. I'm sorry I didn't do it earlier."

She sniffed into his neck, tears rolling down her cheeks. I hugged myself, not able to give them privacy. It was too beautiful to witness.

"H, we're going to have to hire us a new PA. You're going to be too busy to be dealing with our day-to-day necessities. Oooh, hire a sexy little Latina?" His eyes twinkled, and a sexy grin slipped across his lips.

She shook her head. "Oh, hell, no. You'll be banging her in five seconds. I'm hiring a gay man! End of. Nothing to distract either one of us."

Anton shrugged. "Party pooper." He swung her around and set her on her feet. "Now can you call that *bastardo* that's trying to steal you from me and tell him you're off the market, that you've been promoted and to fuck way off? If I see that slimy *hijo de puta* I'm not going to be kind. He tried to take my girl away from me."

Heather chuckled. "He's actually really nice." Anton's head shot around and he glared at her, showing his teeth. "Okay, okay! I'll tell him today I'm not interested."

His eyes softened and he smiled.

On that note, I tiptoed out of the dance studio and headed for my home away from home. Things were now right in the world. Well, in Anton and Heather's world. It was yet to be determined how I'd move on with Weston. Tomorrow would tell.

CHAPTER SEVEN

Studying myself in the mirror, I figured this outfit would do. The top half of the black dress was a ribbed tank-top style, the bottom loose and flowy to about two inches above the knee. It was cute. I scanned my back and front one more time. I felt sexy, young, hip, yet still me. Casual Mia. Instead of putting on sky-high wedges that matched, I stayed barefoot. Wes would be here soon, and I had no idea what his plans were. Would we talk? Make out? Would it be weird since this was the first time we were seeing each other face-to-face since our hookup in March?

Hookup. I cringed. That sounded too "casual ho" for my liking. Besides, Wes would tan my hide if I called myself a ho. He'd probably consider our romp in March an extension of our long-term friends with benefits relationship. It reminded me of a time when we just first met.

"What are we toasting to?" I ask.

"How about to being friends?" He grins, setting a warm hand high on my thigh, much higher than a "friend" would. It feels good there. "Good friends." His eyes drop to my mouth as I bite my bottom lip.

"Friends with benefits?" I inquire, lifting an eyebrow for maximum effect and crossing my legs. That hand of his goes a few inches higher until it brushes along bare thigh.

His gaze focuses on mine, making me feel warm, positively

hot, under his intense look. "God, I hope so," he whispers, leaning closer.

Yes, that was the start of something I had no idea would turn into more. More friendship, more fun, more living, and most of all—more love. The doorbell rang through the apartment, sounding ultra-loud in the cavernous space.

Taking a deep breath, I jutted my shoulders back, clasped the door handle, and pulled it open. There he stood like blazing California sunshine glinting off the Pacific Ocean. Surreal perfection.

"Wes…" was all I got out before he pressed a hand to my stomach, pushing me back away from the door a few steps. He dropped his bag on the floor in a heap, kicked the door shut, and yanked me into his arms. His mouth was on mine in the blink of an eye. His minty tongue dived inside as I gasped. Tongues touched, remembering. Hands groped, reacquainting.

In seconds, I was pressed up against the door, legs wrapped around his waist, his hands gripping my ass, mine twisted into his hair at the crown of his head. I held him close, plundering his mouth like a woman in a drought who hadn't had a sip of water in days. He tasted of mint with a hint of alcohol. Mojitos. I grinned and tugged on his lips. He groaned and pressed his denim-clad length directly against my aching bundle of nerves. Crying out, I tore my lips from his. As I gulped air, his lips were all over my neck, sucking, biting, tasting.

"Can't fucking get enough of your taste. Christ, I need inside…" His growl was muffled when he sucked at the fleshy globes of my cleavage where he'd managed to push down the tank enough to access them.

"Need you too." I lifted up his head and took his mouth again.

Vaguely I heard my panties tearing at the sides and felt the pinch of pain as he tugged them from my body in his haste to get me naked. Then he pressed me harder against the door. I moaned, feeling his knuckles press against my wetness as he unzipped and unbuckled.

"Going to take you. Take it hard. Make it mine again." He bit down on my lip hard as one hand curled around my ass and the other slinked up behind my back where he gripped my shoulder. "Fuck, Mia," he roared as his cock drove home.

"Oh, oh, God..." My mind spun, so filled with pleasure. I tightened everywhere, barreling like a speeding train toward my release. So fast. With Wes, it was always a sure thing. With every draw, release, and thrust back home, I splintered, my body crackling with so much need I was going to lose it any second. "Gonna come..." I warned.

Wes licked up my neck. "Already?" he growled between clenched teeth and sucked in a fast breath. "Fuck, your pussy missed me. Christ, sweetheart, like a vise on my dick. So. Goddamned. Tight. And. All. Fucking. Mine."

That proclamation and one more piercing thrust accompanied by his pelvic bone crushing my O-trigger between our bodies, and that was all, she wrote. Twitching, howling, toes curling, I clung to Wes's body as he rammed home over and over, finding his own bit of heaven on a mighty roar. His body sank deep, planted to the root where I milked him of his release. His breath came in potent punches against the skin of my neck, and I felt the door digging painfully into my back.

Moments later, when our breathing was more relaxed, I pulled his head from its hiding spot against my neck until Wes's eyes sought mine. He grinned lazily.

"Hey, babe. Missed you." I noticed the shy timbre in my voice.

He chuckled and rubbed his forehead against mine. "I got that. Obviously not as much as I missed you, since I attacked you at first sight."

I grinned and kissed him, putting all my joy, happiness, and regret for the time spent apart into the kiss. "It's okay. If you noticed"—I clenched around his softening, still semi-hard member within me—"I was all about it." I winked and unwound my legs from his hips, groaning when we disconnected.

"Want a drink? A nap? Another go?"

He laughed and the sound reverberated like a drum within my chest. I loved hearing him laugh. "Perhaps not in that order but I'm thinking, shower, food, another go, and then a nap." He waggled his eyebrows.

I smoothed down my skirt. "Now that you mention it, I am pretty hungry." Probably because I hadn't eaten anything because I was too nervous about seeing Wes again. "How about I call for takeout while you shower?"

He frowned. "Wanted to shower with you, sweetheart."

"Then we'll never get to the food part of your plan." I cocked my head with a hand on my hip. His eyes took in the stance, and he smiled then shook his head.

"Shower that way?" He pointed toward the back end of the apartment.

"Yep. I'll order us some food. Go wipe off the travel

and, um, you know." I pointed to the general vicinity of his lower half.

"My cock? You want my cock clean, sweetheart?" He grinned, and the sexy quirk of those lips went straight to my pussy where a blossoming throb became a pounding rhythm.

I squirmed, squeezing my legs together, and huffed, trying to pretend that this crass discussion didn't affect me. "Hey, you want a dirty dick, that's on you. I'm most certainly not putting my mouth on it after a six-hour plane ride and a sweaty fuck against the door. Go shower. I'll take care of food, and then we can catch up."

Wes turned on a heel and headed toward the bathroom. "As long as part of that catching up is me spending a great deal of time between your thighs, with this"—he gripped his denim-clad cock in a vulgar display that had me chuckling—"and these"—he wiggled his fingers—"and this"—he tapped his mouth—"my life will be complete."

I rolled my eyes and shook my head, ignoring him so he'd leave, even though he knew it affected me the way he intended it should. That was when I started to feel our combined fluids slipping down the inside of my thighs. Shit. He'd ripped my underwear off. No barrier. I needed a towel, and then maybe I would join him in the shower.

★ ★ ★

Our bellies full of Miami's primo sushi and egg rolls, Wes and I were snuggled up on the couch, his hand methodically running through my hair. I'd let it air-dry while we ate and talked. Now we were content just being in one another's company. I couldn't remember a time when being with a man I had feelings for was so simple. No demands on time, no stress, no drama—just being with one another. It was nice. More than nice—it was exactly what I wanted to set roots around and let grow into something even more than nice, something long lasting.

Without comment, Wes stood up and grabbed my hand. I followed because, well, I'd probably follow him anywhere right now. He led me to the bedroom. The sky outside the windows had turned to a hue of pinks, oranges, and blues as the sun began to set.

Wes turned me around, facing the view. We were in a high-rise overlooking the ocean. The ocean always reminded me of my time with him. He slid his hands around my waist and leaned close. "Tomorrow morning we'll surf."

I smiled and leaned into his back. "I'd love that."

He hummed against my neck and slipped his fingers under the tank dress at each shoulder. I'd thrown it back on sans bra after our shower. Hey, a girl could hope. He pushed the material down until it fell in a puddle at my feet. I stepped out of it and kicked it to the side. Wes's hands went to my waist and slowly slid up my ribcage. Gooseflesh prickled along my skin. His large hands came up to my breasts and he cupped them reverently. Gasping, I closed my eyes and pressed into his hands.

"Missed these. Best tits I've ever seen." He placed tiny kisses along my shoulders. "Best I've ever touched." He squeezed them, setting up a rhythm that had me thrusting my hips forward as if on autopilot. "So sensitive to touch," he murmured against the nape of my neck.

"Only your touch," I mumbled, rubbing the back of

my head against his pecs.

"Is that right?" He hummed again. I focused on the featherlight touch of his fingertips as they played delicately over my breasts and around the nipples in a caressing, petting massage. Heat built all over, a slow, simmering sensation from the tips of my nipples, through my chest, and around, to nestle heavily at the apex of my thighs. Then he spoke again, blowing me away, reminding me of one of the best nights of my life.

"Rule one," he started, and I smiled wide, not able to contain the sheer happiness of what I hoped he was about to do. "We're going to have an insane amount of sex over the next three days." *Three days?* He squeezed hard on each erect peak, cutting off further thought. I cried out, remembering this feeling, overjoyed that I was finally in his arms like this after so long. Any fear or anxiety was completely obliterated by this man. The only man's touch I needed, craved, wanted more than any other. The space between my legs softened and clenched at nothing. I needed him there, right *there*. Taking me to bliss.

"I seem to recall that rule," I said breathlessly, leaning farther back into him, grinding my ass into his thick erection. Oh, sweet mother of all things good, I'd missed that steely length. Even though we'd had sex earlier today, we had some serious time to make up for.

Wes chuckled and reacted by pinching each nip just right. Sparks of electric pleasure rippled through my tits on a live wire to my clit where it throbbed and ached to be manipulated.

"Rule two," he continued, "is that we're monogamous." This time, I laughed, only he retaliated by twisting and running the edge of his nail along the over-sensitized peaks. I moaned and shook in his arms. "Remember that one, too," I choked out. "Only before, it was for the month. How long this time?" My heart clenched. I was unsure if he was feeling the same tension and anticipation that I was. He didn't know things had changed for me, that my previous views about us had flown out the window, wailing like a banshee into the night.

Wes plucked my nips, elongating them to the point that pleasure and pain coalesced in a symphony of heat and need. "Indefinitely." His voice was hoarse, a rough grumble against my spine. His teeth dragged along my shoulder until he sank them into the exact same spot Aaron had. I expected to be taken back there. Instead, my body jolted under his capable hands, obliterating all thought except the desire for him. My Wes.

"Does that mean you cut ties with your other friend?" I closed my eyes, waiting, holding my breath, too afraid to hope for what I wanted. In the past, I'd never gotten what I'd wanted from a man I fell for. Ever. It seemed to be part of my genetic code. I had the fuck-over-Mia gene stapled to my heart. With Wes, I wanted so badly for him to demolish that fear of the unknown that would enable me to trust another man again. Trust *him*. Unlock my heart, break it wide open, and let him in.

"Stopped that friendship when I fucked you over the phone."

That was a full month ago when we sexted. Holy shit, he really was serious. Chills raced along my spine, and at the same time, longing for more filled me to the brim.

"Rule three: We *always* sleep in the same bed. We do

not want to confuse this with something it's not."

I shimmied against his dick until he groaned, placing a hand on my hip and rubbing into my backside, circling. "Mmm. And, uh, what is it this time?" It became more difficult to finish our chat because he was harder than a two-by-four behind me. My panties were soaked through with the ache he'd built.

He pulled his bottom half away from me, and I wanted to sob. I did try to protest, but he held me fast, leaning my head to the side and snuggling into the crook of my neck. That's when he blew my world wide open.

"Sweetheart. You, me…it's paradise. From here on out, no matter where you go, what you have to do for the rest of the year, this paradise will be waiting for you with open arms."

Paradise. Wes did not lie. Our time together, the month we had, the follow-up in Chicago, all the calls, texts, and then some were all part of the bundle. A place I was able to go where I could be me, live life, be happy.

"And rule four?" The words came out in breathless veneration. This was it, the ultimate question. Over six months ago, we stood, just like this, and he set the rules in stone. Rule number four was never fall in love. My heart was in my throat. I arched like a cat. His hands squeezed and caressed each nip with a reverence I hadn't felt in too long. Still, he didn't answer. Worry, panic, and longing built within my soul, and I spun around and clutched him around the neck, fingers tugging on his hair, forcing his face down to mine. His eyes were so green, I gasped at the sheer beauty and grace that was Weston Channing.

An adoring smile filled his features, and I held tight.

"Fuck rule four. I broke that rule six months ago when I fell in love with you."

Tears filled my eyes, so much so that he was blurry. I swallowed reflexively around the knot in my throat. "Wes, I…"

"I know, sweetheart. Something changed in you. From my visit in March, to our calls, texts, the shit with Gi—"

I placed a finger over his pouty lips I wanted to gobble up and burn with repeated tugs and blistering kisses. The last thing I wanted to hear from that sexy-as-fuck mouth was her name spoken here and now when I was about to confess my love for him.

"Not now, not when it's you and me." My voice shook.

He nodded. "Tell me what I *want* to hear, Mia. What I *need* to hear. I *deserve* it." His voice demanded nothing but honesty.

Want. Need. Deserve.

And he did. All of those things were true and finally, after six months of waffling, trying to deny it, wanting to deny it, I let it all go. For the first time in my life I was going to take something for me. Something good, kind, and all mine.

My paradise.

Looking into his bottomless green eyes, running my fingers through the dirty blond layers of his just-fucked hair, and stroking my lips along his stubbled jaw, I leaned close enough so that no matter how quietly I said it, he'd hear it.

"I love you, Wes."

His arms tightened painfully around my mostly naked form as he let the declaration sink in. I could feel the tension pumping off him in powerful bursts of energy. "Not going to let you go this time." His words came out harsh, though I knew the gruffness was driven by the intense feeling behind them.

"I love you." I kissed his cheek, and his arms loosened a bit.

"I love you." I kissed his eyebrows, and he sighed.

"I love you." I kissed his lips, and he opened.

Within seconds, my back hit the bed and his body hovered over mine. "You love me?" He needed me to admit it, eye-to-eye, heart-to-heart.

"I do."

His entire face broke out into an earth-shattering, gorgeous smile. "I'm going to love you so hard, sweetheart. After tonight, baby, you might not be able to walk."

I grinned and squealed as he ripped my panties off and latched onto a nipple. Once he had me squirming and panting, almost coming from his ministrations to my breast, he kissed his way down my body.

"Open up those long legs, baby. Spread them wide. I'm about to taste paradise."

I complied, opening my thighs, revealing everything to him. My love, my body—proving in that moment that it was all his for the taking.

His eyes gleamed, and he ran his fingers through my sex. "So slippery. I love how you respond to me. How your body reacts, making it easy for me to take you. First though, I need a sip of your honey. I've been dreaming about putting my mouth on you, sucking you dry, and starting all over again. Grip the sheets, sweetheart, because I'm fucking parched."

"Filthy bastard," I said before he spread me wide, opened the petals of my sex with his thumbs, and laid his mouth over me. He made a sound that was a cross between a groan and a moan, and then his tongue sank deep. So fucking deep. His hands wrapped around my ass, and he tilted my hips up to his face, going all in. I howled, holding fast to the sheets, and let him take me there. I think it took two and a half seconds and I was coming all over his face. He made carnal noises like an animal feasting before he sat up, licked his lips, and wiped his mouth on his forearm. He centered his cock and pushed in, ramming to the root.

I jolted, my body strung as tight as a drum from the first orgasm and on its way to another. "Jesus, Wes. You'll be my end," I said breathlessly, losing cognitive ability as he thrust in and out. I wrapped my legs around his hips.

"Sweetheart, I hope to be your end, your beginning, and everything in between. Now shut up. I'm making love to my woman."

The "making love" part made my heart squishy. Then Wes set about spending the evening making love to his woman…repeatedly. Though I convinced him in the middle of the night that his woman needed a good fucking, where he promptly turned me on hands and knees, smacked my ass, and pounded me until I screamed in ecstasy.

CHAPTER EIGHT

The waves crashed against the board, water pounded against my face, and I couldn't have been happier. Wes's toned form paddled farther out like a machine, intent on catching air this time. In a split second, he was up on his feet and slicing through the water. I followed his lead and, lo and behold, caught my own much smaller wave. Still, it felt amazing, and together we rode the waves back to the shore.

I tucked my board into the sand as Wes road his all the way until he was able to jump off. He pulled his board up under one powerful arm and made his way to me. His hand slid behind my head, and his lips slanted over mine. Tongues and teeth gnashed as the kiss became more indecent. The hand not on my head dropped the board in the sand and he grasped my neoprene covered ass, squeezing rhythmically. With a growl, he pulled back and shook his hair, which sent saltwater droplets flying. That finely muscled chest of his dripped with water as he unzipped and let the top half of his wetsuit fall down around his golden brown chest. I wanted to jump his bones as I took in all the hotness that was Wes. *My Wes*, I reminded myself.

"Someone likes what she sees. Keep it up, sweetheart, and your ass will be hitting sand and my dick sinking home."

Thrills, chills, and bells clanged all around me as I responded to the heady promise, not at all alarmed with the plan. Moreover, ready to take the next steps toward seeing that warning come to fruition.

Wes shook his head grinning like a schoolboy who'd gotten the girl. He definitely had the girl. "You're off today, right?"

I nodded. "Yeah, I told Anton I needed another day, but tomorrow I've got to rehearse because we're taping the video the next day."

Wes hooked an arm around my shoulders. "Then you're all mine." Instead of admitting how very true that now was I just grinned, completely content to be held in the crook of his arm as we waded through the sand.

"Back to the apartment?" I did not even try to act coy, my intent clear. I'd been away from Wes, enjoyed the pleasures of the flesh with Tai and Alec after I'd left him, but it wasn't the same. Love was never involved. Before, with the other men, it was fun. Meaningful, yes, a part of my journey, absolutely. With Wes though, it was just…more.

He picked up his board and then mine. Chivalry indeed wasn't dead. We walked back to the hut on the beach and turned in the boards and suits. I tugged on my jean shorts, tank and Converse shoes. He had his cargo shorts, boat shoes, and T-shirt on and clasped my hand when I finished winding my hair into a messy bun on the top of my head.

Wes had rented an open four-by-four Jeep. He put the car in motion, a hand to my bare thigh as if reminding himself of still being there, gave me a cheeky grin, and zoomed out onto Ocean Drive. I decided it was best to soak in the sun and Miami heat and enjoy being young and in love. It wasn't a new feeling, but it was the first time in a long time I had any faith in or desire to have that feeling filling my pores, roaring through my veins, and zipping along my heart.

We drove up a path leading to an enormous mansion.

"Where are we?" I asked Wes as he got out of the car, came around, and opened my door. I clasped his hand and hopped out, pushing the sunglasses up on my head to take in the lush gardens along with the historical-looking architecture of the building.

"Vizcaya Museum and Gardens. I've been wanting to come here for a while. I've done a lot of research on it, and I think it could be the perfect location for an upcoming script I'm working on." He grabbed my hand, and we entered. Once we were settled with the touristy requirements with the staff, we had free rein to roam the house and gardens. Wes led me through room after room. I could hardly take it all in. The art collections, the ridiculously rich bedrooms that were fit enough for a king to live in. Who knew these types of places existed beyond those of the exorbitantly rich and famous? Then it hit me. Shit. Wes was rich and famous. I couldn't remember if he was just a millionaire or a billionaire. Not that it mattered to me. Money was only good to get you what you needed to live and a bit more to have some fun with. I didn't need colossal amounts of cash to be happy. Only enough to get my Pops out of hock and move on with my life.

Wes didn't speak for the longest time, both of us taking in the opulence, history, and attention to detail that the designers had put into something so unique. Each room in the mansion was special in its own way, laying out the foundation of one family's life. A family that had died out and donated the private Miami estate to Dade County that took excellent care of it. The estate brought in money for the county and was a place for folks to get married, where movies were made, and allowed the other ninety-nine percent of the population to ooh and ah over the extreme wealth of the previous owners. It had a magical, unreal vibe that places of extreme opulence had. Like a castle would, I imagined.

"Would you take me to a castle?" I was trolling down the long hallway. The art collection in Vizcaya was damn near priceless, some pieces dating back to the Renaissance.

He lifted his chin, closed his eyes, and then opened them as if he were clearing something from his vision. "Sure. There are a couple of amazing ones in Germany. We can plan a trip."

Just that easy. We could plan a trip. *To Germany*. And that is how the one percent lived. The farthest I'd ever been was to Hawaii. There was pretty much never an opportunity where I'd likely be making the kind of money it took for the cost of plane tickets to fly internationally.

"Isn't that expensive?" I tried to hide the anxiety that went with the simple response, "we can take a trip."

He shrugged. "Not to me. Drop in the bucket, sweetheart."

Drop in the bucket. Taking a trip to Germany was a drop in the bucket for someone with Wes's affluence. Shit. Eventually we'd have to talk about his outrageous wealth and my lack thereof. Suzi, my crotch rocket, was the most expensive thing I owned, and that didn't even equal the cost of a newer used Honda Civic.

I took a deep breath and clenched his hand tighter. Right then, I promised myself that I would not allow money to get between us. If he wanted to splurge on a trip to Germany, he knew what he could afford and what he couldn't. Emasculating my man was not something I would do in any way shape or form, but I did want to have a conversation about it when all this was over.

We stepped through a set of French doors, and nothing but intricate lawn carvings and greenery spanned as far as the eye could see. "This is the former villa and estate of businessman James Deering, of the Deering-McCormick-International Harvester fortune," Wes finally said.

That meant nothing to me, but I listened and nodded. He was obviously into the history behind the place, and I had to admit, I felt as though I entered the book *The Secret Garden*, which was a very cool feeling.

Wes stood in front of a staircase leading down into one of the many gardens. "The Vizcaya estate includes the Italian Renaissance gardens, a native woodland landscape as well as the original historic village outbuildings surrounding the compound. It's magnificent isn't it?" He asked while we walked hand-in-hand.

The gardens were definitely magical and the county had to spend a mint on gardening. Everything was trimmed neatly and to pristine detail, most of it in intricate designs that reminded me of mazes as well as country style lace. Wes pointed over to one area. "The landscape and architecture were influenced by Veneto and Tuscan Italian Renaissance models and designed in the Mediterranean Revival architecture style, with Baroque elements. Paul Chalfin was the design director," he confirmed.

I sucked in a breath and took in the many floral scents combined with that of fresh cut grass. "It's truly beautiful."

Hand-in-hand, we walked and walked until we found a strange waterfall. It was a series of steps on two sides with giant pots at each level of incline. Water fell down the center of the stone and concrete. Moss and minerals colored the blocks a vibrant orange and green as the water slid over each level.

Wes placed me next to the backdrop, stepped a few paces back, and lifted his phone. I smiled, and he took a photo. "Want to remember this, sweetheart," he murmured as he took me into his arms and kissed me just under my ear. Tendrils of excitement pranced along my nerves, bringing that giddy feeling back to the surface. I gave him my wide, unencumbered, all-teeth smile, and before I could stop him, he took a selfie of us smiling at the camera.

"I want a copy!" I announced, and he hugged me to his side as we continued our stroll, only this time, our bodies touched from shoulder to hip. Couldn't have asked for better.

We found ourselves in front of a rectangular structure. "You see that?" He pointed to it excitedly.

"Um, yeah, it's pretty big, babe." I snorted and he ignored the jab.

"This was featured in *Iron Man 3*! Take my picture in front of it."

I laughed, took his phone, and he pumped his arms out in front of him in a very superhero-esque pose and I snapped it. "You're so goofy!" I smiled, and he once more took me into his arms.

"And you love it." His green eyes dazzled, his face softening into an expression of serenity and joy. That was the face I wanted to look into forever.

"I love you," I countered.

He inhaled sharply. "The things those words do to me. Christ, Mia, I can't describe it. Just so damned lucky to be hearing it. I feel like I've waited my whole life to hear it."

I smacked his chest playfully. "You've only known me seven months." I sashayed out of his arms, swaying my hips from side to side, putting on a show, trying desperately to lighten the intense moment. "Come on. We have a million miles of lawn to traipse through."

He caught up to me as I picked up my pace. "You are unbelievable."

With a hip bump to his side, he staggered. "You better believe it! It's all real."

Wes reached for me again and caught me close. "And all mine." Then he kissed me. Not a soft kiss. Not a hard kiss. A downright knock-down, drag-out precursor to boning type kiss that made me pant, moan into his mouth, grip his hair, and pull him closer. I wanted more, and I didn't care where we were or how I got it, just that he gave it to me. Now.

"Want you…" I whispered between licks and sweet drugging sucks of his succulent mouth.

He grinned, and I could feel his smile against my teeth, his hand locked into my hair. "I know," he whispered and then tugged on me and gripped my hand. "Come. Like you said, we have a million miles of lawn to traipse through, and I, for one, want to get you back so I can ravish you."

I followed, a little dazed and a bit annoyed play time was over, yet equally anticipating more play time when we got back. "Where's the exit?"

He tipped his head back and laughed, a deep, throaty sound that I absolutely adored. Wes gave good laugh. Then again, Wes gave good everything. "Soon, baby. Anticipation, sweetheart, makes everything more intense. We've got all night."

Pinching my lips together, I sneered. "But one of us has to work tomorrow and wants her man to exhaust her tonight, not by trailing through unending paths and lovely gardens, but by plundering her garden." I wiggled my eyebrows suggestively.

"Wicked woman!"

"That's right. No rest for the wicked. So come on. Make me tired." I grinned, and he lifted me up in a princess hold and spun me around in a circle. It was fun. It was carefree. It was Wes and me.

★ ★ ★

The instant the elevator doors closed, he was on me. His hands were all over my body, his tongue in my mouth. Claiming, consuming, devouring. The hand rail around the elevator dug into my back, and I mewled and winced. Wes's hands roamed down my back until he felt the offending bar and slid his hands over my ass and down to my thighs, where he promptly lifted me. I was happy about this for two reasons. One, the bar was no longer digging a hole through my spine, and two, it put his cock exactly where I wanted it, pressing hard against my love button. It was wild, wicked, and just what I wanted.

The doors opened, which should have stopped the very overt public display of affection, but we were too far gone, until the sound of laughter and the elevator not moving pierced through the fog that was Wes. He too moved his head infinitesimally from my mouth and took in the two bodies standing there, Anton holding the door of the elevator open and Heather holding her hand over her mouth to try and contain the escaping peals of laughter.

"*Lucita...*" Anton's voice was laced with humor. Then he looked at Wes. "I'm guessing you're the man in her life." His voice as smooth as honey and just as sweet. His eyes danced with mirth and his lips pursed into a pout. "Glad you finally showed up. At least you can touch her." He took in the display before him not even a little flummoxed. It was as if he saw this kind of thing every day. And knowing Anton and his penchant for women—lots and lots of women, in his bed or otherwise—I could see why this didn't bother him a bit.

Heather waved hysterically from a foot behind Anton. Wes made an uncomfortable noise from deep in his throat that sounded like part growl, part annoyed boyfriend. I chuckled and unwound my legs from his waist, and he let me down but didn't allow me to go far, probably because he was sporting serious wood. And by serious, I meant a massive, long, hard cock ready to go. I pouted, missing it against me as much as I think he did right then.

Wes's eyes narrowed at Anton as he held out a hand, and we stepped off the elevator on my floor. Anton shook the outstretched hand. "So Mia didn't mention you were coming, but I imagine after that *cabron* attacked her last month, you needed to see your girl. Respect man. Mad respect." He clapped him on the back.

"Excuse me? What guy? Attacked Mia?"

Anton's face jolted back. The shit was about to hit the fan. I tried to give hand signals, throw up flares, wave down the plane, but nothing stopped him. He gripped Wes by the shoulder. "Ah, don't worry. Her secret is safe with me. The no-touching thing though, shit, man, she's beautiful, and a man wants to put his hands on her even in a friendly way, you know. Well"—he grinned pointing to the elevator—"you know." He winked. "That *bastardo* that did it uninvited put her in the hospital. You must have been downright *loco,* eh?"

Wes stopped on the way to my temporary apartment. His eyes narrowed, and both hands turned into white fists. He shot a guarded glance my way. "You were attacked? A man put you in the hospital? A fucking client?" The calm way he asked was scary, downright frightening because it was laced with venom. "Mia? Answer me."

I stood still, tears forming in my eyes. "It wasn't that bad," I whispered.

"Did this guy also try to touch you uninvited?" He hooked a thumb over his shoulder toward where Anton stood, obviously misunderstanding what Anton meant to say.

My eyes widened, and I opened my mouth to speak, but something on my face registered wrong, and he flipped around and had Anton by the throat against the wall. "Did you fucking touch her?" Wes slammed his body once against the wall. Anton recovered quickly and put his hands to Wes's forearms. I feared he'd start a brawl. He didn't. Anton went still and allowed Wes to hold him against the wall. Wes's arms shook with the effort. "I asked you a question," he shouted.

"No." A single word, his eyes directly on Wes, challenging him not to believe the truth.

I placed my hands on Wes's back, not knowing what to do. I didn't want to make it worse. Tears scuttled down my cheeks. "Wes, baby, Anton has been trying to help me get past what happened. Please, let him go. We'll talk. You and I. He didn't hurt me."

"What's this about you not being able to touch her? Why the fuck would you even say that?" he thundered, right up in Anton's face.

Again, Anton showed the patience of a Saint, which was odd, because I knew he boxed for sport and worked out like a mad man. He could probably take Wes, or at the very least, destroy this hallway trying. "When she came to me, she couldn't even handle a simple hug. It was bad, man."

I sank to my knees.

No. No. No. No.

Wes wasn't supposed to know. I didn't want this ruined. It was too new, too important. Now he would see that I was damaged. Not good enough for him. I hadn't had enough time with him. Heather shouted something I couldn't even hear through the roaring noise in my head. I was lifted up in a flourish, held in the cocoon of the only arms I ever wanted to be in again. Wes.

"Sweetheart, I'm sorry. Baby, it's okay, it's okay." I trembled against his chest. Somehow he got into my apartment and sat on the couch with me curled up in his lap. He held me for a long time while I cried. He soothed me, petted my hair, whispered sweet nothings to me. Finally, parched, he got me to take a few sips of water from a glass that appeared from out of nowhere.

"We'll leave you. *Amigo,* I'm sorry. I didn't know. *Puneta! Lo siento.*"

"If you need anything, I left our cards on the counter. I'll touch base with you later. Take care of our girl," Heather said.

Our girl. They thought I was their girl, but the only girl I wanted to be was Wes's girl. I sniffed against Wes's neck, enjoying the ocean scent, wishing we were at his place in Malibu, not in Miami in a strange albeit nice apartment.

"Hey, you okay?" He tilted my head up and wiped away the remaining tears as I nodded. "You hungry?" I shook my head. "Thirsty?" Same response. "What do you need?"

"I need you to love me."

"Mia, I've loved you from the moment you took off your helmet at the beach. Hell, maybe it even happened before, when Mom showed me your photos on the website. I knew then I had to have you. And not just in my bed." He squeezed me tight. "Though I love that too." He grinned wickedly. "With you, Mia, it's always been more. Everything about you calls to me. Your body makes me weak with desire. Your love of life and new things makes me want to set the world at your feet just so I can see you smile. I'll love you today, tomorrow, and every day after that."

"Prove it."

He groaned and then sighed. "Sweetheart, we need to talk."

"Prove it," I pleaded, my voice bordering on begging.

He ran a hand through his dirty blond layers and down his face. "Fuck me," he grumbled.

"Exactly. Fuck me."

He shook his head. "Not tonight. Tonight I'm going to worship you."

CHAPTER NINE

Back and forth. Back and forth. Stop abruptly. Tug the hair. Scowl. Mumble profanity. Turn. Repeat.

I watched Wes pace the floor, figuratively burning the tread off his shoes in the process. He stopped suddenly, clenched both hands into fists, and faced me. "I'm going to fucking kill him. I'll *ruin* him. Political career"—he made a slashing gesture with his hand—"over. He's going to pay in blood!"

"He already did." I glanced up when the chill in the room turned white hot. Wes's eyes were dark pitch black with only a tiny ring of translucent green around them. "Mason beat the hell out of him," I whispered, the words trailing off. Gulping down the dry ball of newspaper that had built like papier-mâché in my throat, I tried to speak, but the look in his eyes kept me silent.

Wes's eyebrows narrowed so severely a gnarly pair of eleven's worked its way above his nose. "Mason? Who the fuck is Mason?"

I blinked at the grating tone of his voice. "Uh…uh, Mace is an ex–client…" Wes's eyes went dead flat, devoid of feeling, and then widened. "Friend," I amended.

Back to pacing.

"I can't believe this. My girlfriend gets attacked, by a scumbag"—he turned on a heel and kept walking—"and ends up in the hospital, and I'm not told jack shit about it! Jesus Christ, Mia! This is so fucked up." It probably wouldn't do any good to point out that we hadn't officially determined the status of our relationship until yesterday. I thought it might go over worse than a hole to the head. He stood still, his eyes closed, jaw ticking with the extreme way he was holding his mouth so tight. "I don't know what to do."

Jumping up, I grabbed his hands, brought them up between us, and rubbed out the tension until they loosened. "Baby, there's nothing you can do."

He bit down hard on his lip, so much so that I worried he'd break through the tender flesh until he drew blood. "Mia, I'm so angry." His voice was raw and pained. "I need to do something." His eyes opened and found mine.

"No. You need to see to *me*. Help me. That's what you can do. It's over."

And it was. I had spent the last hour going over in excruciating detail what happened, the moments leading up to the assault and the fallout. Through it all, Wes held my hand, sat patiently while I retold the horrific experience, and caressed my back, wiped my tears and more. He listened and didn't react until afterward. Once I'd told him an acceptable version of what Aaron did to me that night and the time before, when he inappropriately touched me while I slept…that's when Wes started the pacing. And profanity. Next came anger.

Wes shook his head and clutched at his hair for the umpteenth time. "It's not over. There's a god damned whole in my gut. Sweetheart, the only thing that's going to fix this is me taking that fucker down. Don't you see?" His eyes blazed as his hands shook. "He hurt the woman I love. Badly.

He needs to feel that pain."

"Like I said, he is. He has to go to a therapist, AA, and more. Baby, if this hits the news or anyone finds out about what happened, the ramifications will hurt a lot more people than just Aaron. Hundreds, possibly thousands more in other countries. Warren, his Dad, he'll have to pull out of the project. His investors would never support a man whose son is a sexual predator and a drunk. Please try to understand."

And back to the pacing. I knew by the slump of his shoulders that he got it. We'd already been over it. I told him about Warren's business, about the work he was doing, about the contributions pouring in and how all that could very well stop if something this heinous came out. The good ol' boys' club would crucify him and take their money with them. Weston knew that. He agreed to it because, if faced with the same circumstances, he would pull funding.

"Wes, there's also the backlash…" I tried to broach the very sticky subject of my work and how the rest of the world would view me.

His eyes narrowed, and he leaned against the edge of the chair across from me. "Backlash?"

I nodded. "Yeah. On you, on Alec, Mason, Tony, Hector, the D'Amicos, Tai, Anton. It's too much to risk to go for a full–court–press–style justice for what he did."

"Sweetheart, you're losing me. Who are all those people?"

And that was when it got real. Very real. The kind of real that either made couples stronger or broke them forever. I had no choice.

"Wes, you know I'm an escort. The general public

thinks that means I'm a well-paid hooker, and in some instances, that information could be inferred as correct." He huffed and let out a long breath. "Also, securing me as an escort means that the people who can afford me are all big in their own right."

"I'm not following. Explain it." He spoke in a way that I found rather ruthless. He wanted to go there? Fine. I'd take him.

I shrugged. "You asked for it."

Looping a finger around the opposite hand's first finger, I called them off. "Aside from Warren and his help the poor in third world countries, the clients immediately before him were the D'Amicos. I did the Beauty Comes In All Sizes campaign. News that they hired an escort to model for them could destroy what they built."

Wes pointed at me. "I actually saw the campaign. Was really proud of you, sweetheart. You looked great. Amazing really." I beamed under his compliment. It made me feel amazing that Wes was proud of the work I'd done. "Next?"

"Mason Murphy." Wes's eyes widened in recognition. "Yep, the famous baseball player for the Boston Red Sox. Was hired by him to be his girlfriend to perfect his image. In the end, it actually worked, and he did find his mate in his PR representative."

Wes moved to the bar at the side of the room. He lifted the whiskey, and I nodded. I'd need a drink to get through all of this. He took two tumblers and filled them with three fingers full of the amber liquid. Yep, it was going to be one of those nights. A straight confessional. I could only hope he wouldn't crucify me for my sins.

He handed me the tumbler, and I took a sip. The liquor

burned down my throat like those Hot Tamale candies, leaving an even thicker aftertaste that sizzled on the tongue and warmed the belly nicely.

"Did you sleep with him?" He sat in the chair opposite me. We were separated by a long slim glass table. The distance he put between us, whether intentional or not, wasn't lost on me. Didn't matter. This is what needed to happen.

I shook my head. "No, I didn't. Not that he didn't try." I grinned, and he frowned. Okay, moving on. "Then before him was Tony Fasano."

He cocked his head. "The food guy?"

That made me smile. "Yeah."

"What did he hire you for?" This time when he spoke, it was a little lighter, carried less of that nervous weight.

"To be his fiancée." I snickered, and Wes cringed. "Best part is *why* he hired me." I grinned.

The grin must have given Wes relief because he gave a half-hearted smile in return. "Why's that?"

"I can't believe you don't remember what we talked about in March or staying in their house. I mean, yeah, they weren't overt at the bar, and we did toss back a few too many, but really? You don't remember anything about Tony and Hector?

Wes shook his head and shrugged. "Not really, no. I recall what they look like, meeting them, and drinking too many with a couple of cool dudes. However, what I mostly remember is your mouth, taking you up against a wall, that amazing shower, and having drunken monkey loving all night with the sexiest woman alive."

"Monkey loving?" I snorted.

He nodded. "So what's the big deal about why he hired

you to be his fiancée?" he asked, bringing me back to the topic at hand.

I pushed my feet under my booty and got comfortable, setting my glass on the arm of the chair. "In order to tell you that, I have to set the scene."

Wes's lips lifted into a crack of a smile, and

I thought that was definitely a tiny victory.

"Okay, shoot." He leaned back and took a swallow of his whiskey.

I loved watching his neck and Adam's apple bob with the effort. Everything about Wes interested me, especially now that we were together. Hopefully together for longer than this conversation.

"After I arrived in Chicago, the house help put my bag in a room. It was a huge room, much bigger than I expected, even though Tony lived in a penthouse apartment in the city."

Wes didn't say anything just waited for me to continue.

"When the guy left me there with my luggage, I heard the shower running. You can't imagine how freaked out I was, knowing that I was in a room, probably the master bedroom, and a guy I didn't know, a stranger, was in the shower."

For a chick, this would be entertaining and funny. For Wes…not so much. His jaw clenched, and he worked a nice grinding motion while I rushed to continue. "So he opens the door, and this huge hulking dude is standing there in a towel, and that's when things get really interesting…" I tried to lead into the whammy, but Wes just looked pissed off.

"I won't hold my breath," he said.

I rolled my eyes. "Well I stood there like a fish out of

water, not knowing what to say, and then, out from behind him, another guy with a towel wrapped around his waist hugged my client. As in bare-chested hugging. As in they'd been in the shower…together."

That's when Wes gave me the full, beaming pearly whites. "He's gay!" He shook his head and shrugged.

"Don't you read the news? Pay attention to the gossipmongers?"

He licked those perfect lips and tipped his chin. "Not at all. I avoid that shit like the plague. It's rarely based on truth, and usually just ends up hurting the person they are featuring."

I rolled my eyes but continued, "Tony is gay. Been in a long-term relationship with an amazing attorney named Hector Chavez. Actually, during the month I was there, I became really close with Tony and Hector. More Hector than Tony for obvious reasons." I winked.

"Obvious," he mouthed.

I drummed my fingers against my leg and took a drink. "Then before Tony was Alec." Remembering my time with Alec put that pit back in my stomach. I gave a piece of myself to Alec that month. A piece I never wanted back. Simple truth: I loved my filthy talking Frenchie, and I enjoyed being in his bed just as much. Not more than with Wes, but way up there on the list of great people to have sex with, same as Tai.

"And Alec was the artist," he grumbled. How he knew that, I couldn't recall. It's possible that I mentioned Alec and our time together, but Wes wasn't giving anything away.

Pursing my lips, I looked away and down at my half-filled drink and took another large wallop of whiskey.

"You had a sexual relationship with him," Wes said in a way that wasn't accusing, which I hoped meant it would be okay.

I nodded.

He shrugged and looked out at the setting sun. "But it was just casual, like Gina."

The mere mention of that bitch's name made the jealousy flags wave, the green-eyed monster sing, and the two-faced bitch shake hands with the devil. "Alec was special. He means something to me." I'd become defensive, not realizing I was showing my hand in a way I hadn't been ready to deal with.

Wes inclined his head, leaned forward, and rested his elbows on his knees as he steepled his hands together under his chin. "Is that so? Special how?"

Tears pricked at the edges of my eyes. "Alec made me feel beautiful."

"And I didn't?" he challenged.

My hackles rose. "You did, but he made me feel like the Mia that everyone didn't see, the same one I was with you, but not the rest of the world, was okay to let out. Forced me to put down the mask and let the world in. I learned a very valuable lesson from Alec."

"And that was?" His tone was hurt and scared.

"To love myself."

Wes closed his eyes, inhaled, let out the breath and relaxed. "Mia, you have every reason in the world to love yourself."

I shook my head. "I didn't believe it. Not before Alec. Not before his art made me see what everyone else saw. Even though I was broken, was struggling in life, that I'd become an escort because my gambling, drunk father couldn't hold his shit long enough to take care of his own debts, that I"—I slapped my chest"—"Mia Saunders, the waitress from Vegas, deserved more. I deserved happiness. Deserved love."

"And I don't give you that?" His voice cracked when he said it.

"You do, only at the time, Alec did too. In a way, he still does."

Wes's eyes hardened, and then sadness swept across his features. "He loves you."

I nodded and he closed his eyes. I was quick to respond. "Alec believes that you love the one you're with for however long you're with them. That it's okay to take a piece of each other with you as you carry on throughout your life."

"Does he want you back?"

And there was the jealousy on my normally laid-back movie-making surfer. "No. Not in that way. Alec loves every woman he's with, or he wouldn't be with her. There are probably hearts all over the globe breaking daily because he's loving someone new right this very moment."

"That's not how I operate. Mia, I'm a one-woman man when I commit, and I'm committing to *you*. To *us*. In order for this to work, you have to commit too." He cleared his throat. "And we have to get past all this history. Because, honey, that's what it is. It's history."

I thought briefly of Gina, but I didn't know the timeframe of when he was fucking her and making love to me. I only knew that now he wouldn't be, and I believed him.

"That's all the months. So you only slept with one man since we've been together?" His gaze was incredulous. He had reason to be so.

Closing my eyes, I braced for it. "No. I was with Tai Niko, the male model, in Hawaii."

"Hawaii? In May?"

"Yeah."

"Like a one-time thing?" There was so much riding on my response.

My voice shook. "No," I admitted, because if anything, I wasn't a liar. There was no way I was going to start out my first real relationship in years built on lies.

"Fuck!" He stood and started pacing, tugging on his hair and cursing. This seemed to be his go-to response.

"You don't understand. Wes, it was just fun! He's already with someone else right now. Someone he plans on marrying!" I yelled to get my point across. Wes was too important to not get past this.

Wes shook his head from side to side. His shoulder slumped once more. "Shit. Sweetheart, you're killing me. You spent a month in paradise loving someone else?"

He used the word paradise to torture me. Playing fair was off the table. "And you spent the last how many months fucking Gina DeLuca, America's goddamned sweetheart, hot throb, sexiest woman alive, and I'm supposed to be okay with that?"

Like a shot from a cannon, he backed up several steps and clasped the side-table behind him. "Mia, she means nothing to me!" He clutched at his chest. "Nothing!" he reiterated.

"I find that hard to believe. You've been *casually* fucking her for months." I gestured with air quotes at the word casually. "You don't think she believes it's something more?"

116

He shook his head. "She doesn't. I swear."

"Whatever. Tell yourself that until you believe it. At least I can say that I've had my time with Alec and Tai and moved on from it. I'm in a different place. I. Love. You! I never said those words that way to them. I may love them as friends, as people I care about who I know care about me in return, but I'm not *in love* with them. Monumental difference. I've never been *in love* with them. Can you say the same about Gina? Huh?" My voice was at a screech, and I knew I'd lost it when I stood up and threw my tumbler at the wall. It didn't even break. No satisfaction whatsoever. Damn Anton and his love for quality glassware.

I groaned, flopped back down to the couch, and cradled my head in my hands. "This is why I never fall in love." I said the words aloud and repeated them in my head, over and over like a chant.

Without warning, Wes pulled me up and turned around so that my knees hit each side of hips in a straddle.

"Don't you ever regret loving me. That would hurt worse than anything you could ever say or do to me." He cupped my cheeks. "Is that all? That everything? Two guys? One attacker and a handful of new friends?"

I licked my lips and nodded.

"Okay, sweetheart." He swallowed and admitted his own truths. "For me it was just Gina on and off. We can both move past this." The words made my heart sing. Like a bedtime lullaby, I softened. Being with him, like this, in his lap, his hands caressing my sides, made me that easy.

We can work with this.

My eyes filled again with tears. His thumbs swiped them away as they fell. "No, no, baby. Right now, from here on out, it's just you and me. We put it out there and it's done. I know what I need to know, you know that Gina is gone. G-O-N-E," he repeated, spelling it out. "Only thing left is this. You and me. Now we can build on it."

I nodded and shoved my head into his neck, inhaling that ocean and Wes scent I adored. "I love you." I spoke the words to him so that he could hear them and know that I needed to hear them in return.

"Sweetheart, I love you too. Me and you. Just me and you."

CHAPTER TEN

The trill of my cell phone woke me from the best dream. Wes and I were touring castles in Germany, hand-in-hand, a young couple very much in love. Until the ringing started. As soon as it stopped, it would start again.

Wes leaned over me, grabbed the offending object, and answered it. Shit. No. Bad idea. It could be anyone. If it was one of my ex-clients, friend or not, it could go bad. Really bad, insanely fast.

He yawned. "Yeah, yeah. Okay, just a sec. It's Ms. Milan."

I rolled my eyes. Aunt Millie.

I grabbed the phone and held my hand over the speaker, muffling any sound. "She's actually my Aunt Millie. As in, her name is Millie, not Milan."

"Really?"

"Thought I told you that."

"Pretty sure I'd remember that." He leaned up and kissed the top of my shoulder. "I'll go make us some coffee before you hit the studio today."

I squeezed his bicep, caught him behind the head, and kissed him sweetly. He grinned and pulled back.

I put the phone to my ear. "Aunt Millie. What on Earth would make you call so early? I mean, it has to be ridiculously early for you."

I heard her fingers tapping in the background. "Yeah, yeah, haven't gone to bed yet. You've ignored my calls all week, and I needed to give you the details on your next client since I'm heading out on vacation tomorrow. Want to make sure it's booked in advance. This one is...I don't know. Something's off about it." Aunt Millie had never sounded anything other than one hundred percent self-assured.

"What do you mean? Why is it off? The guy a creep?"

She sighed. "No, no, it's actually that he's too clean on paper. He's been insistent that he reserve you as soon as you're available. Checks in every couple weeks to see if you've had a cancellation. Which you haven't, of course."

"Okay, so he really wants me. Did he say why?"

"Apparently, he needs you to be his long lost sister. Something about a business landing in the wrong hands if he doesn't produce his sibling for the investors, blah, blah. Her name popped up in some random agreement regarding the business, but he never knew her. They couldn't really discern the scribbled name. It could be Mia Saunders or Mia Sanders, or Sonders with an O, but you share the individual's birth date exactly, and your name is Mia Saunders. Hence, why he had to have you."

I plucked at my lips. "This is weird. Did you check him out?"

Millie gave an overwrought sigh that seemed to strangle my heart in the process. "Do you think I'd ever risk your safety?"

Laughter sat at the tip of my tongue, especially after the Aaron debacle, but she didn't know much about that. Basically nothing. I'd hidden that whopper well. "I know you have my best interests in mind, Auntie. Sorry."

She tsked, and all was well again. Pushover. "He's been thoroughly vetted. Young. Only thirty, and he's been at the helm of one of the top oil businesses headquartered in Texas."

"Wow. Oil's big money, right?"

Aunt Millie hummed. "Yesiree. I don't know all the details aside from him being very anxious to meet you. And you'll love this, too. He's not an old stodgy gentleman caller. He's a hot cowboy, lives on a ranch and everything!" She paused. "Haven't seen the extra twenty-five grand come through for our Latin-Lovah. Guessing you haven't been having as much fun as I'd thought you would."

"Millie, that's none of your business, but no, I'm not. And I'm not going to."

"You might change your mind when I send you a picture of this cowboy. I was never into cowboys myself, but something about him is familiar, speaks to me in a way I haven't felt in a long time. Perhaps that's why I'm feeling off, because the young man gives me a déjà vu vibe. Hmm, no matter. Your plane from Miami to Dallas will be booked tomorrow. Do you want to stay a few days in Miami, Dallas, or go home before you head to Texas?"

Home.

That thought made me smile huge. So huge that, when Wes walked into the room with a cup of coffee, he stopped in his tracks, tilted his head, and an eyebrow rose in a silent question. "What?" he mouthed, but I shook my head grinning like a loon.

"Millie, I'd like to stay in Malibu for the few days before I have to meet my next client in Dallas. I'll fly out of LAX."

Wes did a little hip sway and ab curl move that made me want to remove his boxer briefs and suck on his cock. Straight up.

"Okay, dollface, I'll set up the arrangements. It's good you're coming home for a bit. Let's do lunch."

"Sounds good. Love you."

"Yes, dear. And I you."

Millie hung up, and I clicked off the cell and turned to my guy. "After this week, I'll be in Malibu for six days. Wonder if there's a place I could stay."

With an absolutely blank face, Wes responded, "You have an apartment."

I cringed. My apartment. I needed to just empty that place and put my stuff in storage. As a matter of fact, maybe I should add that on my list of things to do while I was in LA. No reason to pay rent for a place I hadn't stepped foot in for the last seven months.

"Baby, I thought—" I was cut off by Wes slamming me into the bed.

"Gotcha!" He kissed me full, deep, and so completely I forgot I was supposed to be getting up to prep for rehearsal. "I so had you." He nuzzled my nose with his and laid a series of sloppy, wet kisses on my neck. "Of course I want you with me. My parents have been bugging the crap out of me to get you back."

"Get me back? You never had me in the first place."

He sat up and placed his hands on my ribs where he pushed at the hem of my camisole and lifted the fabric inch by inch. "I had you." I shook my head. "You were mine even then." Another shake. "No?" Instead of pushing up the top and going for my needy, achy tits, he did the exact opposite and tickled me. His fingers dug into the sensitive area between each rib, causing loud bursts of laughter. "Admit you were mine!" he demanded. It was hard to hear over the peals of laughter exploding from my body. I shook my head and tried to grab his wiggling fingers. I couldn't breathe. My body was no longer my own, but dammit, he was right. Ever since the first, he had me.

"Okay, okay," I begged.

He shook his head. "Not good enough." He pulled my hands to rest above my head. "Say it."

I took about twenty deep breaths to try to stop the racking, jittering feeling strumming along each nerve. Then I looked up into his eyes, and somehow I could tell that whatever answer I gave was really important to him. "You had me in January, Wes," I choked out, my voice filled with emotion. "I didn't want to believe it. Tried so hard to deny it. Shove it in a closet, high on a shelf where no one would find it. Not even me. Especially not you. But these things have a way of breaking free. I'm so glad they did."

A single tear tracked down the side of my face. Wes leaned forward and licked it. "I love the taste of your tears. And you know what?"

"What," I choked out, wiping at my cheeks while his gaze focused solely on me.

"You had me too, sweetheart. Even then."

★ ★ ★

Yesterday's rehearsal was brutal. It didn't help that Wes was there watching, growling, sending daggers toward Anton every time he rolled his body against mine and placed his hands on my hips. The role of seductress in this video was to entice the man, make him bleed with desire for her. Now secure in my own skin, Wes's love gave me the confidence

I needed to get past another man's touch. Simply put, I was on fire. Scalding hot and burning bright. Maria was beside herself, and that happiness continued through each step as we filmed.

"Yes, yes, cut!" The cameras stopped rolling. Anton's hands were digging in my hips, his face near my belly in a very suggestive pose. He popped back as if he weren't just rolling his nose from my knee, up a stocking-clad thigh, pushing the tiny dress up with his teeth. Yet when they called *cut*, it was done. *Poof.* Back to chill, friendly Anton who made a point to keep his distance. That plan worked, because the fear of his touch, the anxiety I'd felt most of the month had dissipated, having mostly worked its way out.

Maria was right. Talking to Gin by phone and going over it with Wes—two people that knew me in a way the others didn't—had helped get me through. I figured out that it wasn't just the touch from another man that triggered the response. Guilt drove the flashbacks, the anxiety, the niggling fear that crept into my experience with Anton. In the end, I had to accept that I'd made the right call. When it came down to it, saving everyone else with the decision I'd made essentially saved myself. I could never have lived with the knowledge that those I cared for and thousands of people in need would have also suffered the consequences.

I walked off the set to the area where the stylist was. She held up the last outfit. This was going to be the test of all tests. A designer that Anton knew made the garment— if you could call it that. Essentially, finely woven pieces of fabric were tacked together in a patchwork that made it easy to tear. The makeup artist and costume designer fussed over me while Wes stood to the side and held his tongue.

As a man who made movies and dealt with actors every day, you'd think he'd be a lot more considerate and accepting of the fact that I was playing a character and not think too much about it. Totally wrong. He kept quiet, a solid, respectful professional in the industry, but I knew it cost him. The tight way he held his frame, the thin line of lips, the way his eyes flicked from naked pieces of my flesh to where Anton had been touching them. All these were signs that Wes was barely handling it.

"You know you can go back to the hotel. We'll shoot the last scene, and we can have dinner with everybody." I tried once again to get him to leave, not really wanting it.

Wes shook his head. "Sweetheart, I'm here. Just do your job, and we'll take it from there."

His tone was flat, holding no emotion. I tried a different tactic. "I'm really glad you've stayed. Made it easier." I blinked away the sensation of tears.

He came to me, lifted up my chin, leaned forward, and kissed me lightly. The makeup artist behind me groaned and cursed. I smiled against Wes's mouth. "You're going to get me in trouble."

Finally he grinned and waggled those brows. "I like getting you into trouble. I'm sure there are all kinds of ways we can get into more of it."

Snickering, I pushed him back, sent an apologetic glance to the makeup artist, and blew Wes a kiss. Wes licked his lips and petted the plump bottom one with his thumb. I loved that. So damn sexy.

"Pay attention, *hermana*. The final scene is a doozy. You ready for it?"

Wes would lose his mind when he watched what was

planned for the finale. "Ready as I'll ever be," I confirmed, but wanted to add, *for a woman who is about to be naked in front of room filled with dancers, crew, Anton, and my man.* Briefly, I considered telling Wes what was going to happen in the scene, but decided against it. If we could get it done in one shot, the entire thing would play out organically, and he'd have no choice but to deal with it.

Everyone knew that it was easier to ask for forgiveness than permission. This was absolutely one of those times.

The stylist walked me to the new stage, hemming and hawing over the pieces of fabric, glitter, and jewels. When I say jewels, I mean those bedazzled rhinestones with the flat bottoms and the multicolored tops. The tips of my breasts were covered in gemstones that were glued in a way that the nipple and areola were covered but the fleshy globe was enhanced. A tiny thong, again made of sparkly gems, and a line of diamonds around each hip covered my hairless sex. Another thing Wes didn't know about yet, as we'd done that horrific part in the private bathroom while he had lunch. All of that was hidden beneath the slip of fabric that really couldn't be called a dress. Especially since I knew it was going to be ripped to smithereens in a couple of seconds once those cameras started rolling.

Carefully, I climbed up onto my pedestal. The heavy beat of Anton's song surrounded us. Lighting flashed, blinked in a strobe effect, making it hard to see without blinking. The wind machine hit me with that soft sensuous flow, making my hair move wild and free. The loose curls drifted in the current of air in what I'd hoped gave the appealing result Anton and his team desired.

Wes stood in the darkness directly in front of me. I

could primarily see his face, mostly those green eyes. His arms were crossed over his chest and his gaze focused on me. The room fell away. Dancers mingled around me as I pumped my shoulders, swayed my hips, and inhaled and exhaled as Maria had taught me to in order to achieve the breathy affect that made men stupid. Her words, not mine.

Anton's character started in the back. I felt his hand stroke up the side of my body. I closed my eyes and opened them again, seeing nothing but Wes, and what I saw ricocheted up my spine and landed heavily in my gut. Lust. Carnal need so strong it hardened my nipples, the jewels pinching favorably. In the middle of a scene with a hundred people around me, Wes lit up my body like a torch. Anton continued to dance around me, touching me, lip syncing, begging. Every so often he'd touch a piece of the outfit and make a point by ripping a shred off. I jolted as instructed, as if he were tearing off pieces of my armor. I guess that was the abstract view. Him removing the armor of his seductress so she would be his.

The dancers dressed in swaths of black gaping holes showing glittery skin whirled around me like phantoms. The metaphor in the choreography that Maria crafted alongside Heather's suggestions was truly one of a kind. As the song came to a crescendo, the dancers crowded around me. The cameras were at every angle. At a hard thrust of Anton's hips as he stood directly in front of me, each dancer tore away a piece of my outfit, and the rest fell away, leaving me in my jewelry lingerie. Anton dropped to his knees. I acted confident and powerful, really getting into the part. When Anton lifted his hands up, as if in prayer, begging to be mine, I cupped his cheek with one hand, pressed the other against his chest, and the camera zoomed in close. With measured movements, I puckered my lips and mouthed the last words of his song perfectly in sync with the female voice on the soundtrack.

"Forget me."

Then, as the cameras backed up, I crossed an arm over my breasts, shoved him back, and moved the other hand down to the apex of my thighs. Then I closed my eyes tilted my head to the side and down. The lights faded out.

"Cut, cut. That's a wrap!" the director called out. A robe was thrown over my shoulders, and I was in Anton's arms.

"*Lucita*, you were a genius!" He kissed my cheeks, my forehead, temples, hairline, and finally, cupping both cheeks, he stared deeply in my eyes, his intent clear. He leaned forward and kissed me softly on the lips. A mere whisper of a kiss, but it was enough. The best part of the kiss was the fact that there was absolutely no fear. No flashback, just the comfort of a friend congratulating me. He held onto my biceps but then dropped them suddenly, and a grin played against his features.

"I think that's quite enough of you touching my girl, eh, amigo?" Wes spoke in a monotone.

Anton turned around and pulled Wes into a man-hug complete with hard slaps to the back. "You're good for her, amigo. Now we celebrate!" One arm across my shoulders and another at my waist nestled me between Anton and Wes even in spite of Wes's earlier warning remark. Anton didn't seem to care. He lived life in the moment and ignored Wes's initial pissy attitude. That alone made Anton a special man. He lived life in the present, enjoyed his friends, his work, and celebrated it as often as he could.

Heather and Maria met us at the edge of the set with hugs and a bottle of Cristal. "Big spender," I noted dryly, yet I sipped the awesome liquid, letting the golden, bubbly nectar swirl against my taste buds and dance on my tongue.

"You were amazing!" Heather pulled me into a tight hug.

"I had a great teacher." I beamed at Maria, unable to contain my enthusiasm. Having this video play all over the world, knowing that people everywhere would see me... there really wasn't a way to describe it. Amazing. Wonderful. Unbelievable. It was all of that and more. Couple it with having Wes and three new friends—the world as I knew it rocked!

★ ★ ★

Bags packed, TV on low as the news reported the happenings around Miami. I zipped up the last bag filled with all the clothes Heather and Anton had picked for me. I'd take them to California and put them in storage along with all the other crap I needed to box up and move out of the Cracker Jack box apartment I rented.

I thought about the last week of my time here. Like Hawaii, one of the best of my life. Wes's visit and our newfound relationship and commitment to one another were the highlights. He'd left the day after we finished filming on the video. Said he'd do his best to take the days off that I had available but would likely have to work a little. Mostly in his home office. For me, I only cared about being with him. Resting up for the next job.

Dallas, Texas and an oil tycoon. I didn't know much

about what he wanted me to do other than pretend to be his long lost sister. One he'd never met. So apparently, my appearance didn't matter, only that my name and birthday were the same as hers. It took me a few days to realize that Millie had not mentioned his name. Turned out, he was Maxwell Cunningham. I did some quick research on the cowboy. He owned fifty-one percent of Cunningham Oil & Gas, one of the top twenty-five oil companies in the world. For a man only thirty years old, it was quite an accomplishment. However, during my research I learned that he inherited his half of the company only a year ago. It didn't say who the other forty-nine percent belonged to, but I knew in most giant companies, smaller percentages were often owned by the investors. Either way, he was paying me to be his sister, Mia Saunders. It was definitely odd. When I pulled up his photo, I felt as if I'd met him before. Made me wonder if he and I had been at one of the same swanky shindigs over the past six months.

Figuring I'd found out soon enough, I went over to my bag and pulled out my stationery.

Anton,

How does a person thank someone for helping her deal with a trauma? It's not like I can go to Hallmark and pick out a card that says, "Hey, you helped bring me back from the ledge. Thanks buddy!" tee hee

Honestly, though, you handled me with care and respect, the way a true friend would. Sharing your history with me, allowing me to share my experience with you, saved me in ways I cannot express. I'm thrilled that you worked out your business and personal relationship with Heather. She's a beauty with a ridiculous work ethic. You'll never be able to pay her what she's worth because even you don't have that kind of money. Just make sure you pay her back in praise and love for a job well done. Even hard-assed managers need a pat on the back once in a while. Especially when they are from your best friend.

The video experience was one I'll never forget, but the memory I'll hold most dear was our motorcycle ride. Pure thing of beauty. Thank you for sharing your toys with me. ;-)

I know this next song is going to set the world on fire. I'll buy it the minute it goes live.

Until next time.

Your Lucita,

~Mia

Heather -

Meeting you was a gift. I hope you know that no matter where I am, I'll always be your friend. Call, text, bug me as often as you'd like, and I'll do the same. Why? Because that's what friends do! I look forward to hearing about all the shenanigans Anton puts you through. I'm also glad you worked things out with one another. Best friends, the kind that last a lifetime, always find their way back to one another.

Good luck in the new job!

Your friend,

~Mia

On that note, I gripped my suitcase handle, left the key to the apartment on the table, locked the door, and left. Anton and Heather thought they were meeting me here in two hours, but goodbyes weren't my thing. I preferred to fly off into the sunset to my next destination, knowing that the next adventure is just around the corner.

I'd taken back my life, and I felt good about the decisions I'd made, where I was and what my future held. The possibilities were endless, especially as I imagined my movie-making surfer in a pair of swim trunks, sand around his feet and stuck to his ankles, waving me into the open expanse of the Pacific.

Time to go home…at least for a little while.

CALENDAR GIRL

AUDREY CARLAN

CHAPTER ONE

The second I stepped out into the California sun, I was body slammed, swooped up into the air, and spun in a dizzying circle. Moist lips found mine. Sunlight, the ocean, and the scent of my man permeated the air around me. Comfort, exhilaration, and relief swarmed through my emotions as I sucked Wes's bottom lip like a greedy leech—wanting more of him, needing his imprint from the top of my head to the tips of my toes.

Surround me in you. It was all I could think while Wes turned my head from side to side, taking the kiss deeper, staking his claim far beyond the bounds public decency allowed.

"Get a room!" A young kid's voice barked, breaking through our happy "welcome home" bubble. I slid my nose against his, relishing his scent, the way his eyelashes fluttered closed as if he, too, was having trouble with the overwhelming idea that was us. Wes and Mia. A relationship.

"Hey, baby," I said low, my voice belying how very much I missed him.

Wes's fingers tunneled from my nape up into my hair, holding the back of my head loosely. "My girl," he whispered in awe, shaking his head before kissing me sweetly once more. There might have been less heat in this one, but it was no less meaningful. "Come on. I wanna get you home. Ms. Croft has a spread for your homecoming."

"Really? You told Judi I was coming?" I smiled and squeezed his hand.

He swung my arm, leading me to the limo. "Of course. Had to tell her my *girlfriend* was coming for a week. Make sure she's prepared."

I hummed. "How very thoughtful of you, Mr. Channing…" I put one foot on the floor of the limo, popping out my ass for maximum gazing. Like bees to a flower, his focus went unabashedly to my bum. I wiggled it for the hell of it and grinned when his eyes found mine. "… The Third," I mouthed and winked.

He shook his head and smacked my ass, hard. I'd be rubbing that imprint for a while. "Get in, sweetheart. Time's a-wasting, and I want to fuck you before I feed you."

Wes entered the limo with practiced grace. He was a thing of beauty. Tall, long, lean in all the right places. The well-defined abdominals and pecs were slightly visible through the thin fabric of his polo. He wore cargo shorts befitting the surfer he was, not the movie-making rich socialite I knew he could be, at least when he needed to. His feet were stuffed into a pair of Vans.

The moment the driver took off, Wes rolled up the privacy screen and pounced. There was a second where I wasn't sure if he was going to make a move, but I should have known. We were far too eager. It had been a week since we'd last seen one another. Within half a breath, Wes had me on his lap, straddling his legs, his large hands on my ass, rubbing, caressing, and kneading the flesh deliciously.

"You gonna make a dream come true and let me fuck you right here?" His green eyes were blazing with a fiery ball of lust.

I shook my head and pressed lower, grinding into his stiff shaft. Rocking my hips back and forth, I set up a rhythm that had us both gasping. "Nuh-uh. I'll be doing the fucking." A grin that likely matched my own slid across his lips.

Wes's hands moved up my flowy little skirt where he pushed his hand down into the back of my underwear, gripping my ass more fully. "Sweetheart, I'm all yours for the taking. Any way you want it, you can have it. As long as that tight cunt is wrapped around my cock, I'll take any orders you throw out."

Hearing Wes say the word cock was like zapping my clit with a white hot poker. It sizzled and throbbed, wanting attention.

Without taking much time, I pushed off his thighs, removed my underwear, and dropped to my knees on the limo floor where I yanked and tugged at his shorts. His cock sprang free. *Eureka!* I wrapped a hand around the root and squeezed. Wes groaned, his eyes closed, and his head fell back against the leather seat. A pearl of pre-cum beaded at the tip, and it looked too good to pass up. Wes's eyes looked down just as I licked the tip of his dick.

"Christ!" He gritted his teeth, but I held his legs wide. Then I glanced at his face and saw a man who was on the edge of losing his cool. In seconds, I'd be pulled up and slammed on his cock. I knew it. He knew it. Wes was used to being in control, and any time I tried to take the reins, he'd try—like the gentleman he could be—to allow it. However, the second I got my lips around his cock, I had little if any time before his control would snap. Don't get me wrong. Wes loved my mouth, enjoyed head immensely, but usually, a blow job was something he'd be interested in after he'd pounded me into next week. My man expected intimacy first, filthy fucking second.

Holding firm around the base, I sucked on the wide knobbed head, flicking my tongue against the slit and sipping the fluid that gathered there. Just when his hips thrust, I took him down my throat. When his considerable length hit the back, I swallowed around the fat crown. Like I'd predicted, Wes lost it. His hand caught me around the neck, and he pumped hard into my mouth a few more times, losing his ability for coherent communication.

"Fuck your hot mouth." He thrust, his hand holding me fast on his dick.

"Oh, yeah." I felt him pull back a few inches.

"Take it," he snarled, thrusting again as if he were mad at me for sucking his cock.

"So good." His teeth clenched as he retreated again.

"Once more down your throat, baby." He thrust hard, and I relaxed my jaw and breathed through my nose. He stopped right there in a place of suspended pleasure. "Take me so deep. Christ, Mia. Love you." He pulled back, and this time, all the way out. Doing an ab curl, he reached under my arms and yanked me up over his knees to straddle his thighs. My legs wide, pussy open, he centered his cock. "Now, take what's yours, sweetheart."

And I did. Hard and deep, the way I'd imagined all week. As was his way, he slipped one talented thumb between our bodies and circled. I gasped. He circled. Holding my breath, I picked up my pace, taking him into my body until I wasn't sure where he stopped and I began. Time slowed. All that surrounded us was heat, pleasure, and bone-melting kisses.

Wes held my shoulders, pushing me down on his cock at the same time he thrust up into me. I screamed into his mouth, but he swallowed the sound. An orgasm tore through me. I was wholly unprepared for the blistering pressure and heat that consumed every nerve and pore as he continued to pound into me.

When I stopped helping, lost in all that was him and us, he leaned forward, wrapped a hand across my back, leaned a knee down on the floor, and laid me out. I was nothing but sensation, synapses firing in all directions, building to the precipice again. "Wes, baby," was all I could say. He responded by pressing both hands behind my thighs, pushing my knees toward my chest, and shifting another inch or so deeper into me. It was impossible and possible at the same time. A cry tore from my mouth, and he didn't try to muffle it this time, just kept up a brutal pace. His hips pistoning wildly, his cock grated along every nerve delectably.

"God, I missed this cunt. Love your pussy, baby. Want to die here. One day, when we're ninety, I'll die fucking you. Just. Like. This." He swirled his hips in a circle and leaned over, pressing his weight and his cock so far into me, I could feel his dick at my navel. "Give it to me," he growled through his teeth.

"Already gave it, baby." I reminded him of the earth-shattering orgasm, which had led to me to the floor. Jesus, the man was a machine, moving his hips, taking me nice and slow in even thrusts.

Wes shook his head. "No, need it again. Want your pussy squeezing my cock in that vise. Want to come with your cunt on lockdown. Together, sweetheart." He kissed me and tugged on my bottom lip, and then started again. Knowing

AUDREY CARLAN

exactly what I needed, he slipped that hand between us once more, twirled his magic thumb, and gave me long, slow thrusts until the muscles of my core clenched, and then my groin, limbs, and everything in between did exactly as he said. Locked down. "That's it. Oh, Mia, so good." He pressed deep, held still with the base firmly planted within my body, and let his release go. My sex milked him dry. When the aftershocks left him, he fell over me, rolling to the side and taking me with him.

A goofy grin slid across his face while what seemed to be a sense of peace washed over him. "Feel better?" I asked on a giggle.

He opened his eyes and lifted a hand to my cheek, cupping it. "I'm always better when I'm with you."

"Me too."

★ ★ ★

"Poppet!" Judi greeted me, her arms open wide. I trotted over to her and hugged her. She moved back and focused on me, her eyes assessing. "I am so very pleased to see you, love." Her English accent was sweet and made every word that fell from her lips sound like sugar and spice and everything nice.

I smiled. "Happy to be here, Judi." I inhaled the scrumptious scent of garlic, grilled onions, and green peppers. "What's for dinner? Smells divine." My mouth watered at the thought of food. I'd not eaten anything on the six-hour flight from Miami to Malibu except for a granola bar, and after the limo romp, I needed some serious sustenance. There was no way I'd be able to keep up with

Wes's insatiable appetite for me if I didn't carb up.

Judi's eyes twinkled as she walked back into the kitchen. "Comfort food. Something to remind you of home." She glanced at Wes and rolled her eyes. "Pork chops, fresh grilled veggies, a parmesan cous cous, and warm garlic bread. How's that sound?"

"Heavenly." She had me at pork chops. I'd been eating most meals out the entire month. Anton and Heather were not big on eating in, mostly because they didn't have time to grocery shop, and since they moved around so much, they didn't employ a cook. Anton had enough money though. He should definitely look into hiring a nutritionist to help keep that body fit and healthy. He worked on it enough. If he ate less rich foods, he wouldn't have to work so hard. I made a mental note to tell Heather my thoughts the next time I texted. Now that she was officially Anton's manager, she'd need more time to focus on that and not what he wanted to eat for breakfast, lunch, and dinner.

Judi led me to the breakfast bar. "Come, come." She patted the high-back stool. "Tell me about what you've been up to the past year."

Tell her what I'd been up to? Hmm. A filtered version would work. "Well, I've been all over. Portland, Chicago, Boston, New York, DC, Hawaii, and Miami."

She nodded and stirred the sauce she was warming in the skillet. "And did you meet anyone of interest?" Her neck quirked, but her eyes bored into mine.

I grinned. "I met a lot of someones, Judi. Made a bunch of new friends."

"And my Sonny, is he your friend?" She asked in that motherly way only someone who was your nanny before she was your house attendant would do.

Leaning forward, I put my elbow on the counter and placed my head in my hand. "I think you know Wes is more than a friend."

Her eyes rose, and a hand went to her chest. "Do I? I know no such thing. Enlighten an old woman of the coming and goings."

I giggled at the phrase *comings and goings,* thinking about the wild limo sex we'd had minutes ago, but stopped when her eyes cut to mine. "Sorry. Um..." I tugged a lock of hair and wound it around my fingers. "I guess you could say that Wes and I have come to an agreement. We're together."

"Together." Her tone was accusatory, and I didn't understand why, and then she added a full-on harrumph. What happened between walking in, hugs galore, and dinner offers, to an all-out attitude problem?

"Is something wrong with us being together?" I asked tentatively.

She shook her head. "No, no. Whatever would give you that impression?"

"Uh, you're acting a little off, Judi. Did I say something that offended you?"

Judi leaned forward and patted my hand that was resting on the counter. "Not at all, love. It's just that I know when you left, my Sonny missed you terribly. Then that snobby woman came around now and again, and I worried."

Ah, I see. "Gina. It's okay. I know all about her."

"And you don't care?" Her eyelids slanted into slits.

I thought carefully about how best to respond. Not a lot of people would understand our relationship. Hell, I didn't understand it half the time and definitely not now when it was so fresh and new.

Licking my lips, I inhaled deeply. "Wes and I have always had feelings for one another." She nodded as if this information was not at all surprising. "And we'd not lost touch this entire time, but we weren't in a committed relationship. He was free to do as he wished, as was I. Now that we've come to terms with what's happening between us, we're taking the time to feel it out and just appreciate it day by day. Does that make sense?"

She shrugged. "It's none of my business, but I do like to see the smile on my boy's face when he walks in with you on his arm. He's been planning all week for your arrival. Making sure you had some things to wear, which he put into *his* closet, I might add." She grinned one of those knowing smiles that only motherly types could. The kind that said she knew something you didn't, or had some awesome wisdom to impart to you that would blow your mind.

At her words, I laughed. "So he moved me right into his room, eh?"

Her smile was beaming. "Yes, and I've got instructions to take you to your apartment tomorrow with a couple of helpers to box up and move all of your things. He wants you to bring them here."

"Um, what?" Shaking my head did not help me assimilate any faster what she'd inferred. "He wants me to box up my apartment and move in, move in? As in, *move into* this house permanently?"

Her eyebrows narrowed. "Isn't that obvious?"

I smacked the counter. A stinging pinch rolled up from my palm and out. I clutched the sore hand with the other and rubbed out the sting. "Looks like Lord Channing and I are going to have to have a little chat later. Don't make those plans tomorrow."

Judi patted my hand again. "Oh, love, you really don't know what you're dealing with. That appointment will stay with the movers tomorrow. I'll be ready to lead the pack at ten."

This time I was the one with the narrowed gaze. "I'm telling you it isn't happening."

Judi chuckled. "Okay, honey, you go ahead and believe that."

"Why don't you? It's my apartment. I say what goes, and I definitely say where I move to"—I pointed a finger to the granite—"and it won't be here." Even though I would love living here. Having dinners made for me, scrumptious meals every night. Sitting on the veranda enjoying the ocean view, or the opposite one that looked out over the hills. Sleeping in the blissful cloud that was Wes's bed. But there was no way I was going to do it now because my new boyfriend demanded it.

Judi stopped stirring, turned down the heat, and leveled her gaze at me. She set her elbows on the counter and leaned forward. "Love, I've been with Weston a long time. Since he was a wee one. There are very few things that he doesn't get when he sets his mind to having them. You would do well to learn that now. If you are what he wants, you are what he will have, or he'll die trying."

When I thought about it, really thought about it, it was kind of nice to be coveted in such a way. However, I was not, nor would I become, some rich man's possession. If he thought he was just going to get me to move in without any discussion, he had another think coming. "Well, my dear boyfriend is going to have to ask me himself," I said with a determination I tried my damnedest to feel.

"Ask you what?" Wes walked back into the room from his office where he'd gone to check on some work before dinner.

"Judi tells me you want her and some movers to go pack up my apartment and move it all here during my stay." I cocked a hip and braced my hand on it. My super-serious-nothing-is-getting-by-me pose had been perfected over the years.

Wes frowned and then shrugged. "Don't you want to be with me?"

Jeez, when he said it like that, I had no response other than, "Yes, of course."

"And you want to live here eventually?" His head tipped to the side, a non-defensive gesture.

"Well, yeah," I said, not getting the point of where he was going with this.

"Okay." He walked over to me, caged me in by placing his long arms on each side of the counter behind me. He brought his face down low so I could look him straight in the eyes. Green-on-green. His breath puffed against my lips and made other parts of my body start paying very close attention. "Mia, sweetheart, will you move your stuff into my house and let this be your home?"

I licked my lips and stared into his beautiful eyes, noticing the way the fine lines around his eyes and lips made him seem distinguished. Beautiful. More handsome. I sucked in a breath, and he waited, cool as a cucumber, until I gave him my answer. I was completely powerless to his brand of charm. "Okay, I'll move in."

He grinned that heart-stopping-melt-your-panties-into-a-puddle-at-your-feet smile, and I swooned. "Love you." When he followed up anything with *that*, he was bound to get his way. Seriously, I needed to start preparing for the future of softly said love yous and their effect on my rational mind.

"Love you," I responded.

He kissed me, the barest of touches before he pulled back, stepped away, and clapped his hands. "All right. That's settled. Dinner ready, Judi? Everything set?"

I spun on a toe and planted my ass back in the chair. Judi smirked as she plated our dinner. "Everything is just right, Sonny." She glanced my way and winked. I wanted to hate her for being right, but I couldn't. The love she had for Wes stemmed from eons together, and at the end of the day, she knew him better than I did.

For now...but not for long.

CHAPTER TWO

Box number five was taped and ready to go. I moved the giant box of clothes to the stack I'd already prepped. Judi was humming in the kitchen, taping up her stash of stuff.

"Done here," she called cheerily. I scowled. "Poppet? What could possibly be making you so blue?"

I twisted my neck from side to side, waiting for that crack signaling release of tension, and frowned when nothing came. "I don't know. I hate moving days. It always feels so final. Like when you take this step, you can't take it back."

"Oh, pish posh. You'll settle right in with us like you've always been a fixture."

A fixture. Great. Something stagnant and unmoving. But I would be moving to my next client's house in a few days. Wes knew it, and we'd still not discussed it. I needed to know that I could finish doing what I had started for my family without being given a pile of money from my ridiculously rich boyfriend. The last thing I'd ever want to be was a mooch. People hated mooches. I hated mooches. They sucked rotten eggs, and I was determined never to be one. Wes, on the other side of the coin, must very much like mooches and wanted me to mooch away. Not going to happen.

When the morning was over and we'd packed up my entire life in the span of three hours, my mood had not improved. I opened my cell and hollered at a bitch.

"This better be good. I've got my eyes on a high-roller," Gin said into the phone.

My scowl likely deepened when I added the choking, gagging, gurgling noise.

"What? Don't judge. I'm not sitting sweet on hot mother fucker number one hundred and twelve, in the span of—what—six months? A girl has to look out for her future, you know!"

"Gin, seriously? A high-roller? You were the one who told me there was no such thing as a high-roller out on the floor. That those bastards were all just losing their home, their wife, and their kids' college tuition in the hopes of winning against the house. Don't fall for that garbage. A true high-roller would be behind closed doors having clandestine poker tournaments with his other Monopoly-playing rich buddies, not showing off to a Vegas girl. Cool your jets and talk to me."

Her gum smack sounded loud in my ear, and even though I think it pierced an eardrum, I'd rather hear that sound than the sound of her giving herself cancer one breath at a time smoking those cigarettes. "I've moved into Wes's house."

The gum-smacking stopped. Everything stopped. No sound at all came from the line. I pulled the phone away and looked at the display. No, still connected. "Gin? Hello?"

"You fucking moved in with bachelor number one? Get. The. Fuck. Out!" Her tone was astonished and laced with a heavy dose of 'holy shit.'

"Er, not exactly. I mean, kind of. Yeah. Maybe. Um... yes?" I worried my nail with my teeth and waited.

"You moved in with Malibu Ken?"

I blinked and waited.

"Mr. Rules?" She scoffed.

Again, staying silent was the only option. I'd known her for a lifetime, and these things took time to process.

"Golden god on the surf board?" Her tone turned dreamy this time. Okay, now we were getting somewhere.

"Movie writer guy, the one that changes characters so they look like my hot BFF guy? You moved into his house, in the Malibu mansion?"

"It's not really a mansion…" I started, but she cut me off.

"Zip it! Are. You. *Insane*? Do you need your head checked?"

I rubbed on my dome and felt around. "Not since the last time I checked."

She groaned. "Okay, tell me one thing. And it's gonna hella suck to have to ask you this babe, but I gotta." On a slow inhale, I braced for whatever she would throw at me. "Are you doing this because of that needle-dick prick that assaulted you in DC?"

I closed my eyes and hugged myself. "No, honey, no. Not at all. When I was in Miami, Wes came down for my birthday."

"Yeah, yeah, I know. I sent the smooth operator, remember?"

"While he was there, we both admitted some feelings— things that we'd been going back and forth about since I was here in January. Gin, I love him."

"Oh, Jesus Christ on a fucking pogo stick. Not the love-him shit again!" She started mumbling something I couldn't quite hear but knew was a full-on rant. "You love *everybody*,

Mia. It's part of your DNA, your genetic code. You meet hot guy. You fuck hot guy. You fall in love with hot guy. This is not the first or the last time you will repeat this pattern."

Ginelle had a point. In the past, that was my MO. Not now, not with Wes. "I didn't with the other guys I fucked this year. Explain that?"

"Explain a roll in the hay. Okay, when a boy and a girl meet, there is this chemical that puts off pheromones…"

I groaned and blew out a harsh breath. "Ginelle! Focus here." I almost stomped my foot in exasperation. Shit, I'd called the wrong sister. I should have called Maddy, the blood sister, not the soul sister. She'd have been over the moon. Mostly because she had found her one and only and was engaged to be married. People like that wanted everyone else to be in the same place they were: happy and in love.

"Mia, I…I just don't want you getting hurt. Again." She sighed long and deep. So much so that I could feel the rumble of her distress even at this distance.

"I know, Gin. I do. It's just, you know I've been going back and forth with him for months. If I hadn't had Pops's shit to deal with, I'd have still been here."

"If you hadn't had Pops's shit to deal with, you would have never been there at all!" Touché. Point well made. "And what about that va-Gina chick? What's the deal with her?" Her tone was hoity-toity, not hiding her distaste.

"Gone."

She harrumphed. "Gone. That's it. End of." The exaggerated way she said it indicated she didn't believe it.

I shrugged, but she couldn't see it. "According to Wes, yeah."

Another choking sound came through the line. "At

least he has good sense."

A laugh bubbled up, releasing the constriction that had been pressing on my chest. The tightness that felt like I had heartburn started to dissipate, bringing relief with it. "Be happy for me," I whispered. A hint of begging lingered at the edge of the request.

"Honey, I am. Always will be, but you know that your best friend has to play both sides. Protect you even when you won't. It's in the fucking book of best friends, right under the part that says pat them on the back and make them feel better when they've had a one night stand and can't remember the name of the guy they fucked, totally making them a whore. It's my job to make sure that even when you're being a whore, you don't feel like a whore."

Her logic had merit. Fucked up, twisted merit, but still, she cared. Ginelle loved me more than most people, and I knew that the same way I knew I loved kick-ass concert tees and my motorcycle, Suzi. "Thank you. For caring and worrying...even though you're a two-bit skank."

She sucked in a breath. "I see. So we're back to that. Okay." She clucked her tongue. "I got you. I *so* got you, wackjob hussy."

There was my girl. I smiled. "At least I don't shake it to make it," I threw back.

She feigned a gasp. "At least I don't lie down on my back and open my legs for cash, hooker!"

"I love you, Gin."

"Love your ugly face. See you soon?"

"Hope so, pancake ass." I hung up superfast. That was the rule. I win. I pumped a fist into the air and did a little touchdown dance, complete with wiggling my knees in and out while rolling my ass the way Maria De La Torre taught me back in Miami. Hell, this white girl could dance. Now, whether I looked like a chicken with my head cut off or not was an entirely different story. At least I got the last word in with my best friend. It rarely happened, but this round… all mine.

* * *

"I don't want you to go." Wes rolled his hips, pressing deep. He was rapidly hardening again while inside me, even though we'd just finished a very active round of mind-blowing sex.

"We've been through this already. You agreed."

He frowned and thrust his hips ever so lightly. The sweat on our bodies hadn't even cooled, and he was already working toward round two. Insatiable. I was a lucky, lucky girl.

Wes's fingers tightened around the meaty part of my hips. "I know we did, but I figured maybe I could sway you in another way, a more pleasurable way." He leaned up and took a pink tip into his mouth. The heat of his mouth around my nipple combined with gentle flicks of his tongue made me instinctively grind into his pelvis, forcing his hard flesh between my thighs even deeper. We both groaned. "See, you're already starting to get it." He grinned and pushed up while pulling my waist down. Fully hard inside me. I placed my hands on his chest, used the strength of my thighs to lift up, and slammed down.

"Ugh, Jesus! Warn a guy next time. Baby, you'll unman me before the fun's even begun." He lifted up, pressed into his heels, and shifted back to the headboard where he lay back and cuddled me into his arms. Lifting up both his knees into ninety degree angles forced the steely length of him into a new position, a beautiful position. I'd marry this position if I could.

Sighing, I looped my hands around his neck and brought his lips to mine. Tongue-to-tongue, chest-to-chest, and heart-to-heart, we made out. Neither one of us moving our position, he was thick and long, still buried deep inside. I kissed Wes, giving it my all. I wanted him to know that this thing between us was real, and no matter where I went, I was committed to it. To him. To us.

Wes growled and nipped my lips. "You're going to leave on that plane tomorrow, aren't you?"

I nodded and rubbed my forehead against his. Our mouths were so close we were alternately breathing one another's breaths. It was intimate and private. Being this close to him, sharing life-sustaining air, him deep within my body. All of it was beyond magical.

As he'd said before…paradise. And that's when it dawned on me. Wes and I would have years of this, a lifetime of sharing, of loving, of living for the other. Unfortunately, right then, I had to do some living on my own, for Pops and for me, before I could stay in this bubble forever.

"Wes, honey, you know I have to. Our relationship needs to be clean of my father's debt."

He shook his head. "It would be so easy to just take the money. Pay off the goon and stay here, with me. Don't you want to stay here? Start your life over, fresh?"

"I'd love to, Wes, but I know me." I pressed my hand into my chest over my heart. "I know that in my heart, I'll always feel like I owe you something. A half a million dollars is not something I'll ever be able to pay back. Ever. We can't start our relationship with one beholden to the other. It's not right. That's not a fresh start."

His shoulders slumped, and he cupped both my cheeks. "It kills me to know you're going to be spending time with another man. Allowing him to woo you, fall for you."

I cupped his cheek this time. "That's not going to happen."

"No?" His eyebrow quirked defiantly.

Rubbing the soft brow up and along the arched shape, I shook my head. "No, it's not."

"But it happened to me. I fell for you. I'll bet half the men, if not all of them, fell for you in some way. Who's to say that over the next five months one of them isn't the most amazing man you've ever met? And what if he wants to sweep you off your feet? Huh? What then?"

I sucked in a sharp breath. "Not possible."

"But it is…" he started, until I placed two fingers over the lips I was dying to nibble on.

"No, it's not possible because I've already been wooed. I've already met the most amazing man I'll ever meet, and I've already been so completely swept off my feet that the ground now feels wrong to stand on." He smiled that sexy-surfer-boy smile I wanted to look at every day for the rest of my life. I took it as the signal it was, time to show him just how much he meant to me. Hovering my lips against his, a scant hairsbreadth away, I whispered, "My heart belongs to you. My body belongs to you because I love you. You need to take a leap of faith and trust me."

Wes closed his eyes. He looked like an angel when is

eyes were closed. Stark black lashes against sun-kissed brown skin. His hair, a golden blond messy tangle of layers, struck my heart with a wave of devotion so deep I could hardly breathe. I swept a lock of hair over his brow and caressed his temple with one finger, trailing it down the side of his face and chin, where I held it between thumb and forefinger. I lifted his face up until he opened his eyes. "I love you, Wes. *You*. Please trust me to do what I need to do and know that I'm going to be faithful." Then I kissed him.

I knew the moment the kiss changed. His lips were firmer, mouth open wider, tongue greedier, and when his teeth came into play, his hand wrapped around my neck and he took the kiss from me. Led the way through a fiery trail of lust and a desire so fierce, it stole everything but the need to mate. Our bodies melded until all thoughts of anything but the other fled on gossamer wings a hundred miles from where we loved.

"Want you all the time," Wes growled, his fingers digging into my shoulder at the same time his hips pressed up, piercing me stroke after stroke. Mind-numbing pleasure was so intense my teeth rattled with each thrust.

I sipped from his lips, rubbed my mouth along his cheek in a wet trail of kisses, reaching his ear and sucking on the soft cartilage until he moaned and his body tightened. "Want more always," I confirmed breathless, mindless as I lifted up again, squeezing his dick tight within the sensitive walls of my center, attempting to wring as much pleasure as possible, not only for me, but also for him. When I clenched down around his cock, using the muscles of my pussy like a vise, his jaw tightened. I loved making him grin and bear it. Bear so much pleasure he'd forget any woman who had come before me.

Thrust after thrust, we hit one another with as much as we could take. This wasn't making love. It wasn't sex. It was hard-core fucking, not exactly angry, but definitely not filled with butterflies and rainbows and soft vows of love. The dirty things he said in lieu of those frilly vows made me hotter, wetter, and downright insane for his cock.

"Gonna make that pussy so sore." He rammed up into me. At this point, I was holding onto the top of the headboard while he thrust his hips up, and I sat my ass down, coming together in a crush of naked limbs and moist privates.

He fucked me so hard and with such intensity that I lost the ability to speak coherently. A litany of grunts, mumbles, and moans left my mouth as I rode Wes, a breath away from my second peak of the night.

Wes sucked a nipple into his mouth and bit down on the furled tip. I cried out, holding his head to my breast like a mother would her brand new babe. I didn't want him to stop sucking, or biting, or sending those lightning jolts of ecstasy straight to my clit with every tug.

"Someone likes her tits worked over, huh, sweetheart?" I couldn't respond, too lost in the beauty that was fucking Wes. He switched breasts and sucked, bit, and tweaked that nipple until I was circling my hips, so wet even I could hear the noise of our slick bodies coming together. The slide and pull of his cock as it burrowed deep and then grated along hyper-sensitive tissue on the retreat made me dizzy. It was heaven and hell rolled into one. Every thrust was so good, I sighed. Every retraction the same, only with the incoherent worry that his body was leaving mine, and I never wanted it to go.

"Want you coming on my cock, sweetheart. Need to feel that sweet cunt when it locks down around me. So fucking sexy the way it never wants me to leave. Don't worry…" He thrust hard, and I gasped, feeling the ripples and tingles of the impending orgasm just on the cusp of exploding. "I'm going to fill you so full, you'll be feeling the slickness trickling from between your legs for days, proving who owns this pussy. Me. Now give it to me!" he commanded, and lo and behold, my body responded.

I tightened every muscle, every nerve ending sparking, each new wave crashing over me. Every inch of my skin felt alive, loved, and most importantly, worshipped. I clasped my hands around Wes's neck, sealed my lips over his, and kissed him with everything I had. Long sweeps of my tongue, nips of my teeth, until his own body turned rock-hard and he moaned, groaned, and convulsed underneath me. I held his mouth to mine, tasting his desire, his passion, and his love as he released his essence, pumping into me.

"Love," he said into my mouth with those plush lips, moist and bruised from my kisses.

"Love," I repeated.

"Mine," he gasped, the last of his orgasm racking his large frame.

"Mine," I agreed, mostly because I was his and he was mine. There would be no other definition needed from here on out. I only hoped it would stick, that he'd finally come to terms with my job and our position as a couple. I wasn't leaving, yet I couldn't stay. For now. Soon, though, and hopefully for the rest of my life, I'd be in this bed, with this man, doing this very thing a year from now, ten years, fifty, until I took my last breath.

"You're still going," he said, placing kisses along my neck and clavicle, massaging the back of my head, and soothing me into a state of pure bliss. Not that I wasn't there already after the two rounds of life-affirming sex.

"Yeah, but you know what?" I tunneled my fingers through the hair at the nape of his neck.

"Hmm?" he said a little melancholy.

"I'll be back in just three weeks. I promise to come home between jobs."

A huge smile broke across his face. "Home?" He grinned, not at all hiding the fact that he loved it when I used that word in a way that no one could dispute meant this house here in Malibu. The one he'd sneakily gotten me to agree to move into.

"Yes, home is where you are." I laid my head against his chest and kissed his heart. "I'll miss you though."

He sighed. "I'll miss you, more." And even though I doubted that, I loved how much it meant to hear him say it and believe it.

I'd never been someone's *more* before, but now that I was, I understood why people did it. Committed to the person they loved. Knowing I was someone's choice, his light, his good ending to a shit day, gave me a feeling of power that couldn't be darkened. It would always be there, shining bright, for his love would light my way home.

CHAPTER THREE

I arrived at the airport with a crick in my neck and a heavy heart. Leaving Wes to meet my new client in Dallas did not go over well. He'd wanted me to stay, take the money he kept offering, and call it good. Stubborn man could not accept that I needed to do this. Pay this debt to Blaine on my own, as much to save my dad as to save myself. Finish one thing from start to finish and come out the victor. Knowing that once and for all, I was the owner of my destiny. Every decision I made from here on out was because I made it. Me.

It was my journey, and I intended to finish it. Did I want it to cost my relationship with Wes? No, not in a million years. However, he needed to cool his jets and understand that not everything was about him and the way he sees things. It's not as easy as just handing someone a cool half-million and all the world's problems are solved. We were still new. Learning one another. In that newness, somehow he'd staked his claim and moved my ass in. Worse yet, I let him.

Without any real fight, I'd packed my tiny shit-hole apartment up in Los Angeles, stored my boxes in one of his five car garage bays, and set a box of my prized possessions—yet to be unpacked—in my old room. Really all the rest of my crap could disappear and the items in a small two-foot by two-foot box held all that ever mattered to me. Not wanting to waste the little time we'd had left with one another, I didn't ask about adding my stuff to his home to make my mark the way a woman normally would. Maybe I needed the time to realize that I'd technically just moved in with Weston, but planned to continue my job as an escort for the rest of the year. Not exactly something you wanted to tell your friends and family about your new girlfriend.

My thoughts were a jumbled mess. I walked out of the airport, distracted and feeling hollow, lost in my own head. While I walked along the sidewalk muttering to myself, a warm hand curled around my bicep and stopped me. I looked up, and up, and up, until the rim of a Stetson cowboy hat blocked the sun, and my eyesight adjusted. Pale green eyes came into view. The eyes were so pale they resembled a green amethyst, much like my own. Damn near exactly like my own. Weird. A smile complemented his rugged square stubbled jaw. White teeth gleamed as he said something, but I didn't hear it, too lost in my own thoughts. Golden blond tufts of hair could be seen at the back of his neck, proving whatever was under that hat was unruly, likely curly, and needed to be cut.

"Mia? You're Mia, right?" the man said, but the rumble in his voice hit my heart and squeezed. Not with desire but a faint hint of something else. A familiarity shimmered across my senses, like a long lost dream I'd had, remembering it when I awoke, but unable to place the pieces appropriately. "Sugar, you okay?" Another large hand held my other arm. I glanced at both of his huge hands. The nails were clean, cut straight as if he'd recently trimmed them.

I stepped back, but he clasped my arms tighter. "I'm uh, okay. Sorry." I blinked several times, trying to clear my head. "Do we know each other?"

His grin widened. "No, but over the next month, I reckon we will get to know one another mighty well. I'm Maxwell Cunningham. Max for short." He held out a beefy hand. The calluses rubbed along my palm, scratching the tender flesh sharply. He wore a yellow polo shirt stretched tight over a broad muscled chest, if the contours through the fabric were any indication. The trim of his shirt sleeves around his bulging biceps looked as though it would tear at any moment with the sheer size of his muscles. With the polo, which incidentally, looked really good on his frame, he wore dark Wranglers with a wide leather belt complete with a silver buckle that was at least three inches wide and two inches tall with a gold star dead center. His feet were covered in a pair of dusty rust-colored cowboy boots that matched his belt. My guess, he'd made an effort to match them. As I took in his attire, he took in mine. Those green eyes, so like my own, scanned my simple sundress and sandals. My hair was loose and black curls flowed everywhere.

"You're so beautiful," he whispered, his voice coming out gritty as if he'd said the words but hadn't meant to. His eyes were haunted, wounded in a way that made me want to reach out and hug him. I didn't know why I had that desire, especially after what Aaron had done to me back in DC.

I looked around at the people passing by and gripped my sundress just to have something to do with my hands. The air between us was uncomfortable, thick, filled with things unsaid. When a man tells a woman she's beautiful and looks at her in a way that nearly guts her, a response of some kind is mandatory. "Um, thank you."

His eyes widened. "Oh, uh, sorry. I didn't mean that the way it sounded. It's just you're pretty, *real* pretty, and even though I saw your picture, I wasn't prepared for the living, breathing thing. Hot damn, that didn't come out right either." He rubbed the back of his neck and looked down at his feet, a scowl marring his plump lips.

"Sir, this your truck?" An airport security man wearing a fluorescent vest interrupted our awkward conversation and pointed at the silver Ford F-150.

"Yeah, some kind of problem?" he asked.

The man nodded. "If you don't get a move on, there will be. You're obstructing traffic. Get going." He gestured once more to the truck.

"Oh shoot. Sorry. Mia, this way." He picked up my suitcase, opened the quad cab door, and tossed it in. Then he opened my door and held out his hand. I looked down at the hand as if it were dipped in acid. "Mia, sugar, I'd never hurt you. I'm a little out of sorts, but if you come back to the ranch, we'll get you set up and Cyndi will make everything better." He offered a small smile and kept his hand out.

When I put my hand in his, I felt that weird sensation again, and something nudged at the frail edges of a memory. It was just on the surface, like when you can't recall the name of a song, but it's on the tip of your tongue.

I stepped into the cab and sat down.

"Who's Cyndi?"

He smiled huge, a big megawatt smile that was unnervingly familiar. I was sure I'd met this man before. Had to. Maxwell wrangled his large form in behind the wheel, put the truck in gear, checked his mirror, and eased out.

"Cyndi's my wife."

★ ★ ★

161

Two hours in the truck and we were finally driving up a gravel driveway. A two-story yellow ranch house, complete with bright blue shutters hugging each window, stood at the end of the drive. A white picket fence surrounded the front of the home where a small child played with dolls on a blanket out in the late summer sun. A woman wearing a long sundress leaned against a white wooden column next to the stairs that led up to a wraparound porch. Her dress was myriad blues and greens, reminding me of the tropical waters I'd seen in Miami. One of her pale hands moved and pressed along a large, rounded belly. She had to be almost ready to pop. Her belly was the size of a basketball under the maxi dress. The woman's light brown hair blew in the soft breeze, untamed by a tie or ribbon. Her entire being, the fertility she so effortlessly displayed, seemed ethereal in this setting.

When the car stopped, she waved at Max, and he smiled back. That same giant smile he had in the car a couple of hours ago when he spoke of his wife was plastered along his jaw once more. Since then, I'd learned his wife's name was Cyndi, and he had a daughter named Isabel and a baby boy on the way. He was ecstatic about being able to pass down the Cunningham name to a son.

I found out he was an only child, raised by Jackson Cunningham who had recently passed away and left him fifty-one percent of the business. The other forty-nine percent was supposed to go to his sister. One he'd never met. One he'd been told shared my birthday and name. The details about what he wanted me to do were still hazy, but he said over the next month, things would become clearer.

Me, I was just thrilled he was married, and happily by

the looks of it. I didn't have to pretend to be a love interest. With my relationship with Wes so new, it felt like a godsend to find out I'd be playing the part of a long lost sister. There would be no hand holding, pretend snuggling, or chaste kisses for anyone.

This was going to come as welcome news to my movie-making surfer. A pang punched at my heart as I thought about Wes. It had been less than a day, and the distance between us felt far more acute than I thought it would be. In the past six months, I had been able to be in different places for weeks on end without hearing anything. Hell, in May, I didn't even have a text exchange with him, both of us too raw after the Gina debacle. I ground my teeth, thinking about Hollywood's sexiest sweetheart and how she'd had her clutches into my man. Before I realized it, Maxwell had the door open and was helping me down.

"Darlin', come meet Mia. Bell, come meet Daddy's friend," he hollered at the little girl. His wife waddled down the steps, one hand holding the banister and the other her blossoming belly. The moment she got close, he put his hand to her stomach and the other wrapped around the back of her neck. He lowered his face and looked his wife in the eye. "How you doin', darlin'? Okay?" She smiled prettily and her cheeks pinked up when she nodded. "And our boy?" He rubbed her stomach.

"Right as rain, Max. We're okay, I promise." She leaned forward and kissed him softly, just a peck on the lips before pulling back. Her bright blue eyes, the color of sparkling sapphires, took in my appearance. She held her hand out. "Cyndi Cunningham. Welcome to our home."

I shook her small hand. "Mia Saunders. Happy to be

here." The little girl was hiding behind her mother's legs, a little arm looped around her knee. "And who's the pretty thing I see hiding there?" I pointed to the shy child.

Maxwell took a breath, his chest seeming to puff up even wider and higher. "That's my first born, Isabel. Bell, honey, come out and meet your daddy's friend."

The small child peeked her head out from behind her mother's leg. Pale green eyes and golden blond hair like her father's framed her heart-shaped face like a halo of light. Cherub lips puckered as she wiggled out from her hiding spot. I took in her eyes and hair, and that sensation of familiarity piqued again. I must have run into this family before now, but I couldn't place it.

"Hi, I'm Mia." I waved with one finger as Isabel tugged on her mom's dress and swayed from side-to-side, her feet kicking dirt around. Her dress was covered in rainbows that suited a child of her age, which I knew from the car ride with Max, was four years old. "I like your dress."

Her green eyes got darker. "I love rainbows. They are so purdy."

"Yes, I agree. Have you ever seen a rainbow in real life?" I knelt down so I could look her in the eyes. She nodded with the exuberance only someone her age would do. "Me too. You know what they say about rainbows, don't you?" Her sweet little eyes widened and she shook her head.

"Well, Irish myth has it that at the end of a rainbow is a pot of gold. And the pot of gold is protected by a leprechaun! A little happy fella in a green suit and top hat!"

She laughed. "Maybe we can find one while you're here?" she said, hope thick in her tone.

I shrugged. "Sounds like a worthy adventure. Next

rainbow we see, we'll be on the lookout. You and me. Okay?"

Isabel grabbed my hand. Cyndi and Max looked down at the two of us holding hands. Surprise clear in the astonishing way they tried to speak but didn't say anything. "I'll show you our house. Do you like pancakes? Oh! What about Care Bears? Which one is your favorite?"

When you had a child happily dragging you along, there was little that could be done other than follow, which I did. "Um, I love Lucky Bear, the one with the clover on his belly. And pancakes are yummy. Especially when you add chocolate syrup."

She stopped walking and turned around, crossed her hands over her chest, and stomped her tiny sandaled foot. "How come we never have chocolate syrup on our pancakes?" Isabel asked her parents, clearly thinking this issue deserved the full attention of anyone in earshot.

Both Cyndi and Max laughed and shook their heads. "We'll try it Mia's way in the morning, Belly Boo," Cyndi responded, petting her daughter's hair. "You were going to show Mia her room, remember?"

Isabel spun on a toe and giggled while running up the stairs. "Come on, Mia!" she yelled.

"She always have this much energy?" I asked her mom and dad while trooping up the stairs after the exuberant one.

"Yes!" They said in unison, and we all chuckled.

"It's going to be a fun month, I can already tell," I said and turned around to see if they were following.

Max rubbed at his neck and glanced at his wife. She looked away, not making eye contact with either one of us. "We're glad you're here, Mia," was all he said, but the way he said it was odd, telling, and anxiety-inducing. I got the feeling that sooner rather than later I'd be thinking the exact opposite.

★ ★ ★

Settled into my room that night, I pulled out my phone and called Wes.

"Hey, sweetheart. You tucked in for the night?" he said without preamble.

I smiled and snuggled deeper into the down comforter. "I am. How about you?"

He yawned. "Not quite yet."

"You sound tired though."

Wes hummed a simple 'mmm' and the sound went straight through my body, softening and moistening the way I always did for him. Traitor.

"I am. It's been a long day. I miss you though. Less than a week, and I've already gotten used to having you in my bed."

Laughing, I played with a string I found hanging off the seam of the blanket. "You just miss fucking me."

"True. Having you naked in bed next to me definitely has that side effect. It's nice not going to bed alone. I think that's going to be the hardest part, alongside your snuffling breaths when you turn over and rub your nose and mouth into my arm and then proceed to drool all over it."

"I do not drool!"

He laughed heartily, and it sent a shimmer of sadness through me, knowing it would be another three weeks before I saw him again, provided he was in town and not on location for a movie.

"No, you don't drool, but you do cuddle into me. As much as I thought I'd hate that, I actually love it."

"I love you," I butted in.

He sighed. "I know." The sound of his breathing simmered around our call as I imagined I were there, my head against his bare chest, listening to that sound as his breath floated like a breeze across the top of my hair. Turning over, I rubbed my face deeper into the blanket, loving it's softness and lavender-smelling detergent. "So tell me about the client. Have you figured out yet why he needs you to be his sister?"

"Not really. He told me on the drive from the airport that his father, Jackson, passed recently and left him fifty-one percent of a company and the rest to a sister he's never met and didn't even know he had."

"Weird," Wes added.

"Right? Anyway, apparently, according to some hand-written testimony the father put into his will, the sister had my name and birth date. Which is also strange, though Mia is a pretty common name. There were two of them in my age group growing up. And Saunders is common. Although, according to Max—that's my client—the name was handwritten in a way that it could be with an "o" instead, so that makes the pool of potential people larger. He said it was a real coup that he'd found me and I was hirable. Whatever that means."

"Huh, it's just odd that you have the same exact name and birthday, and he found you. I mean, how did he find you anyway?"

That hadn't entered my mind, but it was an excellent question. "I don't know. I'll find out though."

"What else do you know about this guy?"

I could tell by his tone that he was going to have him investigated. Secretly, that thrilled and pissed me off in equal measure. Millie had already vetted him and said he was harmless. Uber rich, but nothing to worry about, certainly nothing that Wes needed to investigate.

"Wes…" I started with a warning so he'd know how I felt. "Really, this guy is harmless. He's thirty, a cowboy, lives on a normal ranch without all the fancy dancy items you'd think a wealthy person would have. His wife, Cyndi, is lovely and pregnant with their second child, a son he's over-the-moon happy about. Their daughter, Isabel, is four and a darling little girl. They're normal."

"Then why did a normal family hire an escort? Sweetheart, it's odd. I get the name thing, but still, he could have hired anyone to pretend to be the sister if it's his company's interest he has at stake. Why you? Why someone who absolutely has the same name and birthday?"

"It could be a different spelling." I tried, but knew I'd failed when Wes groaned in that way I knew he was tugging at his hair. "Don't pull on your hair!" I fired off.

He laughed. "How did you…"

"When you're frustrated, you start pulling on your hair. I love your hair and want to continue to see it for the rest of my life or at least for another thirty years, so stop ripping it out! You'll go bald prematurely."

Full-bellied guffaws could be heard through the connection. He gasped and chuckled as he responded. "Okay, okay, but I'll have you know my father's hair is doing well at his age, so I don't think you have anything to worry about."

Imagining Wes thirty years down the road made me all warm and squishy inside. "Don't worry about me, okay?"

"Not possible. Until you're home, sleeping in my bed next to me, I'm going to worry. Oh, and where did you say the ranch was?"

This time I laughed. One track mind, my guy. I gave him the address and I could hear the clacking of a keyboard.

"No shit," he whispered.

"What?" I sat up, suddenly worried.

"His ranch is next door to a friend of mine. Well, the wife is a friend of mine, but she lives there half of the year. I attended their wedding on that ranch."

"Who?"

"Aspen Bright-Reynolds." I'd heard the name before but couldn't place the face. "Well, technically she's Aspen Jensen now. Married Hank Jensen who literally owns the ranch property adjacent to the Cunningham's. No way. I've met Maxwell," he said with a hint of surprise. "You should connect with Aspen if they're in town. I'll give her a call."

My guy mentioning a woman he knows with such familiarity caused the green-eyed witch to pop her head out of her hidey-hole. "How do you know her?"

"She's in the business. Owns AIR Bright Enterprises. You think I'm rich? Honey, she's on the tippy top of the list of wealthy women in business and young, too. Maybe thirty now and recently had a daughter. I know they visit the ranch house as often as possible because Hank is the cowboy type. Needs open spaces and all that. I'll have to contact her. Set something up if you'd like."

"Um, maybe. I don't know. It's not like you're here to introduce me. Might be weird."

"Well, either way I'm going to find out more information about the Cunninghams."

"Baby, really, Millie already did all that—"

He cut me off. "My girlfriend, my concern. It will make me more comfortable. If you're spending time away from our life and home, I need to know you're safe. Besides, the whole thing is fishy to me. Admit that at least, Mia?"

Honestly, I kind of lost everything he said after the *my girlfriend, my concern* part. Having a man care enough about me to have the people I'm working for investigated was a new level of love for me. One I'd certainly never experienced before. The mere thought had me wanting to hop on a plane, drive to his Malibu mansion, and jump on his cock. Unfortunately, I'd be doing none of those things, so I responded vaguely with, "uh huh. I guess. Whatever makes you able to sleep at night, Wes. Just don't worry about me. I'm gonna hit the hay."

"Hit the hay? They're already transforming my girl into a cowgirl?" He snickered.

I giggled. "Love you."

"Dream of paradise." His voice was a throaty rumble that I missed so much at that moment I clutched the cell phone tighter.

"You mean being in your arms?" I waited until I could hear him sigh. "I'll call you tomorrow."

"Love you. Be safe."

CHAPTER FOUR

Maxwell drove us the forty-five minutes it took to get to the headquarters of Cunningham Oil & Gas. The building was enormous. It looked more like a small university than a corporate headquarters. I'm not sure why, but I expected it to be out on a dusty ranch, something a true cowboy would call his workplace. Everywhere I looked, sleek white pillars and glass walls protruded. Trees dotted the perimeter as we drove through a guarded gatehouse.

"Wow, how many people work here?"

Max paid attention to where he drove, slowly maneuvering his truck through the lot until he parked up near the front doors in a spot clearly marked Maxwell Cunningham, Chief Executive Officer, on a bright white sign with bold, black lettering. "Here? There are approximately twelve thousand employees on this campus."

"Campus?" I chuckled. "Fits. Looks like a college."

"We do a lot of good work here. But the company as a whole employs over seventy-five thousand."

"People? Holy shit. And you're responsible for all of them?"

His brows came together, and he tipped his hat. "It's not as glamorous as it sounds. Or rather, I don't allow it to be. Come on, I'll show you around. There's a lot to see."

I clambered out of the vehicle. He stopped with his hand on the door. "A gentleman opens the door for a lady," he admonished.

His statement instinctively made me put hands to hips, one hip jutting out with attitude. "Dear brother," I joked, trying the endearment on for size, "I am not your woman. I am your sister."

He grinned, yet something serene came over his features before he quickly shook it off. "So you are, sugar. Come on, there are people interested in meeting my one and only long lost sister." Max crooked his elbow, so I laced my arm through and pushed the sunglasses on top of my head.

"Your dad built all this from scratch?" I scanned at the campus, at least what I could see of it from the parking lot.

He shook his head. "No, no. The business was started ages ago by my gran'pappy, a real old west John Wayne-type of fella. Then it grew with the generations. Now"— he held out one arm wide, expressing the vastness of the property—"it's truly something to behold. Growing up, all I ever wanted was to run my ranch and work at this company. I've always been Dad's right hand, but now that he's gone, I'm taking the helm." His lips pursed together, and the mood turned melancholy.

I rubbed his shoulder and bicep. "Hey, I'm sorry about your dad. If he was anything like you, he's probably missed by a lot of people."

"Yes, I do believe you're right. Though why he'd keep a secret like me having a sister all these years is beyond me."

"So your mom must have remarried then?"

He huffed and opened the wide glass door. "My mother never married Dad, not for lack of trying. Dad said he asked her many times over the years they were together. Even downright demanded it when they had me. Instead, she just

172

up and disappeared. Left a baby book she'd made of me, some pictures of her and Dad together. and that's it. Never to be heard from again. At least that's what Dad said." His shoulders tightened, and the skin around his jaw seemed to tighten. It was obvious that talking about his mom wasn't his favorite subject.

He led me with a hand at my lower back, into the elevator. We went up the five flights to the top. Though the company employed many people, the building wasn't tall. I guess, though, if they wanted to keep the charm of the country, they probably didn't want skyscrapers jutting into the sky and blocking out the sun.

"Hi, Diane, how are you?" Max said to a pixie of a woman sitting at the desk in front of a set of double doors. Her hair was white and pulled back into a sleek bun. A pair of rose-colored glasses were perched precariously on her nose. She smiled wide and held out her hand. Max grabbed it, leaned forward, kissed it, and then patted the top. The woman was old enough to be his grandmother, but I could tell from the intelligence in her gaze that she was sharp as a tack.

"And who is this lovely young lady?" She glanced at my body, checking me out, or at the very least evaluating my clothing choices. Her blatant regard didn't feel alarming or rude, more like she was curious about me.

"My sister, Mia." He said it with such a sense of pride, it hit my heart like an intense bone-breaking hug and squeezed tight, making me wish I were this man's sister. Any woman would adore a brother like him, so caring, obviously a family man, and seemingly a strong leader.

She stood up, proving she was even smaller than I'd

suspected. Her arms opened wide and her smile could brighten any dull day. She pulled me into a full body hug. "So good to meet you, Mia. Welcome to the family, dear girl." She cupped my cheeks. "Now you don't be a stranger, you hear?"

"Um, okay, I'll try not to be."

"Thanks, Diane. Let her go now," Max encouraged as he tugged my hand. She released her grip and crossed her arms over her chest, smiling happily as if she were hugging herself. As we retreated, I could hear a couple sniffs in the background and a muttered, "Never thought I'd see the day."

Max opened the door to his office, and what an office it was. Huge didn't quite describe it. The room was in at the corner of the building and overlooked the rest of the campus. Hundreds of acres of land spread out, and different buildings were nestled among the trees. "We try our best to be environmentally friendly, but there's always the activists that want to protect the Earth. I get it, but that doesn't change our need for natural resources." His tone was soft, not at all damning, simply matter of fact.

"Do you get a lot of issues running a business like this?" I asked, looking out over the vast landscape.

He leaned against his desk and stared at the view alongside me. "We get our fair share. There's always the need for transparency, accountability, sometimes issues with conflicting materials."

"What's that?" The rest I understood, but the material thing, not so much.

"Supply sources dealing in gold, copper, tin, tungsten, and tantalum are often essential to use in production or functionality of the products. There's always the energy and environmental policies to deal with in our government and that of our plants in other countries."

I nodded. "You're global?"

"Yep. Remember, we employ over seventy-five thousand people. They're not all in the US. Though I have people to run each branch. My cousins as well as some executives we've hired. In every branch, there is a Cunningham in top tier management ensuring the family's stake."

"And the investors?"

"We have plenty of those as well, but they don't own pieces of the company, just interest in it. The more money we make, the more money they make. Unfortunately, that's part of why you're here."

I turned and took a seat in one of the leather lounge chairs. "Explain that to me."

He sighed and sat down in the chair opposite me. A glass table with the bottom made of what looked to be dried out wood from a dead tree comprised the base that separated us. The table added to the rustic western appeal of the space. I liked it. Suited the man that worked there. "Well, in Dad's will, he left forty-nine percent of the company to my sister."

"The one you haven't met yet."

He looked away and responded. "Er, yeah, you could say that. Basically, he left this woman close to half of the company and has given me a year to find her. I've been looking for months." He laughed. "This is going to sound so ridiculous, and you're probably not going to believe it, but I heard your name in the entertainment news my wife watches. They mentioned it tied to man I met a couple years ago. Friends of ours, so I asked them about you."

"And who is this friend?"

"My friend is Hank Jensen. He's our neighbor, and his wife..."

"Is Aspen, who's friends with Weston Channing. Am I getting warm?"

His mood shifted again, like a wave crashing over him, and the melancholy I'd felt before left completely. "Yes, exactly! Met the fella at their wedding on the ranch a couple years ago. Nice guy. Movie man. Anyway, saw your name on the entertainment show and then confirmed it on a tabloid at the supermarket. So I uh, had you investigated."

And there it was. Honest. Simple. There was nothing nefarious lurking in the corners ready to bite me. He's just a guy looking for his sister who just happened to share my name. "Imagine my surprise when I found out you were an escort. I will say that shocked me a bit." The words came out grumbled, almost angry, not at all matching the man. "Why are you an escort anyway?"

I held up my hand. "Wait a minute. Don't try to change the subject. You had me investigated, and what did you find besides the escort part, which you know to be true?"

"A little of this, little of that. Know your dad is in the hospital in convalescent care. Know you worked a string of waitressing jobs in Vegas and in California, where you also did a small stint in acting. Saw a couple of your commercials. You're really good."

Aww, he saw my acting. "Thank you." I smiled and then realized I was getting off the subject. "What else?"

"That you now work for Exquisite Escorts and you were noted in the smut mags for being the girlfriend of Weston Channing. But then a month later, you were working for some French guy who painted. And after that, you popped up connected to the Fasanos, the folks who own all the Italian restaurants. Wish they had one close to here. I've eaten at one of their locations, and damn, it was good."

Again, he had me chuckling and thinking about my time with Tony and Hector and the entire Fasano clan. "They're an amazing family. I care very deeply about them. Is that all?"

He shook his head. "You were noted again in the papers as the girlfriend of that Boston Red Sox player. Not sure why in the world you'd get with a guy who played for that craptastic team. Should have been someone on the Texas Rangers. Now that's a team!"

"Seriously? You know my entire life history, and you're worried about the team my client worked for?" I could feel my temperature rising and the wall of frustration right along with it. People shouldn't know this much about my life, my private life. Especially a client.

"So that wasn't your boyfriend?" His head jerked back. "But I saw you kissing him in the papers. That Weston fella, too."

I groaned and let out an exasperated breath. "They are all clients. Except Weston. He's my boyfriend, but he wasn't then. We just got together recently." I straightened my shoulders. "Doesn't matter. What is it that you need from me?"

He licked his lips and rubbed at his jaw. "Simple. I need you to be my sister so that the investors don't get to take a stake in the company."

"But how would that work? Eventually they're going

to figure it out."

"No, I don't think they will. It's too close. Imagine my surprise when I found out that the Mia Saunders I saw on TV and in that super market magazine not only shared the same name but the birthday my father noted as well. For now, your driver's license will suffice, and then, by the time we need to get into birth records and DNA testing for the courts, I'll uh, hopefully have found the real Mia Saunders. My Mia. I've wanted nothing more my whole life than to be part of a huge family. Dad never had more children. That's why I married Cyndi young, and we set about having a baby. I want a brood of children running my family's company one day. And right now, I need to protect that. It's why you're here."

Hearing him say, "my Mia" made my heart ache again. I got it. What he wanted—a real family with a mother, father, sister, brother, all of that. I had Maddy, and now I had an extended family in my friends, but it had always just been me and Maddy and Pops, when he was sober enough to even attempt to be a father figure. A real family environment was something I also craved. That deep blood connection with people, what Maddy and I had, meant everything to me.

"I'll do whatever you need. Just let me know."

"That easy? You'll agree to help me, share your information, and pretend to be her?"

The decision really wasn't that hard. I'd been a girlfriend, muse, fiancée, model, arm candy, and seductress. Why not the sister of a good guy who just wanted to protect his family's business? I held out my hand. "Agree to name your next daughter after me, and I'll do it," I said with the straightest face I could muster.

"Really? That's all you want? A namesake?" His eyes turned soft, and once more, I was hit with that buzzing, the sense that I knew him, had seen that exact look before.

I dropped my hand. "You really would name your kid after me, huh?"

He shrugged. "You save my family business, I figure it's the least I can do. Besides, you're my sister." He said it with such conviction I almost believed it.

"I can tell that you're pretty straightforward. I was kidding though. You owe me nothing. Just give your family a good life."

"You don't want more money? Blackmail me? You know you could. For a lot. This company has billions in revenue every year. I could set you up for life."

With a conviction I felt down to the soles of my shoes, I shook my head. "A good deed is done because it should be, not because it's being paid for. You've already paid the fee to get me here. I've sent that to my debt collector. It's all good."

His eyes went from a pale green to a harsh dark forest color. "Debt collector? That money I sent went to a debt? My investigator showed no debt under your name. You had very little in your checking and savings, though checks had been written to a college fund. I figured you were using the money you made for back tuition. That money was supposed to go to you!" His tone bordered on vehement, and he clutched his hands into fists. Not exactly the response I'd expect.

I groaned. "Look, Max, my debts are not your problem. Hell, they're not even my problem." I spoke on autopilot and shouldn't have.

"What do you mean? Whose debt are you paying?" He stood and placed his hands on his hips. The sunlight struck his shiny belt buckle, momentarily blinding me.

"None of your business." I squeezed my eyes shut, trying to avoid the light. That brightness shone as though it were piercing me with much more than a blaze of sunshine, but the truth, right at the heart of its wicked arrow.

"Of course it is. You're my sister."

"Pretend sister," I reminded him with a warning tone. The kind that usually made people listen. Not him. He wasn't fazed by it at all.

In a flourish, he pulled off his Stetson, set it on his desk, and ruffled his fingers through his unruly hair. When it fell down, all golden blond layers around his ears, he looked beyond familiar. He looked like my baby sister Maddy for the briefest of seconds. Jeez, even he had me drinking the Kool-Aid.

"Look, I'm not going to go into the debt details. Just know I'm handling it."

"But what about college? If you're here, you're obviously not in school."

I pressed my fists against my eyes. This really was none of his business. Most of my clients didn't get this close to the personal details of my life this soon. Only Wes, but that was different. In the back of my mind, I knew he was someone more. It just took a while to confirm it. Now, I had this giant cowboy all up in my business, and from the looks of his tight jaw and firm stance, he was not going to budge until he got some answers.

Taking a deep breath, I leaned forward. "I dropped out of school long ago, Max. The tuition payments are not for me."

His hand went to his jaw. "Then who are they for?"

"My sister, Madison. I'm paying for her schooling."

His hand dropped to the desk where he leaned heavily, the wood creaking under the pressure. "You have a sister?" he gasped.

"Um, yeah, five years younger. She goes to school in Nevada, going to be a scientist," I said with absolute pride and affection. My baby sister was my one true claim to fame. Everything I did in life, I did for her, because of her. She would have everything that life could offer, and I'd done my best over the years to make it so. Then I laughed, realizing a tiny important detail and taunting the cowboy with it. "I thought your little investigator would have mentioned that." I wagged a finger at him.

When our gazes caught, I noticed his eyes were tortured and hardened. He swallowed a couple times, opened his mouth, and then closed it again. "Another sister," he whispered. "Madison." He said her name as if it were a prayer, something to be held up high on an altar and worshipped. "Two sisters. All I've ever wanted. I'll be damned." He shook his head, closed his eyes, and a tear slipped down his cheek.

What. The. Hell. Just. Happened.

CHAPTER FIVE

"Max, what's the matter?" I asked as he stood, walked over to the window, and ran his monster-sized hands through his golden locks.

He cleared his throat. "Uh, nothing." He sniffed, trying to pull himself together. I was at a total loss. He'd gone from talking oil business to invading my personal life and then a one–eighty-degree spin to tears. It didn't make sense. I mean, I'd kind of figured out that he had a soft spot for family, but nothing I'd said would warrant a big man like him to breakdown and cry.

I got up, went to the window where he stood, and placed a hand on his shoulder. It was firm, denoting his physical strength. He definitely didn't sit around on that farm and put his feet up. No, I got the impression that Max was the type who worked with his hands, and often. "Is it your dad?"

His eyes were absolutely tortured when his brows narrowed, and he shook his head. Tension radiated off his form like a physical wall of magnetic energy. Before I knew it, I was pulled into his arms, my face planted in the center of his chest. He held my head while his enormous form quaked. For a guy his size, that meant the whole ground seemed to shake with him. What was a girl to do in this situation but hold on for dear life or get swallowed whole by the sheer force of his grief? I held on and whispered words of comfort.

"It's okay, Max. You'll be fine. He's in a better place." That last comment seemed to cause him to squeeze the life right out of me. I figured a different tactic might be in order. "Calm down. Remember, you've got a beautiful wife, an adorable daughter, a family who loves you." His arms tightened, and then loosened incrementally with each breath.

Max coughed, took a step back, and turned around. He wiped at his cheeks, cleared his throat, and coughed. Wanting to be considerate of his needs, I moved around the room, giving him some space to clear his head, compose himself.

After a bit, he spoke.

"I'm sorry, Mia. I uh, didn't realize I had that locked under the plate of armor." He battered a fist against his chest. "It would be kind of you not to mention it to anyone." He glanced down and away.

I shrugged. "Hey, we've all got shit to deal with, Max. Yours is just more recent."

His stance and the way he held his jaw showed the power nestled under the surface. "Come, let me show you the rest of the campus."

"Lead the way." I extended my arm, showing that I was ready.

We passed Diane on the way out of his office. Her smile was bright and big. Her hands were clasped together and held to her chest. She beamed as Max crooked his arm once more for me to hold. I giggled and leaned toward him for his benefit as much as mine. I think he needed a friendly body to lean on. Even if he wouldn't do the leaning, I would on his behalf.

For a couple hours, he walked me from department to department, introducing me as his sister over and over. I could have sworn that, with each introduction, the level of pride in his voice went from fake to genuine in a less than half a heartbeat. The entire scenario boggled the mind and made me feel strange, as though I were a boat on a lake with no anchor and no paddle. I had nothing but the strength of my arms paddling endlessly in the cool water to get me back to land.

Maxwell took me to the engineering department where he introduced me to a willowy woman with long brown hair tied back in a French braid. She wore a set of rimless glasses and a pinched expression. The moment we entered the office, a haze of distrust swirled in the air around her. I knew instantly that she was going to pose a problem to our little game of hide-the-real-sister.

"Mia, meet my cousin, Sofia Cunningham. She runs the engineering department here and sits on our sponsor committee as she has a vested interest in the company."

I offered my hand, and she looked at it with disdain before clutching it so hard I cringed and stepped back, yanking it from her clutches.

"Good to meet you," I lied.

"I'll just bet. So, Mia, the missing sister that no one knew about." Her snide comment hit its target, which was Max, not me. He groaned. Me, I could hold my own, so I stared at her with a blank expression, allowing her no hint of my feelings. "Where have you been hiding all this time?"

My eyes instantly rolled. I couldn't control them any longer. "Uh, Vegas?" I answered truthfully, since that's where I'd been the bulk of my life. If anyone looked that information up, he'd find it was true.

"Is that right?" She cocked a hip and pushed her glasses up from the tip of her nose to the bridge. "Interesting how all of a sudden my uncle dies and leaves you half of what we've all worked our asses off for over the past decade."

Knowing that with this type of chick I couldn't back down, I swiped my hair off my face, hooked my arm through Maxwell's, and snubbed my nose at her. "Guess I'm just lucky, huh?"

Sofia harrumphed and then waved us over to a table. She pointed at a big sheet with a bunch of stuff on it that very well could have been in another language for all I could understand of the lines, formulas, and marks. "Max, these schematics need to be reviewed by the committee, Legal, and a check cut by Finance in order to get ahead on the project for the East Asia plant. When are you going to be available to check them?"

Max curled an arm over my shoulder. "Sof, I've just met my sister. We've had a day together. Maybe you can give me a couple days to get to know her before you bust my balls on work issues? I warned you, once she was here I was going to be out of pocket for a while."

She sighed and her lips went down into a pout. "You know I don't like to get behind. This is important, Max. More important than some stranger," she half snarled.

His body went rigid. "Sofia, you know what family means to me, and I'll not have you talking that way about my sister. She's family too, same as you. Just because we haven't known about her until now doesn't change that simple fact."

"Yeah, well we'll see about this sister business."

"You going to look into her credentials?"

Her eyebrows rose into her hairline. "Maybe I will. What would you say to that?"

He leaned a forearm on her desk and got right into her face. "Iron clad, cuz. Look all you want. Ain't nothing to find. Feel free though. Do your searchin'. I know what you're up to. I know you have a stake in the ultimate prize of getting that forty-nine percent, but the will is fact. Talk to Legal. Check on the specifics. Dig all you want. You ain't gonna to find nuthin' but the truth." He rolled up the schematics she had displayed and put them under his arm. "I'll give these a gander when I have a chance. When I'm not busy visiting with my sister."

On that note, he turned, put a hand on my back, and led me out of the room.

"So, your cousin, she always been a bitch?" I asked with absolutely no malice in my tone. The last thing I needed was to piss him off after that interaction.

He started laughing and hugged my shoulders, bringing me close to his big body once again while we walked down one of the ridiculously long hallways. I hated to admit it, but I enjoyed the closeness of what felt like bonding between a man and a woman, one without the sexual aspect to cloud the simple human connection. With Maxwell, it was easy. It worked on a level I wouldn't have expected had I not been here to experience it myself. Max was a good guy, and the more time I spent with him, the more I found I really enjoyed his company. Liked that he was straightforward, no nonsense, a real man's man.

And of course, on that thought, my mind drifted to my

own modern day cowboy. I thought he'd get a kick out of Max. They actually had more in common than not. They both held their family in high regard, enjoyed the simpler things in life while being able to easily afford more lavish luxury. They both worked hard, and as far as I could tell, loved their women beyond compare. The memory of Wes's arms around me as we headed to the airport rushed through my subconscious like a freight train.

Wes's arms looped around my waist loosely. His fingers made dizzying circles along the sensitive skin of my lower back. "I don't want you to go," he said plainly, as if I didn't already know what he was thinking. Ever since we'd admitted our feelings for one another, I could sense his moods and work out his thought processes much quicker. Maybe before, I'd been blocked from that side of our relationship, not wanting to allow that level of closeness.

"I'll be back in three weeks, and we'll talk every night."

"Promise?" The way he issued the request made my heart thump, pounding in a rhythm that weakened my knees. I leaned heavily into his chest. He hummed that content sound, the one that made me purr, and I rubbed my nose into his shirt, ensuring his scent was all over me so that all I'd have to do on the flight to Dallas was inhale deeply and he'd be there.

"Three weeks and I'll be back here. Unless you tell me to meet you somewhere else, I'll plan to go home."

Every time I mentioned his Malibu house as home, *a ridiculously beautiful grin adorned his face. "I love when you refer to our home." He slid his hands down to my ass and squeezed, pressing me into his groin, where his erection was at half-mast.*

"I know. I can also tell how much you're going to miss me." I thrust against his hardening shaft, and he grumbled a profanity

and slid his hands up into my hair, tugging at the roots, forcing my head back. I was completely at his mercy and loving every second.

"You're so easy to be around, Sis." Max broke through my two-day-old memory. I glanced around to see if anyone was watching. The hallways were quiet. Murmurs came from each door as we passed. The chatter from someone on the phone, a too-loud speakerphone, a person smacking a rolled up magazine against his hand as he paced the floor. Even the clickity clack of a computer keyboard sounded extra loud, but there were definitely no bodies around.

So why had he called me his sis? Perhaps he was just trying to get used to the new endearment. Although I realized, rather belatedly, that I enjoyed hearing it far more than was healthy, and if he kept it up, I would lose sight of the fact that I wasn't really his sister, but someone playing a role. An actress for hire.

I played it off, nudging him in the shoulder, which was more like his bicep since he was so damn tall. He maneuvered me through the vast building to the cafeteria. Only it wasn't a normal cafeteria you'd see in the movies. This place had four restaurants, a snack cart, and plush wooden tables and seating for those who had brown-bagged it.

Max pointed to each restaurant. One was Italian, one American Cuisine, another Asian, and the last Tex-Mex. "Where would you like to eat? They're all free."

"Free?" I said, shocked, while considering my options. I was in Texas. I'd be remiss if I didn't have Tex-Mex at least once, so I pointed to the restaurant with the big chili pepper and a sombrero on the sign.

"Yep. My employees often work twelve to eighteen

hour shifts. Heck, some of them stay overnight in what we call the bunker to grab a few hours of shuteye and then get back at it."

I cringed. "Why do you work them so hard?"

He led me through the restaurant that was a full service business except there was no cash register or hostess. We sat where we wanted and the menu was already on the table.

"It's not on purpose, but sugar, some of our projects are extremely time-sensitive. Could mean the difference in the cost of oil per barrel the longer the project lasts. That's time and money lost to us, which inevitably gets passed on to the consumer, the average Joe at the gas tank." I nodded and sat down, pulling out a menu. "It's hard work; I won't lie, but my staff is paid very well for any inconveniences. For example, the food in these restaurants is free. There's an onsite daycare, gym, and game room for folks to let off some steam when the pressure gets too much. Heck, there's even a Zen garden for people to walk through to feel in touch with nature."

"Wow, sounds like you do a lot for your staff."

He smiled and waved a hand at one of the waiters passing by. "We try. I want my team, regardless of where they fall on the scale, to work hard and know that they are appreciated, valued, you know?"

I nodded. "I mean I get it in theory, but I've never experienced that myself. Well, until now. Millie takes good care of me."

"Millie?"

"Oh, sorry. Ms. Milan, as she prefers to be called. She's actually my aunt."

"On your dad's side?" he asked immediately.

Twiddling with the saltshaker, I shook my head. "Nope. My mom's."

Max put his elbow on the table and rested his head in his hand. "Tell me about her."

If I'd been thinking normally, not swayed by the coolness factor of the environment and the ease with which I found myself talking to Max, I would have found his interest odd. Who cared about someone's random aunt? "Um, I guess for starters, I'd say I got my looks from her and Mom."

"That's true," he said, and I narrowed my eyes. How would he know if that statement were true?

Before I could ask, we were interrupted by the waitress. We both ordered the same thing: a combination plate with a tostada and a cheese enchilada, but Max added two tacos. The guy was a massive wall of man. It had to take a lot to fill him up. He probably ate his wife out of house and home on a daily basis.

"So continue. Aunt Millie is your mom's sister and she runs Exquisite Escorts. Right? And that's how you got into the business?"

"Yeah, I needed to make money and fast."

"Can I ask why?"

I huffed. "I just don't understand why you care."

He looked away, his cheeks pinking. "Call it curious. I like you as a person, Mia. I can tell already you're good people, and I want the rest of your time here to be worth something. At the very least, when you go home, you'll have another person you can count on. I'd like to be that person."

I'd learned through this journey not to be so cynical about these things. Tai, by nature, was the same way. A man who protected women, all women, not out of some kind of outdated, old-fashioned idea, but because he cared. Max had that vibe as well. I took a deep breath and decided I'd be honest. Lay it all out there, and if he thought differently of me for it, so be it. I had to take chances in life. Real chances with people and relationships, if I wanted to have any that mattered in the long run.

"My pops got into some trouble. He's a drunk most of the time, but a gambler all of the time. Usually he'd bring home just enough to cover the rent. The rest—food, utilities, the other things people needed to live comfortably—had to be paid in other ways."

Maxwell's eyes turned icy. "And how did those things get paid while you were growing up?"

I tipped my chin and focused on the tea the waiter set down in front of me, adding my heaping dose of sugar and squeezing in the lemon. "Usually, I worked to make the extra. Bought clothes for Mads and me at local thrift stores. I'd be really careful with my clothes, knowing that I'd need to pass them down to her one day. And you know what, she never once complained. She's the better of the two of us, my girl."

Talking about Maddy made my heart hurt. As soon as we got back to his ranch, I was going to check in. It had been too long, and I needed to give her an update, especially the fact that I'd moved in with Wes. Maybe I could get her and Matt to fly out for Christmas. I guess that all depended on where I'd be during the holidays. I still had a fat debt to pay.

"You two must be really close." His voice was gravelly, emotional in that way I'd come to recognize with him.

"Yeah, as close as two people can be. We pretty much

only had each other after Mom left and Pops went on a bender. He never really recovered from losing her."

Max scowled and grumbled something I would have sworn was, "I know the feeling," but I dismissed it instantly. He didn't know our mother, but then again, he'd said he didn't know his own, so maybe that's what he meant.

There was a long pause as Max ripped at his paper napkin and I got lost in the past. Remembering some of the times when Maddy and I would have loved the solidarity of a mother, a female to look up to as we grew into women.

The waiter delivered our food, and for a few moments we were content to just eat together. Eventually, Max took a ginormous bite of his enchilada and then put down his fork. When he'd chewed and swallowed, he clasped his hands in front of him, leaning his chin on them. "Will you tell me about Madison?" His voice came out soft, almost needy.

Since I was like a proud mama bear, I had absolutely no problem speaking of my girl. "Maddy, or Mads, as I call her"—he smiled and picked up his fork once more, almost as if he was hunkering down into the story and the meal at the same time—"she's beautiful. Long blond hair, super tall and slim with eyes like mine. Though she's turning more womanly every day."

"She's not a brunette?" He scoffed, which I thought was strange, but I didn't mention it.

"Nope, she's my opposite." I looked at his shocked face and clocked each of his features. "You know"—I laughed—"she looks more like you than she does me! You should have had her pretend to be your sister!" I giggled and his jaw clenched.

"Is your father blond?"

I shook my head. "No, his hair is also dark. Mads is a throwback to our grandmother, I think. At least, that's what Pops said."

"Hmm. Okay, what else? You said she's in school?"

I sat up a little straighter. "She's going to be a scientist and a doctor!" There was absolutely no shame in my game. My baby sis was going to make something amazing out of her life, and I couldn't be more proud.

"You sound really excited about this."

Tilting my head to the side, I watched him while he pushed his food around, no longer seeming interested in his plate. "Why shouldn't I be? I've been raising her to be something incredible my whole life. I've had to be her mom, dad, and sister for the last fifteen years. And I'm paying for her schooling, peddling my ass around from state to state to do it and to save our dad."

His brow narrowed and his eyes turned into slits. "Tell me about what kind of trouble your dad got into. You said he was into gambling. Did something happen?"

I plopped a bite of tostada into my mouth, appreciating the crunch of the lettuce and the mixture of the asada, cheese, green sauce, and beans. So good. Max waited patiently while I chewed. "Turns out he owed some loan sharks a hefty bill. He couldn't pay up, as usual. They beat him within an inch of his life. Put him in a coma. Cornered me in the hospital and told me if they didn't get their money, they'd kill him for sure, and if he died, they'd go after me and Maddy. Something they called survivor's debt." I shifted in my seat and pushed my hair back from my face. "Unfortunately, I know the bastard that loaned him the money. He's my ex, and he's ruthless. He'd take me down just as easily as my dad and sister if he doesn't get his cash. So I'm doing what I need to do to pay him off."

"What do you owe?"

A normal person would probably keep this bit of information to herself, but I'd had enough of keeping secrets. Sometimes a person needed to let the shit out or it would swallow her whole. "A million dollars."

Max's eyes widened.

"I know. Crazy, right?"

He closed his eyes and leaned his head back against the booth. "And your fee is a hundred thousand a month. So you're paying installments?"

I put a finger to my nose. "Bingo was his name-O!" I laughed, but he didn't even crack a smile.

"How much do you still owe?"

Shoveling in more food, I thought about it. "Including this month, four hundred thousand."

He huffed. "And that's why you don't have any money in your account. Any bit of extra you send to your sister, right?"

"Right again. You're getting good at this game, Maximus!"

He laughed. "Maximus."

I scanned his giant frame. "Have you seen you? You're huge. Name fits."

"Mia." Max's tone was deadly serious. When he put a hand over mine on the table and held it, I knew something was up. "I'd like to pay the debt free and clear. The entire million. Then you can have your money back. You shouldn't have to pay for the sins of your father."

Licking my lips, I pulled my hand away and looked

him straight in the eye. I'd never understand why men like Max thought they could solve all the world's problems with money. Had to be the damsel in distress and knight in shining armor trait all the men I'd come into contact with lately had about them.

"Why would you do that?" I said it flippantly, though Max did not take it well. His entire body went tense, and he clenched his jaw so tight, I worried he'd crack a tooth.

"Because I can." The words came out through his teeth the way garlic goes through a tiny handheld grater.

Sitting back in my chair, I looked him in the eye, ensuring he knew I was dead serious. "That will never happen."

He also leaned back in his chair, put a long arm out as if he were getting nice and comfortable. "It would be wise if you learned how to accept a gift."

A gift. He was insane, downright certifiable, right up there with people who charmed rattlesnakes. "Tell that to my rich boyfriend. I've got an idea. How about the two of you start a club? The 'we have more money than sense club' and share your 'gifts' with people who actually need a handout. I'm just fine, and I'm going to keep being just fine after I've paid off this debt, moved my happy ass to Malibu permanently, and watched my baby sister walk the stage accepting her bachelor's, her master's, and then her P-H-fucking-D. Now, can we let this go? You're pissing me off, and I was enjoying a nice complimentary lunch. Which by the way, for free food…" I bent my head back and moaned over another bite of the crunchiest, most tasty tostada ever. "Amazing!"

Max looked at me as if I'd sprouted another eye in the

center of my forehead. "Whatever you say, sugar," he said with a smirk.

Sugar. He gets Maximus, which admittedly is a super cool nickname, and I get sugar? Lame.

CHAPTER SIX

The next week or so we spent getting to know one another. I met with different members of his team, spent a lot of time just being visible at the offices, but mostly I hung out with their family as one big unit, which was strangely wonderful. If Maddy and Wes had been there, I would have felt right at home. Max took me to each of the free gourmet restaurants. I'd have been hard-pressed to pick a favorite. They were all that tasty.

Today, when we finished lunch, Max showed me around the other half of the campus. The side we hadn't spent a lot of time in. I found it mostly contained the corporate boring stuff, HR, Legal, Public Relations, and Marketing. If I had a pedometer, I'm pretty sure we'd have clocked ten thousand or more steps throughout the day. Eventually, we loaded back into his truck and drove to his ranch.

Exiting the vehicle, I was surprised to see another giant of a man with his arm curled around the bottom of a toddler at his hip. The other looped around the waist of a statuesque blonde. Her hair was like spun gold and trailed in a flat sheet down her back. She wore a pencil skirt, a sky blue silk blouse, and a pair of flip-flops. The footwear aside, she was far more put together than most people I knew. Looked like she might have thrown the shoes on instead of replacing what was probably a pair of ridiculously expensive heels.

As we walked up the steps, we could hear the tail end

of the woman speaking. "…in thanks, we'd love to have you over for dinner sometime soon."

"Well, look what the cat dragged in," Max stated in jest, smacking his thighs while grinning at the couple standing on the front porch.

The man turned around and his smile widened. I stopped and looked at the specimen of utter man candy who stood in front of me. He was built like a Viking. Sandy-brown hair, chiseled jaw, even white teeth, and just the right amount of scruff to make a girl stutter. The sleeves of his tight-fitting polo stretched around a set of massive biceps, wider around than my thighs, and I was no stick. His blue-green eyes sparkled as he took in my form much quicker than a male usually did. I mean, I wasn't a model or anything, but I'd never lacked for a man's interest in the past, and admittedly, the rack was definitely something to write home about.

This hunk of heaven scanned me as if he were assessing me, not checking me out. I wanted to pout, complete with a lip quiver, until the blonde turned around. Then I got it. Her eyes were a stunning blue and reminded me of the Hawaiian water off the coast of Oahu. Those eyes were set into a pristine pale face with pouty red shapely lips, high cheekbones, and a small nose. Essentially, one of the most elegantly gorgeous women I'd ever seen. All that attached to a thin yet womanly shape, and it clicked why he only had eyes for the blonde. Every few moments, he glanced at her like he was about to take a bite. There was a hunger there, simmering. I knew that sensation because it's the way Wes looked at me, like he'd never ever get enough. I could tell the blonde appreciated it fully by the small smile she gave him in return.

On the man's hip was the most adorable little girl. Aside from little Isabel, that is. Isabel and I had become fast buddies. This morning, I woke up to her little hand playing with my hair while she lay beside me in bed. "How come you have black hair?" she'd asked. I laughed, rubbed the sleep out of my eyes, and told her that it was because my mommy had black hair. Her little mouth had formed an "o" as she connected the dots. "And my daddy has yellow hair so I have yellow hair!" I cracked up and laughed with her, told her how smart she was, and then let her play with all my stuff while I got ready to hang with Max at his office.

"Hank and Aspen Jensen"—Max pointed to the male sex-on-a-platter in a pair of tight fitting Wranglers, and then to his wife, God's perfect woman—"their daughter, Hannah." He tickled the little girl's tummy, and she squealed delightfully. "This is my sister, Mia Saunders." Max once again announced with more pride than the situation deserved.

I put out my hand and shook theirs and was pleased to find that Hank didn't strangle my hand. Loved it when a man gave a firm handshake but catered it to the person. "Pleasure to meet you. Funny thing, you actually know my significant other, Weston Channing," I said.

Aspen's eyes lit up. When I say lit up, I mean the sun came out, birds sang, and butterflies fluttered around us. She was just so damn pretty. If she didn't seem so nice, I'd probably sit with Gin and talk shit about how perfect she was and how unfair it was that bitches like her drove all the good men to their knees. "I love Weston!" She brought both her hands to her chest.

Her husband grumbled next to her, a real carnal, "me

Tarzan, you Jane" type growl. "What's this about loving another man, angel?" His tone was dead serious, though she raised a hand making a flippant gesture to shoo him away.

"I didn't know he was seeing anyone. He's so kind and definitely a looker."

At that comment, Hank's mitt of a hand curved around Aspen's waist, and he tugged her back to his chest. "Now you're insinuating you're hot for other men, darlin'?"

Aspen rolled her eyes and patted his hand over her belly. "Never so much as had a date, a kiss, or anything other than a business dinner, and that single dance with him... at our *wedding*, so relax, big guy." She emphasized the word wedding. He slid his hand to her ribs, perilously close to her breast, and she gasped as he laid a set of open mouth kisses to her bare neck, not at all concerned with the overt public display of affection, or rather, ownership. She rolled her eyes and smiled. "Caveman," she said in a breathy timbre. Then she bummed her booty back, throwing him off his mark. "Go hang out with Max and the kids while we girls catch up."

His jaw clenched before he nodded, but as she started to turn around, he curved a hand behind her neck, brought his woman close, and slanted his mouth over hers. She squeaked and then hummed into his kiss and melted on the spot, completely taken away by her husband. It made me miss Wes in a fierce, bone-aching way. It was as though each and every day that went by, the distance seemed to grow. I didn't know if it was the fact that we were so newly in love or the need to be connected to someone who knew me intimately, knew who I really was and loved me anyway, that made the distance a world away, even though, in truth, it was only a couple of states and a short plane ride.

Cyndi led us through the house to the back veranda where there was a fan blowing soft air, a set of cushy wicker chairs with billowy seats, and a glass pitcher filled with a pink liquid. "Spiked pink lemonade." She grinned.

I tucked an arm around her shoulders and brought her close. "Woman after my own heart." I smiled.

Her response was strange. Instead of laughing, she mumbled, "I hope so," and then pulled away, setting about pouring us heaping glasses of the fruity alcoholic beverage. There was another pitcher marked with a sad face. I pointed at it and frowned, matching the symbol that was written on it with washable marker.

"That's for me." She rubbed her rounded belly. "No booze for another two months," she pouted. Holy shit. The woman still had two months of her pregnancy to go and she was enormous. Then again, I didn't really know enough about these things to gauge what a pregnant woman was supposed to look like in her seventh month.

I patted her on the back before sitting down. "Bummer."

She shrugged. "It will be worth it once he's here."

Never being one to skip out on a free drink, I took a sip and let the cool lemony vodka-flavored drink rush over my taste buds. Not only was it delicious, but it allowed a sense of calm to creep over the strange mood of the day, forcing a lighter more relaxed vibe in its place.

The three of us sat and talked about menial things at first—the weather, and the latest fashion trends, which I knew absolutely nothing about. Aspen admitted that she had her personal assistant pick everything she wore, one who would be freaking out if he saw her in flip flops. Apparently, he despised them with a passion that warranted her talking about it. His name escaped me as the liquor continued to warm my gut and loosen my tongue.

"My sister London is also pregnant. Twins!" Aspen said with a merriment that proved how truly excited she was about becoming an aunt.

When the word sister hit, I jumped up to get my purse and pulled out my cell phone.

Cyndi's eyes narrowed in concern. "What's the matter?" she asked.

I shook my head. "No, nothing. Just Aspen talking about her sister reminded me that I needed to call Maddy. I'd meant to days and days ago."

"Who's Maddy?" she asked with a hand on her belly. Since she'd sat down, her hand was constantly rubbing in different spots. I was too freaked out to ask why she did that and nervous that it would make her feel uncomfortable if I did. Pregos are a strange breed. I figured I'd probably go down that road someday, I guess, if Wes wanted them. It was yet another thing my new boyfriend and I needed to discuss in the future. It felt good, though, to have those serious discussions to look forward to. I'd never had them with any of my other boyfriends, and I'd thought the sun and moon rose with them. I was such an idiot. Now, I had a new path, and it was all sunsets, surfing, and snuggling in the Malibu hills with my personal hunk.

Giggling in that way only two fully loaded glasses of vodka-flavored lemonade could make me do, I responded. "My sister, silly."

Cyndi's face paled, and her hand came up to her mouth. Instantly, her eyes filled with unshed tears. Shit.

What did I say? "You have a sister from your mother?" Her voice croaked as I nodded. "Max didn't mention that." She choked on a half-sob. What was with these people? It was like mentioning the word sister was a hot button to emotional breakdown.

I let the phone ring but responded while I waited. "Makes sense. I only told him about it last week."

She stood so quickly that she swayed. Aspen caught her around the arm and hand to the belly. "You okay?"

"I have to get to Max. Jesus, this is the reason he's been so strange."

I looked around, not knowing what the big deal was. "If you say so," I said, not sure why the air had become so strained. Everything had been fine as far as I could tell.

"Hello?" Maddy answered. "Mia?"

Aww, there was my light. "Hey, baby girl," I responded and turned to look out onto the open landscape. The hills rolled in swaths of green speckled with orange flowers here and there. Way off in the distance, I could see the back of a red barn. To my right, I could see an outline of another barn, only this one was a pale yellow that matched the house. A big "C" was scrawled on the front above the doors. A few horses meandered around near the building at least two football fields away from where I stood. There were more animals I could barely distinguish in the distance. I made a mental note to go check out the barn and all the farm animals. I'd never been on a farm before. Maybe Max would teach me how to ride a horse. Two things I'd check off the proverbial bucket list. Farms and horseback riding.

"Where are you now, Sis?" Maddy asked.

"Dallas, Texas, on a full-on farm." Full-on farm. Farm

full. Farms full of farm. I snorted as I tried and failed to rethink how to say what I wanted to say correctly. The alcohol made things a tad fuzzy.

"Oh, no way! That's so cool. Do they have animals?"

I nodded, though she couldn't see it. "They do. And horses. I'm going to see if Max will take me for a ride."

"Man, you're so lucky. Matt and I just finished up an intense day of signing up for fall classes." Her voice changed, a hint of sadness so subtle it just barely lurked within the happiness she always exuded.

Turning around, I realized I wasn't alone. Cyndi and Aspen sat, watching me. Mostly Cyndi, as though she were hanging on every word I'd said. Aspen, on the other hand, would glance my way, smile, and suck down more lemonade. Hank would have a handful of tipsy blonde tonight if she kept up the drinking at the rate she was swallowing them down.

If Maddy was signing up for fall classes, that meant she was puttering around not doing much. In the past, when she was between semesters, we'd spend the time together. Now though, with me working for the service, I didn't have that luxury. "I'm sorry I can't come to Vegas and spend the break with you." I slumped back into the chair and put my hand to my temples rubbing out the thrum of stress that slowly crept in while thinking about how much I missed my girl.

Maddy sniffed, and I knew she was crying. "It's okay. I have Matt now…I guess."

"You guess? What changed?" I asked, instantly sobering up, the mama side in me coming fast and quick to the surface.

"Nothing. We're good. Really good, actually. Mia, he's

started talking about moving up the wedding."

Fear, heartache, and a devilish dose of anger hit me like a wrecking ball to the face. I felt like Wile E. Coyote chasing after that pesky roadrunner and never catching him, but always getting hurt in some ridiculously violent fashion.

"Maddy, you cannot marry him so quickly..." I swallowed down the giant lump in my throat, trying to let the voice of reason come through and not the overbearing sister.

Again with the sniffing, only this time, I could hear her let out the small snuffling sound I knew to be the waterworks. I'd spent years wiping those tears and comforting her enough to know exactly when she was dealing with something bigger than she was able to handle alone. I cursed our bastard father once more internally. If it wasn't for him, I'd be there now, helping her deal with whatever life changing thing was plaguing her. "I don't know, Mia. I want to be with him, but it's too fast." I shook my head along with her words. "We're so young, and just moved in together."

Trying to put on my sister hat and not my mama bear Fedora, I asked her the million dollar question. "Are you happy?"

"Oh my God, Mia, so happy. Everything's perfect. I mean, living together the past couple months has been a dream. We just click, you know?"

"I do." I felt that way about being with Wes, but didn't feel now was the time to mention my life change when she was struggling with something far more involved.

Cyndi scooted over close to me, her eyes worried. She pressed a hand to my knee, and I covered it with my own, needing the womanly solidarity as I worked through this with Maddy, hoping against all hope that I could convince her that she needed to wait. Take the time to be young and in love and not rush into such a huge life change.

Maddy sighed. "I feel like he just wants to hurry it all, and even though I know I want to marry him, and that he's it for me, I still want to take it slower, you know?"

I nodded rapidly and pushed my hair back behind my ear. "Did you tell him that?"

A groan came through the line, and I heard a plop. Almost as if she'd fallen back on a soft surface like her bed, cradling the phone to her ear, the same way she used to when she was a teenager living at home with Pops and me. "Yeah, but then he got all sad like, thinking I didn't really love him because I wouldn't elope. He wanted to go to the strip and do one of those quickie chapels all by ourselves. Said we'd keep it a secret and then do it big when we graduated, like we planned."

No, no, no, no. I pressed my thumbs into my temples so hard I might actually have left marks. With extreme effort, I took several slow breaths before responding. "And what did you say to that?"

There was a long pause before her voice cracked. "I told him that I could never get married without you there. That it would break your heart, and I'd rather walk across hot coals than hurt you. I love you, Mia. I could never do that. I promised you."

I sighed and gripped my hair at the crown so hard the pain brought a little clarity. "I love you too, Sis, but you can't make your decisions based on how I would respond. If that's what you want to do, even though it would make me sad to miss it, I'd support you."

The sob that tore through the phone broke me into a shattering mess of emotions. I wanted to be there for her, to hold her, help her through this confusing time in her life. "No, it's not just that. I do want you there. Period. And if Matt can't understand that, well, tough titty."

"Tough titty?" I snickered and repeated it on a chuckle. "Tough titty? Maddy I can't believe you just said that!" My prim and proper little sis had a bit of a mouth on her. One she'd never before used in front of me.

She laughed. "It just came out."

"Well, it was funny. And honey, don't worry. You and Matt will work this out. Part of being in a relationship, a real one, the forever kind, is working through the good, bad, and the ugly times. This is just one of those times where you're going to have to agree to disagree. Tell him how you feel. Explain that you want to wait, spend more time being engaged and focused on school. The rest will come. If he loves you, honey, which I know he does, he'll understand. Eventually. Don't let him pressure you into something you're not ready for, okay?"

Another sigh, and then I heard a noise in the background. Maddy gasped and then the phone crackled with static. "Baby, I'm sorry. I'm so sorry. I should have never tried to force you to get married now. I just love you so much. Forgive me. Forgive me. Don't leave me." I heard Matt's muffled plea through the line.

Then Maddy whispered, "I gotta go, Mia." Her voice was choked up again.

"Go get your man, baby girl. I love you." I wiped an errant tear that had trickled down my cheek.

"I love you more," she said and then hung up.

I clicked off the phone, crossed my arms over my chest and let the tears fall. Before I knew it, a set of big arms were around me, cuddling me close. "I miss her so much," I said into the rock-hard chest I found myself against for the second time that day.

Max squeezed me tight, and another hand rubbed up and down my back. Smaller, more feminine. Cyndi, I gathered.

"Let's bring your girl out to Texas," Max said into my hair where he kissed my temple the way I imagined a brother would do for his real sister. But I wasn't his sister and that thought made the tears come even harder.

Sniffing in his leather and male scent, I pressed my palms into his chest. Damn, he really was hard as steel. "I can't do that. You need me focused on the business, and besides, you've been so nice."

He shook his head, and his wife repeated the gesture. "Nope. We'd love to have her out if she can get away."

Technically, she was on school break my subconscious supplied helpfully. Then I remembered Matt. "She'd never come, anyway. She and her fiancé live together, very new, and I doubt he'd be okay with letting her come to Texas to be with a strange man."

Max frowned, and his wife looked around the room as if trying to find something else to focus on.

"I'm not strange to you. Besides, we'll bring them both out. We have plenty of room. The more the merrier," Max said.

I shot out of his arms, needing the space. The man's arms and comfortable nature clouded all judgment. "What? No. You can't do that. You don't even know them. Besides, why would you want to have my sister and her fiancé here? It doesn't make any sense."

"Would it make you happy? You said you missed her."

I shook my head, expecting a moment of clarity to hit at some point, but nothing happened. Just more fog and confusion. "Well, yeah, but this trip is not about me. It's about you and saving your assets."

That's when nice, sweet, down-to-earth Max changed. His eyes narrowed into slits, his lips pursed so tight they were a thin line, and he clenched his jaw so tight he could probably cut glass. "My assets mean nothing without the love of my family. So we'll bring your sister and her fella here. End of story. Cyndi, darlin', will you make that happen?" His request brooked no argument.

"Yes, honey. Mia and I will make it happen tomorrow. Go on, go calm down. Have a cigar and a scotch with Hank. I'll talk with her," she responded as if I weren't in the room. In the room, hell, as if I wasn't on the same god damned continent.

The stress of the day, spending quality time with Max, drinking the pink lemonade, talking Mads through her life decision, and now Max pushing his decisions on me had taken its toll. Stick a fork in me, I was done. D-O-N-E. I needed bed and about ten hours of sleep.

Without a word, I stormed off toward my room.

Cyndi called after me, catching me at the stairs. "Mia?"

"Tomorrow. Right now, I need some space and sleep. Can you just give me that, or do you need your husband to order you to leave me alone?" I snapped.

She gasped, and a pained expression stole across her features. Licking her lips, she nodded, turned, and waddled out of the room.

With a heavy heart, I climbed the stairs. I'd apologize to Cyndi tomorrow. She didn't deserve my wrath. It was just that not one thing since I'd come to Dallas made a lick of sense. Between Max's constant need to call me his sister, to the emotional breakdowns of not only Max but Maddy, I was drained. Now my client, the man who had hired me to do a job, wanted to bring my sister and her fiancé out to stay with us in Texas. Who the hell does that?

If I thought about it, really thought about it, most of the men I'd been hired by would have done the same thing if they'd seen me break down. I shouldn't have done that, had that conversation with Maddy in front of an audience. Only, when I was talking to her, and she was so stressed, reality was stripped away, and the one thing that mattered was making sure she was okay.

Maddy's happiness had been the one thing most important to me. Now it seemed as if I had all of these people around me who actually cared about what I thought, what I needed. I was barely getting used to Weston giving me that kind of attention, let alone a horde of other people I now considered friends.

Friends.

That was it. Is that how a friend responded? I mean, if I took Ginelle for instance, that crazy broad would move Heaven and Earth to ensure I was safe and happy. Whatever she could give me within her power, she'd attempt. Was this situation the same thing? Max and Cyndi attempting to be friendly? I guessed so. Hell, I didn't know. We hadn't been what one would consider friends very long. Was there a time limit on how long you needed to be friends before they started offering expensive plane tickets and week-long stays with extended members of your family? A month, a year, a decade?

Rubbing my eyes, I belly flopped onto the bed and snuggled in. Why did they care so much about a person who really wasn't their family? Overwhelmed and emotionally drained, I decided there wasn't anything I could do about it tonight. Sleep was in order. Tomorrow I'd deal with the overly generous Cunninghams, and I'd apologize to Cyndi for snapping at her and being rude. Everything would be clearer in the light of day.

CHAPTER SEVEN

Apparently the Cunninghams had absolutely no concern for another person's privacy. By the time I'd woken up and checked my phone, there were texts from both Weston and Maddy. I scanned them both while rubbing the sleep from my eyes. Maddy's message proved my point perfectly.

To: Mia Saunders
From: Maddy
OMG Matt and I are so excited about coming to Texas. Yee-haw! We'll be there Friday! Your friend Cyndi was really nice BTW. Totally cool. Booked us on a private plane!
To: Mia Saunders
From: Maddy
Did you get my last text?
To: Mia Saunders
From: Maddy
Private plane!! Eeek! So cool!

Jesus! It looked like little miss Cyndi-farm-girl worked fast. Somehow she got Maddy's number from my phone without me noticing it. Then I looked around the room. My outfit from yesterday was folded up and sitting on the dresser, and a quick tug at my clothes showed I was in a man's T-shirt. A really big T-shirt. Huge in fact. I exhaled on a long sigh. She'd changed me. Oh, man. Now I felt like a serious bitch. The sweet prego came into my room, found me face down, shoes and all, and took care of me. Even gave me one of her husband's shirts. Crap. I hope she didn't have Max help her. That would be doubly embarrassing. Then again, she did steal my phone and invade my privacy to do her husband's bidding, which put her firmly in the not all together peaches-and-cream category.

To: Mia Saunders
From: Wes Channing
Hey, sweetheart. Missed your voice last night. Let me know you're okay.

Without delay, I hit Weston's name and called him, needing that connection I only had with the man I'd now come to love with my whole being. Sitting on the bed and crossing my legs, I waited rather impatiently for him to answer.

Just as I thought I'd have to leave a message, his breathy tone came through the line. "Mia," he said in lieu of a greeting, "you okay?"

I snorted, thinking I was pretty far from okay but not in any real danger. Only the losing my mind kind. "Yeah. Sorry I didn't call last night. I think I fell asleep before my head even hit the pillow. It was a really long day. Unbelievably long."

"Oh, yeah, tell me about it. I've got some time now, and I missed you."

Hearing him say he missed me made my chest tighten and my sex quicken. Damn, the things this man did to me. A couple more weeks and I'd be doing something about it. At that point though, without the benefit of having his physical form to work out the tension I carried, I went through the entire day, even breaking boy code and telling him about Max's collapse at the company, even the way Cyndi reacted strangely around me as if she were walking on eggshells. I also told him about Max's cousin Sofia Cunningham and how she was less than pleased about my sudden appearance in the family, right when she was about to get a fat portion of that forty-nine percent take of Cunningham Oil & Gas. Then I explained the situation with Maddy and what went down last night, including how Cyndi had taken care of me and then invaded my personal things and contacted Maddy without asking me.

For a long time Wes didn't say anything. "Babe, you there?"

"Oh, yeah, I'm here. Just not too happy about everything you said. I knew it was odd when you told me about the job initially, and my investigator has found nothing but good things about the guy. He's solid, a family man, big in business and heir to the Cunningham Oil & Gas fortune. Apparently, the Cunninghams are keeping the sister and percentage deal under wraps because my guy said he couldn't find a word of it in his research."

"Really? Hmm, I guess it makes sense to keep it quiet until they figure it all out." I pushed a lock of hair back behind my ear and worried my lip. "Wes, it's hard being here. The more time I spend with this family, the more I wish it were real," I whispered, afraid if I said it any louder the truth might swallow me whole.

Wes exhaled loudly. "Sweetheart, I know you crave that connection. Just don't get too attached. Besides, you've got me and Maddy. We're your family. You'll always have a home with me, babe, and my family. And someday down the road, we'll be making that legal." His tone was matter of fact, but the words hit my heart like a shock to the system, fraying the edges of my nerves beyond distinction. I was now a ball of nervous energy awaiting the next magnetic pulse. *Holy fuck*. Did he just insinuate what I think he insinuated?

"Wes…" I warned, not wanting to address it at all, but knowing if I didn't, it would fuck with my head something awful.

"I know, I know. You're not ready for marriage talk." He chuckled, and it lightened the intensity of the conversation. "Just know, sweetheart, that I'm committed to you for good. Your home is with me and we are family now. Okay?"

Family. The mere suggestion of it prickled against my skin in a rather pleasant tingling sensation. "Yeah, baby. Okay. How's the movie-making biz going?" I asked, not wanting everything to always be about me and my problems.

"Good. Though I'm working through a romantic section I could use some real world help with." His voice took on that gravelly swallowed-a-box-of-rocks timbre that made me giddy with lust and achy for his touch. "Know any hot, long-legged brunettes with tits so big I salivate just thinking about them and an ass I could write an entire ten-page scene to?"

I laughed and twirled a lock of hair around my finger. "Hmm, I could think of someone," I said, using the sultry, raspy lilt I knew drove him wild.

He groaned. "Christ, sweetheart, I'm already hard."

"Mmm, pull it out." I could hear the sound of a zipper sliding down and a shuffling of clothing.

"Okay," he responded. The needy tone set my confidence-meter spiraling into space.

Leaning back against the headboard, I held the phone close to my ear so I could capture every breath. "Wrap your hand around the base and pretend it's my hand. Squeeze with just enough pressure, but go easy, not too much." He groaned. "Now lick your thumb and circle it around the tip. Think about my mouth sucking at the crown of your hard cock. Flicking my tongue against the little patch of skin that makes you crazy."

"Fuck, it's making me crazy now. Need you here, sweetheart," he moaned.

"I'm licking up and down your shaft, smooth and swift. I reach my hand down to cup and fondle your balls, and then take you down my throat in one swift suck. It's so deep I can hardly breathe, gasping around your length until you take mercy on me and pull back, giving me more room. You taste so good, like the sea and man. My man. Oh, baby, I'm so wet for you." I gasped and Wes's breath came in labored pants as I set the scene.

Throwing caution to the wind, I snaked a hand between my own legs and under the lace of my undies. "I'm soaked for you, Wes."

"You touching that pretty pussy?" he growled.

"Mmm, yeah, thinking about you tugging on your hard cock, imagining it's me is such a turn on, baby." I groaned and worked my clit in fast, tight circles. It didn't take long for me to start humping the air, reaching for a body that was fifteen hundred miles away.

"You almost there?" I asked when he groaned.

"Oh, yeah, you fucking that sweet cunt with your

fingers, nice and hard like I would?" The mental image roared through me, and thinking about how large his fingers were inside me sent a fresh flood of moisture through my sex.

"Yeah," I rasped and held my breath, pushing two fingers into the wet heat. I let the base of my hand crush my clit, sending tremors of pleasure from my center, up my chest, and out each limb. "Gonna come…"

"Me too. I'm yanking hard on my cock, thinking about how I'm going to take you up against the front door the second you get here a couple weeks from now. I'll tear your panties off and shove into you, pierce you with my dick so hard you'll never want to leave me again."

"Wes, Wes, Wes…" I chanted, lifting my hips, fucking myself, imaging him pounding me into the wooden surface. My guy loved fucking me against walls and doors. I pressed hard on the bundle of nerves that literally throbbed in time with the sound of his harsh breathing through the line, and my orgasm ripped through me. My entire body tightened, the sensitive tissue between my thighs clutching at the two fingers I still had imbedded deep inside. "God, yes! I love you," I whispered in the phone just as his voice rushed out in a stream of profanity.

"Fuck, baby. So good. Sexy, fucking woman. Christ. Mine. All mine," he roared into the phone, and I leisurely fingered my clit, letting the little jolts of pleasure work their way out as I listened to my guy get off on the thought of fucking me. Soon his breathing slowed. "Sweetheart…I love your voice. It's like liquid sex on the phone."

I giggled and held the phone tight to me ear. "I enjoyed hearing you come for me. Thanks for reciprocating."

He hummed. "Mmm, pleasure was all mine, Mia. I'll be busy tonight, but call me anyway. Leave me a message before you go to bed so I know you're okay. And remember, I love you."

I smiled huge. Being intimate with Wes, even by phone, gave me the second wind I needed to figure out how I was going to deal with the well-meaning Cunninghams.

"I love you too. Have a good day at work."

"You too, sweetheart. Call if you need me."

I wanted to tell him that I'd always need him, but that was too mushy even for me. Instead, I just waited until he hung up, clinging to the phone like it was my own personal lifeline.

★ ★ ★

That evening, a dream I'd had a few times over the years came back. I was around four years old and playing at special park-like area connected to one of the local Vegas casinos. A young boy with a mop of yellow curls on his head led me around by the hand.

"Dad says I have to keep an eye on you because he has a real important meeting with your mom." The boy was older than I was, maybe two times as old. He had funny looking hair and big teeth with a gap between the two front ones. *"How old are you?"*

"Four and a half," I answered as if I were much older than I looked.

He climbed up a small rock wall, went down on a knee, and held out his hand to help me climb. I put my foot on the nub tentatively until I realized that I could balance pretty well.

218

"I'm ten already. Double digits," he said with a sense of pride as if aging were something a person could win an award for, and he'd already gotten his trophy.

Instead of grabbing his hand, I pulled myself up. Even though I was really proud I'd made the climb, I pretended it was easy. "My pops says age is only a number. One that's best served on one of those black-and-white-and red wheels they have at Mommy's casino."

"Roulette?" His eyebrows came to a funny point.

I shrugged, not really sure, though Pops liked to hang out at the table that had it. That's where he was now. Playing that game. Mom was working her fancy show with that man. I knew it had to be really important because she wore these outfits with diamonds all over them and big feathers coming out of her hair and behind her back. The ones from her back almost touched the floor, and they were so soft. She would let me pet them, but I was never allowed to play with her fancy clothes. She said they were too expensive and worried I'd mess them up.

"My dad likes your mom," The boy said as he swung from one rung on the monkey bars to the other. I stood at the edge of the spot where he'd swung but couldn't reach the bars even on my tippy toes.

"Everyone likes my mom. She's an act-tress." My tongue got stuck rolling around the word Mommy said all the time. "If people don't like her, she's not doing her job right." I repeated what Mom told me before.

The boy nodded, his hair flopping over his eyes. He pushed the strands away, and his intense green eyes stared back at me. People told me all the time that my eyes were like a cat's, but I thought this boy's eyes looked more like a cat's. Kind of like Mom's. "Well, my daddy says he wants to marry your mommy and be a *family. That would make you my sister."*

I frowned. "He can't marry my mommy because she's already got my dad. With a ring and everything."

The boy's eyes narrowed. "Really? I don't think he knows that." His happy face turned sad. "I was hoping for a mommy and yours is pretty and nice."

I shook my head. "She's not very nice, just good at pretending to be nice."

His head tipped to the side. "Is she mean to you?"

Walking over to the swings, I sat down. "No. But she doesn't like me as much as my friends' mommies like them."

He got behind me, pulled back the swing, and pushed me forward, giving me a good head start. I would be able to keep it up now that he got it going. Then he went over to the other swing and sat but didn't move it. "Then I don't want her as my mommy."

"Yeah, maybe your daddy could pick a nicer one?" I offered.

"That's a good idea. I think I'll help him find me a really nice and pretty one. Maybe you could help me?"

I smiled wide and dragged my foot on the ground stopping the swing. "That would be fun."

The boy and I spent the next hour or so walking around the casino, holding hands, pointing out women that could be his new mommy. Unfortunately, we couldn't agree on the right woman before his dad and my mommy found us. She was crying, and when she got down on one knee, she shook me and screamed that we were supposed to stay at the playground. The man got down at eye level with the boy, put both hands on his shoulders, and scolded him, but the boy didn't cry. He apologized, and his dad told him how scared he was and hugged him tight. My mom didn't hug me at all. The boy looked at me with sadness in his eyes over his dad's shoulder, mouthing, "sorry." I waved and watched as the man grabbed Mom's hand, pulled her close, and kissed her.

The boy's dad kept kissing Mommy until she shoved him away and told him to stop. He asked her to come with him, to bring me and run away, leave this life and go with him. Right then, my pops walked up, showing Mom a bucketful of chips. He lifted me up, spun me around, and hugged me hard, the way he always did. My pops gave the best hugs. Then he showed Mom the bucket and pulled her into his side, saying we were going to a steak dinner. She smiled and turned away from the boy and the man as if she'd never even known them.

I watched as the man's shoulders slumped and his head hung forward. He put his hand on the boy's shoulder and the boy waved goodbye to me.

I woke with a start, the dream still so vivid it was as if I could hear the ping and trill of the casino all around the room, see the slot machines and the bright lights blinking on and off. Closing my eyes, I slumped back down under the duvet, flattened my pillow, and turned it over to the cold side. Usually, I could control my dreams enough that I could go back to them or think about what I wanted to and dream of that. This time when I closed my eyes, I went head first into another memory.

Mom and Dad were fighting again. Maddy was with Aunt Millie back at the house. It was her fourth birthday, and we were picking up her present. Pops wanted to visit Mom at work and make sure she was going to be home in time for the party. Mom didn't think it was fair that she had to cut work short to celebrate a four-year-old's birthday. Said that Maddy would never remember it anyway, so what did it matter?

That's when a man bumped into the two of them on the street. A teenager stood next to him and caught Mom around the waist. She turned, ready to yell at the intruder even though they were being helpful. I knew instantly it was the boy from the past only much older. The father looked unchanged. He even wore a big cowboy hat like he'd worn that day a few years before. When Mom saw his face, she turned white as a ghost and backed into Pops. He caught her this time.

"Meryl?" the man said to my mom, whose hands shook at her side. "My God, it's been years. Uh, this is, this..."

"Maxwell." Her voice broke as she said the young teen's name.

Max. That's right. His name was Max. Only I'd forgotten that before. The teen tipped his own cowboy hat and responded, "Ma'am," before shoving his hands into his jeans pockets. I could still see the blond curls of his hair peeking out from beneath his wide black hat. Then he glanced at me. Those pale green eyes sparkled with kindness as he tipped his hat toward me. "Howdy, little miss," he said, and I smiled. I'd wondered if he remembered me from before, but I doubted it.

"Who's this?" Pops asked Mom.

"Uh, this is an old friend. Jackson Cunningham and his son...Maxwell." It was as if her voice cracked under the sheer pressure of having to say the boy's name. Pops held out his hand and introduced himself. Jackson's blue eyes never left my mom's. Hers never left Max's. There was something there within her gaze, a secret hidden so deep, I knew the truth would break us all if it came out into the light of day.

The five of us stood there awkwardly, Jackson staring blatantly while Mom seemed to shrivel into herself. Pops finally broke through the moment by tugging my hand and announcing we were late for an important event.

"Um, yeah, we have to go. It was good seeing you, Jackson. I hope you and Max, uh, your son, have been well."

"Wait, Meryl, let's exchange numbers." Jackson *reached out a hand as Mom shook her head and skirted his grasp, trailing after Pops and me.* "Don't, Meryl. Not again..." *His plea was almost a whisper in the wind.*

"It's for the best. You're better off."

The alarm clock sounded, but all I could hear were those seven words rolling around and around within the clutches of the dream, but more recently, in my very own walk down the hellish path that was memory lane.

"It's for the best. You're better off." I squeezed my eyes together tight, trying not to remember.

"It's for the best. You're better off." Her voice was soft, sounding almost like a song.

"It's for the best. You're better off." The scent of her perfume swirled through the air of my bedroom long after she'd gone.

"Mia, my darling..." I vaguely remembered her petting my forehead while I clung to sleep, only ten years old with my princess-themed comforter, too hot, but tucked tight around me. She kissed my hairline and whispered those very same words. *"It's for the best. You're better off."*

That was when my mother left and never came back. For a long time, I'd blocked that memory, thinking it wasn't real, that I'd imagined it. The same way I'd blown off the dreams about the boy and his father. Only they weren't dreams. They were memories, ones that made one thing clear as day.

I knew Maxwell Cunningham and his father knew my mother.

CHAPTER EIGHT

"Max, we need to talk," I said as I entered the kitchen. Cyndi was making a big belly breakfast, complete with pancakes, bacon, and eggs. My stomach growled loudly as the scent of bacon wafted around the kitchen.

Cyndi pointed to an empty plate at the table while Max loaded it up full of all the fixings. I sat like an elephant— my legs, too tired from holding the weight of my burdens, collapsed beneath me. "Here, eat. We do need to explain a few things," he said gruffly.

Before I could start, Cyndi interrupted. "Now, I know you're probably mad," she started while setting down a steaming cup of coffee in front of me. With an efficiency I knew I'd never had, she plopped in two teaspoons of sugar and a splash of cream, remembering exactly how I took my coffee. Things like that added to her overall lovely nature. She paid attention to the small things. The little tidbits that made a person feel comfortable, like how they took their coffee in the morning. "I'll start by saying I'm sorry," Cyndi announced.

"No, you're not," I stated plain as day, watching her face closely to see if there truly was even a speck of remorse.

Her blue eyes rolled, and she stopped and pressed a hand to her belly, the egg crusted spatula hovering in the air in the other hand. "You're right. I'm not sorry. You need your sister here, and we need to meet them."

They *needed* to meet them. That was the part that threw me for a loop. "Why? What goes on between me and my sister has nothing to do with you or your husband or his business." I glanced at Max and he looked down, doing a great job of avoiding the conversation and pushing his uneaten eggs around his plate. Max not shoveling the food down his gullet was another thing that stuck out. The man liked to eat. Meaning, every time I'd ever seen him eat, he'd clear two plates of food before anyone else in the near vicinity could remotely finish one.

Max sighed deeply, his entire body heaving with the effort. "We've come to care a great deal for you, Mia. Can you just accept that and let the rest go?"

I huffed, picked up a fat slice of bacon, and shoved it in my mouth. The crisp texture and salty, meaty goodness flowed over my taste buds like a blanket of perfection. Bacon. God's perfect food. I chewed thoughtfully for a few moments, thinking about how I wanted to address this. Yes, they were being kind, overly so. But—and it was a pretty big but—they had done this without consulting me. It's my life, my family, not theirs. They needed to understand the severity of what they've done.

"Look, Max, Cyndi…" I gestured to them both. She put down the spatula, turned off the burner, and waddled over to her husband. He looped an arm around her waist while she gripped his shoulder. They presented a united front, and something about that didn't sit well with me. Regardless, I had a point to make, and by God, I'd make it. "You cannot meddle in my life. I am here to do a job. One you've paid a hefty fee for. Even though we've become friendly, it does not give you the right to home in on my problems. You are my client. I am essentially a hired hand, not your family. What you did, bringing Maddy and her fiancé here, was so far out of bounds, outside of anyone's comfort zone…" I shook my head, not knowing how to finish what I needed to get across without crucifying them.

"You overstepped a line." My own voice shook with the anger bubbling at the core of the problem.

Max inhaled and nodded. "I'll speak for my wife and myself when I say that we regret the way we invaded your life, but please know that our intentions were in the right place."

"Yeah, well, the road to hell is paved with good intentions." I pursed my lips together and brought a knee up to my chest, balancing it on the chair. "Please remember your place. I think the lines are getting blurred here. I am pretending to be someone to help fool your investors until you find your *real* sister. As much as I wish it were true…I'm not your sister. You do not get to act like the big brother saving his little sis."

Saying that put it out there in black and white. Max clenched his jaw and closed his eyes. Cyndi leaned down, kissed his temple, and whispered something that sounded a little like, "Tell her," into his ear, but I couldn't be sure.

Several excruciating minutes of an uncomfortable silence passed until, finally, Max opened his eyes and loosened his hold on his wife. "Okay, Mia. I get it. We'll play it your way."

"Max honey—" Cyndi started, but Max threw a hand up cutting her off.

He shook his head, eyes laser-focused on me. "Can we move on from this?" he asked me, his tone now that of a hard and fast businessman.

I nodded and played with my napkin, suddenly feeling as if I were in the wrong somehow. The conversation turned so quickly that I didn't even have a chance to bring up the dreams, or memories rather, before he stood abruptly, his chair grating along the tile floor. "Got to get ready for work, Mia. Today is a suit day."

"A suit?"

His chin jutted. "We're meeting with the investors. Time to put that sisterly facade into place." He grumbled in a way that sent pointed spikes deep into the tough barrier around my heart. The one that I'd just barely put in place this morning after finding out they'd duped me. Admittedly, his words stung. No, they downright hurt. My concerns were valid, and he was the one that overstepped his authority, not me. So why did I feel like the scum on the bottom of a landfill worker's shoe?

"When do we leave?" I asked around a mouthful of eggs.

"Forty-five minutes. Cyndi honey, I'll be on the porch. I need some air," he muttered and walked off.

I finished my breakfast and thought about how I was going to get him back into the jovial mood he'd been in most of the time I'd been here, but I couldn't come up with anything. And of course, now with tension between the two of us, we had to meet with the committee of investors and present this new sibling relationship, making it believable enough that they'd forgo transferring the ownership for the time being.

★ ★ ★

The ride to Cunningham Oil & Gas was suffocating. Max turned on the music and didn't utter a word to me the entire ride. Every once and a while the air would shift, and I'd see him tighten or loosen his grip on the wheel. It made me think he was going to say something, but then he'd exhale and focus on the road again.

When we exited the truck, he still came around to my side, ever the gentleman, and helped me out of the vehicle. The suit I'd worn fit like a glove. I felt strong, powerful, and ready to take on a bunch of stodgy businessmen. The pencil skirt reached an acceptable length with a slit in the back at a decent height. Nothing too provocative. The blouse I'd paired it with was a mint green, showcasing my eyes. The blazer nipped in at the waist and the gray color set off my hair beautifully. Whoever picked it out had done a great job.

As we entered the building, every woman within a fifty-foot radius checked out Max. He did look scrumptious in his black suit and pristine white dress shirt. At his neck, a bolo tie of black twisted leather met at the top in the shape of a star, one that matched the company's logo. He'd finished off the look with a perfect pitch black Stetson, his blond hair peeking out the back. I smiled and clasped his hand. He inhaled sharply and curled his fingers around my hand. A jolt of electricity and familiarity sizzled at the center of my palm.

"Do you feel that?" I asked, wanting more than anything to know he felt that connection between us. It wasn't sexual in nature like I'd experienced with other men I'd been intimate with. It just felt right, holding his hand. As though the universe had stuck us together and we were supposed to be there at that moment, unified—connected in a way I couldn't seem to fathom.

He tipped his head toward me. "Sugar, I've felt the connection to you for eons. Ever since I met you that first time when we were little."

I swallowed down the sob that wanted to tear through my lungs. "You knew?"

He nodded. "I remembered you the moment you got off the plane, but it's more than that. A tug, if you will. Like a missing part of myself is somewhere else, moving around the earth. A piece I can't touch or see, but I know is there."

I shook my head and squeezed his hand tighter. "I don't understand. It's like I know you, but I don't know you."

Max put his arm around my shoulders and pulled me close to his chest. A warm sense of peace and serenity filled my heart and my entire being. "It will be okay. We'll figure it out. First, we need to get through today and this meeting. It's go-time, darlin'." He ushered me off the elevator. My mind was a mix of nostalgia intermingled with the present.

I briefly closed my eyes and saw the boy from my dreams, his eyes so closely matching my own. Shaking the thoughts away, I lifted my chin and tightened my jaw. Jutting out my ample bosom while straightening my spine, I readied for battle. No matter what was going down between Max and me and our convoluted past, the present was now. His birthright, the company his family had owned for generations and built from the ground up, depended on these investors believing I was his sibling. I clutched his hand tightly as he opened the glass door to the enormous boardroom that overlooked the lush landscape and campus beyond the acres of trees.

"Bring it," I whispered, and he chuckled.

Max led me to a chair at the front of the room. There were only two empty ones left, and at least two dozen more filled with bodies also wearing suits. In the seat three down from the one that Max held out for me was Sofia Cunningham. Her sneer and distaste for me was palpable as I smoothed down the back of my skirt and sat tall. Max didn't sit. Instead, he stood behind his chair and placed his hands on the backrest.

"Ladies and gentleman, I have called today's meeting to bring to light a most exciting development. As you all recall, several months ago, my father, Jackson Cunningham, surprised us all with his will. At his passing, we were informed that forty-nine percent of Cunningham Oil & Gas was bequeathed to my biological half-sister, a woman five years my junior who I'd not known existed." Murmured chatter picked up between small groups throughout the room.

"Quiet, please!" Max spread his arms out wide, and the talking stopped. "My father's last wishes noted the name and birth date of the woman with whom I share a lineage. Her name is Mia Saunders. Born July fourteenth, five years after I was born. This person to my left is that woman. I am immensely proud to introduce you to my sister, a woman I have only recently begun to get to know, but already feel that familial bond, Ms. Mia Saunders. Stand up, Sis."

I stood and every single pair of eyes in the room zeroed in on me. A bunch of whispered comments reverberated through the room.

"They look nothing alike."
"I can see it in the eyes."
"She's beautiful."

231

"The resemblance is there."
"No way that's his sister. Look at her."
"Her hair is black. His is blond. They are not related."

This time, when Maxwell quieted the room, it was on a mighty roar. "Enough!"

The faces around the table looked chagrinned and some completely put out. Finally, Sofia raised her hand.

Maxwell tipped his head. "Sofia? You have a comment?"

Sofia placed her hands delicately in front of her on the mahogany conference table, the perfect picture of reason. "As a member of this family and an investor, you cannot expect all the members of the committee and investors around the room to take your word as fact on this matter. There are billions at stake, and generations of Cunninghams have put their good name to this. What proof do you have that this is indeed your blood relation?"

I stared at Max and watched he tightened his fingers, digging into the black leather chair enough to leave crescent-shaped indentations from his nails. "My word, and my honor as this company's CEO and head of the family, should be enough, is it not?" He challenged Sofia in front of a roomful of their peers.

Her eyes were blazing hot, and her devilish smirk proved what I already had guessed. Nothing but solid, irrefutable proof would be enough to get her to back off. The woman was out for blood and her share of the money. A shockwave of fear scuttled down my spine as I worried my fingers in my lap, twisting them back and forth, wondering how Max was going to get her off the trail.

He tipped his head and stared at his cousin. "If proof

is what you need, proof is what you'll get." He waved a hand and little Diane, his cheerful personal assistant, briskly entered the room with a remote control clutched in her hand. She was followed in by a sharply dressed African American woman in a winter-white suit. The suit was so bright against her ebony skin that a wave of jealously stole across me. Black women had the best skin, and this woman was breathtaking. Her hair was done in a series of braids tight to the scalp and tied back at the nape, where they fell in ropes down to her bum. Beautiful.

"Thank you, Diane." Maxwell smiled, and she beamed, patted him on the chest directly over his heart, and crossed over to the two chairs in the corner of the room and sat in one of them. The gorgeous black woman followed, sliding her briefcase beside her chair, and taking her seat, her back ramrod straight. The bright red sole of her sky-high Louboutins gleamed when she gracefully placed one knee over the other. I needed hot "sista" girlfriends. They always seemed to know how to dress. I could take some serious notes on business chic from a woman like that.

Max clicked a few buttons on the remote control, and an LCD screen zipped down from the back wall, the light at the center of the room shining onto the blank screen. A few more presses and a picture of my Nevada driver's license popped up.

Without missing a beat, Max spoke. "You want proof. Exhibit A. Mia Saunders's driver's license proving not only her name is exactly the same as what was written in the will but her birth date as well." That confused me. I'd thought Millie and Max confirmed that the name was written in a way that you couldn't confirm what was stated. I'd have to check on that after the fact.

"Is that enough for you, or do you need more?" His question was directed at Sofia.

"Anyone can fake a license." She waved a hand at the screen, seeming utterly put out.

"Okay, then, Exhibit B. Mia Saunders's social security card proving her name and her citizenship. Shall I continue?"

Sofia huffed and responded haughtily, "By all means. You're doing such a great job. Though I haven't seen anything that couldn't be refuted in a court of law."

The next slide stole my breath. Tears built and threatened to fall. I tapped the corners of each eye and stared at the screen, lost in a tornado of memories.

"That is a picture my father had of my mother holding me, next to a picture of Mia. The resemblance is uncanny," he croaked and cleared his throat.

How could that be? That image was absolutely my mother, much younger, but her nonetheless. I would know her anywhere. And in the picture, she was holding a toddler, perhaps around a year old with blond curls like a halo around the baby's head. I shook my head, and the tears fell unchecked.

The volume of chatter had reached a fevered pitch.

Sofia's voice was strained yet she plowed ahead. I had to give it to her. She was the definition of tenacious. "A lot of people look alike, Max."

He nodded. "True, but there's more." He held a hand out to the smart-looking woman and waved her over.

"Members of the committee, my name is Ree Cee Zayas, and I'm the attorney for the late Jackson Cunningham and Maxwell Cunningham. Mr. Cunningham hired me to prove the legitimacy of Mia Saunders's birthright and familial lineage." Her voice was cool, calm, and educated. I liked her instantly, but immediately feared the next words she was going to say.

"If you will look at the screen, you will see a copy of Maxwell Cunningham's birth certificate from Dallas, Texas next to Mia Saunders's birth certificate from Las Vegas, Nevada. As you can see, the woman listed as mother—one Meryl Colgrove and her social security number, shown clearly on both legally binding documents—is exactly the same. This document would be binding in a court of law and proves that Maxwell Cunningham and Mia Saunders share the same birth mother."

The room went silent. Absolutely nothing could be heard. A shockwave of sensations hit me hard. I stopped breathing and trembled under the proof staring me in the face. Unaware of the tidal wave of emotions battering me into a loopy mess, the tears poured down my cheeks. Maxwell heard the shift in my voice as I swallowed a sob. He crouched next to me, one knee on the floor, clasping my hands painfully. I didn't care. I was numb, shaken to my core.

Max placed his lips over my hands and kissed the tops over and over again. "I should have told you the truth," he whispered. "For-Forgive me." His own feelings overwhelmed the words so much that he stuttered with the effort to get them out.

I was incapable of responding, but that wasn't the end. No, the beautiful woman I would later come to think of as the "dark angel of life-changing events" didn't stop there. "Due to the extreme nature of the birthright and the monetary amount at stake within the company, I felt it prudent to go deeper and a DNA test was done. A sample of hair was taken from Ms. Saunders's hairbrush and the results were compared to the results from Mr. Cunningham. You'll see on the screen that the results are conclusive: Maxwell Cunningham and Mia Saunders share identical maternal genetic markers that prove beyond a shadow of a doubt that they are indeed half brother and sister, issue of the same mother."

That's when I lost it, as did the rest of the room. I couldn't hear myself think over the roar of conversations at the table. I just sat there, unmoving, trying to pull the pieces of my life into something resembling a reality I could understand. Nothing came. No amazing bouts of wisdom, no perfectly placed analogies to explain away how the little boxes and lines on the screen in front of me had ultimately changed my life...forever. I was no longer Mia Saunders, the girl who raised her baby sister, whose mother left her at ten, with a father who was a knock-down drag-out drunkard. I wasn't just the woman who was ass-over-tits in love with a man far better than she was. It was all becoming clear to me that I was more.

I, Mia Saunders, was Maxwell Cunningham's biological sister. A man at the helm of an empire and family I knew absolutely nothing about. The documentation could not be denied. Max was my half-brother.

"Mia, Mia, sugar, please, say something. Anything," Max pleaded from his position on his knees in front of me. I looked down into the exact same pale green eyes that my mother gave to me, to Maddy, and also to him.

"You're my brother." The words came out of my mouth on a gasp.

Max nodded. "I am." He scanned my face, as if he were looking directly into my soul and seeing a piece of himself.

"My *real* brother," I repeated.

"Yes. And you, you're my baby sister." He swallowed and licked his lips. The lines around his eyes seemed more pronounced, under the weight of what he'd been keeping hidden inside.

"Oh my God. I can't…" I sucked in a breath. "Maddy!" Tears fell down my cheeks, and he cupped my face and wiped them away with his thumbs, caressing my cheekbones.

"Yes. Now you understand why it was so important to get her here. She deserves to know the truth."

I closed my eyes and thought about Maddy and what this information would do to her, to our family dynamic. In a flourish, I pushed back the chair, Max's hands going to the floor to catch the weight of his large frame. Standing, I scanned the area for the nearest exit.

The need to flee was strong, a prickly, painful sensation, like an exposed nerve being zapped with electrical pulses, and I realized the full severity of the situation. This was no longer pretend. Max had brought me here because he'd known this information all along and waited until we were in front of all of these strangers to disclose the truth.

I'd wanted to be Maxwell's real sister. Had contemplated it several times over the past ten days. At that moment, things were so jumbled up in my brain I wanted to scream, scratch, and howl until everything, my life, but more importantly, the truth was put back together and Pandora's box closed tight and buried never to be found again. I bolted out of the room with the single thought—*be careful what you wish for, because it might come true and leave your entire world hanging in the balance.*

CHAPTER NINE

The hood of the truck was cool to the touch, chilling my palms as I leaned against it, bending over at the waist, looking down at my feet.

Just breathe. In…Out…In…Out. Repeat. It will all make sense soon.

I repeated the mantra over and over until the sound of gravel crunched underfoot behind me and a pair of black cowboy boots entered my vision. He didn't speak for a long while, which I appreciated. Eventually the jack hammering of my heart dulled to a normal rate, and I stood and turned around, allowing the front of the truck to hold me up.

Max stood before me, shoulders slumped, and a deep frown marring his otherwise handsome face. His eyes, mirrors of my own, were cloudy and uncertain. "Mia, I—"

I held up a hand to stop any further excuses. "You knew, and you didn't tell me."

He inhaled, brought both hands in front of him, and cracked his knuckles. "There's no excuse. It's just I wanted to get to know you, spend time, maybe allow the truth to come out naturally…"

"Naturally, as in a room full of fucking strangers when I can't react! What the hell were you thinking, Max?" I yelled, not holding a lick of anger back. "Right now, all I can think is why would you want to hurt me?" I sucked in a harsh breath as the tears threatened again.

Max lifted his hands and walked over to me. I couldn't back up or flee as his arms bracing me in against the hard metal of the truck prevented further movement. "Mia, I'd never willingly hurt you. That wasn't supposed to come out like that. I didn't know Sofia was going to ask all those questions, and it all happened so fast." He shook his head. "Christ on a cross. You're my sister. Sugar, I already love you." His pale eyes turned dark and stormy as his jaw clenched, and a muscle at the dip of his chin ticked. "Mia, I'd die before intentionally allowing anything to hurt you."

I closed my eyes, not able to watch the honesty break us both. He loved me. My brother. I had another living, breathing sibling. Holy shit, this was intense and I didn't know the first fuck how to handle it. All I knew is that I had to get out of there. "Take me home."

"To Vegas?" His voice broke.

"No. God!" I blew out a breath. "Back to the ranch. I need time. And I need to figure out how the hell I'm going to tell Maddy about this."

Max nodded, unlocked the truck door, and opened it for me. He got in and started up the truck. When we were about ten minutes from the ranch, he covered my knee with his hand. "I know this doesn't mean much right now, and I know you're trying to digest all this, but I'm really glad you're my sister. After Dad died, before we found his will, I was completely lost. When I found out I had a sister, someone who shared my blood, it gave me a new purpose. Something good and right to focus on. When I saw your picture on that site, looking exactly like my mother... I knew it was all going to come together as it should. That finally, I wouldn't feel alone."

"But you have Cyndi and Isabel, and soon, your son. You're never alone." I covered his hand over my knee and squeezed, the ice in my heart melting at his admission.

He nodded. "Yes, and they are the most perfect part of my future. But there's something special 'bout sharing a parent. Like we're two sides of the same coin. I also had this feeling, like I told you. Then when I saw you and remembered that we'd met a couple times a long time ago, I just knew it was true."

I licked my lips and stared out the window. "My entire life I've dreamed about you. Well, I didn't know it was *you*, but a boy who played with me at a playground." Then I laughed, remembering the hunt we'd been on. "And how we walked around looking to find you a new mommy."

He grinned. "Yeah, I've thought about that first time a lot, wondering whatever happened to that woman Dad seemed to be taken with and her daughter. Now it makes more sense. The way I see it, Dad was chasing after our mother when she didn't want to be caught."

I huffed and crossed my hands over my chest. "Yeah, well, my pops couldn't hold onto her either. Do you know where she is?"

Maxwell shook his head and maneuvered the car around a dead skunk on the road. "Never tried to look for her."

"With your money and connections, I'd imagine it would be pretty easy for you."

He glanced at me from the corner of his eyes but kept his focus on the road. "It would. Only problem, sugar, is that when a woman up and leaves her baby and then remarries, has a family for a decade, and up and leaves them too, she obviously doesn't want to be a part of any of their lives or she wouldn't have left. Sometimes people just don't want to be found, or they wouldn't have run away in the first place.

I rolled the logic around in my head as we drove up to his ranch. He definitely made sense, but the lingering feeling I had about the way Mom left, especially after recalling it in the dream last night, made me consider another alternative.

"Do you ever think that maybe she wanted someone to come running after her?"

Max turned off the truck, removed the Stetson, and ran his fingers through hair. "You know, I never thought of it like that. What do you think?" He turned sideways in the truck. We stared at one another for a few moments.

"I think our mother screwed up a lot. When someone is used to screwing up, a lot of times they don't want that trouble to taint the only good things they have in their lives. Maybe she loved us more than we ever thought possible."

Max closed his eyes and frowned. "If that's the case, maybe we should at least look into it."

"I agree." Decision made. Max would use his resources, and we'd track down our mother. I had a few choice questions to ask her. Number one being why she never told us we had a brother.

★ ★ ★

The moment the limo door opened and my sister's blond hair went flying in the breeze, I lost my ability to breathe. Madison Saunders, my baby sister, was a vision in cropped pants, wedge heals, and a simple tank. Maddy held out her purse, and Matt barely grasped it when she was off at a run toward me, arms as wide as her smile. I braced and waited for her weight to hit me. When it did, it was like a cloud of love had wrapped its arms around me and filled my entire being with joy.

Maddy squealed in my ear. Usually I'd spin her around and play the goofy big sister, but this time I held on so tight it would take a crowbar to break me away. The sense of fear that came with letting her go, not having her close, swarmed around me in a thick fog. The girl had always been my everything, and I knew as excited as I was to see her, there was the burden of information and truth weighing this visit down.

Easing out of my arms, Maddy frowned, cupped my face, and pressed her forehead to mine. "What's the matter? Why are you sad?" She brushed the wetness from my cheeks, wiping away tears I didn't know were there.

Clearing my throat, I took a slow breath. "Just missed you is all." I attempted to pacify her.

Her eyelids narrowed into slits. "You're not being honest with me. I don't like it, but I'll grill you when we're alone."

I half-laughed half-snorted. "Okay, baby girl. Let me look at you!" I held her at arm's length, and she brightened like the sun peeking out on a cloudy day. "Most beautiful girl in all the world but…"

"Only when she smiles," Matt chimed in. He tugged her waist, pulling her to his side and out of the comfort of my arms. He'd pay for that move.

I narrowed my eyes at him. "That's my line!"

He chuckled. "I know." He waggled his eyebrows. "Maddy has told me that a million times! I can't wait to hear her say it to our children one day." He nuzzled noses with my sister, and I wanted to gag and hug him in equal parts.

A booming voice behind me cleared his throat or cursed. I wasn't really sure.

"Maddy, there's uh, some people I'd like you to meet." Turning around, I found Maxwell holding his wife Cyndi. Isabel was jumping up and down the porch steps behind them lost in her own world, as was the way of most four-year-olds.

Max's eyes were huge, his mouth open unattractively. Cyndi's eyes also had that deer-in-the-headlights look, only she had a hand covering her open mouth. Neither of them said a word as I clutched Maddy's hand and took her closer.

"Uh, guys, hello?" I waved my other hand in front of both of them, and they seemed to snap out of it at the same time.

"Jesus…" Max whispered.

Cyndi gasped a throaty, "Oh. my god."

I turned to Maddy. "They're usually not so weird, but this is Maxwell Cunningham and his wife, Cyndi. Guys, this is my baby sister, Madison Saunders, and her fiancé, Matt Rains."

Maddy's eyebrows rose as Max and Cyndi continued to stare. Maxwell's eyes didn't leave her face. It was as if he'd been stunned with a Taser, his mouth slightly ajar, his eyes bouncing around unusually slow.

Cyndi spoke first, but what she said wouldn't make any sense to Maddy. "She looks… Jesus, she looks exactly like you." The statement was made as if she had also been struck with the stun gun.

"It's unreal," Max finally said, his head tilting to the side.

Matt looped an arm around Maddy's waist and tugged her back a step. "What's going on here? You two look like you've seen a ghost."

He said the exact words I was thinking myself. Though, it had to be strange seeing your sister for the first time, especially one that looked so similar to you. I clutched at my fingers as the two sized up my sister awkwardly. I worried that they'd spill the beans without even trying to before I had a chance to tell her myself. Finding out she had another sibling needed to come from me.

Eventually, Isabel pushed between her parents' legs and looked up at the new guest. "Wow! You're pretty like a princess." Isabel patted Maddy on the leg. She bent down to one knee so the little girl could see her face-to-face. Both Maddy and I had always been good with kids, but Maddy had special kid-friendly powers. They were attracted to her like a teenager to his game system. The little girl grabbed hold of a lock of Maddy's hair. Her little eyes went big. "Yellow like mine and my daddy's!"

I looked at the little girl's face and saw the similarity between Maddy and the little girl, and then looked up at Maxwell with new eyes. Their hair was the same golden blond. Even their skin tone and the shape of their faces matched. If anything, *they* actually looked like siblings, whereas Max and I had some minor similarities. Side by side, these two were eerily alike.

Maddy glanced at Max and smiled. That's when it happened. Recognition. Not only did the sizzle of familiarity buzz in the air around our huddle, but seeing little Isabel's face next to Maddy's, their twin smiles exact matches of the other, I saw a third in Maxwell. It was like looking into a

AUDREY CARLAN

microscope and reading genetic code, only this was live and in living color. Physically, Maxwell, Maddy, and his daughter Isabel shared the same smile, but not with our mother or me. I had been told over and over that Meryl and I shared the same exact smile. I'd always thought Maddy had some of Pops's features, but at that moment, I couldn't remember a single time I'd compared the two and found them similar.

Maddy petted Isabel's head. "And what's your name?" she asked.

"Isabel, but also Bell, too."

Maddy tapped Isabel's nose. "Well, I think you're the prettiest little girl I've ever seen, so if you think I look like a princess, that must make you the queen!" She gasped and put her hand across her chest. Isabel giggled sweetly. "Maybe we can play some games while I'm here visiting, after I've gotten to know your mom and dad and spend some time with my sister. How does that sound?"

"So much fun!" she squealed and clapped her hands. Then like a shot in the night, she twirled around and ran up the stairs hollering, "I'll get my crown!" as she clomped up each wooden step and slammed the screen door as she ran into the house.

Maddy chuckled and stood, putting out a hand. "Happy to meet friends of Mia's. And thanks again for sending a plane and a limo. It's the first time I've been in a limo!" She grinned.

Max shook his head as if he were shooing away flies. "The pleasure was all mine, sweetie. Come, come on in." He held out a hand, leading the way up the porch. "Cyndi has a full spread of some of her best country dishes. Chicken fried steak, fried okra, homemade mac-n-cheese, and fresh baked pecan pie."

Having spent the last two weeks eating Cyndi's meals, my mouth started to water. "Seriously, her food is the best. Come on."

"Lead the way," Maddy responded.

I clasped hands with my sister and nudged her shoulder. "Thank you for coming. I missed you."

Maddy leaned against my shoulder the way she had a hundred times before over the years. "Any chance I get to see you is one I have to jump on. Especially flying on a private jet!" She laughed. "Oh my God, you should have seen it. Matt and I were served champagne…on an airplane!" Her voice rose along with her excitement. "And they didn't even check our IDs!" she whispered so only I'd hear what she said.

Sister secrets were commonplace between the two of us, only that was about to change. A pang hit my heart. Max was her sibling now too, and I had the huge, overwhelming responsibility of figuring out a way to tell her that.

It had only ever been Maddy, Pops, and me. The trio of lonely hearts whose wife and mother left them for God only knows what. Now I knew there was an entirely new part of us, a piece that had far reaching repercussions on who we were and what type of family we were going to be in the future. Even the addition of Matt had been something I hadn't had a chance to get used to yet. I wondered if Maddy had even had that chance herself with her school load and all the recent changes to her life.

It was a lot for a young woman of only twenty to deal with. Her father in a coma, her sister gallivanting around the world as an escort, newly engaged, living with said fiancé, and now a brother comes into the mix. A sibling that she never knew she had. It was hard enough for me to wrap my head around it. I worried that it would be the tipping point for Mads. She was fragile in ways that I wasn't. It was that part of her that made her special, though she often reminded me that she wasn't a china doll and wouldn't break every time bad news came her way. Only, it had been my job for the last fifteen years to protect her from all the shitty things life could throw her way. I still hadn't figured out whether this was crummy news or not.

Thinking of Max and his family as another one of our problems made me feel like a cold-hearted bitch, but it was the God's honest truth. We'd been dealt some pretty harsh realities over the past decade and a half, and this one was right up there with Jerry Springer-style bombs being dropped on us.

A brother. Worse, an older brother that we'd had before we were even born. Mom knew he existed and never once bothered to mention it to us. Hell, I'd met the boy twice. She had her chance to come clean and she'd chosen not to. Made me wonder if Pops had any idea. I dismissed that thought instantly. No, he must not have known. If he had, he would have told us. Family was too important to him, even if he had a funny way of showing it.

Then again, what about poor Max?. Mom had left him when he was barely a toddler. So young, he'd never remember her. Kind of like Maddy. She didn't remember anything about our mom. Me, I remembered everything. Every last fucking detail. The more I thought about it, the angrier I got. How dare she leave Max the way she did? Disappear to Vegas, have me, marry Pops, have Maddy, and then repeat her abandonment pattern with us? What was it about her kids that made it so easy to leave?

I looked at Maddy laughing at some joke Max was telling her, holding Matt's hand on top of the dinner table. The light in her eyes as they twinkled with humor was ethereal and hard not to be taken with. Her smile, jeez, I wasn't a poet, but I felt as though I could rock a few Shakespearian sonnets of my own over how just seeing it could turn any dark mood bright. I'd never in a million years forsake Maddy's love and trust. Yet our mother did it not to just one, but to three children. And worse, she'd neglected us in a way that was more unforgivable by not telling us about each other. Max was thirty years old. I was twenty-five and Maddy was twenty. That was over two decades of sibling time we'd never get back.

As I sat and thought about all the holidays, birthdays, graduations, family gatherings we'd missed out on, a fiery rage started to build within me. A clawing, evil, snarling revenge monster grew in the pit of my belly. It took everything I had not to act on it. Meryl Colgrove-Saunders, my mother, had committed the worst sins a woman could.

Broken the hearts of two men, shattering their belief in love after her.

Abandoned her three children.

Denied her children the love of their siblings.

Watching Maddy and Max interact, thinking back to all the times she should have been there, made the monster in me growl and snap, ready to fight, maim, and harm. More than ever before, I wanted to find my mother. Needed to, in fact. This time she'd be held accountable for her actions, if not for the men she broke down, but for her children. I no longer felt bad for her. I felt bad for me, for Maddy, and for Maxwell. The three kids she abandoned.

Over the years, I'd often wondered why she left. What had I done to make it so bad? What could sweet little Maddy have done? What Pops must have done to make her leave us? Now that I knew she'd left Jackson and Maxwell waiting in the wind too, a deep-seated hatred spilled into every nerve and pore within my body.

"Mia, snap out of it." Mads handed me a cold beer. "We're toasting."

"What should we toast to?" Max questioned, our gazes meeting across the table. His eyes were happy and sad at the same time, and I thought I'd probably looked like that for the last fifteen years.

"There's nothing more important than the present. That's why they call it a gift," I said, and everyone held up their beers.

"I'll drink to that," Max said, his words clouded by emotions only Cyndi and I caught on to.

"To the future—may it be as awesome as today!" Maddy said, bliss coating her tone.

"To the future."

May it be everything we ever dreamed of.

CHAPTER TEN

Dammit! For the fifth time, I attempted to call Wes. Nothing but voicemail. Unfortunately, I'd gotten a text the same day I found out about Maxwell being my real brother that Wes had to jet off on location. This time it was to a remote locale deep in the heart of Asia. Apparently, an actor on the set had been in a pretty severe car accident, which meant they needed to recast some of his parts on the battlefield. I figured that meant he'd be out of pocket for a while, but that didn't stop me from trying to reach him every day for the last five days.

Not having Wes to bounce this new development off of hit me hard. I'd come to count on the man so much in such a short time. Maybe that was the way real love was. The couple leaned on each other to the point where no other source would do. Sure, I had Ginelle back in Vegas, but I wasn't about to burden her with this yet. Besides, Maddy deserved to be told before my best friend. This affected her, and I still hadn't figured out the best way to tell her that Maxwell was our half-brother. What I did do, though, was steal her hairbrush and request that Max have his people do the same DNA test. I wanted something with her name on it that verified he was indeed her sibling. Not that I didn't believe it to be true. Hell, the more time I spent with the two of them, the more I felt like the outsider.

Not only did they look alike, but the gestures, the way

they tipped their heads while thinking, how they ran their fingers tirelessly through their hair for no other reason than to touch it. The easy and often way they both smiled. These two shared something that I couldn't begin to grasp. I didn't want to. Maddy had always been mine, and now I'd have to share her. Of course, Max was awesome.

He already treated me like his little sister, even though he deferred to me regarding Maddy. Thankfully, he respected the relationship and what I'd given up over the years and didn't attempt to stomp on that. Only every day, he'd asked when we were going to tell her. We had two more days before she and Matt flew back and another couple before I headed back to Malibu. At this point, I wasn't even sure Wes would be there. I didn't even know how that would feel. To be in the big house alone. Sure, it was supposed to be my home now, but I hadn't had enough time to make it feel like mine. Right now, it was where I hung my hat in between clients. Eventually, I'd make an imprint.

A knock sounded on my bedroom door.

"Come in." I closed the journal I'd been writing my thoughts in and smiled when Max shuffled in. His frame was so large he almost filled the width, but what surprised me was the woman who followed him in. It was the attorney, Ree Cee Zayas. Damn, she looked chic too. Here I sat in a pair of yoga pants and a tank with bare feet, hair in a messy bun and no makeup while she entered rocking a red power suit with matching crimson lip stain. Her charcoal-black eyes seemed soft as she entered and placed her briefcase on the bed.

"Uh, what's going on?" I looked from Max to Ree Cee.

"I have some startling information about the DNA

test you and Mr. Cunningham requested on Ms. Madison Saunders."

The way she said it sent a cold lick of fear zipping up my spine, straightening my posture painfully. "What, what is it? She's okay, right?" I had no idea what a DNA test could show medically, if anything, but even the mere suggestion that it could be something "startling" made me grip the coverlet with both fists.

Max sat down next to me and put an arm over my shoulder. "Sugar, relax. Maddy is right as rain. It's what she found in the test as it pertains to our genetics that's shocking. I brought her here to tell you directly, and I wanted to be here to let you know that I'm with you every step of the way."

I swallowed and clutched his hand, bringing both of mine to my chest. "Max, you're scaring me." His shoulders sagged, and he cupped my cheek and brought my forehead to his lips where he planted a lingering kiss.

"It's okay. Everyone is fine." He cleared his throat. "Go on, Ms. Zayas, share what you found."

The entire room seemed to go dead quiet. The air around my body felt thick, like fog had settled around us as I watched the woman pull out a set of papers and lay them out on the bed.

"It's easier if I show you." She placed three sets of paper down in a neat line facing me so that I could easily see them. One had the name Mia Saunders, the next Maxwell Cunningham, and the last Madison Saunders. They were the same sheets that she'd shown on the LCD screen at the meeting last week. The squares and lines familiar from that slide alone. "See here where your genetic markers match up with Mr. Cunningham's?" I nodded. She moved to Max's sheet and pointed to Maddy's. "Now see how these genetic markers match up?" They were nearly identical, carbon copies of the other.

"Yes. So what does this mean?" I frowned while trying to put all the pieces together to make the final image.

"Okay, now compare yours to Ms. Madison Saunders." She moved mine next to Maddy's. Not all of the boxes matched up, but a whole lot of them did.

I shrugged. "What does this mean?"

Max rubbed my back while I tried to find the answer they obviously wanted me to come to without using words.

Ree Cee sighed. "Ms. Saunders, this test was done three times to be sure. Mr. Cunningham requested the three tests so that the results could not be disputed."

"And?" I shook my head. "Spit it out already. We already know that Maddy is Max's sister too. What is so surprising?"

Maxwell closed his eyes but waited for the attorney to respond. "Ms. Saunders, this shows that Madison Saunders and Maxwell Cunningham are one hundred percent blood-related. They share the exact same mother *and* father. You share the same mother with both of them but have a different father."

The world around me stopped. Every muscle, every breath, every atom within me sat on pause. For several moments, my vision went in and out, and my heart pounded so hard I thought someone was standing on my chest.

"Christ, she's fainting," was the last thing I heard before the world went black.

★ ★ ★

I awoke later to warmth over my entire side and my right hand completely numb. Something was holding my hand in a vise grip while the left side of my body was hot as hell. I blinked a few times, seeing the ceiling of the guest room at the Cunningham ranch. The room was darker, lit now only by a soft lamp in the corner.

A murmuring sound came and went like gusts of wind carrying sound in snippets. Straining, I could hear it coming from my right. "Please make her okay. I can't lose her now that I just found her. I can't lose her now. I can't. Please make her okay." It was Max saying those soft muffled words. Turning my head, I could see him leaning over the bed, his forehead planted on our clasped hands. He held it so tight, I was pretty sure there was no blood circulating. I wiggled my fingers, and his head snapped up. "Thank God!" He moved to the head of the bed and scattered a halo of dry kisses against my brow. His eyes were moist as he leaned back. "You scared the hell out of us. You've been out for an hour."

I tried to roll, but my left side was still pinned down by the heavy weight. I turned my head and found Maddy snuggled up along my side, an arm wrapped tight around my waist. Her head was pinned to my ribcage and her breath came out in soft puffs against my neck.

"What happened?" I whispered, not wanting to ruin this moment. It had been too long since I was cuddled up with my girl like this.

"You fainted and then went into an exhausted sleep. I even had a doctor down the road come check on you. He said you were fine, just sleeping really hard. Said the body sometimes does that when presented with extreme information the mind can't yet handle. I'm sorry, Mia. I didn't know that what she said would do this to you."

I shook my head. "Nonsense. I'm fine. I haven't been sleeping, worrying about all this." I gestured generally over the room, but he knew what I meant. "And I've been concerned about my boyfriend. I haven't heard from him in several days, and he's in Asia on location. Then your attorney hit me with this, and I think I just shut down."

He nodded his eyes, sympathetic and understanding. Maddy stirred, and her eyes blinked open. "Hey, you okay?" she asked sitting up.

Running my fingers through her hair, I took in every lovely facet of her face: the eyes that matched my own, the pert little nose, and the cherub-red lips. No matter what, she was still my sister, even if by half, which posed an entire new set of problems. "I'm fine. Come sit up. We need to talk to you about something."

I pushed back up against the headboard and fiddled with the strings on the quilt. I'd bet good money that Cyndi had sewed this herself. Wouldn't surprise me. She was the picture-perfect country wife. Max sat down at the foot of the bed and put a warm hand over my knee. I was starting to get used to the comforting gesture from my big brother.

"Maddy honey, some information has come to light about us and our family."

Her eyebrows narrowed. "Like what?"

"Well, it turns out that our mother had a child before us." Her head snapped back and her mouth opened. "I know, believe me, it shocked the hell out of me, too. But uh, baby girl, Max here, he's our brother." I tried to soften it in a way that would hopefully get through to her compassionate side. Of the two of us, she was definitely more kind.

Maddy's eyes widened, and then she did something I hadn't expected. A slow smile slipped across her face. "You're our real brother?" she asked, awe filling every word.

Max nodded. "Yeah, sweetie, I am."

"But how?" The words came out breathy and uncertain.

"I found some information in my late father's will leaving close to half of my family's company to a woman by the name of Mia Saunders."

"No way!" She put her hand over her mouth.

Max chuckled softly. "Yes way. Anyhow, I had an investigator research for Mia Saunders with the appropriate information. When I saw your sister's image, I knew she was my sister. We'd even met before in the past when my father went to Las Vegas before you were born."

"And Max had DNA tests done on me and you and confirmed biologically that we are indeed siblings."

Maddy scooted up onto her knees and planted her hands on her thighs. Her entire body lit up like a firecracker. She was taking this way better that I'd imagined. "This is so cool!" She threw her arms around Maxwell. "I always wanted a brother!" She squealed in delight. Yep, way better than I thought. And I had been stressing about this all week. Only this wasn't the end of it.

I patted Maddy's back, and Max released his hold on her. She wiped tears from her eyes and smiled. "Baby girl, there's more, and I'm not really sure how to tell you this."

Her smile faded and she tilted her head to the side. "Just tell me, Mia. What you've already revealed is awesome news. Our family is bigger. It's not just you and me. We now have a brother and a sister-in-law...and oh, yeah"—she clapped her hands together—"we have a niece and a nephew on the way! I cannot wait to tell Matt and Pops! This is going to be the best year ever. Matt will have you in the wedding, I can have Isabel as the flower girl..." She went on and on.

I sighed, and Max placed a hand on her shoulder. "Sweetie, your sister is trying to share some information that might not be so easy to swallow. I'm glad, hell, I'm elated that you're so happy we're family. I share those feelings."

Maddy beamed at him like only she could. Fuck, this sucked. Why the hell did it have to be so hard! It's like I was always the bearer of bad news. This one time I wish I could have left it at Maxwell being our brother, let's celebrate, and start having family reunions and get to know one another, etcetera No, it has to come with the whopping side of the man you thought was your father your whole life is not your real father. Oh, and by the way, the man that is your real father is dead so you'll never get a chance to know him.

Tears flowed unchecked down my cheeks. I inhaled deep and let it fly. "Mads, the attorney found something else about your genetics." I flicked at the tears, pissed that they were falling and that I was not able to hold them back.

Max reached out a hand to me, his eyes betraying his sadness. He knew what saying this cost me, and he was there, sharing in my grief. He hated knowing I was in pain and that what I had to share would only bring more. He'd always wanted a big family, and now he was getting two sisters to add to his fold.

"May I?" he asked, and it became clear then and there, I truly wasn't alone. Max might have been my brother for only a week but he was ready to jump right in and dish out the hard stuff, say what needed to be said, take the brunt of the pain for me. I nodded, not knowing what else to do.

My form was racked with emotions so damaging it was as if each sob were a punishing blow to the chest.

"Maddy, sweetie, what Mia is trying to tell you is that the attorney found out that you and I have the same parents."

She blinked a few times but didn't move. "You mean the three of us have the same parents? But that would mean Pops is your dad, too, and he didn't even know it?" Her eyebrows rose to her hairline.

A gut-wrenching sense of dread bubbled up as I spoke the words that would change her life forever. "No, baby girl. Pops is not your dad. You and Maxwell share the same parents. That means your real father was Jackson Cunningham."

A tidal wave of tears hit her hard, rushing down the smooth lines of her face in rivulets. It was like watching a mudslide down the face of a California mountain, seeing her face crumble into a mess of tears, snot, and wracking sobs. "But, but, Pops…I don't understand." She shook her head and covered her face as she cried. I pulled her into my lap, and her face went straight for my neck as it always had during times of turmoil. "But you're still my sister." She hiccupped.

"Yes, baby, yes, we are biologically still sisters but only by half."

"Not by half to me!" she cried, wetting the skin of my clavicle with her hot tears.

I kissed her hairline and pet her over and over, whispering that I loved her, that I'd always be there, that nothing would change between us. I tried to spin the side of having Maxwell as our brother to help bring her out of her emotional breakdown. Eventually, she stopped shaking, and her breathing became slow and even. She'd cried herself to sleep. This was not an unusual reaction. When she dated boys in high school and they broke her heart, this was much the same response.

Max stood and paced. "Is she going to be okay?" He looked like a caged animal. His form was taut, hands clenched into giant fists, and his stance ready for battle. He didn't even know us and he was on the defensive, ready to go down swinging to protect his new family.

"Yes, she will be fine. I imagine this is a heavy blow to her. Same for me, but we're used to surviving difficult things."

That was the wrong thing to say because he scowled and looked at me, his pale eyes a frosty ice-green shade. "Not anymore. You now have our family money and connections."

I frowned. "We don't want your money or connections."

He shook his head. "Doesn't matter. You're getting it. The attorneys are already working to change over the forty-nine percent to you."

"What? You've got be kidding?"

He stopped and put his hands on his hips. "Nothing's changed, Mia. The will is iron clad. My father obviously didn't know about Maddy, but you're getting nearly half the company."

"I don't want it!"

"You don't want to be part of my family?" His voice was strained, pained even.

"Of course, we're going to be family. But I don't need your company to be your sister. Besides, what about Maddy? She's your real sister!" My tone was harsh and unrelenting.

"So are you! Half or a hundred, it's all the same to me."

I closed my eyes and tried to think, but there were too

many emotions swirling around my head. "I want to give my half to her then."

Max laughed. Full on tipped his head back, held his stomach, and belly laughed, overtaken with hysterics. "You're going to give billions of dollars' worth of stock and all that comes with it to our little sister?"

I cringed and my lips tightened. "She's the only person that matters."

He huffed. "Yes, you're working your ass off to pay her schooling, and going from place to place to be whatever a stranger needs you to be in order to pay off your father's debt but you won't take money that's rightfully yours? You are somethin' else, sugar."

"I'll tell the lawyer myself."

"Too late. I've already told the lawyer to draw something up to split the company three ways. Soon, you and Maddy are going to be very rich women, but it will take the next six months to a year to satisfy the conditions set in the will, and then we'll both have to sign over a portion."

"But Jackson wasn't my father. Why should I have any stake in this? Divide it between the two of you."

He shook his head fervently. "Not what Dad wanted. He knew who you were, knew you weren't his, and he wanted you to have it anyway. Now if he'd known Maddy was his, I know in my heart of hearts that he'd want it split among the three of us. That's just the type of man he was. Honor and family meant everything to him."

"You're not going to change your mind, are you?" I retorted.

"Nope."

"Are you always like this?"

"Like what?"

"Bossy, obstinate, unwilling to see reason?" A slow smirk slipped across my lips even though I didn't want it to.

He smiled, sat on the bed, and picked up my hand. "When it comes to my family, you'd better believe it."

★ ★ ★

The buzzing phone woke me up from a dead sleep. The kind of sleep that happens after popping a couple of Benadryl. I grappled for my phone and answered without checking the caller ID. It was probably Millie. I'd shot her text, telling her to send me the details of the next client, but to give me a few days in Malibu before I left. She'd agreed, and I hadn't even bothered to check who my new client would be. It didn't seem to matter before, but she was probably checking in with me since I'd be flying to Malibu tomorrow. Maddy and Matt were heading back to Vegas today on Maxwell's private jet with the new information that she had a brother, was about to become a rich woman, and the knowledge that the man who'd raised her was not her father.

"Hello, hello, is Mia Saunders there?" A nasally voice broke through my sleepy bliss.

I cleared my throat. "Uh, yeah. I'm Mia Saunders, who is this?"

"This is Wilma Brown from Kindred Hospital and Convalescent Homes in Las Vegas, Nevada."

I sat up as if a pail of ice cold water had been thrown on me. "What's the matter with my dad?" I asked, rushing the words and needing to hear that he was okay.

"Ms. Saunders, I'm afraid your father took a turn for

the worse. He contracted a viral infection that worked its way through his nervous system. Unfortunately, we didn't have any previous medical files as your father hadn't had much in the way of medical treatment, and we gave him the strongest antibiotic possible to counteract the infection."

Oh, no, oh, no. I could hear the in the tone of her voice that this was bad. Really fucking bad. "Is he going to be okay?" I cut in.

"I'm sorry, Ms. Saunders, but the antibiotic ended up being something he was allergic to. He seized several times before we could give him additional medication to counteract the seizures and the allergic reaction. He was also allergic to the ant seizure medication and he went into cardiac arrest."

His. Heart. Stopped.

His heart stopped.

His heart...stopped.

No matter how many times or different ways the phrase rolled around in my head, it still had the ability to rob me of breath. "Ms. Saunders? He's alive, but he's in critical condition. It doesn't look good. I'm sorry to say, but it's touch and go right now. You and your family should probably come as soon as possible."

"What?" He was fine the last time I saw him. Maddy just told me he looked great, that the doctors were baffled as to why he hadn't woken up.

"He may not have a lot of time. You'll need to come soon if you want to say goodbye."

"Thank you. I'll be on the next plane. Please, do everything you can," I begged.

"We will. Goodbye, Ms. Saunders."

Critical condition. It doesn't look good. Come soon. Say goodbye.

I closed my eyes, and the words moved across the back of my eyelids like the scrolling newsfeed at the bottom of the television on the local news stations.

No matter how many times I saw the words, repeated them silently over and over, the end result was still the same. My father was dying.

September

CALENDAR GIRL

AUDREY CARLAN

CHAPTER ONE

White walls. Nothing but white walls with cracked, chipped paint and ceiling tiles with gnarly rust-colored splotches. Blinking several times, I lifted my head and turned it from side to side, forward and back. The knot in my shoulder was the size of Mount Everest and had been there for almost a week.

> *"I'm sorry, dear. He's not getting any better."*
> *"Mia, we're here for you."*
> *"We'll continue to pray for a miracle."*
> *"Your father's chances are very slim, I'm afraid."*
> *"Make sure you notify the rest of the family."*
> *"Talk to him. Say goodbye."*

Snippets of condolences and responses from the doctor whirl in my head as if on an old time spinning record. I just keep picking up the arm and placing it back down until it repeats the melody.

With too tired eyes, I stare at the only man who's always loved me. From the very first breath I took, to teaching me how to play baseball, rooting me on through my studies, all the way until Mom left before he broke down. Even when his face was bright red, his speech slurred, and his eyes a hazy gray, he loved me, and I counted on that love to get us through. For the most part, it did.

Sitting next to his bed, I clutched his hand, hoping my grip, the warmth I pressed into his palm, would worm its way into his body's recognition and tell him to fight. Fight for his daughters. Fight for *me,* his flesh and blood. I'd spent the last decade and a half fighting for him, for Maddy, and now he needed to man up. *Be there.* Work hard to come back to us. We might not have been much, just two young women trying to find their way, but we were his, and I had to believe deep down that we were worth the fight, or he'd be lost to us…forever.

The new morning shift nurse entered. She was light on her feet, seeming to not make a sound as she checked Pops's vitals and marked something on his chart before sending me a remorseful smile. That's all I'd received for the last several days. Apologies, frowns, tentative condolences. I looked over at Maddy curled up in a fetal position on the tiny loveseat, asleep. Like me, she'd refused to leave for more than a speedy shower and change of clothes. If our dad was going to take his last breath, we'd be there to witness it.

We still hadn't talked about the elephant in the room. The one that weighed so heavily on my chest, I swear it had broken a few ribs in the process. Taking a full breath was impossible, knowing that Maddy was hurting. The information about Jackson Cunningham being her real father had been a blow, one that hit us both upside the head so hard we knocked into one another. The knowledge had us tiptoeing around the other, separating us in a way that made my skin crawl. I needed Maddy now, more than ever before, and she seemed to be slipping away, uncertain of the space she occupied. I hated that and hated our mother even more for making it our reality.

The only benefit to all this was Maxwell. He'd sent us here on his private jet and called every day. Even scored us a hotel for the next month that was walking distance from the convalescent hospital. Our new brother had thought of everything, and he made sure money was no object. All of a sudden, we had the best doctors—teams of people coming in to check on our father, scouring over his medical records. They looked for clues as to not only his neurological status to be sure he wasn't brain dead, but also whether he'd be able to overcome the physical ramifications of a viral infection gone bad, including not one but two heart-stopping allergic reactions to treatment.

A few of the doctors feared the worst. Until the new teams of specialists arrived, the convalescent hospital had written off our dad. Told us there was nothing more we could do and recommended taking him off life support.

Life support.

Removing the support that gave him life. I couldn't do it. If I were in a similar circumstance, would Pops give up on me, stop the machines from giving me that life-sustaining air? Hell would literally turn to ice before that happened. That man would stand over me and pump my chest and give me CPR nonstop if it would keep me alive even for one minute. I had to give him the same chance.

"Good morning, Ms. Saunders," Dr. McHottie said as he pulled Pops's chart from the end of the bed and scanned it. For a few minutes, he'd make notes, check some things, flip pages, and repeat.

I stood, stretched my arms above my head, and did a small backbend, trying to relieve the constant ache in the center of my spine, the kind that comes from sitting in a plastic chair for nearly a week. My back protested, and I winced. Dr. McHottie shook his head, staring at me over a pair of black-rimmed glasses. His dark, curly hair was cropped close to his head and almost seemed to shine. It looked wet, and by the fresh scent of Irish Spring, he'd just left the shower. Smelling the soapy goodness reminded me of how ripe I was getting. It had been two days since I'd left the hospital. No amount of deodorant could mask the funk beginning to germinate under my arms.

"Morning, Doc. What's the prognosis? Any better?" I tried not to sound too hopeful because every day for nearly seven days, he'd frowned and simply shook his head. Today though, there was a moment. One where I knew, I just knew, our luck was changing.

The slick, young doctor met me on my side of the bed and placed a hand on my shoulder. He squeezed, and I tried not to moan at the scant release of tension that small grip provided. I was wound so tight any touch, no matter how brief, felt like a momentous occasion. "According to the readings, at some point in the night, your dad's lungs started to move *against* the machines. It's a slight positive response indicating he might breathe on his own, but I don't want to put the cart before the horse.

There weren't words to express my gratitude for this tiny speck of hope. Instead, I plowed into his body and wrapped my arms around his waist. I poured everything I had into that one hug, holding on as if my own life depended on it. He didn't seem to mind. In fact, he held me. Wrapped his arms around my body, keeping me against his chest. We stood there, a wrecked woman and a man of medicine, a healer. I leaned against that man and prayed God would grant him the ability to save my dad regardless of whether or not he deserved it. I had to believe that everyone deserved a second chance. If he made it, I think Pops would agree. Maybe this would be the wake-up call he needed to realize that life was indeed worth living.

A cell phone ring blasted into the euphoria that was my single positive moment in the better part of a week. I jumped back and looked into the sky-blue gaze of Dr. McHottie. "Sorry. It's just a lot—" I started but he cut me off.

"Mia, never be sorry for needing a hug. I can tell you're a very strong young woman, but everyone needs someone to lean on. Let's keep praying for a miracle. I'll be back to check on his status in a couple of hours."

I nodded and turned around to find Maddy with her cell phone crushed against her ear.

"Uh, yeah, she's right here, Auntie." Maddy held out her cell phone as she pushed the blond layers of bedhead back off her face. She looked the way I felt, though I'm certain if a mirror were anywhere near me, I'd look like the night of the living dead revived.

Blowing out a long breath, I lifted the phone to my ear. "Hello?"

"What the hell is going on? You haven't answered my calls, you didn't show up for your flight, and you certainly didn't show up in Tucson, Arizona where client number nine was expecting you!"

I tried to form a reply, but nothing came out. I should say sorry, should say something, but I didn't have it in me to care. "Millie—"

"Don't you Millie me. You are in deep shit, young lady!

If you read the fine print in your contract, you'd know that if you stand the client up, not only do you lose the hundred thousand dollar fee, you owe them a hundred thousand for their trouble!"

Moving as fast as my tired legs would take me, I left Pops's room and went down the hall to the outdoor garden area. It was early so the there wasn't anyone out just yet. "Are you telling me I now owe some rich motherfucker a hundred thousand dollars?" I roared into the phone.

"You're yelling at me?" Her voice was laced with venom and just as lethal. "You got yourself into this."

"I had no choice! Pops is on his death bed!"

"So you just up and leave and don't tell me? Mia, had I contacted the client in advance, this might have been avoided. Right now, you are two hundred thousand dollars in the hole. You did not have enough in the master account to send Blaine your monthly installment."

Oh, no. My body started to shake, and my legs couldn't hold me up any more. Quivering, I slumped into the nearest bench. "I missed my payment…" I choked out, fear controlling my tongue.

"Yes! I've been calling several times a day. Finally, I got in touch with Maddy, though she'd ignored my calls until today."

"My phone has been off. It's been touch and go with Pops for the last week, Millie. He's still nowhere near out of the woods. I can't leave him." I ran a shaky hand through my hair and tugged on the roots, the instant bite of pain bringing with it a clarity I was desperately trying to wrap my mind around.

"I can't bail you out, Mia. My money is tied up in the

business and a new venture I just sank everything into. You're going to have to talk to one of your rich friends. Maybe one of the ones that paid the extra fee?" she suggested—as if that were so easy. Sex and money. That was the name of her game.

Ask Wes or Alec for two hundred thousand dollars? Absolutely not. No way. "I'll figure something out."

"All I know is you'd better figure it out fast. Your next client is Drew Hoffman."

The name bounced around in my mind like a game of Plinko until it sank into a winning number. "The doctor to the stars? The one with his own daily TV show, line of vitamins, workout clothing, and DVDs? You've got to be kidding."

"The very same. Apparently, he saw your swimsuit campaign about beauty in all sizes. Wants you to appear on his show for a daily segment he's going to call 'Living Beautiful.' Mia, if this goes big, you could end up securing a regular spot on the show at the start of the new year. He'd only have to wait a couple months for you to start. No pressure." She cackled. Straight up witch-like screech you see in the bad B-movies. If I had been standing next to her, it would have taken a Herculean effort to peel my boney fingers from around her throat.

No pressure. Millie said that as if this weren't the break of the century. I pressed hard against my temples. All the blood in my body seemed to rush to my heart and make it pound far harder than normal. If I weren't here with Pops right now, this would be amazing news. The press I'd received had given me a small *in* with the world of acting so far. The media had taken notice, and when Anton's video went live next month, it would definitely coincide nicely. This opportunity though, to be a regular on a TV spot with Dr. Hoffman? Crazy town. This is the big break I needed to find me, my own path.

Goddammit, I needed to talk to Wes. Get his opinion, see if he knew the famous doctor personally and whether he'd heard anything. Of course, I couldn't do that because I hadn't heard from him in two weeks. Didn't know where he was, when he'd be back, just that Judi had said he left overnight one day. Told her he wouldn't be back for a two to three weeks and to tell me he'd call. That was all she had for me. I'd received a scratchy voicemail from him that broke up so bad I couldn't hear much of anything. Be home soon and that he loved me. Outside of that, nothing.

Of course, there was a whole new issue of figuring out how I was going to come up with two hundred thousand dollars or a way to get Blaine to give me more time.

"Hopefully, Pops will be out of the woods soon. Don't make any cancellations on the October job until you hear from me. I'll try not to be so unavailable, but it's hard right now, Millie. There's also some family shit I need to talk to you about. Serious stuff that has to do with Mom."

"Have you heard from Meryl?" Her voice went as low as a whisper, so much so that I had to press the cell harder against my ear.

Shaking my head at the ridiculousness of that question confirmed that I did not want to get into this. Pops was here, fighting for his life. Our mother, Millie's sister, and the whopping bad choices she'd made for the last three decades didn't get to take center stage. The last thing I wanted to deal with was Mom and her secrets. "No, I haven't. Just some stuff came up. When Pops is in the clear, I'll call you, okay?"

Millie sighed through the line. "Is…uh…he going to be okay?"

An annoyed snort-chuckle slipped from my mouth. "Don't act like you give a damn what happens to my father. You've always hated him, resented him for not bringing us to California when Mom up and left us in the lurch. He did the best he could."

Her own disbelieving grunt came through the line. "The best would have been actually giving you a life. When my sister was there, you were all happy. He couldn't keep anything together when she left." Her voice was icy and chilled me to the bone.

A deep defensiveness for Pops swirled heavily in my gut. My aunt or not, she was poking the bear and needed to be set back in her place. "At least he didn't leave. That was your sister. The woman you miss so much walked away from her ten-year-old and five-year-old daughters, but I guess that's okay, huh? Wasn't the first time she left a family hanging. Hell, for all we know, she's got a whole slew of them around the nation. I probably have a handful of other siblings I don't know about."

Millie sniffed, and her voice shook. "Your mother was never well, dollface. You know that. Deep down, you know that she was never meant to be saddled with children and married life. Her spirit needed to roam free or she would feel imprisoned within her own life."

"You're making excuses for her?"

"Mia, she loved you."

I huffed. "Is that what you call it? Up and leave your daughters? Love. She didn't know the meaning of love."

Now that I had Wes, I knew that for a fact. When you loved someone that much, you cared more about their happiness than your own. You made sacrifices that benefitted them, not yourself. Sure, there was give and take, but it was all part of sharing your life, of having a family. "Mom didn't know the meaning of love, Millie," I repeated.

"Don't say that. Meryl just wasn't all there in the head all of the time. It has been that way since she was little."

Right then and there, I decided she needed a fat dose of reality about her dear sister. "I've heard enough. Do yourself a favor. Why don't you go look up the name Maxwell Cunningham one more time?"

"Your last client? I vetted him. You know that." Her tone was bored, annoyed.

"Just do it, Millie. Look up his birth records."

The line crackled as I walked towards the door back into the hospital. I needed a caffeine drip, stat.

"Mia, you're not making any sense. His birth records?"

"Yeah."

"And what do you expect me to find?"

I laughed. A full-on piggy snort, hyena chuckle, all over body heave. A variety of medical professionals who passed me in the hall looked at me like I'd just sprouted wings and told them I was a fairy. I didn't care. Delirium was not a fair-weather friend these days, and I figured these folks dealt in enough mental illness to offer a cold shoulder as they passed.

"You're going to find that Maxwell Cunningham's mother's name is Meryl Colgrove. His father, Jackson Cunningham."

"What! This must be some type of joke. That can't be. He's lying to you. Someone's lying to you." The dread and shock in her voice was believable. At least she wasn't in on her sister's depravity.

"Yeah, Meryl up and left her son when he was a year old. Three years later, she married Pops, and a year after that, she had me."

I wasn't planning on going through the fucked up family tree, but she'd pushed every last one of my buttons defending the one woman who didn't deserve it.

"It's not possible. I'd have known..." she said on a gasp.

Once I made it to the cafeteria, I shuffled to the coffeemaker, plunked in the fifty-five cents, and shoved a paper cup under the spout. The coffee was wretched, but it helped keep me awake. Well, it did for about an hour, and then I'd make my zombie walk back over to the machine once more. This was another one of those routines I repeated several times a day.

I took a deep breath and planted my forehead against the machine as it whirred to life, spilling out the coffee. The buzz and hum felt good against my aching head. "Believe it. It gets worse, though."

"Mia, no." She sobbed, sniffed, and hiccupped into the line. Frankly, at that point, I didn't care. I'd been through more shit the past couple weeks than any normal person should. She needed to share this burden of truth.

"Maxwell Cunningham. Not only is he our brother, he's Maddy's biological brother from both parents. You know what that means, Millie? Huh?" My voice rose, the anger and defeat controlling every word. "That means your sister cheated on my dad. She had an affair with Jackson Cunningham a decade after they had their first child, and she got pregnant with Maddy. That lowlife bitch passed off

Maddy as Pops's child, and she never bothered to come clean. That's the type of woman your sister is. Learn to live with it. I sure as hell have."

I clicked the phone off, grabbed my cup, and sucked down the entire thing in one go. The coffee was hot enough to burn my tongue, obliterating every taste bud in its wake. Not that I cared. Pain would give me something else to focus on besides the absolute dire straits my father was in.

Pulling out a dollar bill from my pocket, I fed it into the machine, added ten cents, and put my now empty cup on one side and a cup for Maddy on the other. Again, I pressed my forehead against the whirring, which lasted longer. For a minute, I succumbed to the blackness.

"Jesus Christ, sugar, come here," came the sweetest sound, next to my Wes's voice, before I was turned around and hauled into the massive arms of the man I've now come to know as my brother.

"Max," I choked into his chest. I gripped onto his back and let the tears fall. They came fast and furious. Like a torrential downpour they fell, soaking Max's black Henley, but he just held on tighter. For the first time since I received that call, I felt safe. Protected. "Thank you. Thank you for coming," I said between sobs.

If possible, he held me closer, tighter. More warmth surrounded my frigid core. "Nowhere I'd rather be than here seeing my sisters through a hard time. You just lean on me, sugar."

And for a long, long time, I did.

When a sob scraped its way up from my chest and out my mouth, he held strong. As my knees weakened and I lost the ability to stand, he lifted me up. When I begged and pleaded for my father to live and prayed to God, he whispered the words right along with me.

I'd never had someone to fall back on, a person who dropped everything to be there when I needed him. Right there, locked in the haven that was his arms, he imprinted on my soul. I had a brother, and now that I did, I never wanted to find out what life would be like without him.

CHAPTER TWO

"Mia, sugar, you're dead on your feet. You have to get some shut-eye or your body is just going to stop working for you when you least expect it."

I pulled back from the warmth of his embrace, wiped my eyes on the sleeve of my shirt, and sucked in several calming breaths. "I'm okay. Really, Max, I'll be fine."

"No, she's not," came Maddy's voice from about ten paces behind us as she made her way over. She looked at the coffee machine and pointed. "One of those for me?"

I nodded and followed her movements while she prepared both coffees. She actually made an effort to add cream and sugar. I'd just taken it black even though I hated black coffee. I couldn't taste it anyway. Same with food. Pretty much everything had not only lost its flavor, but the world around me had lost a lot of its color.

Maddy shuffled over to Max and walked right into his chest. This was a first. Max put his arms around her and tentatively held her close, petting her hair. He closed his eyes as if the moment were a bit much emotionally. I knew he wanted to be close with Maddy and me, but everything in Texas had happened so fast they didn't have much time to connect. From the moment we found out that Maxwell was our brother, to finding out she was his full biological sister, we got the call about Pops and had to bail.

She lifted her head, resting her chin on his chest.

"Thank you for coming, Max."

"Like I told your sister, there is nowhere I'd rather be right now."

"*Our* sister." Her voice shook a bit when she said the two words.

Max frowned and his eyebrows furrowed. "What's that, sweetie?" Sweetie. Since he'd met us, he'd called her sweetie and me sugar. I kind of liked my endearment better.

"Our sister," Maddy repeated. "Before, you said *your* sister. I was just correcting you. We're all related, and I want to make it clear right now that no matter who's got more matching blood running in their veins, Mia will always be one hundred percent *our* sister."

Max's lips pinched together. "You're absolutely right. I didn't mean to say it that way. I apologize."

He apologized? What? "Max, no need to apologize, really. Maddy is just being a little oversensitive. Emotions are really high right now."

Maddy's eyes narrowed. "No I'm not. I'm telling it like it is. The same way you have always taught me growing up. Never hide behind a lie. Never hold your tongue when important information needs to be discussed. I don't want to stew in this any longer. Max needs to know that you are more important to me than anyone else in this world. If we're going to be a family in any way, no matter what, where you are in the lineup is where I'm going to be. And that's just the way it is. Period. I don't care who my biological father is." She pointed down the hall. "That man in there is my dad. No blood test is ever going to change that."

Max took a slow breath, and I scuffed the linoleum floor, leaving black streaks while I figured out how to best deal with this outburst. She was obviously feeling strange about her place, defensive over our relationship, and conflicted about Pops and her lineage.

"Maddy... Max, his wife Cyndi, and baby, Isabel, as well as the little guy on the way, are all now an *addition* to the Saunders clan, okay? Don't think of it as a change as much as an addition. Just because they are Cunninghams doesn't mean you are."

That's when Max made a fatal error. "Well technically, she is a Cunningham but didn't know it."

I could see the moment the statement hit my girl. Her body went ramrod straight, her chest puffed up, and daggers seemed to fly from her eye sockets as she stormed in front of Max, got out that pointing finger of hers—the one I absolutely hated to be at the other end of—and shoved it against his chest several times. *Ouch.* I knew from experience that boney ass finger hurt.

"Are you certifiable? I know they do things different in Texas, but hear me and hear me well. I am, always have been, and will always be Madison Saunders. Got it? I was fine in my skin before, and I'm not changing it because some DNA test proves something. I'll admit that I'm shocked that I have a brother and am actually happy about that fact, but you will not win me as some kind of Meryl Colgrove consolation prize. Got it?"

"Baby girl..." My own voice was unrecognizable with the amount of sorrow rushing through it as I put an arm around my sister. Her whole body slammed into my chest, and her face went right into my neck.

"I'm Madison Saunders! I'm not a Cunningham," she sobbed, the thick veil of my hair covering her face.

"Hey, baby, nobody's trying to change you, your name, or who you are. You'll always be my sister. You'll always be Pops's daughter. Now, we just have a whole other part of our family to love and get to know. Nothing changes, Mads. Nothing. It's still me and you against the world, okay?" She nodded but continued to cry. "I mean that. Max is not here to change anything, are you, Max?"

Maxwell cleared his throat and put a giant paw on the back of my sister's head. "Sweetie, I already love you and Mia very much. You're my little sisters, and from the moment we all met, I felt that tug of awareness, of family. I wanted you and your sister my whole life. Wanted that family. Now I have it, and I'm happy, honey. Cyndi, Isabel, and baby Jack are going to have some seriously awesome women in their lives, and I just feel fortunate. That's all, darlin'. That's why I'm here. To lend support while you and Mia take care of your dad."

After a few moments, Maddy lifted her head. I cupped her cheeks and wiped her tears. "Nothing's changed, okay?"

"F-Feels l-like a lot has c-changed." She wiped her snotty nose on her sleeve. Yikes. We were both disgusting.

"Even though it feels that way, it really hasn't. You're still in school, you're on the road to being Mrs. Matthew Rains, and you have me forever. Now, you just have a big, badass, rich cowboy brother."

"Well, we're all rich." Max supplied helpfully, which really wasn't helpful at all.

Jeez Louise. There had to be a shut-off button. Weren't brothers supposed to come with one of those? I hadn't had a chance to discuss the Cunningham Oil & Gas business when the news of Pops taking a turn hit.

Maddy's eyebrows came together, leaving a cute little wrinkle above her nose. When she was little, I'd kiss that little wrinkle and tell her not to frown because it would stay that way and she'd hate it later on in life.

"We're not rich, Max," she scoffed. "Far, far from it."

Maxwell directed a harsh look my way. "You haven't told her?" He crossed those massive arms over his even wider chest.

I wanted to slink down into a puddle of goo at his feet. There had been way too much drama to deal with to be having this conversation right now. First Millie, now Max and Maddy. Criminy.

"Told me what?" Maddy pressed.

"Max, we've had some pretty severe shit going on. The last thing I needed to do was add yet another complication."

"What complication?" Maddy asked.

"It's really not a complication. More a benefit," Max added.

"And that would be?" she asked.

Instead of participating, I was just too damned tired to figure out a way to ease into it, and Max seemed gung-ho, so why the hell not? Sipping on my coffee, allowing the creamy liquid that admittedly always tasted better when someone else made it—or it could be the addition of cream and sugar—I watched as Max explained to Maddy that we were all three going to own a piece of Cunningham Oil & Gas, though I did get him to agree to split Maddy's and my amount in half so he'd still carry fifty percent of the company. It was his birthright and his legacy, not something we ever grew up wanting a piece of. The two of us would each have twenty-five percent, which would give us a crazy amount of money, but also not force us to make the everyday decisions and work the business if we didn't want to. I sure as hell didn't want to. Maddy on the other hand, with her degree, might be interested in the option in the future.

After Max spilled the details, she stood there, maybe in shock or lost in thought. I couldn't be sure at that point. Eventually, the lights turned on and someone was home because her face lit up. A rosy hue covered her cheeks, and the sunny personality that was my baby sis came to the surface.

"I own twenty-five percent of one of the largest oil and gas companies in the nation."

"Yes, ma'am." A little smirk stole across Max's lips.

"Get out!" Her hands came to her chest and she clenched them together. "That's unreal."

"Having sisters is unreal. It's your birthright to be part of the family business," Max announced proudly.

"So when I'm done with college, if I want, I could just come work for the company?" Just as I suspected, my book-smart, scientist sister would be all over that.

Max laughed. "Of course. I'd love for both of you to come work at the headquarters in Dallas."

I cringed and shook my head. "Sorry, this Vegas girl is now a Cali girl."

"We'll see." Max grinned and put his arms around Maddy and me. "For now, though, I need to get a real meal into both of you." He sniffed my hair. "And showers. And at least four hours of sleep."

Both Maddy and I were going to protest, but he walked us right past Pops's room. Nothing had changed in the fifteen minutes or so we'd been in the cafeteria and he'd been alone.

"We can't leave Pops alone," Maddy said.

"You're not going to. I ran into your fella. He and his mother we're heading in to relieve you both anyway. They're going to sit with your dad while you guys rest of up for a bit. No arguments. You're no good to him like this. He'd be mad as hell if you weren't taking care of yourselves, I'm sure." Max's tone was firm.

I made a sound that was between a laugh and a huff but didn't respond. Pops cared. He definitely loved us, but usually he was so far gone in the drink that he wouldn't notice if Maddy and I had gone days without food.

One time we didn't eat for two days. I was twelve and not old enough to work, and Maddy was seven. We'd gone through all the food in the house, including the dry and canned stuff. After two full days had passed with nothing to eat, I was desperate. So I walked down to the main drag to an overly busy casino buffet and loaded my tote up with rolls and pieces of chicken when people weren't looking. I made sure I stood real close to a family that had other kids, and no one was the wiser. I slipped out of the buffet, and Maddy and I ate for three days on what I'd pilfered until Pops came back from his binge and filled the house with food again. I did that several more times over the years when it got bad. The answer to Max's statement before would be a resounding no. Pops likely wouldn't have noticed we were hurting, tired, or any of that. He'd known me a month and Maddy a week and could already see what we needed.

Led by an overbearing brother, Maddy and I let him drag us across the street to the hotel with the plush two-bedroom suite he'd secured for us a week ago, a suite that hadn't been slept in once. We'd only used it for showering, and not enough if the rank smell that filled the space was anything to go by. Max flicked on the air and sat on the bed. You two, showers, now." He pointed at Maddy and me. Then he picked up the phone. "Yeah, I'd like…uh hold up. You two like burgers?"

My mouth actually watered at the idea of a meaty, cheesy burger. For days I'd lost my appetite. The same went for actually having eaten anything remotely close to a meal. It had been a strict diet consisting of coffee, Snickers bars, and trail mix, and that was when I could force myself to choke down something. Oh, Maddy's new perfect mother-in-law-to-be had come bearing food every day, but I hadn't been able to bring myself to partake. Pops wasn't eating. Why should I? Now, a good few pounds lighter and a stomach eating itself, I knew I was no good to anyone like this.

"Burgers are fine, Max, thank you," I answered, and Mads simply nodded. I could tell from her gait and the slump in her frame that she was losing her grip and the weight of everything was starting to show.

Since it was a two-bedroom suite, there were two bathrooms. I showered in one, Mads in the other. When I exited, a man's T-shirt and a clean pair of boxer shorts sat on the vanity. It didn't even dawn on me to think of pajamas and I definitely hadn't packed any. I shuffled my way into the living area where Maddy sat, hands around a giant burger. She too wore a T-shirt and a pair of boxer shorts.

"Twinsies," I joked, and Maddy almost choked on her burger when she giggled.

"Had to give you guys something to wear. You ain't got nothin' for bedclothes. What have you been wearing to sleep in?"

I gazed at the window, basically anywhere else in the room, to avoid the question.

Maddy went the route of honesty. "Max, we've been holding down the fort at the hospital."

His head jerked back, and he gripped his knees. "You mean you haven't slept in a bed since you left the ranch?"

Maddy, God love her, did not catch on to the warning hitch in his voice. "Nope. Most nights, I nod off on the love seat in there and Mia on the chair."

His gaze cut to mine. "You've been sleepin' in a chair for a week?" He pointed to me. "And you must have contorted into a pretzel to fit your length into a love seat," he directed at Maddy. "For Christ's sake, no wonder you two look like death warmed over. Where the hell are your men in all this?" He scowled deep and gripped his knees tighter.

"Good fucking question," I mumbled around a salty French fry. It was the perfect crispness, salt to grease ratio, and potato awesomeness. After inhaling at least ten of them, I picked up the burger.

Maddy chewed and then spoke. "Mia refused to leave. I refused to leave Mia. We're in this together, right, Sis?" she said as if watching our father die were something we needed to mark off our sisterly solidarity list. It was sweet though. I knew she wanted Pops to pull through this as much as I did, but we also feared what would happen when he found out that he wasn't her biological father.

Max stood, paced the room, and shook his head. "Well, I'll be here for up to two weeks or unless he turns the corner on this thing. Then I've got to get back to Cyndi. Can't be gone in the last month of her pregnancy. Shoot, maybe I should bring the girls out here now. Then we'd all be together during this, no matter what happens."

Could he have been more of a kind, generous human being? I didn't think so. I'd never known a man like him, and I probably never would again. Yes, I'd met some pretty special men this past year, ones that would go down as best friends, exceptional lovers, and *more* in some cases. Max, though, was unique. His love for his family warred with Tai's and his Samoan clan of Nikos back in Hawaii. They were a tight bunch, but the fierceness coming from Max, the way he held himself, doted on Maddy and me, took care of us like he wanted to and wanted to forever, meant so much more. There really wasn't a way to describe it without sounding like an overly sappy Hallmark card.

We ate for the next ten minutes, Max pointing at the plate every time one of us would take a breath, push back, and lean against the couch. He wanted the plates cleaned, and he wasn't going to take any lip. Finally, Maddy and I had stuffed ourselves to the gills. Before I knew it, we were leaning against one another shoulder-to-shoulder, our eyes so heavy it was impossible to keep them open.

"Girls, come on." Max nudged me, but I just leaned into Maddy's side more. Her weight left my side, and I shivered at the change in temperature. My eyes were still far too heavy to open. I needed a few minutes to rest my eyes, and then I'd be golden.

Out of nowhere, I became weightless, as if flying on gossamer wings to an unknown destination. After a few jarring jolts, I was placed on a cloud, soft crisp layers of cotton and a squishy down comforter tucked all around me. I rubbed my cheek against it, never opening my eyes.

"Just a few minutes and then I'm going back," I mumbled.

Something warm and moist pressed against my forehead. "Okay, sugar, a few minutes. Sure." Max said something else, but it was garbled, and I couldn't make it out.

★ ★ ★

When I woke up, it wasn't quite dark yet. I sat up and looked over at the bed beside mine. Maddy was sleeping soundly. Shifting, I moved and crawled out of bed. The second my feet hit the lush carpet, I got dizzy and woozy. I was beyond tired. Downright exhausted. It was seven o'clock.

Holy shit. We'd been out for over eight hours. Pops!

Remembering my dad was across the street fighting for his life moved me straight into action. I threw on some jeans and a clean V-neck shirt, a new pair of socks, and my converse. Out of bed, dressed, and on the move, I was up and ready within five minutes tops. On the nightstand, I found a hair tie, grabbed it, and fastened my hair back into a long ponytail as I left the room. Max was sitting on the couch watching TV.

"You're awake."

"I've been out for eight fucking hours, Max!" I growled, making my way over to the counter where the room key and my wallet were sitting.

Maxwell didn't look fazed by my little outburst. "You needed it."

There are times in your life when you want to sock a good person in the face. This was one of those times, but I didn't act on it. "I *need* to be with my father. What if he wakes up and he's alone? Worse, what if he…" I couldn't even think the words, let alone say them.

Max stood and put his hands out in front of me in a shush gesture. "Relax. I just got off the phone with Matt and Tiffany Rains. There's been no change."

"You were supposed to wake me in a few minutes!" I yelled and put my hand on the doorknob. "How can I trust you if you don't listen to me when I ask you for something as simple as that?" was my parting shot as I left the room and attempted to slam the door. Only, since we were in a hotel, the damn thing did the slow crawl to a close due to the efficient hydraulics. The level of anger simmering within me rose exponentially.

"Mia!" I heard Max yell as I hoofed it to the elevator and smashed the button over and over. It never made the thing come any faster, but it made me feel better, dammit!

Max exited the room and walked cautiously to my side. "Mia, I'm sorry. You really needed sleep. I stayed up to date with calls to the family to make sure that if there was any change at all, we could be there in two minutes. I'd never attempt to control you."

I rolled my eyes and crossed my arms over my chest. "Yeah, well, what do you want me to say? I'm worried about my dad. I don't know exactly where my boyfriend is, and I haven't heard from him in two weeks."

"You haven't heard from Weston in two weeks?"

"Did I fucking stutter? Jeez." I pressed my hand to my forehead where that ever-present ache was coming back.

Max frowned and put a hand to my bicep. "I'll make some calls. If anyone can get the goods, it's Aspen. She's got a lot of connections in the movie-making industry. Would that help?"

A peace offering? I'd take it.

I nodded. "Yeah, thank you." The elevator door opened, and I entered. He remained in the hallway.

"I'm going to wait for Maddy to wake up," Max said.

"Don't wake her up. She needs the rest."

His eyes widened, and he smirked. "And you didn't? I see how it is. You can call the shots for Maddy, but when I try to help you, I'm the jerk?" He smiled that crooked one that I knew made Cyndi swoon.

"I'm the big sister," I countered as if that answered all the questions of the universe.

He pointed a thumb at his chest. "Big brother." He grinned, and I smiled for the first time in a week.

"Yeah, well, that's a new title. You've got to earn that kind of clout, Maximus."

His eyes twinkled as he kept the elevator door from closing. "I intend to for the rest of my life, sugar."

He let the doors close and waved before turning around and heading back to the room. Max had made his point. He was in for the long haul and had no intention of us not being a big, happy family. He'd gained a pair of sisters. A blood relation to his mother and father. Something he didn't have a few weeks ago. The type of guy Max was, he'd make the most of it and give both Maddy and me his all. Hell, he already had in spades, but I was too far into my own head and my heart was carved out with worry, so I couldn't express how much him being here meant to me. How, when this year was over, I planned on making a very big effort to be a part of his regular life and looked forward to it. I'd work on it when I could. There would be time. Hopefully.

CHAPTER THREE

"I come bearing gifts!" Ginelle strutted into the hospital room. One arm held a plant, not flowers, and the other carried a mysterious brown paper bag.

Ginelle set the potted array of desert succulents near the few bouquets of flowers, walked over to Pops, and kissed his forehead, mindful of the tubes all around him. "Wake up, old man. Your girls are aging, watching you sleep," she said.

Leave it to Gin to be sweet and snarky at the same time. She watched his face for a moment as though she were waiting to see him do what she'd asked and open his eyes. He didn't. With a shake of her head, she turned and looked at me, head cocked to the side. She gave me a once over and then she clucked her tongue.

"Well, you look a little better. Still like shit, but you must have gotten some decent shut-eye and finally blessed us all with a shower." She leaned forward and sniffed my head, loudly making her point. "Yep, fresh as a daisy."

I shoved at her chest and smiled. "Shut up, skank. What's in the bag?"

Blinking rapidly, she lifted a finger to her cheek. "Whatever do you mean?"

I half-chuckled, already feeling lighter in her presence. Gin swayed her hips and arms, making a real deal out of sitting on the loveseat and pulling items out of her bag of goodies.

"Okay, since it's been over a week and you're flabby ass hasn't left this room, I figured some serious shit to pass the time was in order." Gin grabbed each item and showed them to me. "Deck of cards, crosswords, Sudoku…"

"Sudoku? What the heck is that?"

Ginelle shrugged. "It's some type of math game."

"You brought me a math game? *Me?*"

She grinned and flipped a few pages in the book. "I don't know. There was this really cute guy working at the grocery store, and we kind of got to talking. I told him what I was looking for so he pointed to all this shit. And I just grabbed and flirted." She looked out the window as if she were remembering the moment. "Anyway, he said it was his favorite, loved trying to break all the puzzles, blah blah. Really, I was more interested in watching his mouth move and wondering how he could put those plump lips to use on my…" She pointed to her crotch.

"Gin!" I looked over at Pops. "Girl, he can hear you."

Her brows furrowed. "Really? You think so?"

"Yeah, I do. So don't talk about wanting a grocery store clerk to you know." I gestured to my own hoo-hah.

Ginelle rolled her eyes. "Whatever. Anyway, Mads can work on that one." Good point. Maddy was the brains in this family. "I've also got some fashion mags, and of course, your favorite…" She held up an issue of *Street Bike Magazine* and made it dance in front of my face.

There was a smokin' hot Playboy Bunny on the cover, dangling over the side of the brand new Yamaha YZF-R1 super bike. The street bike was as slick as the desert highway after a first rain. It had bright royal blue trim and plenty of shiny chrome to blind the eyes of the dudes scoping it out when they should be driving. The bike's 4-cylinder, 16-valve engine was a technical marvel with its cross-plane crank, titanium connecting rods, and compact combustion chambers. The sexy beast tipped the scales at around four hundred and forty pounds. I'd give my left breast to own something that beautiful. Eh, not really. Well, maybe.

My eyes started to fill. Damn, I had the most amazing best friend. "Thanks, Gin," I said, my voice clouded with emotion.

She crossed her petite and toned-as-fuck legs over one another, leaned back, and laid her arms out wide. "So update me. Where's Surfer Boy? Why isn't he here?"

With that one question, the emotional weight of the world was back on my shoulders. I'd contacted Judi, his house attendant, and even reached out to his sister, Jeananna, and his mother, Claire. Neither had heard anything, and everyone was starting to worry. They didn't think it was that unusual for Weston to be out of pocket since they'd go a month sometimes not hearing from him, but that fact that I hadn't heard had made their hackles rise. Me? Not so much. Especially not since we'd committed our lives to one another and I'd moved into his house. We were looking forward to spending time together. He was supposed to be home when I was done in Texas, and then I'd hoped to be able to meet him before moving on to client number nine. I'd heard nothing.

Finally, I called Jennifer, the director's wife. She was in her last month of pregnancy so her husband hadn't left with Wes, which was also why Wes had to go and for much longer than expected. Turned out he was taking on the primary director's role. Last thing the director heard was from an assistant who'd said things were going smoothly, but they didn't have any service to make calls or hit the Internet. They were deep in the Southeast Asian islands with a small filming crew, only about fifteen people—one of whom was Gina DeLuca. It made sense, even though it made my teeth hurt and my heart squeeze to hear it. I knew her character was in the middle of a love triangle in the storyline and since one of them passed away, she had to reshoot all the scenes, but that didn't answer when they were due back or why he couldn't find a way to make a call.

"All I know is that he's deep in Asia on a re-shoot but no additional information has come out."

"He should be here, Mia. This is not scoring him any BFF points. Every day he's not here, he gets higher and higher up on my shit list."

I sighed and rubbed at the back of my neck, trying to work some knots out. "Believe me, he'd be here if he knew what was going on. His voicemail on his phone is completely full. It doesn't even ring anymore, just goes right to the message telling me that the box is full and to try back later."

"Do you think something's really wrong?" Her eyes turned soft and her pretty lips were compressed in a flat line.

I looked out the window and then to my dad. As much as it pained me to say, I admitted to her how bad I thought it was. "Yeah, Gin. I think something really bad has happened and nobody knows."

"Should we call the police or something?"

"It's too soon to tell. I asked his family, and they don't want anything hitting the media if a cop leaks the information, but frankly, I don't give a flying fuck. The more people who know the better, in my opinion, but maybe that's self-serving. I don't know enough about the business to know if this is unusual. I'm totally over-reacting. I'm sure everything is fine. Just fine." I said it twice trying to convince myself even though I couldn't shake the ugly feeling I had.

Gin clasped her hands together, placed her elbows on her knees, and rested her chin on her laced fingers. "What are you going to do?" She didn't say it in a way that was meant to harm, but knowing there was nothing I really could do sent an arrow straight through the heart. The man I loved was missing, had been incommunicado going into three weeks, and no one had heard from him. And worse, I seemed to be the only one really worried. Maybe that alone was my clue that I was making a mountain out of a molehill.

I shrugged and leaned back in the chair, leaning my head back on the hard plastic ridge and staring at the ceiling tiles. "I don't know. Max has a call into Aspen Reynolds, a friend of his…"

"Wait, what? Back the truck up. Put that fucker in reverse! *The* Aspen Reynolds. Aspen Bright-Reynolds of AIR Bright Industries? The ridiculously beautiful blonde, big cowboy husband the exact opposite of her, Aspen Reynolds? Has the most adorable toddler in the world named Hannah?"

"Um, yeah. And that's really weird that you know that much about a woman I just met."

She stood. "You met her?" Her hand went to her hips and she struck a seriously pissy pose. Oh, no, man, I did not need this shit today. Gin's attitude can only be handled in small bursts, and I didn't have the mental wherewithal to deal with it today. "I can't believe you. I swear, all the time, you get put in these positions where you could help me, your bestie, your top skank, and it's like my name is Skipper! As in...Skipped Her!"

I pressed both hands into my temples. "Gin, tell me why me knowing Aspen is such a big deal."

She made a sound between a groan and gag. "She's the biggest in the industry. Models, magazines, actresses, big time Vegas shows..." She added an emphasis on the Vegas Shows.

"So she runs some shows and you want in on them?" I stated plainly so we could get to the point of her frustration faster. The quicker I dealt with it, the better.

"You make it sound like I'm being all greedy or something. Seriously, Aspen runs a lot of stuff in both our industries. Everybody knows her. She's like one of the richest women in the world, and she's only thirty!" Her voice rose as her excitement grew.

I remembered back at the ranch, when I'd met the leggy blonde. She was sweet, wore really nice clothes, but paired them with flip-flops. That right there told me that clothes were something she put on just like the rest of us, but she enjoyed the creature comforts after a long business day. The blonde also lived on a modest ranch out in the boonies just outside Dallas—next door to Max. They had a nice ranch, but it wasn't like the *Lifestyles of the Rich and Famous* or anything. It was a nice country place with awesome land, horses, a few steers, but mostly it was just a quiet place to live for the small family of three.

"Woman seemed pretty normal to me."

Ginelle sliced a hand through the air. "She's not normal. Perfect, yes. Normal, no. She's literally my girl crush."

I squinted. "I thought I was your girl crush." I pouted.

A bit of the tension left the room when Gin laughed and plopped back in the chair. "She's my fantasy girl crush. You think you could introduce me?"

"Yep. If we're ever at Max's ranch and they're home, of course I can."

She clapped her hands together and stared dreamily at the wall behind my head. "That would be awesome."

Whatever. "You're a nut."

"Mmm, nuts," she moaned.

★ ★ ★

The next day, my phone rang as I was pulling the dead flowers out of the arrangements Pops had received. The daises that Judi Croft had sent on behalf of Wes, even though Wes still didn't know what was going on, had stayed strong. Their pretty white petals and yellow middles reminded me of really good times. I hoped that was a metaphor for the resilience of our relationship and his love, but more importantly, his life.

I looked down at the phone and the display said Unknown Caller. I picked it up. "Hello?"

"Is this Mia Saunders?" the woman asked.

"Yes, this is she. Who is this?" The little hairs on the back of my next stood up. Something was wrong. I felt it before when the hospital called about Pops and the feeling was the same.

"This is Aspen Jensen. Remember we hung out—" she started, but I cut her off.

"Yes, hi. Sorry, Aspen. I didn't recognize your voice over the phone. What can I do for you?"

A long pause passed through the line. "Mia, I don't know how to tell you this, but Max had me looking into Weston's whereabouts."

Dread. Nothing but a wall of pure black evil dread pressed against my body from both sides as if flattening me between two metal plates. I struggled to find my breath.

"I know. He told me. I appreciate you using your connections. Have you found anything?" I asked, knowing, just *knowing,* what she was about to say would hurt.

"Mia, honey, his team, the entire crew are MIA. Well, not exactly all of them. My intel found out that while they were filming in one of the Southeast Asian islands, three boats filled with men carrying guns arrived. They're known to be part of a radical and religious extremist terrorist cell. The armed men jumped out, claiming they were purifying their land and were going to make an example of the Americans." She paused for a few moments, cleared her throat, and continued.

"Honey, they shot nine members of the crew, seven of whom died, stole their equipment, captured the remaining six. The two wounded were medevaced to a hospital where one died during surgery. The other is still fighting for his life now. Mia, the remaining six are being held hostage. Honey...I'm so sorry. Our government is involved. The President is involved."

Oh. My. God. "I don't understand! Are you telling me that he could either be dead, fighting for his life in the hospital, or is being held hostage by terrorists?" A lump the size of a golf ball formed in my throat as the severity of the situation hit home.

Her voice cracked, and I could tell she was sobbing.

"I'm sorry, I'm sorry…." Then the phone went quiet for a moment and a masculine voice came on the line.

"Darlin', this is Hank. I know you're probably scared as hell, but we don't know if he was one of the men shot or captured. He could be alive. We're doing everything we can to get the information."

I fell to the floor just as Max ran into the room. "What the hell?" He hefted me up, sat me on the small loveseat, and then grabbed the cell.

"This is Maxwell Cunningham. Who am I speaking to?" He stopped speaking and listened for a long time. His body seemed to harden into stone right in front of me. His jaw went tight and he growled through his teeth. "What's being done? I want intel. I need the names of the men who didn't make it and the two who were treated. I need that information yesterday, Hank. Do you or Aspen have any connections to the executive branch?"

While I watched Max pace, his cowboy boots heavy on the linoleum floor, it dawned on me. I had connections to the government. Warren Shipley. And that man owed me a very big favor since I didn't put his son into jail for trying to rape me.

"I do," I said. It came out as more of a whisper, seeing as my throat had that giant ball of emotion clogging the way.

Max kept talking but held a hand over the receiver. "Just a minute. What, Sis?"

Pushing down the crushing weight and desire to curl up into a tiny little ball and cry myself into sweet oblivion, I sat up. "Um, my June client. Warren Shipley. His son is one of the senators for California and Warren runs high government level deals between this country and others all over the world. He knows the president. There's a picture of both of them in his office. He owes me a favor."

Max's eyes narrowed, and his mouth twisted into a grimace. I wasn't about to share why the rich socialite owed me a favor, and I never would. I'd moved on. I was past that and doing well mentally and physically. Until all of this happened.

Having a plan, any plan, helped me believe I could make it through until we got more information. Wes, my beautiful Wes. He could be in the clutches of men who had absolutely no care in the world for Americans, our politics, or our religious beliefs—the type of men who spent all of their time torturing and killing those who didn't share their beliefs. Worse than that, he could be dead already, or fighting for his life in some faraway hospital in Asia.

Dear God, please, please, let him be alive. Please let him come back to me.

★ ★ ★

After I got myself cleaned up at the hotel, I sat down, and shaking like a leaf falling off a tree, I called Warren. He was happy to hear from me until he heard the reason for my call. He promised he would use every resource known to him, including his personal connection to the president, and get back to me within the day, if not sooner. He said he had some resources in the Philippines that were good at getting information about terrorist groups. So good, they'd helped him steer clear of any when transporting his goods through Asia just last month.

I felt the next six hours pass as though I were wading

through concrete. People came and went, gathered around me, but I didn't recognize their presence. Not in the mental sense. I may have nodded, given a few yes and no answers, but mostly I walked around the hospital and the hotel as if I were a zombie. Because I was. The sheer volume of fear was like electricity over the skin of my entire body. If someone touched me, it was as if I'd been zapped by a sizzling hot poker. There was no breaking through it. All I could do was wait, wonder, and worry. Christ, the worry for Wes's safety was a physical, breathing thing, a frightening being that controlled my every thought and action. I was no longer me. I was just it—the worry.

The worry wouldn't let me eat. The worry wouldn't let me hold basic conversations with people who loved and cared about me. No, it wormed its way so far into my subconscious mind that Mia was no longer there. Only *it* lived within me, creeping its ugly, disgusting thoughts into my brain. The thoughts turning to images of my beautiful Wes cowering in a corner, naked, petrified, wounded, in excruciating pain, screaming to be let go, let out. He'd know in his mind that he might never leave, that he would likely die there.

Running to the bathroom, I hurled the small bit of breakfast I'd eaten earlier that morning. I heaved and hacked into the toilet, trying to expel that evil beast within, the one making despair so prevalent I didn't recognize what beautiful looked like. Couldn't even see it anymore, even when looking at my baby sister's face. The one face in all the world I'd found solace in, until Wes.

"Wes!" I screamed and then heaved into the basin. "Come back, goddammit! Don't leave me here. You promised paradise!" I howled, not even aware that I was in the private bathroom where my Pops was fighting for *his* life. My tears flowed alongside the bile and stomach acid working its way out of me.

"Sugar!" Max crouched down. His thighs braced on the sides of my ribs, and he held my hair back. "You're not alone, Mia. I'm here, Sis. I'll always be here. You're not alone," he whispered against my hairline as my stomach stopped lurching. He covered me with his body like a blanket, warding off the chill I hadn't been able to shake since I'd gotten to Vegas over a week ago. Helping me up, he leaned me against the sink, wet some paper towels, and wiped my mouth before getting more and wiping my face.

"I won't make it if he's gone," I whispered.

Max closed his eyes then pressed his forehead to mine. "I'll see to it that you do. Maddy needs you. Your father needs you, and Mia, honey, I need you."

"But Max, I love him."

He let out a tortured sigh. "I know, darlin'. I know, and if something ever happened to Cyndi, I'd lose my mind, but *you* can't. Not now. We don't know what's going on yet. Give it a little time. Let your friend find out what he can. Then, depending on what they say, we'll handle it. Together. Okay?"

I licked my lips and rubbed my aching forehead against his. I looped my arms around his head, shoved my face in his warm neck, and let the tears flow. He held me and let me cry while I whispered all my fears to him—that I'd lost Wes, that I'd lost Pops, that I'd lose Maddy when she got married, and now that I had Max, that I'd lose him too. Over and over, he assured me that none of those things were going to happen. He said we needed to have a little faith in God, in the strength of Pops and of Wes, and that we'd all come out of this smelling like home-baked apple pie.

More than anything, I wanted to believe what he'd promised. For the first time in my life, I gave it up to God, to the universe, to anyone who would listen to get me through this with my loved ones coming out of it alive and well.

CHAPTER FOUR

"Dear God, I uh, I know I don't pray to you very often, and I don't go to church as much as You'd like." I groaned and blew out a deep breath. "That's a lie. You know it's a lie. I never go to church. Can't remember the last time I set foot in one."

Pinching my lips together, I pressed them into my clasped fingers and closed my eyes. I was leaning over the side of the bed at the hotel. The sun had just set, and Maddy and Matt had left to have dinner before doing the night shift with Pops. I was supposed to be resting, but in reality, I couldn't sleep. Wes—worrying about him, scared out of my mind as to what might be happening—was all I could focus on. I wanted so badly to just get on a plane and fly to the island where he was last seen. But I didn't even have the exact details about which island they were on. Warren hadn't called, and it had been twelve hours. Twelve full hours of absolutely nothing.

No word, no hope, no nothing.

And that's what brought me to the moment where I'd knelt in front of the bed, put my hands up in prayer, and pleaded with a God I'd never truly connected with before.

"Let me start over, God. I can do that, right?" I shook my head. "I can do that. You don't care. You know I'm not perfect. Okay, here goes." My entire body shuddered as I started again. "The man I love is missing. I refuse to believe he's dead. I think I'd know if he was dead. Wouldn't I? I mean, You make these soulmate connections, right? Soulmates feel the other in a way that's not describable. Therefore, if my other half wasn't on this Earth anymore, I'd feel it." Waiting to see if God was going to answer left me feeling rather hollow inside. If He could just send a flicker, a zap of energy, a pulse wave, anything to allow me to believe I was on the right track, I'd have been thrilled.

Moments passed as I waited. Nothing.

Groaning, I blew out a long breath. "Here's the deal. Wes means more to me than I've been able to admit to him. If you take him from me, I won't get the chance to tell him." I sighed and rustled up the courage to say what I needed to say to Wes, even if I was channeling it through prayer.

"You make loving someone seem easy, when it's only ever been hard. Being with you is like sitting on the surface of the sun without being burned. The love I have for you has changed me. Made me someone different. A woman worthy of the more you've promised. Our paradise."

Then the tears fell. "Please, God, please don't take away paradise before I've had a chance to breathe in the air, soak in the warmth, delve into the depths of its beauty."

My body started rocking back and forth, the words whispered over and over in a prayer, a chant.

"Please. Please don't take Wes away from me."

"Don't take Wes away."

"Don't take Wes away."

★ ★ ★

Several pings jarred me out of a fitful sleep. I'd fallen asleep while leaning over the side of the bed where I'd knelt to pray. The last thing I remembered was begging the Lord not to take away the man I loved. Time would only tell if He'd taken pity on me.

The display on my cell phone blinked against the wall next to the side table where I'd set it to charge. Like an old woman with severe arthritis, I maneuvered my stiff joints and exhausted body into a standing position. Lifting my arms up high toward the ceiling, I rolled onto my toes and reached for the sky, stretching long unused muscles. Various joints popped and crackled, protesting the last week-and-a-half of sitting in plastic chairs, kneeling by bedsides, and not getting enough rest.

I ambled over to the side of the bed and plopped down, picking up my phone.

What if it's news about Wes?

Equal parts trepidation and anticipation tightened my chest as I glanced down and frowned.

To: Mia Saunders
From: Blaine Douchebag Pintero
Pretty, pretty Mia. I haven't received payment. You owe me.

I owe him! The nerve of that fucking bastard.

Pressing my fingers into my temples did not alleviate the tension that came with the necessity of dealing with Blaine. The simple truth was, I didn't have his money, and there was no way I was going to be able to make it magically appear. Not only was I going to be a hundred grand shy for missing my payment this month, last month's payment went to the client I'd flaked. So technically, I was two hundred thousand in the hole because he wouldn't be getting a payment at the end of this month either. To date, I'd paid him six months' worth at the end of each month, for a total of six hundred thousand toward the million Pops owed. Millie had no choice but to pay off bachelor number nine the hundred thousand I made in August from Max to save her own ass and the company. I usually didn't get paid until the end of the month, and since I wasn't working September, that was another hundred thousand lost. Business was business, and a man with a hundred grand to blow on an escort could wrap Millie up in court for ages. She'd have lost everything. Now I'm the one who stands to lose everything…again. Fuck!

What would I do? If Wes were here, he'd offer to pay the debt. Of course, he would. At this point, I'd have no choice but to accept his offer, at least until I got the extra money from my brand new ownership in Cunningham Oil & Gas. I could ask Max for the money. He'd give it to me… but ugh, I couldn't do that to him. Nothing like a long lost sister begging for cash. "Hey, I'm your new sister. Thanks for twenty-five percent of your family legacy. Can I borrow two hundred thousand until I make money off you next year and can pay you back?"

Falling back on the bed, I stared at the text again. I just needed to ask for more time.

To: Blaine Douchebag Pintero
From: Mia Saunders
Pops took a turn. Not working these two months. Need more time. Five more months and I'll have it with interest.

I figured the adding interest part would do it. If anything,

Blaine was a businessman and money was his kryptonite.

To: Mia Saunders
From: Blaine Douchebag Pintero
Let's discuss over dinner. Our place. You remember.

Instantly, I went from wired to straight pissed off. How dare he try to get me to go out with him when my father was dying and my boyfriend was missing? Okay, he didn't know about the boyfriend part, but still. What angle was he trying to work? Last time I was here, he asked me out. Now again. It's like he forgot that he cheated on me with not one woman but two—at the same fucking time—the very day he proposed. When he asked, I wanted to take a little time to think about it. I needed to decide if I wanted to be a kept woman. Blaine had offered me the world—jewels, a penthouse apartment overlooking the strip. The works. Said I wouldn't have to worry about anything but looking beautiful and taking care of my man. At the time, it had sounded like one helluva deal. Plus, the bonus was that he'd offered to pay for Maddy's college education if I agreed to be his wife.

Being so young, I needed to think about it. On the one hand, it afforded me a way out of one living hell, but could promptly put me smack dab into another. I knew he wasn't just a businessman. I'd seen the clandestine meetings, the strange need for bodyguards all the time. People we'd meet in the casinos or along the street knew him, or knew of him, and what they knew put a look of fear into their eyes—one that couldn't be hidden. That never sat right with me. It was only later, after I'd found him balls-deep in his receptionist's snatch and mouth sampling the wares of her twin sister's nasty pussy that I found out what his main business really was. When he'd told me he was in the lending business, it wasn't for a local brokerage or banking firm. It was a whole different kind of lending where, if you didn't pay up on time with interest, you took a plunge off a pier into shark-infested waters wearing concrete shoes.

That was the type of man Blaine Pintero really was, and I had the lucky job of dealing with his bullshit because he'd fucked over my dad and me in the process.

To: Blaine Douchebag Pintero
From: Mia Saunders
Can't. My father is dying. Name your terms.
To: Mia Saunders
From: Blaine Douchebag Pintero
I don't negotiate in writing. Dinner. Our place. Don't defy me. You'll regret it.

What was he going to do that hadn't already made me wish I were dead? Hurt my father more? Besides, he had gotten six hundred thousand dollars from me already. I'd proven the wait would be worth it. I did some quick math in my head and put my fingers to work, praying he'd take the bait. The sick feeling in my stomach was not helping. I needed to eat something more than a package of leftover saltines from Max's club sandwich from yesterday if I was going to deal with douchebags like Blaine.

To: Blaine Douchebag Pintero
From: Mia Saunders

No. You'll receive the next payment end of October with 5% interest. That's all I can give.

I read it several times and then hit send. I sat, clutching the phone, waiting for the little sign to pop up that he'd seen it. And then I prayed. Hard. *Let him accept the deal.* Just give me this one get out of jail free card.

To: Mia Saunders
From: Blaine Douchebag Pintero
That's two missed payments. I'm sorry, pretty Mia, you give me what I want and meet me for dinner Friday night, or there will be hell to pay.

Fuck! I can't win for losing. A door slamming against the doorframe startled me out of my reverie. Maxwell's large frame entered my room.

"Hey, your father's doing better!" he said with triumph and joy coloring his words. His chest was jerking back and forth as if he'd run the hundred-yard dash.

I stood up fast and then caught myself as a wave of dizziness overcame me. Bright little stars dotted my vision as I blinked rapidly. "What happened?" Once I got my bearings, I walked over to him, and together we made our way out of the hotel room, down the elevator, and across the street.

"Don't really know. The doc just said they were going to take him off the respirator. Apparently, he's breathing on his own."

Stopping in the middle of the crosswalk on a very busy Vegas street was not a good idea, but that didn't stop me from doing it, so taken I was by his statement. The wave of relief that hit me was all encompassing, like a tsunami, controlling all thought and halting my ability to move forward.

Max chuckled and looped an arm around my shoulders. "Come on, Sis. Let's go check on your dad and see what else the doc has to say."

When we entered the room, Maddy was there, snuggled into the arms of her fiancé, Matt. His parents were standing off to the side in silent support. The doctor was pushing buttons on Pops's machines. His gaze lifted to me as I got closer.

"Ah, perfect. Thank you, Mr. Cunningham, for bringing her so quickly," the doctor said to Max and then focused on me. "Now that you and your sister are here, I can give you the information together. Mr. Saunders has apparently begun to try and breathe on his own. His efforts are now strong enough that we can set the ventilator so that it will breathe for him only if his oxygen saturation falls below a certain level."

I licked my lips and inhaled slowly, gathering my thoughts. "Does that mean he's getting better? The medication is working."

The doctor took a breath. "We don't know for sure, but it's definitely a good sign. In my experience, patients who start breathing on their own end up getting stronger far more quickly. The problem in your father's case is that he was already in a coma. One we couldn't explain. All his readings were normal at the time. Until he caught the virus, followed by the two anaphylactic reactions, which were a massive systemic insult. There was also the very real risk that he would become ventilator-dependent. It's good that he's started to try to breathe on his own, but this type of recovery takes time, and we'll just have to wait and see. We should know more over the next few days, but so far, I'd say the outlook is much better," he said before closing Pops's chart, hooking it on the bed, and leaving the room.

Maddy shuffled over to me. "That's good news, right?" Her lips trembled the same way they used to when she was a little girl and was trying to be brave.

I pulled Maddy into my arms. She wrapped her long arms around me and we held one another. "I think so, baby girl. I really do. Pops is strong. He's been through a lot, but he has us to come back to. That has to count for something. It has to be enough."

Max came up behind us and tugged us into the warmth of his broad chest. "It's enough. Believe me, ladies, you two are more than enough."

"Agreed," Matt said and smiled at my sister.

Another point for Matt. He'd been there for my sister the entire way, only leaving at night when the hospital visiting hours were over, but he was back by her side at the first opportunity. His parents came daily for a couple of hours, too. The Rains family definitely had our backs. Maddy would be loved her whole life long by that family, and any children they had down the road would be spoiled and want for nothing.

Job well done, Mia. I mentally patted myself on the back. The one thing I did right. Raised my sister to be something more, to want and work for everything life could offer. She was on the road to having it all, and I couldn't be any happier for her. Now if some of that good karma could shine down on me and bring Wes home and Pops back to the land of the

312

living, I'd have it all, too.

On that note, I yanked my cell from my pocket and fired off the message to the one man I didn't want to see no matter the cost.

To: Blaine Douchebag Pintero
From: Mia Saunders
You'll be eating alone Friday night. Deal with it.
With a swipe of my thumb I hit send. Screw him, and screw his bullshit.

★ ★ ★

Later that night, I got the call I'd been waiting for all day.

"Hello, Warren?" I answered so quickly that the words were a bit of a jumble.

"Hey, Mia." Warren's voice wasn't warm, but it wasn't cold either. It was firm and filled with sorrow. God, no.

I sat on the end of the coffee table and braced for the worst. Max's eyes cut to mine, and he leaned forward, putting his palms on my knees. I clasped his hand with one of mine and held on so tight my knuckles turned white.

"Just tell me. Is he dead?" The two seconds before Warren answered could have been a lifetime. I'd never forget what I felt in that speck of time. Destroyed. Damaged. Broken. Three things I never wanted to be again came to life in a tiny spark of flint against steel. Thankfully, it didn't catch fire.

"No, honey, he's not." He sucked in a breath and cleared his throat.

"Is he in the hospital?"

Warren sighed low and deep. There was nothing left to say. I knew. I fucking knew it. He was alive, but still gone. The man I loved, the man I wanted to spend the rest of my life with, the man it took me seven months to break down my walls for, was being held by radical religious terrorists half a world away, and I was here. Sitting at a table in a hotel practically connected to a hospital where my father was fighting to live. My world right now was more fucked up than it ever had been, and I had no idea how to fix it.

"Listen to me, the president and secretary of state are on this. Now, America does not negotiate with terrorists, but we are talking to other officials in Indonesia."

"Indonesia? Is that where they were when they were filming?" I asked, confused.

"No, they were filming in a very remote area in the northern part of Sri Lanka. The northern part of the island hadn't had a terrorist attack since 2009, and the military does have a solid presence in the country but not that far north. It's considered a dangerous area."

"Why the hell were they filming there if it was dangerous?"

Warren groaned. "Honey, the production team found out about a couple unique spots to shoot a scene, and your guy, he wanted to get the scene just right."

Goddamn it, Wes. Trying to take on this new role to the nth degree and conquer it. "Stupid," I gritted through my teeth.

"Well, be that as it may, the team being held includes Weston and Gina DeLuca, the lead actress in the film."

"Gina DeLuca." I mumbled, her name alone grating along my nerves.

"They have both of them and four other men. It's bad, though. Mia, honey, there's something I need to tell you." His voice took on a harder edge. The kind that meant I needed to listen and what I was going to hear was going to shake the very ground I walked on.

I swallowed down the fear and waited for him to continue. Max's hand was warm, sending support and love, and I strangled it with my grip, but he didn't move a muscle.

"A video was sent to the military and forwarded to us."

"What's in the video, Warren?" Shivers of dread rippled along my spine, and I sat up straighter. A knot in my gut twisted so tight I couldn't do anything but hold my breath.

"In the video, your guy was talking. On his knees, face to face with another crew member. They forced him to say what they wanted." His voice cut off and a few ragged breaths could be heard.

Tears rippled down my face as if my body knew before my mind that the situation had gone from horrendous to life-shattering. Max tried to wipe the tears away but I shook my head.

Warren cleared his throat and stoically continued. "Uh, he said they wanted to show westerners everywhere what was going to happen to them if they soiled their country with their vile liberal politics and disgusting religious beliefs. Honey, as Wes was talking, a masked man lifted up a machete and cut off the head of one of his crew."

A sob tore from my lungs. "God, no. No, Jesus, please no!" I screamed.

Max grabbed the phone, put it on speaker, and set it on the table so he could hear.

"What did he say?" Max growled, his protective bear

coming out in spades.

"They cut off a crew member's head in front of Wes!" I cried, the tears pouring like Niagara Falls.

Max's face turned hard, his lips white as they formed a harsh line. "Get it together, Mia. You need to get it together, darlin'. What else, Mr. Shipley? This is Maxwell Cunningham, her brother. You can speak freely."

Warren coughed and then proceeded to tell us that the terrorists had traveled by boat with the six hostages to Indonesia, a much larger country where it was easier to hide. Our military already had a pretty good idea where they were being held, and after that video was sent, they were going in to every possible location in question. There were five possibilities. Special Forces teams were being brought together, and once information was gleaned on which location held the hostages, they would move forward with a mission to secure them. He said it could be days before we knew the end result.

When the call ended, I sat there in a daze. My laid-back movie-making surfer guy, the man of my dreams, had watched a co-worker and, knowing Wes and how he connected with people, a friend murdered right in front of his eyes. How the hell does someone get over something like that? Whatever it took, I'd be there for him every step of the way. If he survived, God willing, I'd kiss every single last one of his wounds, mental and physical. I'd take it all away with my words, my body, and by loving him more than he'd ever known in this lifetime.

"I love you, Wes." I said the words out loud. To him, *for* him. Even though Wes was nowhere near, maybe, just maybe, those words would whisper along the air into a remote location in Indonesia, where he would, at the very least, *feel* them…against his skin, within his heart, as part of his soul.

CHAPTER FIVE

Two weeks in Vegas and the zombie vibe had taken on a whole new level of creep-factor. Both Maddy and I shuffled around one another like those little robots that cleaned your floor automatically but didn't run into one another. The Roomba, I think it is? As if the two of us had a sensor a foot around our entire bodies, we moved through the maze of our days on autopilot without touching. Maybe we needed the touching, but neither of us could make an effort. They'd taken the breathing machine away a couple of days ago. Pops was definitely breathing on his own, and the medications were finally clearing the infection. The doctors were pleased with his new prognosis.

Maddy and I were as well, but the fact that he still had tubes coming out of every orifice didn't make us feel all that content. In another week, Maddy and Matt would go back to school. She needed to get her life ready for that change. It was her third year of college and she was taking a full load as usual. My over-achieving sister. Secretly, I loved that she put so much on her shoulders because it meant that she definitely wouldn't be tying the knot any time soon.

Remembering that, I still needed to have a chat with goody two-shoes Matt about his issue of pressuring my sister to marry. If he loved her, he needed to wait. Finish up school and show her the kind of man he is. Besides, I wondered how the conversation about Maddy being interested in Cunningham Oil & Gas and working in Texas was going to go. Would it be a deal breaker? Matt had a great family in the Vegas area, the type that you didn't want to stray too far away from. Would he for her? I guessed only time would tell.

My phone pinged in my back pocket, and I pulled it out. It was a video text message from an unknown caller. Frowning, I clicked on the message, and what I saw almost sent me to my knees. I hadn't even opened the message yet, but the square box framed a face I knew almost as well as my own. Ginelle. A black strip of fabric over her eyes, her nose bleeding, blood running down her lip into her mouth.

Without word, I ran, literally ran outside to the garden space and clicked over the little arrow that would play the video.

What the hell had I done?

The video started, and Ginelle's voice was scared, tears coming down her cheeks from beneath the fabric tied around her head. She licked her lips and sobbed. Her bottom lip was cut, swollen, and purple. The video panned back, and I found she was dressed in one of her work outfits. Feathers and sequins were shredded as a man's hand came into view. The fingertips of his meaty hand caressed down the open space between her breasts in a revolting show of power. I wanted to scream, yell, and throw the phone, but I couldn't. Gin was there, somewhere, being manhandled by men I could only assume were Blaine's goons.

The motherfucker had gone after my best friend.

It hadn't occurred to me that he'd kidnap her. I stared in horror as the man put a beefy hand around her jugular, mimicking the hand placement of snapping one's neck.

"Mia!" Gin cried, and I crouched low, the space around me turning black. The sun was gone. The garden disappeared. It was only me, the darkness, and the moment where I watched my best friend cry out in fear for her life.

"Say it, bitch!" The goon's hands tightened around her head and neck.

Ginelle coughed and gagged and nodded. "Mia, uh, dinner at seven...tonight. You know the place. If you call the cops, they'll..." Her voice cracked and the man shook her violently. More blood trickled from her nose and into her mouth. She licked it away and cried out when he yanked her hair tight in his fist. "They'll k-kill m-me if you tell anyone." As the screen started to pan back, Ginelle whispered. "Not your fault. I love you, Mia."

The screen went black, and the ping of an incoming text jolted me into action. I clicked on it.

To: Mia Saunders
From: Blaine Douchebag Pintero
She's a sweet little doll. My friend likes her a lot. 7:00 sharp.
Be there.

As if possessed, I typed my response in record speed and clicked send without reading it.

To: Blaine Douchebag Pintero
From: Mia Saunders
I'll be there. Please, please don't hurt her.

Before I could wipe the snot and tears from my face, he responded and my heart sank.

To: Mia Saunders
From: Blaine Douchebag Pintero
Don't defy me again or I'll let him have her. Dress to impress.
We have plans.

My ass hit the ground, and my tailbone smarted when it banged against the concrete. The pain was nothing compared to the ache in my heart and the vile acid burning a hole through my stomach lining. Blaine and his goons had Ginelle. Terrorists had Wes. Pops was in a coma. Life had become a twisted action thriller movie. I was the unsuspecting character with few resources and I was emotionally jacked up.

There was no other option but for me to follow Blaine's demands. He wanted to meet at what he called "our place," and I'd meet him there. Such a twisted douchebag.

The place he referred to was Luna Rosa, an Italian restaurant he'd taken me to on our very first date. We sat outside on the patio that faced Lake Las Vegas. White twinkle lights wrapped on the palm trees had given his skin an ethereal glow. Back then I was completely enamored with Blaine. Six-foot-four, a few years my senior, with dark hair that looked perfect against a crisp navy-blue suit. He could have been a model with his svelte body and bone structure. His unique green and yellow eyes were one thing that always worked in his favor. He could mesmerize the panties off any girl in a heartbeat with a single glance.

Blaine had definitely gotten under my skin the very first time I'd served him a drink at the casino I was working at years ago. That night, he'd come in, ordered three fingers of whiskey, and watched me for a full twenty minutes while I worked and he sipped his drink. It was the beginning of the end. His eyes were glued to my ass, my tits, and everything in between, making me feel hot, bothered, and desired in a way I'd missed since Benny'd up and disappeared, only to find out he'd actually ditched me to save his own ass.

I delivered Blaine's check, and he tipped me a cool hundred dollars and left the bar without a word or a look in my direction. At the time, I'd shrugged it off, figuring he must not have been as into me as I'd thought since he hadn't asked me out. I guess I was just a nice distraction from the sports and news playing up on the screens in the bar. I gave it little thought, more thankful for the extra hundred that would buy my sister and me a weeks' worth of groceries. Then, when I was leaving after my shift, and I hit the curb for a taxi home, a shiny shoe stepped out the open door of a BMW with blacked-out windows, and Blaine offered me a ride. The car was white-hot, but it didn't even come close to the man who owned it.

Stupid, dumbstruck twenty-one-year old Mia got into the car with the sexy-as-hell stranger and let him take me home. He didn't hit on me that first time. He was a gentleman the entire time he walked me to my door, kissed me on the cheek, and asked if he could take me out the next night. I agreed, and Luna Rosa was where we started our evening. We ordered pizza and an expensive wine, which I thought was cool. He could have taken me to some fancy dancy steakhouse and plowed me full of gourmet cuisine in an attempt to impress or bed me. Instead, we talked, had two bottles of wine, and ate pizza followed by the most mouthwatering tiramisu I'd ever tasted.

Once a month, for the two years we were together, we went back to "our place" and stuffed our faces with pizza and wine. Then we'd stumble into the Town Car, and one of his bodyguards would drive us back to the casino. Sometimes, we'd be so hot and bothered in the elevator, I'd be wrapped around his hips, him already deep inside when the doors opened to the penthouse floor, and he'd proceed to fuck me up against the wall. Blaine had absolutely no concern for the individuals who might live in or have reserved the few other rooms on the top floor finding us. He simply didn't give a fuck, and I loved that about him. Hell, I thought I loved him, and I thought he loved me.

I was so young, dumb, and full of cum that I ate up every line of bullshit he fed me, throwing caution to the wind and living in the moment. Not anymore. I'd learned those lessons the hard way. If Blaine thought he was going to score some points with me for meeting me at Luna Rosa, he had another think coming.

★ ★ ★

I didn't have anything dressy with me from Maxwell's ranch because, well, we'd stayed on a ranch. We pretty much spent our time kicking it at their house, hanging out with their friends and enjoying their ranch.

A pang hit my heart when I thought about Max. When Pops took the turn for the better, he announced that he had to go check on his wife and daughter. Cyndi was a month from having baby Jackson, and he needed to check on the transition of the company ownership and deal with any pressing business activities while he was there. He promised he'd check in daily.

Throughout my life, I had never really aspired to be ridiculously rich, but I couldn't help thinking if the transition moved faster and I was able to get access to my share, perhaps I could pay Blaine off, and this whole mess would be over. I'd live in Malibu and surf, kiss, and make love to the man I wanted to spend the rest of my life with. Unfortunately, Max had warned that the process of finalizing the will and going through the change in ownership to both Maddy and me, using our DNA samples as proof of our relationship, would take some time but it would be worth it in the end.

If I made it alive through all of this, maybe Max would be proven right. For now, I had a really hard time seeing that sparkly light at the end of the tunnel. Right now, it seemed life was driving down a slick road with no streetlights during a hurricane in a car with broken wipers and faulty brakes.

★ ★ ★

I arrived at Luna Rosa promptly at seven. Maddy loaned me a dress I'd given her from my time shopping in Chi-town with Hector. It was a simple number, a dark eggplant with a deep V down the back. The skirt hit mid-thigh, and the fabric stretched across my breasts nicely. If I hadn't been so pissed about who I was wearing it for, I would have felt like a million dollars. Instead, I felt like steam-rolled garbage, although no one could tell it from the outside. Heavy concealer hid the dark circles and bags under my eyes, and blush made me rosy-cheeked. Luckily, I was one of those girls who didn't need to wear a lot of makeup to turn an eye, and I knew exactly what Blaine liked. I wore my hair down and full and over one shoulder, something he once told me he loved.

Making my way through the patrons, I spotted him outside. The patio. Of course, he'd pick the most romantic location possible at the same table where we sat on our first date.

He stood as I approached his table. He gazed up and down my length like a predator assessing his prey, stealthy and quick, never missing a beat.

"Trying to score points by picking this table?" I asked and sat down, a scowl firmly planted on my face.

His features, on the other hand, lightened considerably. "You remembered, I see. That's good, pretty Mia." I cringed. God, I hated hearing him call me that old endearment. When we were together, he'd constantly tell me how pretty I was, how beautiful, and that there would never be another who could catch his eye quite like I had…until, of course, he caught the two-for-one deal with his receptionist and her hobag twin. Who fucks sisters anyway? Gross.

Before I could say another word, the waiter came over with a bottle of wine. I knew that label. I'd recognize it anywhere.

"*Signore*, the Cignale Colli Della Toscana Centrale Cabernet Sauvignon." He poured the dark crimson liquid into Blaine's glass.

He picked it up, swirled it around the bulbous glass, sniffed, and took a sip.

So fucking pretentious, I could gag.

"Two thousand and six?" he queried the waiter.

"Absolutely, *signore*."

Blaine nodded, and the waiter filled our glasses a quarter

of the way full. I grabbed the glass and downed the liquid in one go.

Blaine looked around and smiled before placing one hand on the railing overlooking the serene waters of Lake Las Vegas and the other on the stem of his glass. His eyes were lasered on me.

"I'd like another," I said, and he grinned, leaned forward, and poured another serving. This one I sipped and waited for him to speak. For a long time, he didn't. He just watched me, seemingly cataloging my appearance. Eventually, I couldn't take the silence.

"Where's Ginelle?"

A sharp, dark look came over his snakelike eyes. "She is being taken care of, I assure you." His tone was sweet, belying the subject matter.

I huffed. "Really? Is that what you call kidnapping and beating the hell out of an innocent woman on her way to work? Taking care of her?" I gritted through my teeth. I was gripping the wooden table so hard my nails might have actually left little crescent-shaped indentations.

Blaine waved his hand and leaned closer. "Mia, you and I both know that if I wanted your friend dead, she would be. Now let's relax and enjoy our date."

Date. Did that lunatic just call this coercion a date?

I blinked rapidly to try to clear the red rage. I wanted to grab the knife, so helpfully placed within range of my hand, and drive it straight into his cold heart. Unfortunately, the fucker likely wouldn't feel it. He was already dead inside.

"I don't understand why you want me here. You know I'm good for the money," I whispered and looked around. "There's no way in this lifetime that I'd stiff you."

He grinned. "Oh, but my pretty, pretty Mia, you have already made me stiff." His eyebrows waggled, and I sucked down the vomit I wanted to spew out over the table. Once upon a time, I was genuinely into Blaine. He's devastatingly handsome, ridiculously charming, and a great lay. Now, I could barely stomach the sight of him and what he stood for.

"Blaine, you've taken something very precious to me, and you want to talk about sex?"

His eyebrows rose. "I don't want to talk about it, no. I'd rather being doing it with you, if that's what you're asking."

I clenched my jaw tight. "That's never going to happen, so get that out of your head right now. You fucked your way right off that train...literally. There is no going back, ever." My own voice was low and held a warning.

He shook his head and pursed his lips as he twirled the wine goblet around in a circle. "Those two meant nothing to me. I was just blowing off a little steam since you hadn't said yes to my proposal."

"By having sex with two women?"

"Of course, Mia. A man had needs and pride. You wounded mine." He gave the excuse as if what he had done was his right as a hot-blooded male.

"So you fucked two whores to make yourself feel like a man?"

His eyes got hard then, and his voice turned to steel. "You of all people cannot possibly be implying that I'm not a man."

I shook my head. "Why are we even having this conversation?"

"Isn't it obvious?" He blinked slowly and stared.

"Not to me." I was there for one reason and one reason alone. Ginelle.

Blaine placed his elbows on the table and rested his chin in his palm. He was the epitome of calm, cool, and collected, whereas I was unraveling from the inside out with worry and fear.

"I want you back. In my bed. In my life. As my wife."

Those words dropped like a nuclear bomb damaging everything in its wake. I looked around the restaurant to see if anyone else had survived the blast. It was that monumental, alas, only in the tiny little speck of a thing I called my life.

Saying I hadn't expected this would be an understatement. I would have expected the second coming of our Lord and Savior over *this* announcement.

"Blaine," I whispered, barely able to speak. "You can't be serious."

"Deadly so. And I'm willing to negotiate the terms. Here. Now."

"This has to be a nightmare. Blaine, are you hearing yourself? You just told me you want to pick up where we left off when we broke up."

"I know exactly what I want, and it's you. I think I've made that clear. Now shush and listen to what I'm offering."

I did listen, not because he told me to, but because I was so shocked that the additional thoughts it took to form words were not forthcoming. The man was officially certifiable. Undeniably. Absolutely. There really was no other explanation.

Before he got down to telling me what the offer was, the waiter delivered two steaming hot pizzas, one margherita and one supreme. The smell alone had me salivating. It had been a couple days since I'd had a full meal. The Rains and Maxwell had been trying to get me to eat, but food just didn't have the appeal it once had, since Weston was probably starving to death and Pops was getting his meals through a tube. Tonight, though, I was going to eat for no other reason than to get this over with as fast as possible.

"Now, since you've been away, I've had time to reflect on our relationship and our life together," he said.

Since I've been away? We broke up. I moved out of state, had been an escort for the past eight months, and lived in Los Angeles for six before that. Altogether, that was over a year apart, and he made it sound as if I'd left him last week. I'd been with other men, fallen in love. None of this made any sense.

"Blaine, I've been gone over a year—" I started, but he cut me off with a flick of the wrist.

"No matter the time or distance. You're here now, and I've figured out that you are the woman for me."

"Did you come to that monster conclusion before or after you fucked the twin fun-bags for the hell of it?"

"I'm trying to connect with you here, Mia," he growled. "You would do well to mind your manners. I'm only going to make this offer once."

"No deal. I don't want what you're selling."

He sat back and crossed his arms over his chest. "I think you might find my offer one you won't be able refuse, if you'd just listen. All of your problems would be solved, and everything would be back as it should. With us, together, running all of this." He opened his arms wide, as if he were holding all of Las Vegas in the palm of his hand.

Such a smug piece of work.

"No, Blaine, I had what you offered, and I walked away from it." I stood, my chair falling to the ground with a loud bang behind me. "And I'm walking away from it now. This was a mistake. I'm calling the cops."

"Your friend will be dead by morning," he grated just loud enough for me to hear.

I turned around, my entire body alight with anger. The hair on my arms and neck stood on end. That tone—I'd heard that tone before when he was barking orders into his phone, arranging plans to make people pay. Hurting anyone who dared to cross him in the most vile and violent ways possible. This was the kind of man I was dealing with. Not the ex who used to hug, kiss, and love me to oblivion. That was the man I'd fallen for. *This* was his alter ego. Everyone looked at this side with cold, hard fear. It was his world. The rest of us only lived in it.

"What do I have to do for you to let her go?" My voice shook, emotion controlling me. I lifted the chair and looked around the restaurant. Most of the patrons were openly staring, watching the fireworks evolve. They probably thought we were having a lover's quarrel. In a way, we kind of were.

"Earlier, I was feeling nostalgic, being here, looking at you across from me, knowing that it's the view I want to see for the rest of my life." His eyes hardened, and he squinted. "Now that you've embarrassed yourself, and therefore me, with your antics, I'm not feeling so generous."

"Name your price," I stated plainly.

"The four hundred thousand you owe me, or you, for a single night in my bed."

CHAPTER SIX

Blaine's eyes were a glassy, bright, yellowish green. Those were the eyes I'd looked into every time he kissed me, touched me, and made love to me. The conversation we'd just had that made every facet of my being want to curl up into a fetal position and die...turned him on. God, the man loved to have power over people and things. Got off on it, too.

"So what do you say?"

I licked my lips, took a massive gulp of my wine, and let it burn like acid down my throat. Looking out over the water, I thought about my predicament. I could end it easily by just letting him fuck me. I'd done it before. He was great in bed, always had been. Giving, loving, worried about my pleasure. I could down a couple bottles of wine and let him have his wicked way with me, and all of this would be over. Done. Finito.

"If I let you have me for the night, you'll call our debt paid, let Ginelle go, and leave my family alone? Including my father?"

Blaine's lips twisted into a smug grin. If I thought it would make a difference, I'd punch that look off his smarmy face so everyone in the near vicinity could see how much I despised him. He took a slow drink of his wine and hummed. A shiver ran down my spine, and my belly clenched. I used to adore that sound, worked for that hum, down on my knees while worshiping his cock. Now, the gentle hum was like the warning before an explosion. The little red light that lasered in on the criminal before the SWAT team blows his head off, like in the movies.

Finally, Blaine responded. "Yes. Your father's debt will be cleared, your friend released unscathed, and you and your family will be off our radar." Blaine glanced down at my chest, tilted his head, and licked his lips. "I cannot wait to taste your cunt, hear you cry out when I use my teeth and tongue on that sweet button. It will be music to my ears." He sucked in a breath through his teeth. His eyes were blazing hot. I'd have bet all the money in the world that his dick was hard as a rock as he imagined all the things he'd do to me. Only problem was I didn't have that same response. His filthy words used to turn me on. Used to, but not now. I'd always been a woman whose panties got wet when her man talked dirty to her, and Blaine knew that better than most. It was a trigger for me. Only he was the wrong man, the wrong voice.

I shook my head as visions of Wes and me rolling around his bed, laughing, enjoying one another in a way I'd never experienced with anyone else paraded past my subconscious. Hard, fast sex up against walls until both of us lost our minds. Spending hours using our mouths, kissing every inch of each other's skin. Sucking him off, over and over, until my mouth hurt and Wes couldn't get hard any more. In turn, he'd go to town on me. He'd give me so many orgasms with his mouth that my body ached, the space between my thighs felt strange without his mouth locked on it, and I'd pass out. The nights in Miami where we'd made love, whispered our commitment into one another's mouths, promised forever—all of those things were at the forefront of my thoughts. Everything came back to him, back to the man I loved. There would be no way I could violate that trust.

Even with Ginelle's life on the line, I couldn't betray Wes like that. There had to be another way. Blaine waited patiently, swirling his wine glass between two long fingers as if he had all the time in the world. Overconfident, smug bastard. Why had I not noticed these traits before I got in deep with him?

"Blaine, I'm going to need a little time to think about it." I fluttered my eyelashes, giving him a bit of my flirty nature, desperately trying to sway him.

His eyebrows narrowed. "No. You decide now, tonight." The tone brooked no argument. Even his body visibly tightened. His hand gripped the wine stem so tight I hoped the glass would break, shatter in his palm, forcing him to need stitches.

Daydreaming of his destruction didn't help me get any closer to figuring out how to get out of what he wanted yet still save my best friend.

"What if I added a little something to my request?" I played with my hair, twirling a lock around a finger. "An incentive for you, to give me a little time to think?"

He tilted his head and his gaze focused on mine. "And what would that incentive be, pretty Mia?"

"A kiss." I decided on a whim.

One thing Blaine loved, told me a million times over when we together, was kissing me. Once, he went so far as to say he could survive on my kisses alone, bread and water be damned. That was the only ace I had to play. The rest of my cards were a fat bluff. And if I kissed him and made it believable enough, I think he'd enjoy the challenge. Blaine appreciated a good chase and liked to build up the anticipation of getting what he wanted.

"Hmmm, you play a hard bargain, my pretty Mia. What are your terms?"

"Two weeks, and you let Ginelle go, tonight, now, immediately."

He scowled, and his hand turned into a fist. "And how do I know you wouldn't just up and disappear, leave me hanging?"

I chuckled. "You'd find me."

His eyes lit like the ball dropping in Times Square in New York City signaling a brand new year.

"Besides. It's not like I could check Pops out of the hospital and hide Maddy and everyone else I loved. You forget, Blaine. I know exactly how you operate, and there is nowhere far enough away to escape your grasp. Am I wrong?"

He leaned back and rubbed at his chin before wiping his bottom lip with his thumb—a gesture that used to soak my panties instantly. Now I was dry as the Sahara desert. His charm, good looks, and sexy gestures did nothing for me anymore. A laid-back movie-making surfer who made horribly bad decisions to tread on unguarded land in a third world country did it for me these days and every day. The thought of Wes tore at my heart, but I breathed in and out slowly, cooling my jets so I didn't break down. Having a meeting with the devil did not allow for cracks in my armor. I could cry when I got back, but I knew better than anyone never to let your enemy see you weak. They strike when your soft spots are exposed. I'd never give him that opportunity again.

"No, you're not. And one week."

Excitement and relief poured through my veins. He was caving. All for a single kiss. I wanted to jump in the air and do a touchdown dance, but I settled for a mental fist pump. "Fine."

Blaine took his cell phone out of his pocket, and I held my breath. He pressed a few buttons and lifted it to his ear. "The girl. Take her home. Set her free." After a few beats, he listened. "No, you cannot have her. Do not touch her in any way. I find out she's been damaged, it will be your life on the line. Have her home within the hour." He smashed a button on his phone and tucked it into his breast pocket. "It's done. Your friend will be home soon."

I nodded and sucked down the remainder of my wine. Thank God. Ginelle would be safe. For now.

"I shall enjoy my kiss tonight when I drop you off. Then you will have one week to come to me. In the meantime, your friend will be let go and we will enjoy the rest of our dinner. Eat up. You're going to need your strength for decision making this week."

★ ★ ★

When we arrived at the hotel, Blaine walked me up to the room. "Give me the key." He put his hand out and palm up.

I shook my head. "Maddy's in there with her fiancé."

"Don't you have your own room?" He stepped closer to me, and I took two steps back until I was plastered up against the wall. Not a good position to be in. I wanted to be in control. Otherwise, he could take it further than I could stomach.

"You're not coming in. Remember our deal—a single kiss."

He pressed close, his hands going to the wall beside my head, caging me in. His eyes had darkened, turning a golden shade of green and yellow. I used to love watching his eye color change, especially when he was turned on. Now, I felt dead inside.

"Oh, pretty, pretty Mia, I always remember the details of every negotiation." His head got close, and I could feel his breath against my face.

I closed my eyes and thought about Wes, about how I was doing this for Ginelle, for my dad, my sister, and to give me time—the one thing that had not been in my favor since I started on this journey nine months ago.

Blaine's lips were warm and moist as they touched mine briefly.

Wes. Forgive me.

With slow movements, I lifted my hands to Blaine's waist and stroked up his hard chest. He groaned and nipped at my bottom lip. I returned the gesture by nipping his top and tugging it into the wet heat of my mouth. We always used to play first before getting to the good part. Blaine pushed into me, his cock long and thick against my hip, digging in. One of his hands moved down to my breast, and he squeezed. I opened my mouth to object when he delved in. His tongue wasn't tentative. No, this was the kiss of a lover who knew when to give and when to take. A familiar dance partner. He moved his hand down to my waist, circled around my bum, and pulled my lower half into his, grinding against me. I couldn't help it. I moaned. It had been over a month since I'd had any kind of sexual relief, and even though I hated every second, his movements and the way he touched me were powering through my brain into the pleasure center where Wes lived.

Suddenly, I wasn't kissing Blaine. I was devouring Wes. I lifted my hands to cup his smooth cheeks, and I licked into my man's mouth. Tasting, teasing, enjoying the lush, drugging swipes of his tongue against mine. My imagination supplied Weston's scent, the ocean and man mingling together into a chaos of need and want. I thrust my hips and dipped my tongue, sliding along the surface of his body as if I were a snake coiling around its prey. Wes.

"God, I missed you, baby," I said into his mouth.

He moaned, and ribbons of heat filled my body, setting me aflame. His hands were everywhere, sliding under my dress, gripping my ass. He moved his hips, that hardness pressing perfectly against my O-trigger. I gasped and hiked a leg higher, digging my stiletto into the meaty part of his thigh, forcing him closer.

My eyes were shut tight as I dry humped my man. Missing his touch, his body.

"Mia, you're going to make me come. Let me inside so I can fuck you properly, or I'll rip your panties off right here."

That voice. That was not... "Wes?" I said, opening my eyes and blinking away the lusty haze.

Blaine moved his head from the trailing kisses he was leaving down my neck. Sweat hit my body in a full-blown panic, moisture beading at my hairline as I took gasping breaths.

"Who the fuck is Wes?"

Oh. My. God. I had just rubbed my lady bits all over Blaine against the wall while imagining my boyfriend. My stomach churned while the insides rumbled, getting ready to blow.

The door next to where we stood opened. Max took in our delicate position, and his nostrils flared. Shock at seeing him there in that moment had to have shown on my face as one of panic.

"Get away from her!" Max roared and pressed one meaty palm to Blaine's chest and pushed. Blaine went flying into the wall opposite me.

Shit. Shit. Shit. I swallowed down the vile response my body had when I realized I was about to fuck Blaine again while daydreaming he was Wes. Jesus, I would have ruined everything. Wes would never have forgiven me. Once more, that soulless pit I called a stomach started to whirl like a cyclone in the ocean.

"Are you Wes?" Blaine sneered.

Max's head snapped back. "Who's this joker?" His hard gaze hit mine.

"Um, my ex, uh, Blaine Pintero."

Blaine adjusted his suit jacket, flapping it and then buttoning one button at the center. "Mia and I have a history."

"I'll say. You're about to be history." Max rushed him, had a hand around his neck in a second flat. For a linebacker of a man, he sure could move fast. "You the cocksucker who's been threatening her?"

"Threatening? Is that what we were doing, Mia? I seem to remember you enjoying our little tête-à-tête a moment

338

ago. She was about to go off like a firecracker on the Fourth of July, had you waited another minute."

Oh, sweet mother of all things holy. "Blaine, no!" I tried to get the words out but I missed the mark, by a lot.

Before I could stop Max or say anything to protect Blaine, Max's tree-trunk-sized arm flung back and his fist connected with Blaine's jaw. "Listen to me, you little piece of shit. That's my sister you're talking about."

Max shook Blaine against the wall. His head and body lolled momentarily, but eventually, he blinked a few times before coming back to the present. This was going to be so bad for me. Fuck!

"You have a brother?" His eyes opened wide and he glanced at me.

"Uh, yeah. Max, let him go."

Max ignored me completely. "If I ever see you touch my sister again, I will hunt you down and skin you alive with a blunt knife!" He raked him up against the wall. Blaine's head smacked the surface a few times, making a dull thud noise.

"Fuck, man! Let me go, you side show freak!" Blaine roared, his teeth tinged pink with blood. I could already see the side of his face swelling. Honestly, I didn't feel that bad about it, especially knowing what he'd done to Ginelle and Pops.

"Max, really, I'm okay. Blaine and I came to an understanding tonight. I'm fine."

"He gonna leave you alone?"

Blaine huffed and straightened once more as I led Max away from my ex and positioned him in front of our hotel room door. "Uh, you could say that."

"I did say that, sugar. What I want to hear is this yo-

yo say it." He growled and his jaw went tight. I held onto his bicep and pushed, trying to get him to go back into the room but I couldn't move him physically. If he didn't want to move, it would likely take a Mack truck to make it happen.

Blaine pulled out a handkerchief and wiped at the blood around his mouth. "No worries, big guy. Mia and I have come to an agreement, if you will. Mia, I'll leave you with your, uh, brother." He looked Max up and down with disgust. "Remember, one week." Then he turned and pushed the elevator button. The doors opened instantly, and in two more seconds, he was gone.

I sighed and fell against the doorjamb.

Max ruffled a hand through his hair. "What the hell was that? You were all over the bozo. What about Weston?"

I groaned and pushed against him to get in the room. He let me by but followed me in. I tossed my purse and went to the mini bar, pulled out a tiny bottle of whiskey, uncapped it, and slammed it all back in one harsh shot.

Max leaned on the edge of the couch. "You've had your drink, now talk." As if to make his point that he wasn't going anywhere anytime soon, he crossed his arms over one another.

"Nothing. What you saw wasn't meant to happen." I blew a puff of air out over my too-hot forehead and reached for another baby bottle of whiskey. "What are you doing here anyway?"

"That's a damn good question, darlin'. You see, I was taking care of some business back home, making sure everything was ready for my boy's arrival when I got a frantic call from our baby sister. She went on and on about you being spooked hard enough to worry her. Says she's never seen you that upset. Being the big brother, and the only one who's got your back right now since your man is missing, I high-tailed it back. Got the plane at the ready when I need to."

"You shouldn't be here," I said. "You need to be with Cyndi and Isabel waiting for that baby to come. They need you." With feet that felt as though they were weighed down by a pair of snow skis, I made my way to the couch and plopped down.

"And they'll have me. Just as soon as I get a read on what's going on with you. Maddy tells me something is up and she knows it's not good. Why didn't you call me, Mia?" His voice was tired, filled with that gravelly tone I'd begun to appreciate. The volume and timbre said, "I'm a man who cares about you, loves you, and will do anything to protect you." I needed that in my life. Especially now.

"Ginelle was kidnapped by Blaine's goons. They roughed her up as a way to get to me."

"Why? I thought all of this was working out. You told me it was fine last month. That you had a handle on it." His voice was accusatory, and it sent a knife right into my heart.

Anger rippled along every nerve in my body, and I stood up and paced, needing to get this shit out. "It *was* fine!" I yelled. "And then Pops got worse. I didn't make it to my client this month."

"So?"

"So! In my contract, if a man books me for a month and I flake on him, I owe him the hundred thousand!"

"Jesus H. Christ, Mia!" His voice was as upset as mine even though it wasn't his ass on the line.

I had been dealing with this shit all by myself and doing just fine with it. "Then, because Millie had to pay the client the money you paid me, I missed my payment to Blaine. Next month, I'll work for the entire month before I can send a payment. So I'm behind. And he's proving that he can get to me any way he wants." Tears filled my eyes and poured down my cheeks. "This is all so fucked up!" I flopped down onto the chair.

Max came and sat down in front of it on the coffee table. The wood creaked against his massive weight. "What do you owe?"

I blinked, letting more tears fall. "Right now, two hundred large."

His eyebrows narrowed. "That's all?"

I shook my head. "No, I owe the two hundred right this second. For August and September."

"Darlin', how much do you owe period?" His voice was now soft, tinged with worry.

My shoulders slumped as if I'd carried the money in solid gold bricks directly on my shoulders. "Four hundred." I answered.

"And what type of agreement did you come to?"

Licking my lips, I sniffed, took a deep breath, and looked into his eyes, the same orbs that mirrored my own. "You're not going to like it."

"Sugar, I already don't like it. Just tell me."

Clutching his hands, the tears flowed again, slipping down my face. "Either I can pay him the four hundred or…." I swallowed repeatedly, trying to push that giant ball of ugly down my throat so I could speak, admit the truth of what I'd considered doing but knew I couldn't.

"Or...?" Max's eyes were so kind, his mouth tipped into a little frown.

"Me. A night in his bed."

Max leaned forward and pressed his forehead to mine. "Darlin', that's going to happen over my dead body." He was firm and unbending, one hundred percent serious.

I snorted at the sick, twisted thought that ran through my head. What Max didn't know was that Blaine was the exact type of man who would make that happen without so much as a fleck of remorse.

My phone rang and buzzed against my thigh. I'd been carrying it around nonstop, never allowing it more than a foot from my presence in case there was news about Wes.

I looked down at the display. Sweet Jesus. Ginelle.

"Hello, Gin?" I answered, desperate to hear her voice, make sure she was okay. Blaine had promised that she would be let go and home within the hour.

"I'm home," was her single reply before the line disconnected.

CHAPTER SEVEN

Taxi drivers in Las Vegas rock! Toss them a hundred dollar bill and they will easily break every traffic law in the books. Knowing my best friend was home, had been kidnapped, roughed up, and released in the span of a day had me out of my mind with worry. Every nerve ending was sparking like an exposed live wire ready to zap anyone that touched it.

When the driver stopped at her apartment's curb, I tossed a handful of twenties I kept as my emergency money, including the hundred I'd already promised him, and dashed out of the car and up the steps to her door.

Instead of banging on the door as if my life depended on it like I wanted to, I pulled out my surfboard key ring that held all of five keys. One to Wes's house, Pops's place, Maddy's apartment, Suzi, my motorcycle, and Ginelle's apartment. Five metal reminders of the people that meant the most to me in the entire world, though I had a horde of new friends that were coming in as close seconds.

Slipping the key into the lock, I opened the door and tiptoed in quietly. The lamp on the side table by the couch was on, but no sound could be heard throughout the space. I walked past her giant burgundy couch, one that was far too big for the space but was also the most comfortable piece of future in the universe. When I sat on its puffy goodness, it formed to my thighs, my back, and cradled my body in a welcoming hug. Yep, best ever.

The kitchen and hallway were both dark, devoid of life. I walked slowly down the corridor leading to the two bedrooms. Gin always kept one room as a guest room. She said she wanted to make sure I always had a place to stay wherever she lived. That's just the type of best friend she is. The light to her room was on. I tapped on the door.

"Gin, it's Mia," I said.

"Go away," I heard her mumble through a whimper.

I pushed open the door. She was huddled in the corner of her room, still in her tattered work attire. Dried blood was crusted around her nose and mouth and along her neck where it had trickled down. The pink sequins sparkled in the bright light. She had the overhead light on, the lights on both end tables and the bathroom light shining in the room. The place was lit like the Disneyland Parade, so bright it blinded you to have your eyes open all the way. Squinting, I shuffled slowly over to her and crouched down. Her body shook like a leaf in the wind. I placed a hand on her knee and she jolted back, her teeth chattering. Tears ran down her face in rivulets, leaving black, sticky smudges of mascara and makeup to mix in with the dirty grit on her face. Her cheek was swollen, her eye turning an ugly shade of purple, and her lip looked like it might need stitching.

A rage I'd never known swept over my entire being. It was so hot I worried I'd scald my best friend with a single touch. Knowing she needed me, I clenched my jaw and gritted my teeth, grinding so hard I could hear the grating noise from the inside. Looking at her petite body, torn, battered, worse for the wear, had my blood boiling. Taking deep breaths, I took her hands in mine.

"Come on, honey. I'm going to take care of you."

Ginelle shook her head jerkily. "No, you have to g-go. If they come b-back, they'll take you for s-sure. He said, he s-said he was going to m-make you his, Mia. They want you b-bad." Her hands clutched my biceps so hard I knew finger-shaped bruises would be there by morning. "This time he w-won't s-stop until he h-has y-you," she sputtered through her chattering teeth, her eyes a wild shade of cornflower blue. The girl was frightened out of her mind, and I hated that it was my fault. They'd hurt my best friend because of me. Thank God she was okay. I'd make sure she stayed that way.

I tugged her body into my arms. After a second, the tears turned into sobs, which turned into all-over body heaving as she cried. For twenty minutes, I let her get it out, exorcise the demons of what happened to her. It would never go away. For a long time, she'd probably be looking over her shoulder as well as double and triple-checking the locks on her doors. It was very possible she'd end up needing counseling to get past it. Whatever Gin needed, I'd get it for her. Somehow, some way.

"Come on, honey. Let's get you cleaned up." I petted her hair and her back in long soothing strokes.

She nodded and allowed me to help her stand. When I caught sight of her attire, I almost lost my shit all over again. The front was slit all the way to her belly button, her breasts barely covered by the flimsy fabric. There were new slits cut near each thigh as if the fucker were trying to get a good look at her nether regions. I turned her around and walked her into the bathroom. I bit my tongue so hard I tasted blood, trying not to scream, yell, and destroy everything in my wake, until I'd found the bastards and put them in a hole six feet under with my bare hands.

Turning on the water for the shower, I helped her out of her clothes. She immediately covered her breasts even though I'd seen them a million times. Gin was not shy, and neither was I. We'd known each other our entire lives, but if the modesty helped her, I wouldn't say anything. Making sure the water was okay, I pulled off my T-shirt and pushed off my pants, leaving my bra and panties on. Then I maneuvered us both into the shower.

With extreme effort, I worked around the various bruises, cuts, and scrapes I found all over her, wishing we could press charges, but knowing Blaine and how many men at the local PD he had in his pocket, the effort would be useless. The bastard would laugh in our faces. I squirted copious amounts of her body wash onto the buff puff and instructed her like a child to hold out one arm and then the next, lift a foot and then the next. I put more soap on the loofa and handed it to her. "Clean your front and hoo-hah, Gin."

She nodded and methodically did what I'd asked as if she were a drone just following orders. Getting some shampoo, I washed her long blond hair, rubbing her scalp slowly, hopefully massaging out some of the tension. When I got to the back of her neck she sighed, and finally her stiff shoulders loosened and dropped down. Point one for Mia!

I repeated the process with the conditioner, making sure to move with intent, never touching the rest of her body. As children and teens we'd taken showers together a hundred times, but after today, I wanted her to be confident that she was being loved, not taken advantage of. That I respected her space and would be here in any way she needed me.

This woman was, for all intents and purposes, my sister, and I loved her more than life itself. Had I been able to take what happened away in exchange for me being the one they'd taken, I would have gladly volunteered to save her even an ounce of pain.

"Honey, very lightly wash your face with this, okay?" I handed her the facial soap. She rubbed her hands over the bar as if warming them. I took the bar, and she closed her hands and did as she was told. Each time she got near her lip, cheek, and eye, she'd wince and gasp in pain. Every sound was like another nail in Blaine's coffin. I wanted him to pay for what he'd done to Ginelle. Fuck, I wanted him to bleed for what he'd done to my father as well as my best friend. Taking Ginelle to prove a point tonight had gone too far. I had to figure something out. We couldn't live in fear like this. Worried that every time someone I loved left his home or work he'd be scooped up by one of Blaine's goons and tortured just to fuck with my head.

Once she was washed, I watched the last of the coppery brown swirls of soap and blood go down the drain. I hopped out of the shower and let her have some alone time.

Drying off, I went into her room and grabbed two pairs of undies. I shucked off my wet ones and put on a dry pair and one of her sports bras. She had curves for a little thing, but my boobs were much larger and would never fit into her smaller cups. In the PJ drawer I pulled out two tanks and two pairs of fleecy plaid pants. They'd be high-waters on me, but it didn't matter. Not wanting to leave Gin in the shower alone for too long, I tugged on the outfit and brought the rest to the bathroom.

When I entered, she hadn't moved. As in, not even an

inch. She just stood there, the water pounding on her back, blankly staring at the opposite side of the shower stall. I reached in, turned it off, grabbed the giant towel next to the shower, and wrapped it around her. She didn't protest anything as I dried her, and she kept her gaze off to the side and down, lost in her own thoughts.

"Want to talk about it?" I asked.

She shook her head. The first movement she'd made on her own without being instructed.

"Okay, you don't have to."

Ginelle closed her eyes and took a deep breath. Tears slipped out, but I didn't say anything. If she wanted to talk about it, she would. For now, I would just take care of her and be here. That's the best thing I could do for her. Once I got her dressed, I guided her over to the toilet seat where I sat her down. Then with thumb and forefinger, I lifted her chin to inspect her face. The lip was pretty open but not so much that it wouldn't heal on its own.

"I'll be right back." I said and moved to turn around, but before I could make it a step away, her hands were clutching my tank, holding me there.

"Don't leave me." Her voice shook. I placed my hands over hers and unfurled them from my shirt.

I looked right into her eyes, pale green to cornflower blue. "Gin, I'm not leaving you. I'm getting the first aid kit in the hall so I can patch up your face, okay?"

Her pupils were huge. Like two giant black holes. She trembled all over but nodded curtly. I squeezed her hands and then got up and walked slowly out of the room. The second I made it past the threshold, I ran to the closet and rummaged around until I found the red case with the big white cross on it. Shoving the rest of the stuff that fell around me back into the closet, I hustled back to Ginelle. Again, she hadn't moved, just stared off into space. Gooseflesh rose on her skin as I got close.

"One more thing." I ran to the closet and pulled out her favorite zip-up hoodie. It was hot pink and had bedazzled metal balls on the back in the shape of angels' wings running the length of the back. I put the hood over her wet hair, helped her put each arm in, and zipped it up. Again, she sighed, tucked her hands inside the armholes, and clutched it close to her body.

Trying to be careful, I treated the various cuts with some ointment and Band-Aids where possible and gave her four Ibuprofen. "This will help with the pain. Are you hungry?"

She shook her head, and I helped her stand. Pulling back the blankets on her bed, I led her in. Then I closed up the rest of the house, sent a quick text to Maddy and Max telling them where I was, and got into bed next to Gin. I rolled over, put my arm around her waist, and spooned her backside. I snuggled into her neck.

"You're okay now. I'm here, and Gin, I'm sorry. I'm so sorry this happened to you, but I swear, I swear to God it will never happen again. I promise."

She clasped both of my hands to her chest and held me close. Then once more, the tears came and they came hard. I held her, soothed her, spoke softly to her until eventually she fell asleep. Then, exhausted, I too fell into dreamland.

★ ★ ★

A featherlight caress ran up one arm and back down. I opened my eyes sleepily and was face to face with the only person I wanted to see more than I wanted to take my next breath. "You're here," I whispered, afraid if I blinked, he'd vanish. Wes ran his fingertips up and down both of my bare arms, solidifying his presence.

"Of course I am, sweetheart. Where did you think I'd be?" His head dipped to the side and a cocky grin covered his lips. Beautiful.

I swallowed and choked down the emotion swirling around me. "Gone. Lost to me."

Wes leaned forward and trailed his lips down my neck, over my tank top, nipping and kissing as he moved.

"The only place I'm going, sweetheart, is between these thighs. Spread 'em." He gripped my inner thighs with purpose.

Without thought, care, concern, I did exactly that. Opened my legs nice and wide for him.

He sat back on his haunches. A well-placed thumb pushed down on my hot spot as if he'd had x-ray vision and could see through my underwear to the pink flesh beyond. The digit spun around the aching, hard kernel of need. His eyes were focused on the task in front of him, glued to the space between my thighs. "Look at that. Soaking that cotton right before my eyes."

I mewled and jerked my hips, wanting more, needing more. "Baby..." I said, breathless, moving my hips in tandem with the blessed little circles.

"You think I can make you come without touching your naked body? Having you screaming in release with just my thumb?" His eyes blazed, lust apparent in every slow blink. He licked his lips, and I watched the bit of flesh moisten, wanting nothing more than to kiss him. He moved his thumb in a fluttering flick that made me arch up. "Can you, Mia? I think you can."

He knew what he was doing. Talking dirty, playing with me. The act of touching me with a barrier ratcheted up my excitement to smokin' hot levels.

Wes leaned forward, holding my legs down with his powerful biceps, his elbows resting on each side of my thighs preventing any further movement. He nudged my clit with his nose and inhaled loudly.

"Jesus, baby, you smell so good. I missed this. Having my face buried in this heat. Best place in the world."

He nuzzled my cloth-covered core, his nose rubbing against the erect bundle, his mouth right over where I wanted him most. I could feel the wet heat of his breath through my panties, right over my slit. Then he took it up a notch, flattened his tongue, and sucked on the damp fabric, groaning his enjoyment at sampling me through the weave of fabric. It provided a new sensation, one I'd never had before, but I wanted to rip the panties off. Let him taste me fully with no barrier.

"Wes," I shimmied my hips as best as I could until he put the lockdown over my thigh once more.

"No moving, sweetheart. I want your body forced to accept every ounce of pleasure I give you." And then he went to work. Licking and sucking my lower lips and clit through the miniscule basket weave of cotton covering me. Pretty soon, I was so wet that it didn't matter that he was eating me through my underwear, it felt so damned good. When he rubbed that thumb over my sweet spot and pressed a pointed tongue into my core, the cotton grated along oversensitive tissue, and my body went tight. The pressure started at my core, glided up my chest, wrapped around my heart, out each limb until I convulsed. The pleasure electrified me, but Wes didn't stop. He held me down and forced me to take the pleasure again and again until he ripped off my panties and dived his tongue deep into my slit. So much so his movements pressed me up the bed. He couldn't get close enough and the sounds he made were carnal, animalistic. Christ, I could come from the sounds alone.

Wes growled, licked, sucked, bit, and nibbled me into sheer oblivion, my body rocking against his face. I held onto his dirty blond hair in a death grip as he held open the petals of my sex and sucked me for so long and so hard that I physically couldn't stop coming.

Eventually, he pulled his mouth away, lifted up his arm, wiped my juices off his face onto his forearm, lifted up my hips, keeping them nice and wide, and slammed his rock hard cock home.

I screamed out as my entire body shook with the effort of being filled so perfectly.

"Wake the fuck up, you crazy cunt!" Ginelle was shaking my body the same way Wes was shaking me in my dream, only his was through pile drives into my wet sex.

The new sensation was foreign, like tiny bony fingers shaking my upper chest in an annoying painful jarring.

Opening my eyes, blinking fast, I looked around the room and realized where I was. Ginelle's apartment. I surveyed the room. Wes was gone. Nowhere to be found. Damn, it was only a dream. A beautiful dream that had me slippery as all get out between my thighs, which was the very last thing I wanted to be when I was in bed with my best friend.

"What the fuck?" Her voice sound like she'd swallowed a box of rocks.

"Gin, I'm sorry. Did I wake you?" I lifted up onto my elbows and pushed the long strands of hair out of my eyes.

She sat back on her heels, her hair a wild, wavy mess of blond curls. Her good eye narrowed, the other swollen shut. Seeing her alive, safe next to me, I swear she'd never been more lovely.

"Yeah, you did, while you were trying to dry hump me!" She frowned and chuckled into her hand. "Dirty whore!"

I'm certain my eyes widened so much that they could've popped out of their sockets like one of those squeeze stress dolls—squeeze the body and their eyes bulge out. Let go, and they go back to normal. That's what I was feeling right then.

"No way."

"Yes way! You were all moving around talking in your sleep." She got up on her knees and rubbed her hands down the sides of her breasts and along her waist. "Oh, Wes, baby, yeah." She winced and then her hand flew up to her busted lip. "Ouch." She kicked her leg out and tagged me right in the thigh. Not hard enough to bruise, just enough to get her point across. "Don't make me move and laugh. Can't you see I'm all fucked up?"

I covered my face with both hands. "Uggh, I'm sorry, Gin. It's been weeks since Wes and I were intimate, and then I had this full on make out session with Blaine last night and Max interrupted me, thank God, before it could go any further."

"You made out with Blaine, the fucker that had me kidnapped?" Her eyes changed to dark blue, indicating her instant anger.

"No! Well, yes, but I need to explain. Hear me out."

Ginelle pursed her lips, cringed against what I assumed to be pain from the cut, and then crossed her arms over her chest. "This better be good. Being woken up by a crazy broad humping your back while you sleep needs a solid explanation."

I went through the entire event from the minute I got his text with the video through my date with Blaine and what happened at the restaurant to our agreement of one kiss for the extra week of time with the caveat that he'd let her go. She seemed a lot more even tempered once she realized I'd done it for her. It worried her, though, that I got so into the kiss. It worried *me*, too, but for different reasons.

I definitely did not want to hook back up with Blaine in any way, shape, or form, and had no desire to betray Wes by fucking my way out of debt. All that aside, I still didn't know what to do.

"So you were kissing him and then all of a sudden you imagined Wes?"

I nodded. "It was so real. Blaine kissed me, and then it was like he morphed into Wes. Gin, if Max hadn't broken it up, I don't know what I'd have done."

"You were that deep in your imagination?"

"Yeah. I swear, it's like I could smell him and that ocean scent that clings to his skin even after he's showered when he's finished surfing."

Gin shook her head and smiled the best her busted lip

would allow. "You've got it bad for this guy, huh?"

I thought about Wes. About how much he was probably hurting and I felt a physical ache in my stomach. "Gin, I'm beyond in love with him. He's it for me."

Her non-swollen eye widened. "As in, marriage it?"

Marriage. It wasn't something I'd ever really given a lot of thought to since my parents had failed so miserably at it, along with most of the friends I'd had growing up. But right then, in that moment, sitting on the bed with my battered best friend, my heart bursting wide open for her to see, I nodded.

"I think maybe, yeah," I admitted on a whisper.

"Wow. You are so fucked."

The sad thing was, Ginelle was right, because if Wes didn't make it out alive, I'd lose a lot more than the man I loved. I'd lose my heart and my sanity right along with it.

CHAPTER EIGHT

Gin took a week's leave of absence, explaining what happened to her. Her boss was sympathetic and told her to take all the time she needed. Everyone in town knew who Blaine was and how he controlled the underbelly of Vegas. Since neither of us were in a big hurry to be away from one another after yesterday's trauma, Ginelle followed me to the hotel. She was still a little off, but definitely coming back to the feisty girl I knew and loved with every hour that passed. We'd spent the morning talking about Wes and where I thought we were headed in our relationship provided he made it back in one piece. She admitted that she was worried about me moving in with him, but now that she saw how affected I was over him being gone, about the dreams, and the imagination, she admitted that I was beyond bonkers over him, and just like that, she supported me. That easy.

When we entered the hotel, Max was sitting in the dining area with Maddy and Matt. He'd stayed with her overnight since I was gone. There was a spread of food over the table, enough to feed an entire army.

Max stood when he saw us. He came to me and airlifted me into a huge bear hug. I held on tight, my arms gripping for dear life as he squeezed the living hell out of me.

"Worried about you, sugar. Glad to see you back and with your friend." He slowly lowered me back to the floor and pressed his forehead to mine. "You okay?" he asked.

I cupped both his cheeks, leaned back, and kissed his forehead. "I'm good, Maximus." I smiled for his benefit and he returned the gesture.

Max turned to Gin who stood awkwardly, swaying side to side rocking herself. "Hey, darlin', you doin' all right?" He lifted a hand to her face, and Gin jerked back a step. Max's hand fell to his side, his pale eyes turning hard, his nostrils flaring. "This is so wrong, a man laying his hands on a woman in anger."

I huffed. "You think that's wrong? He almost killed Pops. The man and his goons are pure evil. Now I just need to figure out what I'm going to do to put this all behind us."

Max was about to respond when my cell phone rang. I looked around the room, and all eyes were on me. The raid was supposed to happen last night in Indonesia. Pulling out the phone, I glanced down and saw Warren Shipley's name.

"Hello, Warren?

"Yeah, it's me, Mia. Got some news." His voice was calm yet firm. "You sitting down?"

I beat it to the nearest chair and plopped down, pressing the phone close to my ear. "Okay, yeah. I'm ready. Did they find him?" My heart started pounding out a violent thudding that I swore I could feel in my fingertips and all the way to my toes. It was as if my entire body was one big heartbeat.

"They got him, but the entire mission was ugly. A lot of lives were lost."

I closed my eyes, sending up a silent prayer for all those that didn't make it. "Tell me what happened, and where is Wes?"

"He's safe, being treated in a secret location."

A weight the size of a two-ton anvil lifted off my chest, replacing the worst of my fear with a much smaller weight. Now I just needed to lay my eyes on him. Kiss his lips. Hold him close and reclaim what was mine…forever.

Then Warren's words registered. Secret location? "What? I need to see him!"

He cleared his throat. "Honey, you can't. Not yet. They treat the victims medically, and then they will debrief them about what they might know about the terrorist cell. Any information they have could be incredibly powerful to help fight the war on terrorism. This group was particularly heinous, honey. The things they were doing to women and children not of their faith, you couldn't imagine. That didn't even include the eighteen tourists that were secured and saved through the raids."

"Eighteen tourists? I thought it was just Wes and the five remaining crew members."

Max sat down next to me and put a hand to my knee. It was bouncing like a five-year-old on a trampoline. Maddy sat on my other side and clutched my loose hand, kissing the top. I gripped her hand and held it close to my face, taking solace in her warmth and presence as I listened to Warren.

"Doesn't matter. How is he, do you know?" I waited with bated breath for any scrap of information on how he was.

"All I know is that when the team struck, they started killing hostages. Apparently, they decided that if they were going to die, they'd take the vile Americans and their religious propaganda with them. One man was used as a human shield. He was dressed in their clothing, forced to hold an unloaded gun and walk out of the hut they had him in. The snipers had no idea he wasn't one of the hostiles. They killed him and the man leading him with a gun at his back on first sight."

"Jesus." My heart clenched.

Warren's voice got low. "Honey, the things they did to that woman, that actress, I wouldn't wish on my worst enemy."

Gina DeLuca.

Fuck. I hated the woman—not because I had any right to hate her, but because she'd had a casual sexual relationship with Wes at one time. She had been getting what I wanted from him but wasn't strong enough to go for myself. Even still, I didn't wish her any real harm. Maybe for an ugly picture of her eating a hot dog to appear on the local smut mag but not to be mistreated by the hands of sick and twisted men with nothing but an axe to grind.

"Is she uh, okay?"

Warred blew out a long breath. "Physically and mentally, no. Will she live? Yes."

I blinked away the tears, trying to hold it together as best I could. "Did anyone else make it?"

"Hold on." I could hear Warren sniff and blow his nose in the distance. "I'm okay, Kathy, talking to Mia. Gotta finish this. Yes, some tea would be helpful. Thank you, dear," Warren said to Kathleen.

Kathleen was the woman he'd finally admitted he was in love with after all these years. They were together, and it made me happy knowing that even second chances at love happened in this world.

"Sorry, Mia. Even at my age, this stuff never gets any

easier to say."

"No, I can't imagine it does." I took a breath, squeezed Maddy's hand, and swallowed. "When is he coming home, and when can I talk to him?"

"My sources say he'll be home within two weeks. They are treating him medically and psychologically, trying to be considerate of the fact that they are severely malnourished, have had little to no sleep, and have been tortured, beaten, and seen some incredibly vile things occur."

Every word Warren said was like sticking straight pins through every pore. My skin itched with the need to see Wes, touch him, love him.

"Warren, I need to see him. Talk to him."

"As soon as I know more about where he is and when you can see him, I'll notify you. Just give it a few days, okay?"

I stood up instantly and paced the room. "A few days? You want me to wait a few days to talk to the man I love, the man who has been missing for over three weeks? Are you insane? Warren, this is ridiculous. He goes from being held hostage by radical extremists to being detained by the government? The United Fucking States! The land of the free!" I roared so loud that Max put his hands on my shoulders, once again stole the phone, and put it on speaker.

"Shipley, this is Max here. What is it going to take to get my sister a phone call to her man?"

Warred grumbled and huffed loudly. "A lot of fucking strings being pulled."

"Then I'd say you need to become a puppeteer. From what my sister tells me, you owe her a favor."

"Mia, you told him?" Warren's voice turned to ice.

"No!" I shot back, pissed that he'd even think I'd risk

telling more people, though my brother wasn't just anyone.

Max's eyes went from pale green to a dark forest green, the pupils big and frightening. Right then, Max realized that whatever I held over Warren was big enough to screw a very rich, very powerful man over. Usually, those things were jail worthy. If Aaron so much as fucked up by missing a single anger management class or a counseling session, I had the power to make a formal complaint and he'd lose his status as the Senator for California. Not that it would be a huge love loss for the state. With one phone call I could ruin Aaron Shipley's career. Not only that, I knew doing so would screw over Warren in the process, and I had absolutely no intention of destroying the good he'd been doing with his new business venture to help people in third world countries. Now that I knew what type of crazy shit happened in those countries, it was even more important.

"Mia, I'll see what I can finagle, but I make no promises."

"Anything would be helpful. Anything, please." My voice was low, emotional, and pleading as I said the words through the tears that had started to fall.

Maddy's arm came around me and pulled me close. I held on to her, one of the most solid things I had in life. My sister.

"You need money or resources, you call me," Max stated in his I-run-an-empire business drawl. "Whatever it costs, make it happen. You hear?"

"Loud and clear," Warren answered.

At that point, I was too raw to even think straight, let alone respond. My man had been saved only more lives were lost, but the lives of those tourists had been saved, yet I couldn't see or speak to him. Now the government had him locked away in some secret location for another couple weeks. Jesus. How would I survive the next fourteen days without another word? The simple answer was, I wouldn't.

"Good man. Have him call her cell and see about making it quick," Max demanded and I smiled through my tears.

Leave it to my new brother to move some mountains. Hell, he was big enough to do it single handedly. Now I knew how he could run such a large empire. Not only was he forceful and fair, but when he spoke, people listened. Natural born leader. That's what happened with a father like Jackson Cunningham. I didn't know the man, but the son he'd raised was something to behold.

★ ★ ★

After the call, I went to bed. Ginelle slept in the other, and Maddy cuddled next to me. Apparently, she'd been worried all night even though I texted where I was. She wanted to come and see me. Matt had forced her to stay with him. Matt.

I blinked away the hours of sleep, got up without disturbing Maddy or Ginelle, and tiptoed into the other room, carrying a new pair of jeans and a long-sleeved shirt. Once I'd had a steaming hot shower, and with the knowledge that Wes was safe—unreachable, yet still safe—I felt a lot better. Pops was breathing on his own, the medicines were helping the allergic reaction, and the doctors believed his prognosis would be good.

The only thing I had to do now was deal with Blaine, but first, I settled for a chat with my sister's fiancé. I entered the main area and found Max snoozing on the couch. The balcony doors were open and the breeze wafted through the room, which was lit with the orange-and-pink glow of the sunrise. I could see Matt's feet up on the railing.

Grabbing a bottle of water from the mini bar, I walked outside and made sure to shut the door. Matt turned to me, a pair of black sunglasses perched on his nose. He wore a plaid button-up shirt and nice dark-wash jeans. On his feet were a pair of Converse chucks. The epitome of a college kid. Well, a smart looking one.

"How's Maddy?" he asked when I sat down, his body going tight, alert.

I put my feet up on the railing, fluffed my hair back, and looked out over Vegas. The desert mountains that surrounded the city were something to behold and were part of the attraction that brought out the tourists in droves. That and the casinos, of course.

"Relax, she's fine. Sleeping still."

Matt's shoulders dropped and he laid back into the lounge chair. "She was really worried about you last night."

I chuckled. "I can take care of myself."

"Doesn't hurt to lean on someone who loves you."

Tilting my head to the side, I squinted at him. "You mean the same way you were leaning on her to get married right away?"

His eyes widened. "She, uh, told you about that." He moved his legs to straddle the chair and leaned forward, head hanging down.

Poor boy. He had no idea whom he was dealing with. "Matt, let's get a couple things straight. I've been Maddy's primary protector since she was five. I'm her sister, but a lot of the time I had to be the parent too. We're tight." I held up two fingers pressed together.

"Yeah, I got that, but I thought what happened was private. I made a mistake." His voice was low, apologetic.

"One I hope you're not going to be making again anytime soon."

His eyebrows furrowed. "I still want to marry her. As soon as she'll have me," Matt said, rushed.

I put out my hands. "I get it. I didn't tell her not to marry you. Truthfully, I think you guys are great together. You're good for her, and you've proven that through all of this." I waved my hand in the air. "It's just Maddy needs some time to adjust. You've only been together a few months. Enjoy one another, be silly, hang out with friends, and work hard in school. Don't let the pressure of needing to grow up too fast make you miss out on the best parts. The journey."

I looked down at my foot and the script that had come to mean so much more than I ever thought possible. The letters intertwined with the petals blowing in the breeze reminded me that I needed to touch base with my friends as well as add some new petals. Even though my life seemed out of control, I should make time for the other people that have come to mean so much to me. Alec, Mason, Rachel, Tony, Hector, Angelina, Tai, Heather—Anton, just thinking about each face brought memories of better times and put a smile on my face.

"Why were you in such a hurry to tie the knot anyway?" I asked and focused on his body language. It looked... defeated, and for the life of me, I couldn't imagine why. He wasn't the type that would cheat, and if he did, I'd absolutely kill him so it couldn't be that. The Rains clan was a loving breed, and they didn't seem too pushy about the marriage side. Matt's parents seemed happy that their boy had found a great girl, and they'd been supportive of their decision to move in with one another.

Matt shook his head. "You'll think it's dumb."

I laughed. "Probably, but tell me anyway."

He smiled and then just as quickly as the grin spread across his face, it disappeared. Matt blew out a long, slow breath. "There's this group of guys. Jocks. Big dudes, good looking. They're always chatting Maddy up after class, casually trying to get her to study with them, help them with their homework. Saying they'd even pay her to tutor them."

"And does she do it?"

His expression morphed into one of disgust. "Hell, no. She'd never do that."

I knew that answer before I asked, but I wanted to know his response. Point for Matt. "Go ahead."

"It's just they won't let up. They're successful, all from rich families. They could give her anything she wants, and they play sports. Maddy loves sports. I just watch 'em for her."

That made me piggy snort. "You watch sports for my sister?" I couldn't help but tip my head back and laugh hard. Man, it felt good, too. Of course, Maddy would cling onto the one man that didn't love sports. Just goes to show how much opposites attract.

Matt chuckled. "Well, yeah. She loves it. Says it's what you and Pops do together as a family, and since I want to be a part of her family, I watch it too."

Sweet. Too fucking sweet. My sister had really scored

with this guy. "I'm not understanding the problem. Are you jealous of these jocks?"

His shoulders slumped again. "I don't know, maybe. I'm a plant guy. I'll be working for companies that deal in farming, botany, and the like. They're going to go pro, run family businesses, and be able to give her a life I can't. I'm just a geek with a green thumb. And Maddy, God, she's so beautiful. Kind. Loving. Crazy smart. She could have anyone with the snap of her fingers."

Aw, I got it now. He was insecure. "That she could. My girl is beyond gorgeous. But you know what, Matt?"

His eyes were sad when he looked up at me. "What?"

"Maddy loves *you*. Maddy wants to marry *you*. She gave you something very special, and you're the only man she's ever wanted to have it. Get what I mean?"

He grinned, and his cheeks pinked up. Too fucking cute. Talk about sex and he blushes. Yeah, he was damn near perfect for my girl.

"I think so. I just thought if I could get her to be my wife, then I wouldn't, you know…"

"Lose her?"

He nodded, and I clapped him on the shoulder. "All I can tell you, Matt, is have faith. Have faith in your love, and have faith in Maddy. She'd never do you wrong. It's not who she is."

Matt patted my hand. "You're right. We talked about it. I admitted most of it to her. She thought I was crazy, said I was the hottest guy she'd ever known, and then she jumped on me and proved to me how much she loved me."

And then he lost that one point. "Gross. Did you just seriously tell *me*, your fiancée's *sister*, how you had awesome make up sex? Blech. Sick!"

He laughed. "Too soon?"

"Way too fucking soon. Ew wee, now I need to have my ears professionally cleaned. You're one twisted dude! First plant talk, and then sex talk? God. I don't know how Maddy puts up with it." I grinned and looked at him through one eye.

Together, we spent the next hour bonding, laughing and talking about the funny things that he and my sister did to pass the days, minus the sex talks. I asked him how he felt about moving to Texas if Maddy wanted to work at Cunningham Oil & Gas. He said he would defer to her. Go where she wanted to go. Matt understood that, until Max, Maddy hadn't had a family besides me, and he wanted her to be happy. Plus, he liked Max and liked the area where Max lived. Apparently, he and Maddy talked about maybe looking at buying some land out in Texas and he'd farm the land. Maybe open up his own small business with the local produce, or something like that. All good ideas and solid for the future. He agreed that the wedding would definitely happen after they both graduated.

Knowing that Matt and I had our talk and worked out some of the slight irritation I'd had on hearing that he was pressuring Maddy made one more weight on my shoulders disappear. Last remaining problem, besides getting access to my man, was a doozie. Blaine douchebag Pintero.

CHAPTER NINE

Friday had arrived, and I was no closer to finding out how the hell I was going to pacify Blaine with no money and no desire to get between the sheets with him. Pops was on the mend. Maddy and Matt were solid and back on their life plan. Max was still in town, and Ginelle was safe. For now. I, on the other hand? That was a totally different story. I was a fucking mess. It had been a few days and no call from Wes and no additional information from Warren, even though I'd called him three times a day since he told me Wes was alive. He had taken to ignoring my calls. Once Kathleen picked up and told me he was working on it and wouldn't stop until he got some facts about Wes's whereabouts. For now, though, he couldn't listen to my broken voice and get anything accomplished. I understood that. If it were me, I wouldn't be able to get anything done with a psycho, emotional wreck calling every five minutes for an update.

This must be what hell feels like. Knowing the man I love, the person I'd give my life for was hurting mentally and physically and I wasn't there to touch him, lend a hand, or support his healing process. It sucked…royally.

My neck had a permanent cramp from looking down at my phone incessantly, waiting, hoping for a call from an unknown number. Every time the damn thing rang, it jolted my system into action, all synapses firing, my heart beating wildly only to find it was Max, or Maddy, or Gin. Ugh.

Last night, I'd finally broken down and made some calls to my friends. Hector cried while I told him what had happened to Wes. Tony got angry and asked if I needed money, plane tickets, anything that could help. Such a fixer. I assured them I was handling it and that I had faith he'd be home soon. Pretty much a fat lie. I got strict instructions to check in next week with both men or they'd hunt me down. I had no doubt they'd fulfill that threat. Mason was not nearly as kind. He was pissed. Ready to skip out on the last handful of games in the season even though the Red Sox were killing it and he was their star pitcher. I remembered our call last night.

"Mia, this is bullshit. You wait until things are so fucked up to call?" Mason's voice got more distant, as if he'd moved his mouth from the receiver. "No, Rach, I won't be calm. This is not cool. We're her family."

Hearing him say I was family hit hard. I had no right to keep all this drama to myself. I had people who cared, even loved me the same way I loved them. It was time I started counting on them more, if not physically, at least emotionally.

He came back on the line. "I can't believe you found out you have a brother. That's crazy."

"Yeah, but he's really great, and check this out. I now am the owner of twenty-five percent of Cunningham Oil & Gas."

"What the fuck? You shitting me?"

"Nope. Apparently, Jackson Cunningham knew about me all along and wanted me to have a piece of his legacy as Max's sister.

What he didn't know about was Maddy, who as it turns out, is a full-blooded member of the Cunningham clan. Mom pawned off Maddy as my father's."

"Jesus. Your mom was wacked."

I thought about Mason and his mom, lost to breast cancer when he was younger. His mother would have given anything to have one more day with her children, and my mother walked away from not one, not two, but three children who needed her. That's the kind of life-changing event that is impossible to forgive. Made me wonder if Max had a chance to set his investigator to work on finding where our dear mother ended up. If he did find Meryl Colgrove, would I even know what to say to her? You suck? Throw it in her face how great we are. Well, Max and Maddy are doing great. Me? I'm an escort paying off the debt of the man she left.

When Mace and I ended the call, I promised to be more present in their lives, visit next year, introduce them to Wes. Next was Anton and Heather. Of course, Anton took the philosophical approach to everything, asking how it affected the big picture, how I felt about it. I swear Anton, the Latin Lov-ah, was a hippie underneath all those gold chains. Heather, on the other hand, offered a bunch of "no ways" and "holy shits." Mostly she was worried about me and how I was taking Wes's disappearance. I didn't have a lot to say because if I did, I'd melt into a puddle of tears. If nothing else, I owed it to Wes to stay strong and keep fighting, and that's what I planned to do.

Alec, of course, was Alec. Everything about his voice, his genuine love, made me feel better. He had a way with words, and he told me that he was confident in my abilities to survive another day. On the other hand, if I wanted to, he'd happily whisk me off to France where he'd ravish my body and fill my soul with light. His words, not mine. Though they were said in such eloquent French my entire body broke out in a series of tingles. I had to stop that sexy train with a sweet warning, which my Frenchie understood. Love was love to him, but he accepted the forever kind and would respect my wishes. Hence, it meant no future hanky panky with filthy-talking French artists. I had to say that part in English and repeat it in French to get the point across.

I waited to call Tai until the very last. As expected, he did not take the news well. So much so that I didn't even tell him all of it, because had I told him about Blaine, his threats, and the kidnapping, he would have been on the next plane with a half dozen giant Samoan men out for blood. Blaine's blood. Sure, it would make everything easier for me, but those men would get hurt. Men like Blaine were too pompous to fight with their hands as proven by the experience Max had in the hallway. Blaine didn't even attempt to hit Max. No, Blaine would use goons, knives, and most certainly, guns. Blaine wouldn't stop until the entire Niko clan was dead and buried six feet under in a long lost section of the Nevada desert never to be heard from again. That was not going to happen to my sexy Samoan. No way, no how.

What I told Tai was about Pops and Max. That was enough to set his worry meter to a ten out of ten. We talked long into the night. I briefly wondered what Amy thought about our long chat, but in the middle of it, she kissed him goodnight and told him she'd see him back in bed. There was no concern, malice, or anxiety in her tone whatsoever. When I asked Tai about it, he said simply, "Amy's cool. She understands that you're family."

And there it was again. That word. Family. When I started this journey nine months ago, that word consisted of four people total. Maddy, Ginelle, Pops, and my Aunt Millie. Now I couldn't count on two hands how many people I now considered part of my extended family, not to mention the new real living blood relation in Max, Cyndi, and Isabel as well as baby Jack on the way. Those were four new instant extended relatives. It was hard to comprehend how much life had changed over the past nine months. More so than I would have ever imagined possible in my twenty-five-years.

And then there was Wes. I looked down at my phone one more time. Nothing. Scowling, I got dressed, actually making an effort. If I was going to beg, borrow, and plead with Blaine to give me more time, I wanted to at least look the part.

My phone pinged, and I hurried to check the display, praying it was Weston. What I saw forced an enormous scowl that I felt down to my toes. The life force of my being was being drained, and it pooled around my feet.

To: Mia Saunders
From: Blaine Douchebag Pintero
I expect you're doing well and either have my money or are prepared to agree to the terms. Meet at our place in an hour. I'll be waiting.

Of course he would, the twisted fucker. As I grabbed

my purse and slung it over my shoulder, Max grabbed a set of keys and looked at me.

"What?" I asked.

Max's lips were held in a thin line. Their normal puffy pink was devoid of color. His body language was rigid and confusing. "I'm driving you."

I cringed. "Um, no. I'll be fine. He's not going to hurt me, Max. He wants to fuck me, not kill me."

Max's jaw locked down and a muscle there flickered. "He kidnapped your best friend, Mia. This is not a situation to take lightly."

Sighing, I put a hand to his bicep. It hardened reflexively. "Max, he won't like your presence there. I know what, more specifically *who*, I'm dealing with. I'm worth too much to him monetarily and physically to do something rash. I'll be fine." I looked straight into his eyes and lied my ass off. Blaine was a wild card. I never knew what would tip him off, make him laugh, or when he'd turn downright evil incarnate. I'd hope for the humorous side and planned to work that angle along with his desire to bed me for more time. Maybe use his love of money and promise him more. A lot more. I could easily keep working for Millie, making the money I needed to as well as whatever I'd get from Cunningham Oil & Gas. I know Max didn't want that money bankrolling a criminal, but I had no choice if I wanted to live any semblance of a normal life.

"Trust me. I've got this," I said, shifting my shoulders back and straightening my spine.

Max shook his head and opened the door. "Trust me." He pointed to his chest. "I've got this. I told you before and I'll tell you again, darlin'. I take care of my family. End of discussion."

My shoulders sagged as I followed him to the elevator and into his rental car. Nothing was said on the drive to Luna Rosa. I had no idea what to tell him, and I think he had choice words that I'd rather not hear.

We entered the restaurant, and as usual, Blaine sat out on the patio at our table. Umbrellas had been put up to provide shade. The water from the lake kept the temperature on the patio feeling a solid ten degrees cooler than the normal Vegas heat. As we walked up, Blaine stood. He wore a crisp beige suit that fit him to perfection. A coral dress shirt unbuttoned at the neck highlighted his coloring and made his eyes glow. They reminded me of a cat's eyes in the dark, how they seemed to glimmer with a yellow-green radiance.

Blaine held out a hand to Max and nodded to the table next to us. "I see you've brought your own muscle, as have I." He grinned.

His goons pushed back their blazer jackets. The barrels of black .45s could be easily seen.

Max pulled out my chair and I sat, and then he proceeded to shift his chair back, making sure he was able to see Blaine and his two guards with ease. Smart move. I wished I'd thought of it. For a minute, I was actually thankful that Max had pushed his way into coming, even though I really wanted him out of this mess.

"Would you like a drink?" Blaine held up a frosty-looking pinot grigio. My mouth went dry, and I nodded. He poured me a glass and kept it aloft until Max glanced at it and shook his head. He was far too busy being an imposing character to be bothered with wine.

I took a sip of the wine and hummed. Blaine always

had exceptional taste in wine. It was something he spent a lot of time doing—tastings, traveling to wineries to check on the newest selections and reserves just being released. Back in the day, I used to envy his dignified palate.

"Let's get right to business shall we?" Blaine said, and I practically choked on the sip of wine. I still hadn't figured out how I was going to get myself out of this predicament, but I'd die trying. Seriously, I'd die because Blaine would probably shoot me on the spot, but there was no other choice. I had to trudge on.

"Look, Blaine, I know you said I couldn't have more time, but there's so many things you don't know about what's happening, and well, I—"

Blaine's eyes darkened and he cut me off. "You better be telling me that you are accepting door number two, which leads to my bedroom, because excuses are like assholes, my pretty. Everyone has one, but not many want to get near one."

I sucked in a deep breath, tears pricking at the back of my eyelids. "Then you're just going to have to kill me."

Blaine gasped at the same time that Max's fist came down like a hammer on the table, rattling the glasses and knocking over my wine. I grappled with the glass in an attempt to catch what I could before it spilled over onto the floor.

"This is horseshit," Max growled and stood up. My brother was a giant normally, but when you were sitting, he was a mountain of a man. He reached into his back pocket and the intensity in the room went from a hundred to a thousand. Blaine ducked and his goons moved like ninjas. In a second, there was a gun barrel at the side of Max's temple and one at the back of his head. He stiffened.

"You better have a very good reason for reaching into the back of your pants, cowboy, or my men are going to escort you out of here and take care of you the same way they did in the old west. I own this fucking town," he growled between clenched teeth. "And the cops around here are on my payroll. You think real hard about that before you make your move."

Max blinked and kept his gaze laser focused on Blaine's. "I was pulling out an envelope. The fella behind me can see I'm not packing."

"He's telling the truth, boss," the pudgy one that looked like a B movie mafia impersonator said over Max's shoulder.

Blaine tipped his chin, and Max pulled out the envelope. He leaned forward, set it on the table, and tapped it with his index finger. "There's your money. All four hundred thousand."

I'm pretty sure at that point surprise wasn't the word I'd used to explain how I felt. So many emotions warred with one another. Relief. Fear. Pride. Love. The last, though, threw me for a loop.

Disgust.

Right then, I was disgusted with myself that my brother, quite possibly one of the sweetest men alive, who didn't deserve any of this, was paying off my debt. My father's debt. A rather *large* debt. It wasn't like I'd said, "Hey, bro, can I borrow fifty bucks?" No, this was four hundred thousand dollars. Almost half a million.

"You can't," I whispered. My voice came out garbled, like I was talking through a ball of cotton.

Max's eyes cut to mine. "I have. No one threatens my

sister or hurts my family when I can take care of it."

"Can this money be traced?" Blaine asked looking into the envelope at what must be a check since it was very thin in size. Four hundred thousand, even in hundreds, had to be quite a stack.

Max nodded. "Back to me, yes. It's from my personal account. If you want it in cash, I'll have it by the end of the day waiting for you at the front desk of your casino. I wanted to bring that check to show good faith."

Blaine's eyebrow rose. "You don't mind if I make a call, verify you're good for it?"

Max huffed. "Not at all."

With a tilt of his head, one of Blaine's goons took the check and stepped over to the backside of the patio. For the first time, I looked around and realized there weren't any other patrons and it was lunchtime on a Friday in the shopping district. Guess Blaine was making sure our situation was kept private. Chugging the new glass of wine Blaine poured me, I waited impatiently. I didn't know what to do or say to Max. What could I say to make something like this better?

With jerky movements, I placed my hands over Max's. He held one and topped the other with his big palm. I looked into his eyes, green to green, and tried desperately to convey all the feelings and emotions I had for him, for what he sacrificed to save my life, Maddy's, Ginelle's, and Pops's. "Thank you." I choked on the words. He brought his forehead to mine. The instant his touched mine I felt that sizzle of familiarity. That feeling a person gets when she's with family. It had happened the very first day I met him at the airport and shook his hand.

"I'd do it again. A hundred times over to keep you safe and in my life. I love you, Sis." Max's voice was low, filled with affection. Those words wormed their way right through my chest and into my heart where they took up shop.

"I love you, too, Maximus." I pulled him close and hugged him hard. "And I'll find a way to pay you back."

He chuckled. "Honey, you're going to be a rich woman very soon. You'll find a way." He leaned back, cupped my cheeks, and wiped my tears with his thumbs.

"We're good, boss," said mafia boy.

Blaine put his hands together, fingers in a steeple. "Pity, pretty Mia. I was so looking forward to having you under me again."

Just his words sent a chill through me, and I shivered.

That's when Max had enough. "Time to go, darlin'." He tugged on my bicep, all but lifting me right out of my chair. "I'll have your cash to you this evening by seven. The bank has been notified I might need it on short notice and is putting it together now."

"Splendid." Blaine stood up, buttoned a single button on his jacket, and put his hand out.

Max stared at the hand but eventually shook it. God, the guy was too good. There needed to be a million more men like him running the world. It would be a far happier, more peaceful place.

Max put his hand to my lower back and pressed me forward.

"Wait!" Blaine said, and I turned around. He walked slowly to me, like a lion slinks forward readying to pounce. I inhaled and waited for him to place his cool hands on my biceps. "I believe this is the end, is it not?"

"My debt is clear," I answered.

He stroked my arms up and down. "You are free, pretty, pretty Mia." Blaine leaned forward, and I could practically feel the tension rippling off Max as Blaine kissed one cheek and then the other. Lastly, he lifted a hand, cupped my cheek, and rubbed my bottom lip with his thumb. "I always wanted the best for you. In my own way. Be well."

On that parting phrase, he turned around and strode purposely out of the restaurant. Max ushered me out to his car, but before he could open the door, I gripped his hand, tugged hard, and smashed my face into his chest. I looped my hands around his waist and hugged him hard. I put everything I had into that single hug.

Fear.

Grief.

Relief.

And ended it with heaping dose of gratitude.

I'd never be able to pay him back and I wasn't referring to the money. That I'd pay back no problem between the job and the money I was going to get from the company. I just wouldn't to be able to pay back the gift of *him*. His presence when I needed him. Taking care of me the way he did. All I knew was that I'd spend the rest of my days being grateful and appreciative of everything that was Maxwell Cunningham until the day I died. He'd lifted his position in my life right up there alongside my baby sister, and that was a position I never thought another soul besides Wes could occupy.

AUDREY CARLAN

CHAPTER 10

They say freedom is a privilege, not a right. I don't feel very privileged or truly free. The debt to Blaine was paid, but my heart was still locked away in a dungeon, begging to be liberated. My father was doing well, his prognosis good. Though his own mind was still locked away.

My savior, my brother Max, has flown back home to be with his wife, Cyndi, in the hope that baby Jackson will soon make his appearance. Maddy and Matt have started school and gone back to the comfort of their apartment near the university. Ginelle chose to go back to work, armed with some heavy-duty makeup to cover her still healing bruises. Her own plans have changed since the attack. We got her set up with a counselor to work through what happened, but she told me that, when I got back home and settled with Wes, she too would like to head out. Get a change of scenery, a new job. Basically, she wanted to get the hell out of Las Vegas, and I didn't blame her. There were too many memories of harsh times to live through. I'd do whatever it took to help her heal, and if that included shacking her up in Wes's guest house, that's what we'd do.

I'd thought about the word *home* for some time now. Though Sin City had been home to me for most of my life, I didn't feel like the real me here. Malibu was calling, but who would greet me when I landed? It seemed like everyone's life had continued to move forward. Everyone's but mine. In a week, I was supposed to be starting on the TV show with celebrity doctor to the stars, Dr. Hoffman, but I didn't feel ready for that leap. I couldn't pay him the hundred thousand for flaking though so, no matter what was going on, I had to go. He hired me to do a new segment spun off from my own slice of fame. The segment was aptly labeled *Living Beautiful*.

Only problem, life for me no longer had color. All I saw were shades of gray, black, and white. The beauty surrounding me had disappeared, seeped out until all colors bled away into nothing. I felt like nothing.

Lying on the hotel room bed, I stared out at the sky— dark, covered in clouds, the desert preparing for a summer storm. It fit my mood perfectly. Storms were unusual at that time of year but not all together unheard of. I sat up Indian style, my phone clutched in my hand. Thunder rumbled in the distance and I started to count.

One Mississippi…

Two Mississippi…

Three Mississippi…

Four Mississippi…

Boom! Thunder roared and lightning hit. Somewhere I heard that every five seconds between the flash and thunder meant the storm was one mile away. A blinding white slash raced across the slate sky like a too-bright camera flash, momentarily taking away my vision. As quick as it came, it was gone. Just like Wes.

Weston Channing, III entered my life on a wave. Literally. From the moment he stepped from surf to sand, I watched him walk toward me. A sun god. Tanned skin, spiky wet hair, the ocean's tears falling down a chest that could have been chiseled in stone it was so hard. His eyes, the color of fresh cut grass in the middle of a Californian spring day, met mine, but that wasn't what drew me in. It was his confidence, the quirky smile, the effortless way he walked, spoke, and made love. As if his body were meant to be near mine. Touched by me. Held within the safety of my arms.

Or maybe it was the reverse of that. My need to be near him. Touched by *his* hand, *his* heart, *his* soul.

"Please come back to me," I prayed aloud.

My phone rang. It jerked me out of my melancholy mood, and I looked down.

Unknown caller.

Heat hit the core of my being, burning me from the inside out as an instant prickling sensation made the hairs on my arms stand at attention. The phone rang again and I picked it up, pressed the answer button, and took a breath. "Hello?" I croaked into the phone, too scared to say anything more.

"Mia," came the breathless reply, almost as if it took him extreme effort to say the three-letter word.

Tears rippled down my face. "Wes," I said, not knowing what else to say but needing to say everything in a single breath. My heart was in my throat, my body convulsing with tension. I gripped the phone in my hand so hard and so close to my ear, pain shot through my hand, but I didn't care.

"Sweetheart, your voice. Jesus, baby so good to hear…" He cleared his throat and sighed deep. So deep I could feel the pressure all around me.

"Wes, tell me you're okay." I finally managed to string more than one word together.

He coughed roughly. "I'm okay. Just a little worse for the wear."

Leave it to my guy to be flippant at a time like this. "I need to see you, touch you, to believe you're real."

His breathing became labored as he replied, "I know. I want to see you so bad it hurts. But I can't. I have to uh, stay here a little while, arrrrggghh."

"What is it? What is it? Are you hurt?" My voice shook so hard, I'm not even sure I said what I thought I said. A knife to the chest would have been easier to deal with than knowing Wes was in pain, had been wounded in some way and I couldn't physically get to him.

"Yeah, baby, I'm hurt. Took uh, a bullet to the neck. I'm okay though. Really I'm going to be fine." He groaned and I heard a rustling sound but everything started to become a little fuzzy after what he'd said.

Took a bullet to the neck.

The neck! Who takes a bullet to the neck and lives to tell about it? "Wes, baby, I need to see you. Right fucking now. Where are you? Tell me where you are. I'll be on the next flight out. I have friends that have private planes. My brother could send me in his." I rushed my words, already planning who to call next to reach him the fastest.

"Your brother?" His tone was confused and I didn't blame him.

I pressed my fingers into my temples. "Yeah, I have a brother. A real brother. DNA proved it. And he, uh, he paid off Pops's debt."

"What, who?" he said tersely, but I wasn't sure if it was because he was in pain or because he was hearing such surprising information for the first time.

"Maxwell Cunningham."

He coughed and whimpered. "Fuck!" he said breathily again. "Stop with the blood pressure cuff. I'm trying to talk to my fiancée. Back off. Give me a minute," he growled.

Fiancée? I'd let that go for now. He probably just wanted to make sure the person interrupting him knew it was an important call. Probably. Maybe. "Who are you talking to?" I asked.

"Nurse Ratched!" he said, but I'm pretty sure he wasn't saying it to me as much as to whoever was checking on him.

"Wes, honey, where are you?" My entire being was frantic for any hint of information.

"Australia, I think."

What the fuck was he doing in Australia? "You were in Indonesia last I heard."

"Yeah, when the raid happened, they had to medevac a lot of us out of there, and since we'd been taken to Indonesia and held captive, they wanted to get us to a safer locale where our government had some healthy peaceful ties."

Leaning back against the headboard, I stared out at the dark sky. "When can I see you?"

He sighed. "Honestly, sweetheart, I don't know. They are interviewing the captives as quickly as possible but also making sure we're safe. You're friend Mr. Shipley has been on everyone's ass. Making a real name for himself." He chuckled then made a wincing sound.

God, if only I were there, I could kiss it better. I'd have to contact Warren, tell him how much it meant to me to have used his connection.

My voice cracked when I told him how I felt. "Baby, I want to hold your hand. Watch you sleep. Feel your chest rise and fall. Hear your heart beating. I *need* you home."

"I want nothing more than to come home to you, sweetheart. Soon. I promise. I'll do everything I can to get out of here."

"Can you call me every day until you get back?"

Once again, he chuckled, only this time softly. "They gave each of us a cell phone. We can talk as much as we want."

The elephant sitting on my chest got up and moseyed away. I still felt the remnants of the burden, but over time, that would lessen.

"So…your fiancée, huh?" I couldn't help but mess with him a little. Banter with my guy the way we always did.

He hummed and the sound went straight to my happy place. Wes was back. Thank you, God.

"There's a lot we need to talk about but yeah, you and me, that's just the way it's going to be. I'm not waiting for paradise. I'm throwing you over my shoulder kicking and screaming and taking you there. I will not live another day of my life worrying about you. About what would happen to you if I'd died out there."

"Don't. Wes, just don't even say it." The tears came back on a rampage.

"Mia, we can't hide from life. We never know how much time we have or what could happen to us as we're living it. All I know is I'm going to do it with you by my side. For good. It's me and you. You *will* be my wife."

I laughed through the tears and rejoiced in the feeling of my chest widening, my heart growing so big it could burst with joy. "And what if I say no?" I joked, knowing he'd hear it in my tone.

"No is not an option." His voice lowered, and the sultry tone that made me instantly wet slid across his lips.

"It's yes, Wes. Oh, God, Wes, yes. Give it to me harder, Wes. Yes, I will marry you, Wes."

He hummed again and the sound went through me as if I'd been struck by the lightening flickering in the sky outside the window. "I'm a nice guy. I'll give you options."

I kicked my feet and screamed silently. My guy was something else. Locked away in some military hospital in Australia after having been held captive for almost a month, and he was talking marriage and joking around with his girlfriend after taking a gunshot to the neck.

"I was really scared," I admitted in a hushed tone.

"Me too. And I'm dealing with some of that now by helping save others that may still be out there. I have to help. If I can be here a week more and save even one person, sweetheart, it would be worth it. We have our entire lives together."

"That we do." I said, trying to lighten the situation enough to get through this week. If he could live through a month of hell, I could manage a week.

"I love you, Mia." Wes saying those words, being able to hear them come from his very lips, was like a cool drink on a hot day.

"I love you more, Wes. So much more." I swallowed repeatedly and wiped my running nose against my sleeve.

"Nurse Ratched needs to change my bandage," he stated on a long yawn and an "ouch."

"Okay. Will you call me when you wake up tomorrow?" I'd meant it as a question but it was really more of a plea.

He yawned and mumbled something.

"Wes!" Fear scattered along every nerve when he didn't respond.

"Yeah, sorry, baby. I think she doped me. My eyes are closing faster than I can open them."

"I love you," I said again for no other reason than it felt good saying it.

"Mmm, me too. My Mia." He sounded drunk and half asleep. Then the line cut off.

With heavy limbs, I snuggled into the comforter, holding the phone close. I tucked myself in and watched the light show outside. All my thoughts were of Wes. The relief I felt, knowing he was safe and being taken care of, but frustrated that I wasn't there to help. I also thought about marrying him, living a long life together. It would all start when he got back home.

I had so much to tell him, and I wanted to know all the details about his captivity. Kiss away any hurts that couldn't be seen. I knew from experience from the assault with Aaron, that those things could be long lasting. Mine was so brief compared to what Wes had survived. It wouldn't be easy to move on from something so horrible. I knew for a fact that he'd watched friends, people he cared about, die right before his eyes. Right now, I could only be thankful that he was alive. My guy had survived and together we'd heal. Both of us.

★ ★ ★

Watching someone I love sleep is one of my favorite past times. Growing up, it was Maddy. She'd fall asleep while I read to her, petted her hair, and told her stories. For a long time after she'd fallen asleep, I'd look at her. Memorize the exact golden shade of her hair, the arch of her brows, the pucker of her pink lips. Even in sleep, my girl was angelic. I took a lot of joy in being able to give my sister a peaceful night's sleep. Each and every day it was a new goal. When I was with Alec, I'd play with his hair until he'd wake up smiling, roll over, and ravish me, allowing those beautiful russet locks to lie like a shroud around my face as he loved me. I did the same with Wes. He was the most peaceful in sleep, and when he was face up, he always had a slight curve to his lips. As if whatever he dreamed of was worth smiling for, even in repose. I loved that about him. There was no other man more beautiful in repose than a man you loved with your whole heart and soul.

Now, I watched Pops. The ventilator was gone, as were the tubes in his nose and around his face. He still had the feeding tube, catheter, blood pressure cuff, and IV. Otherwise, he looked as though he was taking a nap. I think that was the hardest part about him having been in a coma for so long. While I waited by his bedside, I kept expecting him to open his eyes. Every visit depressed me more and more because he wouldn't wake up.

The doctors said after the seizures, almost dying from the two allergic reactions, and the viral infection they had hope he'd wake up, but there was no telling. The only saving grace was that, according to the neurologist, there was brain activity but they couldn't be certain what that would mean if or until he woke up. I asked the age-old question repeatedly. When did they think he'd awaken?. And they always said the same thing. When he wanted to. The truth was, they couldn't know. There was no magic "easy" button or master alarm that we could set to make it happen. And believe me, the noise thing? Yeah, I tried that. Banging on the rails of his bed. Putting headphones over his ears with metal music that I knew he hated just so he'd wake up and tell me to turn the devil music off, but nothing. Silence. No movement whatsoever.

That was hard to swallow, too. Holding his hand. It was always warm yet lifeless. Blood was running through the veins, but the magnetism, the energy, the life force, whatever it was that makes us who we are, wasn't there in him.

I sat there looking at his overgrown hair, beard, and mustache. Ginelle had been keeping him looking good in my absence but he needed a trimming—not to mention a dose of sunshine would do wonders for his pallor. He had that pale grayish skin tone that a person gets when he hasn't been outside in a long time. My father had been in a coma for nine months. The length of time it takes a woman to become pregnant and have a baby.

"When are you going to wake up, Pops? There is so much, too much to say." I took several deep breaths before continuing.

"I'm going back to Malibu tomorrow. As much as I'd like to be here for you, our lives can't sit on hold any longer. Your debt has been paid, Dad, but not without a sacrifice. Sometimes I look back on this year and think I should thank you. Without your debt, I wouldn't have met all the wonderful people I've encountered over the year. People who I know will continue to be a part of my life for the long haul. And of course, there's meeting Max. My brother."

I stood up and started pacing the room. "Mom had a child before me, Pops. A boy. Five years older than I am.

Thirty now. His name is Maxwell, and he's the best brother a girl could ever have. I'm sure you picked up on the name thing. Maxwell, Mia, and Madison. Just like her and Aunt Millie. Mom was nothing if not predictable." I thought about how she left each of us, and that snake coiled up and back around my heart at the thought of the woman who'd borne me. Yep, very predictable.

Stopping in place, I looked out the window. The dark clouds of last night had all but gone, leaving a pristine blue sky in their wake. Moving close to Pops, I ran my fingers through his soft dark hair. It had always been silky smooth, and even at rest, it was no different. "This journey has led me to a man, Pops. A man I'm so deeply in love with, I know with everything that I am that he's it. The end-all be-all for me." I stared hard at his face, hoping there would be a flicker of life, a scant smile, anything…but no.

"I'm going to go now. I don't know when I'm going to make it back. Maddy and Matt will check on you. You'd like him. Matt. He's good for her. Treats her like the queen she is. The doctors here are going to do everything they can to get you to come back, but it's up to you, Pops. You need to fight and fight hard. Fight for us." I closed my eyes and took a breath. "If anything with you changes, I'll be on the first plane out." I leaned forward and kissed his forehead.

"I'm glad you made it through this scare. Hell, I'm glad everyone made it through this scare." I walked to the edge of the bed and looked down at the man who raised me. He'd never been perfect, nor did he claim to be, but he loved us, even when he absolutely hated himself.

"You know, Pops, it wasn't right for you to borrow all that money, and it definitely wasn't okay to have that burden fall on my shoulders, but I don't regret the decisions I've made this year or the journey I've taken so far. I wouldn't change what I've experienced for anything. Through it, I feel as though I'm finding myself, more and more each month. Maybe by December I'll have even more figured out. If you asked me, if anyone asks…I'd do it all again. And the ride isn't even over."

THE END

Mia's journey continues in

October: Calendar Girl
(Available Now in eBook)

Calendar Girl: Volume Four
(Coming Soon)

ALSO BY AUDREY CARLAN

The Calendar Girl Series

January (Book 1)
February (Book 2)
March (Book 3)
April (Book 4)
May (Book 5)
June (Book 6)

July (Book 7)
August (Book 8)
September (Book 9)
October (Book 10)
November (Book 11)
December (Book 12)

The Falling Series

Angel Falling
London Falling
Justice Falling

The Trinity Trilogy

Body (Book 1)
Mind (Book 2)
Soul (Book 3)

ACKNOWLEDGEMENTS

To my editors, Ekatarina Sayanova and Rebecca Cartee with Red Quill Editing, LLC, your knowledge knows no bounds. I am constantly surprised at what the two of you together can do. Thank you for making me shine! (www.redquillediting.net)

To my extraordinarily talented personal assistant, Heather White (aka The Goddess), thank you for allowing me to vent, moan, groan, complain, squeal, freak out, and more without losing your stride. You give me peace of mind, and that's a really beautiful gift. Thank you for all that you do every day. Love you always dollface.

Any author knows she isn't worth her weight unless her story is backed by badass betas. I have the best!

Jeananna Goodall—My pre-reader and beta who has the best responses to wild plot twists. I love blowing your mind. Love to love you, lady!

Ginelle Blanch—Not only do you find the quirkiest errors that would make me look stupid, you're the perfect meter to how the readers are going to experience the story. I adore that you give me that. Thank you for your honesty and always being straightforward. It will keep me making great books!

Anita Shofner—I'm not sure where your talent comes from, but if I had to guess I'd go with God-given. Thank you for sharing your gifts with me and helping to make this the best book it can be.

Rosa McAnulty—For saving my bum with all the Puerto Rican style Spanish with the scorching hot Anton Santiago. Thank you for making sure I didn't look like an idiot.

Thank you to the ladies at Give Me Books and Kylie McDermott for spreading this book far and wide into the virtual social world!

Gotta thank my super awesome, fantabulous publisher, Waterhouse Press. Thank you for being the non-traditional traditional publisher!

To the Audrey Carlan Street Team of wicked hot Angels, together we change the world. One book at a time. BESOS-4-LIFE, lovely ladies.